Things Liars Say Things Liars Hide Things Liars Fake

sara ney

This is a work of fiction. Names, characters, places, brands, media, and incidents are either the product of the author's imagination or are used fictitiously. The author acknowledges the trademarked status and trademark owners of various products referenced in this work of fiction, which have been used without permission. The publication/use of these trademarks is not authorized, associated with, or sponsored by the trademark owners.

First Edition: July 2015, November 2015, January 2016
Library of Congress Cataloging-in-Publication Data
#ThreeLittleLies Series – 1st ed
Things Liars Say
Things Liars Hide
Things Liars Fake
ISBN-13: 978-1523739592 | ISBN-10: 1523739592

For more information about Sara Ney and her books, visit:
https://www.facebook.com/saraneyauthor/

Things *Liars* Say

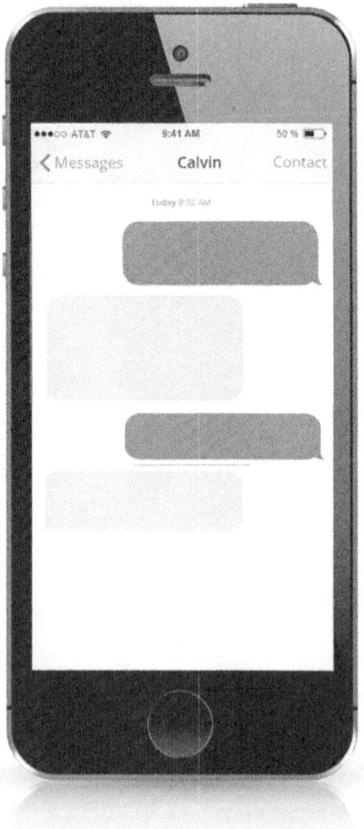
AT&T
9:41 AM
50 %
Messages
Calvin
Contact

Prologue

Greyson

The lie started off innocently enough, and obviously I never meant to get caught up in it—but then again, isn't that what *everyone* says when they lie?

Wait! No. Don't answer that.

Flipping my laptop open, I hit the power button and wait for it to boot, the soft familiar humming of the fan, CD drive, and modem stirring my computer to life, and shuffle the papers stacked in front of me.

I take a bite of the apple on my food tray, chewing slowly as I scan the meeting agenda on the table in front of me and my friends look on.

We're gathered in the university's dining hall for a quick lunch meeting on campus—the only time this week I could get my committee together in one spot at a time that worked for everyone.

"Rachel," I say across the cafeteria table. "Did you remember to call the catering company?"

My sorority sister gives me a victorious smile. "Yup. They have us booked for the third, and we have a tasting on the twenty-ninth at four thirty. It should have updated your calendar in Outlook."

I click open my Outlook and scroll through the calendar to the dates Rachel mentioned. "Excellent. There it is." I cross *catering* off my list and chew on the end of my BIC pen. "Jemma, are we all set with the silent auction donations?"

"Roger that, Greyson. I have ten alumnae lined up for baskets, and another thirteen parents who donated cash, totaling eight hundred dollars. We should be all set once we get everything purchased to put the baskets together."

"What other things do you have left for those?"

"You know, clear cello bags for the baskets, the wicker baskets themselves, labels… Those sorts of things."

"Who's going to be running the auction?" My pen hovers above the blank *auctioneer* spot on my agenda.

"You, Beth, and I can pull the silent-auction sheets at the end of the night."

I nod, crossing both *auction* and *donations* off my list.

"Ariel? Entertainment?"

Ariel, a tall brunette with a serious expression, pulls out an Excel spreadsheet and drums on it with her forefinger. "It looks like Cara put the deposit down for the DJ last week. He's scheduled to arrive a full hour before we start setting up the room so he can get all his equipment in the building without interruptions. I sent him a list of requested songs last night, so we should be good to go."

"As long as Vanessa doesn't request any of those group dances." Jemma snorts.

"Ugh. I hate 'The Electric Slide.'" Ariel laughs. "Should I add that to the do-not-play list?"

"Nah. Because you and I both know if the DJ plays it, you're going to run out onto the dance floor..."

Ariel sighs. "Probably."

I look down at my list and tap a pen to my chin. "So all we have to talk about yet is ticket sales. And getting everyone to sign the guest release waivers for liability."

I pull the form out of a file folder and slide it across the table to Catherine, one of three sisters in the sorority who are pre-law. She scans it with narrowed, articulate eyes and gives a curt nod when she reaches the last paragraph. "Looks great. Solid." Her lips curve into a smirk. "I like the addendum about recovering losses if property damage to the venue occurs by a guest. Good thinking."

Jemma snorts. "Remember what happened last year with Amanda Q's date? He ripped out an entire fern from the foyer of the hotel then threw up in the pot." We all laugh. "To add insult to injury, she snuck him out and then lied about it. Like there weren't security cameras everywhere."

Catherine gives a rueful shake of the head, disappointed we weren't able to charge anyone damages, and says, "Right. But since he hadn't signed a waiver, we couldn't charge him for the damage

"Thank God it was just a few bags of potting soil..."

"But still. She shouldn't have left us hanging."

"Yeah, that was shitty."

Rachel turns to me with raised eyebrows. "Speaking of dates… Inquiring minds want to know: who is Greyson Keller bringing to the Philanthropy Gala this year?"

I shake my head. "I don't have time to worry about a date, you guys. I've been up to my eyeballs in Gala preparations."

"Don't you have to bring a date?" Jemma asks. "As the Philanthropy Chairwoman, you're the hostess this year."

I fiddle with my laptop's power cord and avoid her eyes. "What's your point?"

"Oh, come on, what's his name?" Rachel waves a limp French fry in my face from her lunch tray to get my attention. "Focus here; this stuff is important."

I finally look up, giving my blonde head a shake. "Who says there has to be a guy?"

"Please, there's *always* a guy…" Rachel's voice trails off.

"Just tell us who it is." Catherine prods quietly. Cajoling.

"Spit it out. We're going to find out eventually."

No, you're really not.

Jemma looks me dead in the eyes. "Yes. We are."

What the… Okay, that was freaky. And it occurs to me that they're acting like a gang of unruly hyenas and aren't going to let the subject die until I give them a reason to.

"I-I'd rather not say," I stutter. "We, uh, *just* started dating. It's only been one date. Besides, he's hardly Gala material."

"What the heck does that even mean?" Jemma scoffs.

"Hardly Gala material? If he has a pulse, he's Gala material."

"One date?" Ariel drops her pen on the table. "Why did you feel that wasn't worth mentioning? Why haven't we at least heard about this guy before?"

"I don't want to jinx it?"

"Are you asking us or telling us?" Catherine's eagle eyes are unnerving, and I look away.

"Are you bringing him to the Gala?"

I take another bite of apple and respond with a mouthful. "I don't know yet. He might have... a... game?"

"Game?" Jemma's eyes get wide and excited. "Ooh, what is he, an athlete? Which sport?"

Great question, Jemma. I'll let you know when I figure it out myself. Everyone leans in closer for my answer, and I resist the urge to roll my eyes.

"He, uh... He's..." *Honestly, people. Why do you care so much?* Of course, I don't actually say this out loud.

"Oh, come on, Greyson. Don't get all secretive on us. It's not like we're going to stalk him on social media."

A few of them exchange telling, stealthy glances. What a bunch of freaking liars. The first thing they'll do when they leave this meeting is look for him on Facebook. Twitter. Bumble app... wherever—my point is, they would absolutely social media stalk him. I mean, if he existed.

I lie again.

"Fine. His name is..." I look around the room, my hazel eyes scanning the room, the food posters and the advertising signs adorning the walls. One for fresh, cold Farm Fresh California Milk jumps out at me. California. For some reason, it sticks out at me.

California. *Cal.*

"His name is uh, Cal, um… Cal."

"Cal?"

"That's right," I lie. "Yup. Cal."

"Cal? Cal what? What's his last name?"

Jesus, Rachel. Let it go!

I look at her dumbly. Crap. "His last name?"

"Grey, you're being *really* weird about this."

Again, my eyes scan the dining hall, landing on a girl who just happens to be in my economics class—and I just happened to have borrowed notes from her. Brianna Thompson.

Thompson it is.

"Sorry, I just zoned out for a second. His last name is, um, Thompson?"

"Asking or telling?"

"Telling." I give my head a firm nod. "Yup. Thompson. His last name is Thompson."

Cal Thompson. I roll the name around in my mind, deciding that I like it. Sounds believable.

Legit.

The lie works, because eventually they leave me alone and we go back to our meeting agenda, finish our committee work, and finish our lunch.

An apprehensive knot forms in the pit of my stomach as I swallow the last bite of my spinach chicken wrap.

Little do I know, the lies that so easily rolled off my tongue today will soon become entirely too real.

One

Calvin

"Cal. You there, man? You've gotta come check this out," my roommate Mason calls from his bedroom, the music blaring from his Bose sound system. Combined with the background noise of the television in the living room, the noise pollution almost drowns out his request.

Unfortunately for me, I'm not that lucky, and he calls for me again. "Come here, man. Seriously."

Christ, he's a pain in the ass. "Hold your fucking horses; I'm in the middle of something," I call back.

Yeah. I'm in the middle of something: stuffing my face with a sub sandwich and washing it down with a cold beer. I swipe the other half of my sub off the counter and wrap it in a napkin before sauntering, unhurriedly, to Mason's end of the apartment. I lean nonchalantly against his doorjamb, taking another huge bite of sandwich and chewing slowly.

"What."

He cranes his beefy neck towards me in the doorway, irritated. "I said come check this out. Jeez. Why are you standing there? Where's your sense of urgency?"

Rolling my eyes, I venture in a few feet. "If this is more porn, I'm going to be fucking pissed."

"Whatever. Trust me, this is worth our time."

"Our? No. Don't say our." Skeptically, I sidle up next to his desk chair, and he turns his computer monitor on its base to face me. He has his Twitter feed pulled up, and his beefy forefinger pokes the screen, pointing to a particular Tweet.

It's too damn bad I can't focus on anything with his loud, crap R&B music blasting out of his speakers.

"Would you turn that shit down a notch?"

Mason sighs but clicks a few buttons with his mouse, shutting the radio off. "Okay. So, check it. I follow my cousin Jemma, who goes to State, on Instagram and Reddit and shit."

I roll my eyes. "Okay." *Get to the point.*

"Anyway, Jemma is in this sorority, right? Hottest chicks on campus. I went once to visit when they had family weekend—don't ask me why." My roommate pauses, and for a second I'm hopeful he won't continue talking.

But guess what? He tells me why.

"My Aunt Cindy—Jemma's mom—had her panties in a twist about everyone going. Come to think of it, she probably wanted me there to hook me up with a nice girl and—"

I emit a very irritated and exasperated sigh. "Jesus Christ, Mase, where are you going with all this? Make your fucking point."

"Sorry. My point is, I follow Jemma on Twitter, right?" *Oh my effing God.* "Her sorority has this big fancy dance thing coming up. They do it every year. Anyway, some *dude* named Grey must be helping them plan this event, right? Cause it's a big deal. And see here?" Mason stabs his index finger on the computer monitor again, pointing to another Tweet.

"I swear to all that is holy, if you don't make your point I'm going to lose my shit."

"Some Grey guy tweeted *your* name as his *date*. Check it."

I lean in to scan the screen closely, my brows furrowing into an angry line when I read the tweet in front of me.

Holy shit, the bastard is right.

@JemmaGemini Tweeted: *Theta Gala season is here! Host with the most* @grey_vkeller *and date* @calthompson3192 *are now selling tickets! Get yours here (click on link)* #state #sorority #philanthropy #ThetaGala15

My fists clench at my side. "What. The. Actual. *Fuck.*"

"Wait, hold on—there's more. That was just yesterday." Mason moves his mouse around, clicking until the screen scrolls down. Up pop's Grey Keller's profile and history. "Check this one out." He points to the monitor.

"I'd be able to if you'd get your fucking finger out of

the way," I snap, leaning in closer until my face is inches from the screen. "I can't see."

"You can ask nicely, you know..."

My jaw clenches shut tightly, and Mason moves his finger.

We peer at the Tweets, heads bent together.

@Grey_VKeller Tweeted: *missed you* @calthompson3192 *at* #StateTailgate *knock them dead at your game, honey buns!* #thompsonforthewin

@Grey_VKeller Tweeted: *nothing beats* @starbucks *and* @calthompson3192 *on these cold rainy days* #blahs #raingoaway #soylatte #boyfriend #boyfriendsweater #hugs

@Grey_VKeller Tweeted: *what* @calthompson3192 *needs is a* #queereyeforthestraightguy *as he tries on suits for* #ThetaGala15

There are more, but Mason is reading them out loud over my shoulder, and his commentary is starting to get on my last nerve.

"Did that hashtag say Queer Eye for the Straight Guy?" he asks the silence. "Hey. What's worse than having a stalker?" Mason asks with a smirk, answering his own question when I give him a dark scowl. "Being stalked by a *guy*. Hey. Do you think he's come to any of our matches and we just didn't know it?"

"How did you find these?"

"I told you, my cousin Jemma. She retweeted these, and even though it's a bogus Twitter account—I checked—your name still stuck out at me."

"That is so messed up."

"Sucks to be you, man."

"Shut the fuck up, Mason."

"I'm just saying. He's out there watching you, and you didn't even know it. That's gross, dude."

That's the very last thing I want to think hear, so I prod my roommate sharply in the shoulder with my elbow, narrowly missing his head.

"Shut the fuck up already!" I repeat irritably. "I can't hear myself think."

"But I turned the radio off."

"I meant *shut your yap*."

"Sorry. Just thinking out loud." Then he mumbles, "You're being a real bitch about this."

"Not. Helping."

"Noted." But then he adds, "But you admit he could be watching you at our games."

I narrow a steely gaze at him. "How do we even know it's a guy?" Great. Now I'm using the royal *we*.

He shoots me an impatient look. "What are you, a moron? Grey is a guy's name, bruh. That's how we know it's a guy."

@Grey_VKeller Tweeted: @calthompson3192 *counting down the days until* #ThetaGala15 *and I see your handsome face*

@Grey_VKeller Tweeted: @calthompson3192 *last night was wonderful. Wish you lived closer so I could see you more often* #sexy #stud

"This Grey dude must be blind," Mason says beside me, and I give him another nudge—this time in the back of the head. "Ow, what the hell, man?"

I grunt unhappily.

"You could break a mirror is all I'm saying." Mason mumbles, rubbing his neck.

"Fuck you."

My fist comes down like a hammer on the flimsy wooden door that at one time might have been painted blue but currently looks like shit. In fact, with one swift pull I could probably yank the whole thing off its rusty hinges.

Hovering behind like a couple of chicken shits are my roommates, Aaron Buchanan and Mason, standing down on the loose concrete slab next to the porch. They accompanied me for one reason and one reason only: a good laugh.

Let's not forget to trail along out of perverse curiosity, and if necessary, to pull me off the useless bastard I just drove forty-five minutes to confront.

And beat the piss out of.

"Thompson, you've knocked four times. Maybe there's no one home," Mason rationalizes, checking his phone for messages. His thumb glides over his smartphone, his mouth widening into smirk. He begins tapping away furiously even as he adds, "Time to give it a rest."

I narrow my predatory gaze at the blue door. "Oh, there's definitely someone home. I hear music."

Aaron crosses his bulky arms and frowns. "Well, don't beat the fucking door down. Take it easy."

I shoot him a glare over my shoulder and crack my knuckles. "That's easy for you to say. Some guy isn't impersonating your boyfriend on every social media site known to man."

The thought riles me up, and I curl my hand into a fist, giving the plywood door another hollow rap with my knuckles. "*Come out, come out, wherever you are.* Open the damn door, you little pissant," I chant to myself. "I don't have all fucking day."

"Dude, you sound like a psychopath." Mason laughs without lifting his head from his phone. He nudges Aaron. "Check it out. Sasha Baldwin just sent me a picture of her ass."

My last blasted knock does the trick, because suddenly the music cuts out inside the house, I hear some rustling, and a feminine voice shouts, "Coming!" This is followed by the low sound of hastening footpads advancing towards the entrance, the deadbolt turning, and the door flying open.

"Sorry 'bout that. We didn't hear the door. Obviously." A tall brunette stares curiously through the storm door, a bright smile pasted on her pretty face, hand propped on her slim waist.

She looks at me, eyes darting from me to Aaron and Mason, who are suddenly standing at attention. If possible, the brunette's mega-watt smile widens. "Well, *hello* there. Can I help you?"

Head tipped to the side, I regard her critically as she studies the three of us back with open interest, and I can see her trying to place us in her mind. Trying to figure out if she's seen us before or met us around campus. Or at a party.

No such luck, sweetheart. Today is not your lucky day.

In black yoga pants and a large, baby-blue State sweatshirt, her dark brown hair is pulled back into a loose ponytail. Basically, she looks like the girl next door: fresh faced, normal, and nice.

And did I mention normal? As in *not harboring a known stalker*.

But as we all know, looks can be deceiving, and those keen brown eyes glowing towards my idiot roommates are no exception. Peeved, I want to shake the shit out of them both for being captivated by this pretty, attractive girl. Captivated by her deceptively innocent face—as if she couldn't possibly be a mental person. As if there were a scarcity of pretty girls on our own college campus for them to ogle. There is not.

I angrily snap my fingers in their direction. "Guys, focus. You don't get to drool over this one."

They both have the decency to look embarrassed, and when I catch Mason ascending the stoop, I shove him back down onto the sidewalk. I roll my eyes, turning towards the door.

"Is your boyfriend home?" I cut to the chase.

"My *what*?" Her nose curls up. "I don't have a boyfriend." She presses forward, closer to the screen, and looks out into the yard—at freaking Mason, who's blushing.

Jesus. What a clusterfuck.

"I'm looking for a guy that lives here."

She tips her head at me, confused. "Erm, maybe you

have the wrong house?"

I look down at the address on the screen of my smartphone. "No. This is the address I was given."

"Given by… whom?"

I thumb my hand in Mason's direction. "His cousin Jemma."

The brunette's eyes narrow. "Jemma? Oh *really*."

At that moment, I know exactly what she's thinking: the moment this blue door closes, this Jemma chick is going to get her ass chewed. I have a sister, and I've seen this look a million times.

The brunette looks me over from head to toe, then top to bottom, memorizing the color of my eyes, measuring my height, the color of my hair, and any distinguishing scars or birthmarks. Probably so she can profile me to the police.

Great.

CSI Barbie crosses her arms. "Who was it you said you were looking for?"

"I didn't."

"Are you serious?" The brunette snorts sarcastically, going from pleasant to defensive. "Look, I don't know who you think you are or who it is you're looking for, but there are no guys living here—"

"—I'm looking for Greyson Keller. Is he here?"

Her expression is priceless: eyes wide as saucers, eyebrows shot up into her dark hairline, and mouth agape. A dimple threatens to press into her right cheek.

Busted. I've found my guy.

"Greyson *Keller*?" The girl laughs, tipping her head back. "Oh, this is gonna be good." She looks me up and down, a weird expression on her face that I can't quite put my finger on: amusement. Curiosity. Glee?

Self-consciously, I fold my arms across my broad chest. "Oh, *Greyson* is here all right. Let me go get, uh… *him*. Give me one minute?"

She starts to close the door behind her but peeks her head around it, adding, "Stay there; do *not* go anywhere."

I roll my eyes. "Whatever, make it quick." My fists clench and unclench at my sides, warming up and impatient to get the show on the road.

The door slams shut, but I clearly hear a muted, "Grey! Someone's at the door for you!" This announcement is followed by, "You're what? Oh, okay." Then a muffled, "Make it snappy, chica. You are *so* not going to want to miss this."

Chica?

Then I hear, "Grey, hurry up. Huh? Well, hurry. Yeah, yeah, you already said that."

Soon, from somewhere inside the house, one feminine voice is joined by another—this one pleasant and sweet—responding with a sing-songy, "Give me a second! Be right there!"

Mason appears beside me. "Do my ears deceive me, or was that another chick's voice?" He slips his cell into the pocket of his low-rise jeans.

"That was *definitely* another chick's voice," Aaron agrees, stepping closer to the house.

The door unlatches from within, the knob turns, and the blue front door is pulled open once again on its rusty hinges. Natural sunlight hits the girl who appears in the doorway like a spotlight, her long blonde hair shining around her head like a halo.

Momentarily shocked, I take a step back, and she

steps closer. Like an idiot, I stare. "I'm looking for Greyson Keller."

"Yes?"

I roll my eyes. "Not *you,* sweetie, your boyfriend. Go grab him for me so I can bash his face in."

The blonde bites her lower lip and laughs. "I'm Greyson. As much as I hate asking, can I… help you?"

"No you're not." Confused, my brows drop into a deep V, and I turn back towards my roommates. They shrug uselessly. "Uh, I'm here for Greyson. Greyson *Keller*?"

"Found her. That's me." Her pouty pink mouth gives me a lopsided grin, full of straight white teeth. "You can keep saying my name as long as you want, but no one else is walking out that front door."

"You're a girl," Aaron blurts out.

"Aren't you observant?" The blonde's expressive hazel eyes shine with amusement as she spreads her hands wide at her waist with a light laugh. "Mmmhmm. Last time I checked, I still had all my girly parts."

And what girly parts they were: hands sweeping airily around the flouncy skirt of a tight, feminine sundress, long tan legs accentuated by the short hemline flaring out around her hips.

Around her tan legs. Shit, did I already say that?

"Tighthead, if *that's* Greyson Keller, you are so screwed," Mason mutters into my ear from behind, poking me in the back with his bony elbow. "Walk away, man, before you look like an even bigger douche."

I scowl and elbow him in the gut and am satisfied when he grunts. "Shut the fuck up, Mase. You're not helping."

Not to mention, this is all his goddamn fault. He couldn't have done a little more thorough recon work before raising a red flag?

Fuck.

Running a hand through my hair, I give Greyson a once-over from under hooded eyes.

Long, light blond hair falls over her bare shoulders in one of those sexy, messy French braid things, and freckles lightly dance across the bridge of her straight, pert nose. Her chest rises up and down breathlessly, her cheeks taking on a rosy hue as she lets me study her.

God, she's… she's gorgeous. Not the ordinary, pretty kind of gorgeous. No. She's *make you want to weep into your beer* breathtakingly beautiful.

Or, at least, she is to me.

Fuckity fuck fuck.

"Is… there something I can help you with?" She's biting down on a pink, pouty lower lip. "Are you fraternity pledges?"

I glance at her friend hovering from behind in the living room, hanging on our every word. She looks amused, entertained, and entirely too pleased with herself. Like a gleeful toddler who didn't get caught stealing a piece of candy.

Bitch.

CSI Barbie's laughing gaze shifts to the nitwits standing behind me with unconcealed interest, and I groan. Suddenly, I'm not too thrilled with the idea of confronting *this* version of Greyson Keller in public. In front of our friends.

I clear my throat. "Is there somewhere we can talk? Privately?"

Greyson nods slowly as her roommate shrugs in acquiescence. The brunette stares me down. "I'm blowing my rape whistle if you're not back on this porch in ten minutes, asshole."

She shoots me a cheeky grin.

"Maybe we'll take a quick walk?" Beautiful, blonde, and *female* Greyson Keller puts her arm around her friend's waist. "I'll stay within shooting distance," she teases with a glance at me. "Okay?"

I give a jerky nod. "Yeah. Okay."

"Let me grab my shoes."

She releases her friend's waist and disappears, returning several moments later and a few inches taller, pushing through the screen door and stepping out onto the porch.

Her hot-pink painted toes peek out from a pair of cork wedge sandals, legs going on for miles. Her sundress is everything it should be: tight bodice dipping into a V, giving me the perfect view of her respectable cleavage. The dress is tied in the back with a bow around her small waist, and as she smiles up at me, I swallow back a groan.

Why is she wearing a dress cut like that? Why does she look so goddamn cute? Was she about to go somewhere? Shit, why does she have to look so damn good? Why couldn't she have been fugly? *Why couldn't she have been a guy*?

Why the fuck, why?

Then at least I wouldn't feel so guilty for wanting to pummel her ass.

I am hating myself right now.

Greyson leads me to the sidewalk and takes a right once we hit the pavement. "Let's head this way. It leads to a dead end."

I cram my large hands deep into the pocket of my jeans.

"So…" Her voice hitches in a silent question.

We walk for a few yards before I grow a pair of balls big enough to speak. "Here's the deal. I came here to beat the shit out of you," I blurt out. "I thought you were some dude stalking me on Twitter and Facebook. A guy."

Gasping, she stops in her tracks, shocked. "Why? What! *Why*?" she sputters. "I don't understand. Help me understand."

"On Twitter, are you Grey underscore Keller, Theta Rho?"

She hesitates, turning to face me, biting down on her lower lip. "Yes."

God, I wish she hadn't just given me that look.

"I'm Cal Thompson."

"*What*?" she shouts. Understanding shines in her eyes, and she takes a stumbling step back onto the grassy curbside. "You can't be!"

"Oh, I assure you, sweetheart—I am."

"B-but," she sputters, a blush making her chest, neck, and face red. "I made you up!" A hand clamps over her mouth as she moans. "Oh my God, this cannot be happening to me right now."

"Yet here I am."

I pull out my wallet and produce both my driver's license and student ID, tossing them at her. Because she wasn't expecting the onslaught, she misses, and the identification cards flutter to the concrete sidewalk. "There. Take a gander."

I know it's rude, but frankly, I don't give a shit.

With trembling hands, she bends at the knee demurely, sliding a hand along the folds of her skirt to preserve her modesty, and reaching for the ID's, her long fingers plucking them off the ground.

She studies them both as she stands, her expression crestfallen.

"How? Oh my god, C-Cal. I'm so, *so* sorry. And embarrassed." Her hand flies to her mouth. "So embarrassed," she repeats with a whisper. Grey's full bottom lip quivers, and she glances back towards her house nervously. "My friends don't know I made you up. My friends are the *reason* I made you up."

Aaron, Mason, and her roommate—all within *shooting* distance— watch us from the porch fifty yards away, not even bothering to hide their interest.

Shit. I don't want her to cry—even if what she did was fifty shades of fucked up.

"Explain it to me, then."

She nods slowly.

Greyson

I cannot believe this is happening.

The guy standing in front of me is so freaking angry, a shocking myriad of expressions dancing across his face: Perturbed. Confused. Stunned. Pissed off.

He looks like he came to beat the *crap* out of someone and is disappointed he isn't going to have the opportunity.

I study the planes of his hard face as he walks beside me, a fresh bruise discoloring the rise of his high cheekbone just beneath his left eye, but oddly made less severe by his deep tan. I conclude that he must spend an excessive amount of time outdoors if the sun-kissed tips of the sandy blonde hair curling up from under the lid of his ball cap are any indication.

I take in his eyes: dark pools of cobalt blue made harsh and unforgiving by the severe slashes of dense eyebrows above them. Square jaw with a day's growth of beard surrounding a full, downturned mouth.

Black stitches mend the gash marring his busted-up lower lip.

Tall—maybe six foot one—with lean hips, I can't resist letting my eyes wander down the length of him. They take in the broad, sculpted chest, straining against a tight gray Ivy League t-shirt—a shirt that leaves nothing to the imagination, as evidenced by the defined pec muscles outlined by the sheer threadbare fabric.

If Cal's shoulders are a thing of beauty, then his arms are a thing of *art*, dense and firm and ripped. A large, intricate tattoo snakes up the tendons of his tricep, twisting up his bicep and disappearing under the sleeve of his shirt. Tan, powerful biceps any girl would want to curl her fingers around with a contented, dreamy sigh.

They're arms a girl would blissfully want wrapped around her in a crowded bar. Out in public. Or, let's be honest, a tangle of sheets.

I can't decide if he's handsome or good-looking or not—not by today's definition of classically handsome, anyway. He's too severe. His nose has been broken too many times, his skin has too many scars, but there *is* something about him that I find ruggedly appealing. I just can't put my finger on what that something could be.

However, decision made: I like what I see.

A lot.

"Hmmm." I must have muttered this out loud, because he looks over at me and catches me horn dogging him. I open my mouth to say something then clamp it shut. *Take a deep breath, Greyson. Just take a deep breath and spit it out.*

He deserves an explanation.

"Alright. When I tell you how I ended up faking a boyfriend, I hope you don't…" I wave a hand through the air, listlessly. Nervously. "Judge me too harshly. Please."

We continue walking, reaching the dead end. Cal nods towards the opposite side of the deserted road, and together, we step off the curb and cross to the other side, continuing our meander back in the direction from which we came.

I take a deep breath and exhale.

"To start with, I'm the philanthropy chair of my sorority." He snorts, and I roll my eyes, quite used to non-Greek students mocking my sorority membership. "A philanthropy is a charitable organization we support through fundraising and donations."

I take another deep, shallow breath. "Anyway, this year we're throwing a big gala. The largest one we've put on, with the most number of attendees. It's been… really stressful. I have a committee, but you know how it is. Not everyone is committed. Not everyone pulls their weight. And with everything *else* we have to juggle…"

Cal listens silently as I continue, my explanation rapidly becoming a vent session.

"…school, grades, jobs, athletics. I don't expect you to care, but… you get the picture. Anyway, with all that being said, a few of them are, for lack of better words, boy crazy." I give him a sidelong glance, but he stoically faces forward. "All they want to talk about during the meetings are their dates for the gala, and they won't stop hounding *me* about who *I'm* bringing. So, yada, yada, yada, Cal Thompson."

As if that explained everything.

"Wait. Did you just use yada, yada, yada as your justification? Who *does* that?" Cal sputters a little, and stops short on the sidewalk, trying not to laugh but failing, emitting a short, deep bark.

"You don't like yada, yada, yada?" I shoot him a coy smile. "What's wrong with it?"

"You sound kind of crazy," he teases, his eyes crinkling at the corners with amusement. "I guess the bigger picture is, how the hell did you end up using *my* name? How did you hear about me? We're not even in the same stratosphere."

"Whoa, buddy, it's not like you're famous. Let's not get *too* full of ourselves." I hand him back the driver's license and student ID I've been holding and give a little shiver when our fingers touch.

"Trust me, I had no idea who you were. I pulled your name out of thin air. In fact, you could say I was inspired. There's a sign hanging in the dining hall for Farm Fresh California milk. *Cal*ifornia—Cal. See? So then my friends want a last name, and I'm scouring the room, I see this girl from my econ class, Brianna—"

"Thompson," we both say at the same time.

"Yes. Brianna Thompson." I laugh. "So, there you have it, the day Cal Thompson was born. Or in this case, invented."

"What about the tweets?"

"Well, my friend Jemma is a public relations major and is *all* about social media. She's Theta's PR and Marketing Chairwoman and the one who insisted on the live tweeting. Thinks it's more 'relevant.'" Yes, I use air quotes. "Jemma literally makes us Tweet during our meeting to get people excited, which is great! Good for her. I mean, I love her to death, but now it's getting obnoxious."

"Jemma is my roommate Mason's cousin—he follows her on Twitter."

"Ah. All the puzzle pieces come together." I keep walking and notice Cal checking out my legs. I pretend not to notice; my steps become jaunty. "What does Mason think of all this?'

He peels his eyes away and looks up, down the street towards my yard. "Mason and Aaron are dipshits and get a rise out of seeing me pissed off. They came today expecting a fight."

I ball my fists up and put up my dukes, bouncing on the heels of my four-inch wedges. "It's not too late!"

His dark blue eyes rake me up and down again appraisingly, but not in a creepy, pervy way. "Okay, Mayweather, cool it with your bad self." Cal considers me then, scratching his five o'clock shadow. "You know, I never thought I'd have my own personal stalker."

I laugh, relieved that he's making light of the situation. "Oh, please. If I were stalking you, you would know it. I'd have done a much better job creeping you out than a few measly tweets." I nudge him with my elbow conspiratorially, startled to realize I'm enjoying our banter and warming to the topic. "Maybe driven past your house… found a few of your classes… crafted myself a tiny Cal doll to cuddle at night…" I cross my arms and hug myself, pretending to squeeze a stuffed animal. "Um, yeah. *That* part might have sounded crazy."

"That. Sounded. Terrifying." He shivers. "Well, the weird thing is— it was actually a total fluke that anyone saw my name in your Tweets because Cal Thompson isn't even the name I use on any social media online. I haven't used that since high school."

"It isn't? Don't leave me in suspense. What's your real tag?"

He laughs. "Tighthead Thompson. Tighthead is a rugby thing."

That explains the gashes, scratches, and bruises.

"Ah. Rugby, huh? We don't have that on our campus."

"I'm sure there's an intramural league here somewhere. Most schools offer at least that. It's typically only played competitively at smaller schools, and some Ivy League schools."

"How long have you been playing?" I ask, feeling at ease with him and sincerely wanting to know more.

"Three years by accident." Cal stops on the sidewalk when we're standing across the street from my rental but makes no move to cross the street. "I played football for years and just got sick of it. I had a scholarship to a D1 school, but…" His sentence trails off with a shrug. "I just didn't want that kind of pressure."

I raise my eyebrows. "What did your parents say about you giving up a scholarship?"

"They're supportive; they want me to be happy."

"Wow, they sound great."

"The best," he agrees with a small grin, nodding towards my shoddy little house. "Okay, so… I guess this is you, then." He shoves his hands in his pockets, and we step down into the street to cross.

"I guess. And again, I'm so sorry. It was such a stupid, careless thing to do."

"Yes, but…" he concedes. "No harm done."

"Except the part where you came all this way to kick my ass," I point out gamely.

"Yeah," he agrees. "Except the part where I drove all this way to kick your ass." He gives me an expression full of longing, clearing his throat once his gaze hits my breasts and lingers there. He blushes and looks away. "I'm actually really disappointed I didn't get the chance."

"Well, thank you, then—for *not* whooping my butt.

I'm sure I deserved it." I run a hand over my long blonde braid, and Cal's bright, fascinated eyes follow the motion, sending tingles up my spine. I want to do it again just to see his reaction. "And thank you for not being a total jerk."

"Don't get me wrong. I was really pissed."

"I'll bet..." I tap my chin, and his gaze hits my mouth. "But on the bright side, it was only an hour drive, and you gave your friends something to talk about, probably for *years*. Ugh. Years."

"A few years at *least*. But just look at how happy they are." Our friends are still gathered on the porch, watching us walk back into the yard, chatting happily yet eyeing Cal and me with avid curiosity.

"They're like little puppy dogs."

I giggle. "I can't even begin to imagine what they're going to say when they finally get you alone."

Cal laughs. "Your ears will be ringing, that's for sure."

"For years," I remind him.

"Okay, you little sneak. Who. Was. *That*?" My roommate Melody ambushes me as soon as the screen door closes and the guys pull away in Cal's big red pickup truck. I give him a jaunty little wave from behind the screen before stepping into Melody's eager web of inquisition.

"That was... Well, Mel. *That* was Cal Thompson."

"That was Cal Thompson? Seriously! Where the hell have you been hiding him?" She pauses, the truth setting in. "Wait. I'm confused. If that was your boyfriend, why was he acting like he didn't know who you were?"

"Because… he… Ugh. God, Mel, I'm an *idiot*. That's why." How do I explain this without sounding like a mental person?

"Grey. Just tell me the truth." Melody puts her hand on my shoulder. "I won't judge you, promise."

So I do.

I tell her everything.

Two

Calvin

As soon as the truck door slams shut, Aaron is half out of his seat, punching me in the arm. "Holy shit, Thompson, your stalker is fucking hot. Did you get her number?"

My hands white knuckle the steering wheel. "No." But I wanted to. God, how I wanted to.

Aaron looks at me like I've lost my goddamn mind. "Why the hell not?"

"Uh, because she's a fucking *stalker*," Mason responds.

"So?"

They're still bickering when I enter the off-ramp for the highway, and they're bickering forty minutes later when we pull up to our off-campus housing.

"Her roommate was smokin' hot too, and funny as shit. They're in a sorority, man. Sexy as hell."

Yeah, it is.

Aaron considers this information. "Way out of your league, bro."

"Don't kick a man when he's down," Mason chastises as we climb out of my truck.

Greyson

@Grey_VKeller @tightheadthompson *remember what I said about live tweeting during our meetings? It's happening. Right. Now.*

@tightheadthompson @grey_vkeller *So is this a pity tweet for the sake of your charade?* #ouch #feelings

@Grey_VKeller @tightheadthompson *Shhhhhh. No talking about the charade in public!* #partnersincrime

@tightheadthompson @grey_vkeller *people can read, you know* #notsubtle #publicforum

@Grey_VKeller @tightheadthompson *valid point*

@tightheadthompson @grey_vkeller *I'm usually always right, but I'll let this one slide because you're* #cute

@Grey_VKeller @tightheadthompson *are you flirting with me, Cal Thompson?* #causethatwouldbeawesome

@JemmaGemini @tightheadthompson *whoever you are, could you STOP Tweeting* @grey_vkeller? *We're try-*

ing to be PRODUCTIVE #distraction #meeting #focus

@Grey_VKeller @tightheadthompson *I'm getting scolded* #momsaysicantplay

@tightheadthompson @grey_vkeller *speaking of charades, maybe I should just get your personal info—just to spare you from further public embarrassment* #gentleman

@Grey_VKeller @tightheadthompson *have your people contact my people* @JemmaGemini #giveMasonmyinfo

---

To: grevkeller0143@state.edu
From: calvin.m.thompson04@smu.il.edu
Subject: Circling back

Greyson. Hey. Just wanted to make sure you're not beating yourself up over the whole lying, stalking thing. Because I'm over it and feel much safer knowing I could definitely take you out in a fight. I don't know why your friend would only give Mason your email address and not your cell phone number. – Cal

To: calvin.m.thompson04@smu.il.edu
From: grevkeller0143@state.edu
Subject: Can't even say how sorry I am…

Calvin,

Your concern fills me with warm fuzzies. I'm taking it day-by-day, each day getting easier and easier to look myself in the mirror. That was sarcasm, by the way. I'm guessing the reason Jemma wouldn't give your roommate my cell is because you look ten kinds of crazy. You're big and scary, black eye and tattoos. Thank you for the email, though, and for not holding a grudge against my stupidity. I guess this means I owe you a favor.

Grey

To: grevkeller0143@state.edu
From: calvin.m.thompson04@smu.il.edu
Subject: Don't worry about it.

Greyson, no one has ever called me big and scary. Or ten kinds of crazy—at least not to my face. What does that even mean? And yeah, you owe me. Hell yeah you do. And don't call me Calvin. – Cal

To: calvin.m.thompson04@smu.il.edu
From: grevkeller0143@state.edu
Subject: I'm stressed out and not thinking clearly?

Calvin,

Sorry for the delay. Speaking of ten kinds of crazy, things are REALLY crazy here. Only a few more weeks until our Gala, and I'm really trying to hold it together. We have one hundred and five tickets sold! I can hardly believe it. Confession: although it's a fundraiser, I kind of hope we don't sell any more! That's a ton of people! I want to go to the event and have SOME fun. Anyway, don't let me get started on all that… Tell me, what does a guy like you do in his free time?

Grey

To: grevkeller0143@state.edu
From: calvin.m.thompson04@smu.il.edu
Subject: What is this free time you speak of?

Grey, a guy like me? First of all, every time I see your name in this email, I *still* cannot believe you're a girl. LOL. My roommates haven't shut up about it, and I think Mason has a crush on your roomie. He can't stop talking about how smart and funny she is.

What do I do in my "free time"? My free time is probably spent a lot like yours: homework, studying, hanging with the guys. We like parties. And, as you know, we play Rugby. I've been Captain since last year, as a sophomore. What about you? What does Greyson "not a guy" Keller do in her free time? – Cal

To: calvin.m.thompson04@smu.il.edu
From: grevkeller0143@state.edu
Subject: LAE (long-ass email)

Calvin (sorry, I can't seem to help myself),

Wow, Captain?! Impressive. I don't know much about Rugby except that the players are big, and they get black eyes and banged up a lot. And they drive big trucks. Other than that, I'm pretty clueless. In my "free time"—if you can call it that—I spend a lot of time with my sorority sisters. Home is a 5-hour drive away, so I stay on campus most of the time and don't go home often. My sorority sisters are my family. I like to read and dabble in writing (tweets □ haha). I don't mind hitting the bar scene every once in a while, but… guys are pretty *grabby*, and I can't stand that.

Grey

PS: I also want to add that other than inventing the occasional fake boyfriend, I'm usually always very honest.

To: grevkeller0143@state.edu
From: calvin.m.thompson04@smu.il.edu
Subject: Fake boyfriends are underrated

Grey, speaking of being very honest, I can *honestly* say I'm never intentionally been grabby with a woman. Although I don't mind a consensual handful of ass cheek. Was that TOO honest for you? Just testing the waters. – Cal

To: calvin.m.thompson04@smu.il.edu
From: grevkeller0143@state.edu
Subject: No date is better than a blind date

Cal,

Is there such a thing as too honest? I'll ponder that… As far as ass grabbing goes, I guess I wouldn't mind it if the grabber was my date. Or my fake date. And since we're being honest, the only person who knows you don't exist—I mean, who knows you aren't really my boyfriend—is my roommate Melody. I do feel terrible lying, but we can't sit and talk about guys during our committee meetings. We get nothing done when we do. It drives my friends nuts that I'm single, and I do *not* want to be set up. Blind dates are the worst. Wouldn't you agree?

Grey

To: grevkeller0143@state.edu
From: calvin.m.thompson04@smu.il.edu
Subject: Use me up then spit me out.

So, what you're saying is, you still plan on using me so your friends don't try and set you up on a blind date? And yeah, I agree that those are the worst, although I've never been on one. Speaking of dating: I think it's rude you haven't asked my permission to use me. – Cal

To: calvin.m.thompson04@smu.il.edu
From: grevkeller0143@state.edu
Subject: Request document submitted

Calvin, do I have your permission to use you as my fake boyfriend?

Grey

To: grevkeller0143@state.edu
From: calvin.m.thompson04@smu.il.edu
Subject: Request document received

Greyson, to answer that, I should probably have your cell phone number. – Cal

697-555-5155: *Grey, this is Cal. Thought it would be easier to text rather than email. What was your question again?*

Grey: *Calvin, took you long enough to ask for my phone number.*

Cal: *For the sake of convenience, it had to be done.*

Grey: *That's the story you're sticking with?*

Cal: *Yup, pretty much.*

Grey: *I guess I'll jump right to the negotiations then. Calvin, do I have your permission to use you as my fake boyfriend?*

Cal: *Let me think about it. This all seems so sudden... are you sure we're not rushing into things?*

Grey: *You're wittier than you look, Cal Thompson*

Cal: *THANKS! Shit. That felt like an insult. Or was it a compliment? Dammit.*

Grey: *LOL*

Cal: *LOL? Fucking rude is what you are. You're lucky you're an hour away.*

Grey: *Or you'd WHAT? Come kick my ass or something?*

Cal: *Or something.*

Grey: *So, do I have your permission?*

Cal: *Yes. But when I start feeling dirty and violated, I'm breaking up with you. Also, please don't tell anyone I "put out" on the first date.*

Grey: *I never kiss and tell…*

Three

To: grevkeller0143@state.edu
From: calvin.m.thompson04@smu.il.edu
Subject: Gray skies and stormy weather.

Grey. This shitty, gray overcast day reminded me of you—but not in a bad way. How's it going over there at State? Had a rugby match this weekend, and I've been icing some seriously sore muscles for the past few days. It sucks. Can hardly move. I also have a cracked lip and another black eye—one that matches the shiner you saw last week. But it looks badass, so who am I to complain? I never did ask what your major is. Mine is business. Yawn. Boring, right? My dad owns a commercial construction company, and after working in the field a few years, I plan to take over when he retires. – Cal

To: calvin.m.thompson04@smu.il.edu
From: grevkeller0143@state.edu
Subject: Grey the Procrastinator

Calvin,

Yes, I'm sticking with that moniker. For some reason, it pleases me knowing that you don't like it… Business is also my major, except I'm not sure which direction I want to take it. Unlike most of my friends, I don't really know what to do with a business degree. Choosing a major was one of the toughest decisions I've ever had to make. I actually waited to declare until I absolutely had to. I have passion for a lot of things. Like event planning and team building. Is that weird? Grey

To: grevkeller0143@state.edu
From: calvin.m.thompson04@smu.il.edu
Subject: The Family Business

Greyson, is that weird? Not at all. Isn't diversity a good thing? My dad always says that having diverse interests gives you a leg up in business, so you're already one step ahead of the game. My mom works in the accounts payable department of his office, and my sister is his Field Manager. She never wanted to work for the family but got roped into it two years ago when Dad had a stroke. Sis is Tabitha, and she's pretty fucking cool. A ballbuster, but cool. Do you have any siblings, or are you a lonely only? –Calvin

To: calvin.m.thompson04@smu.il.edu
From: grevkeller0143@state.edu
Subject: Farm Fresh California Milk

Calvin,

Did you think I wouldn't notice you signed that email as Calvin? Cute, cute, cute. Now you're stuck with it :) Do I have any siblings? Yes, I have an older brother (Collin, 29) and a younger sister (Reagan, 18). Reagan is a freshman at State with me this year and sometimes stalks me on campus for a free coffee. I work at the Starbucks on campus part-part-time. Don't even ask why they keep me employed, since I'm hardly available to work. Must be my sparkling wit and personality? So, did you at least score any *TRYS* during your game?

Grey

To: grevkeller0143@state.edu
From: calvin.m.thompson04@smu.il.edu
Subject: A few more cuts and bruises…

Grey. Holy shit, did you actually google rugby jargon and use TRY in a sentence? Wow, Grey, I have gotta say, I'm actually impressed. And to answer your question—of course I scored a try. They're worth 5 points, and that's where the busted lip came from. Those boys from Ohio are brutes. Changing the subject for a second. So what you're saying is YOUR SISTER STALKS YOU????? At the risk of sounding—oh, I don't know—unsympathetic, can I please point out the fact that perhaps this *stalking* problem RUNS IN YOUR FAMILY???? – Calvin

Grey: *I'm sorry, but I can't stop laughing. You can't say funny crap like that during the day. I just choked back a laugh in this class I'm in right now, and the guy in front of me gave me a dirty look.*

Cal: *Fuck that guy AND his dirty look. They can both kiss my ass.*

Grey: *He's trembling at your harsh text.*

Cal: *He would be if I were in that classroom with you.*

Grey: *True. I mean, you with your busted lip and your black eyes and scary glaring. Ten kinds of crazy, remember?*

Cal: *I am pretty scary.*

Grey: *You don't scare ME.*

Cal: *That's because you have a touch of the crazy inside you, too.*

Grey: *LOL I DO NOT*!!!!!!!!!!!!!!!!!!!!

Grey: *HE'S LOOKING AT ME AGAIN. And he is not happy.*

Cal: *Are you wearing a skirt? Maybe he's just trying to see your underwear? In which case, this fake boyfriend WILL come beat his ass.*

Grey: *Okay, now I'm less concerned with my "touch of the crazy" than with your emerging violent streak and wanting to beat people's asses.*

Cal: *Oh, come on. I haven't actually punched anyone in... hours (wink). Fine. It was at last Friday's rugby match, and he deserved it.*

Grey: *Oh lord, Cal…*

Grey: *BTW, no, I'm not wearing a skirt. I'm wearing a dress.*

Cal: *Well, shit.*

Grey: *Is that all you have to say???*

Cal: *No, that's not all I have to say. What else are you wearing?*

Grey: *Oh, heck no, buddy ^^^ I'm not falling for one of those creepy "What are you wearing" sexting messages that lead to no good.*

Cal: *Shhhhhhh. Shush. Just tell me what your dress looks like so I can close my eyes for a second and visualize you sitting in a lecture hall. In a little sundress like the one you were wearing at your house?*

Grey: *Did you seriously SHUSH me via text???*

Cal: *Lol. Shush, woman! I'm not done with my visuals yet.*

Grey: *Wait. You noticed what I was wearing at my house?*

Cal: *Of course I noticed. You're somewhat good-looking.*

Grey: *Cal!!! You brat.*

Cal: *Just stop arguing and send me a selfie.*

Cal: *Please.*

Grey: *Sigh. Fine, here. Since you asked nice.*

Cal: *Shit, wow. I forgot how cute you are.*

Grey: *Cute? Ugh, the kiss of death. Cute is for kittens and grandmas.*

Cal: *Well I can't very well say you look smoke-fucking-hot, can I? That would be weird.*

Cal: *See? That was weird.*

To: calvin.m.thompson04@smu.il.edu
From: grevkeller0143@state.edu
Subject: Crappy night

Calvin,

Can I vent to you about my crappy night last night? I don't want to dump on you, but... Sometimes it's hard to talk to my friends about certain things. Sometimes I feel like I'm the only one with problems—well, not really "problems," but I don't think I'm handling the stress of all this responsibility well. Sometimes I wish I... had someone to share it with, you know? Anyway. A group of us went out last night (Wasted Wednesday and all that) to this bar, Major Dingby's. And even though I have a "boyfriend"—go ahead, make fun—all anyone did was try and set me up with people!!!! Pretty sure they're not convinced you're real? Why would they try to SET ME UP when they know—I mean THINK—I have a boyfriend??? It's so disrespectful. How is that for ironic? There was this one guy who wouldn't leave me alone, and all I wanted to do was leave. I also wish I hadn't worn a skirt, because, HELLO, ASS GRABBING. It did nothing but make me feel less... less whole. Less in control. Less special. It's not that I mind being single, but I will admit, when I see other people in happy relationships, I get... Ugh, whatever. So that was my night. And now that I wrote that all out I feel so much better, even if I am being a big baby.

Grey

To: grevkeller0143@state.edu
From: calvin.m.thompson04@smu.il.edu
Subject: RE: Crappy night

Grey. First of all, I hope you didn't just stand there letting some prick cop a feel of your ass. Hearing you talk about it makes me feel shitty and like a dick, because I've groped an ass or two. You're not saying it, but I can hear the frustration in the tone of your message, and on behalf of all douchebags, I apologize for the guy who made you feel violated. Is 'violated' even remotely accurate? – Calvin

Grey: *Thank you for that email. It made me feel really, really good.*

Cal: *Really? I'm beginning to wonder if maybe I should double major in counseling.*

Grey: *Calvin, has anyone told you you're a very good listener?*

Cal: *No one—in the history of everybody—has EVER told me I'm a "very good listener." Let's not start any rumors to the contrary.*

Grey: *Well, it's not like you have a choice but to listen when it's just me in an email. I'm sure you would have zoned out if you were sitting across the table from me.*

Cal: *I seriously doubt that.*

To: grevkeller0143@state.edu
From: calvin.m.thompson04@smu.il.edu
Subject: Sunday-not-so-Funday

Grey. Feeling any better? I hate weekends. I always feel so fucking restless. Itchy to do something. Just went for a jog, and I think I'm going to take my kayak down to this small lake (that's more of a pond) nearby, blow off some steam. We don't practice on the weekends because sometimes we have matches, so when we don't have anything going on I tend to get cagey. "Calvin has too much energy" is what my teachers used to say. Drove my mom up a wall. I was always up at dawn, rooting through the kitchen in the dark before school, eating everything in sight before taking a run. At least once a week, my parents thought they were being robbed. My mom's grocery bills were ridiculous when I lived at home. Costco has a plaque in my honor from all the pasta my mom used to buy there. So, yeah. On that awkward note—I'm going kayaking. Kind of a bummer that I'm going alone. It's an awesome day out, yeah?

Just thought I'd see how your spirits were. – Calvin

To: calvin.m.thompson04@smu.il.edu
From: grevkeller0143@state.edu
Subject: The countdown continues.

Calvin,

Well, we're less than six weeks from the gala, and tonight we have our sorority meeting. We always have them on Sunday nights. I'll stand and give an update to the entire chapter on the Philanthropy meetings progress, yada,

yada, yada… I have a test tomorrow in my Contracts Law class worth half our grade, so before our Chapter meeting—and after—I'll be cramming for that. Spending the day outdoors sounds (long wistful sigh) *divine.* It's so gorgeous outside. Perfect day, and I'm stuck inside :(

Greyson

Cal: *Here's a pic of the lake I'm talking about. Picturesque, hey? See that little island? Sometimes I paddle over and sit on the log hanging over the water. #nofilter*

Grey: *That is STUNNING, Calvin! So jealous.*

Cal: *I'll admit, it is gorgeous, but today for some reason I'm kind of bored. Like I'm missing something.*

Grey: *I wonder what that could be…*

Grey: *Here's a photo of me NOT on the lake* :(

Cal: *Man, you're pretty.*

Grey: *Here's another one.*

Cal: *Shit, I have to stop texting from this kayak. I just knocked my hat in the water with my paddle because I'm distracted.*

Grey: *Ok. TTYL. Don't fall in*!

To: greykeller0143@state.edu
From: calvin.m.thompson04@smu.il.edu
Subject: Flying solo this weekend definitely sucked.

Morning, Grey. Gotta say, I'm feeling a little guilty I sent you that picture from Lake Holloway yesterday, because you were trapped indoors, but it was so beautiful on the lake. Quiet. There was no one else there except this one couple—they had a tent and were camping on the peninsula of the little island you saw in the picture. Not to be a peeping Tom/creeper/stalker, but I sat and watched them for a little bit before paddling on. Just chilling and lying around in the grass next to their campfire. Looked awesome. It bummed me out though for a second, because it's like you said in one of your emails; I don't mind being single, but seeing that couple made me feel weird. And I'm only telling you this because you're a chick, and I know you have no one to tell—but now I sound like a girl, all whiney and complainey. Haha. – Calvin

To: calvin.m.thompson04@smu.il.edu
From: greykeller0143@state.edu
Subject: Lurker on the lake.

Cal,

Good morning!!!! Yes, I was jealous that you were out on the lake without me. Maybe someday we could... Um. Yeah. LOL. I actually think it's sweet that you were creeping on those campers. It gives me hope that not all guys are commitment-phobes. YOU'RE not a commitment-phobe, are you, Calvin? Sorry, is that too personal? I don't mean to pry, but now I'm curious. Anyway! Moving on—any big plans for the week...?

Greyson

To: grevkeller0143@state.edu
From: calvin.m.thompson04@smu.il.edu
Subject: Resting up and trying to heal.

Grey. Am I a commitment-phobe? The short answer: no.

Big plans for the week? Not really. Just more of the same shit, different days of the week. Studying, homework, studying, practice, and a match this Friday. It's a home game—our first of the season. Taking advantage of the nice weather, because soon it will get shitty and we'll be playing in snow flurries. Which blows. Speaking of which, my foul language doesn't offend you, does it? I keep forgetting you're classy and not some slutty barfly. –Calvin

To: calvin.m.thompson04@smu.il.edu
From: grevkeller0143@state.edu
Subject: Little Miss not-so-Prim-and-Proper

Calvin,

No, you're swearing doesn't offend me. At all. So no worries. Don't censor yourself around me or you'll exhaust yourself. Besides, clean mouth and proper isn't who you are, and I don't want you to pretend you're something you're not. Who are you playing this Friday? Anyone I would know?

Grey

To: grevkeller0143@state.edu
From: calvin.m.thompson04@smu.il.edu
Subject: Assholes and away games

Grey, we're playing a little school called Notre Dame. Ever heard of them? ;) It's a home game, and thank God they're coming to us. I hate being stuck for hours on a bus, even if they're charter with DVD players and shit. You have no idea what these rugby guys are like, myself included. LOL. Bunch of loudmouth assholes. Don't know how we've never been blacklisted by the bus company. I guess there's always still a chance. Glad I can say shit like shit around you and that you're not easily insulted. Gotta say though, if I watched my mouth for anyone, it would probably be you. But maybe that's just the lack of sleep talking. – Calvin

Grey: *Saw the date stamp on your email last night. What were you doing up so late???*

Cal: *Studying. We must have some of the same classes because it's Contracts Law. Actually really love it.*

Grey: *Me too. I wonder sometimes if I should be prelaw LOL.*

Cal: *I don't know. I think you're probably too soft to be a lawyer.*

Grey: *What's THAT supposed to mean??*

Cal: *You don't have the killer instinct. I could tell when you were all 'sorry this' and 'sorry that' when I came to kick Greyson's ass. You should have stood up to me.*

Grey: *And said what? What I did was wrong!*

Cal: *Yeah, but still. Most girls would have at least screamed and yelled at me for showing up on their doorstep.*

Grey: *Well then, I guess I'm not like most girls.*

Cal: *Yeah, I'm beginning to see that.*

To: grevkeller0143@state.edu
From: calvin.m.thompson04@smu.il.edu
Subject: Dentist on call

Greyson. Okay, this week is already going to shit. We had practice today, and I almost got a tooth knocked out. Remember the guy I had with me at your house in the red shirt? His name is Aaron, but for all practical purposes, we'll call him Shitbag. Moron fucking knocked me in the mouth when I wasn't wearing a mouth guard, which was a stupid thing for me to forget. Definitely chipped my tooth, blood everywhere. Emergency visit to the dentist. And let's just put it this way: it's a good thing I'm only your fake boyfriend, because you wouldn't want to kiss this mouth. – Cal

To: calvin.m.thompson04@smu.il.edu
From: grevkeller0143@state.edu
Subject: Face plant.

Calvin,

Does it hurt? I've only been nailed in the mouth once, and it was by my brother when I was 12. Which would have made him 19. We were playing football in the backyard with some of his friends when he came home from college for Easter, and he lobbed the ball right at my face. A spiral toss, full force. Nothing was knocked out but me. Laid me flat out. Fat, bloody lip for almost two weeks. My parents were so pissed. I still refuse to toss the ball around with him LOL. He'll never live it down. Speaking of bloody lips, who's to say no one would want to kiss you? I bet SOME girls get turned on by beat-up-looking athletes. Do you still have that black eye? That's bonus points. Brings your average up considerably, and I definitely find that sexy.

Grey

Cal: *My face still hurts.*
Grey: *Rub some dirt on it.*
Cal: *I don't have any. I live in a concrete jungle.*
Grey: *Poor baby.*
Cal: *>tear<*
Grey: LOLOL

To: calvin.m.thompson04@smu.il.edu
From: grevkeller0143@state.edu

Subject: Nurse Greyson Keller at your service…

Calvin,

How's our patient today? The lip and teeth any better? I hope Aaron hasn't mysteriously disappeared, because that would make me an accessory to a crime. And then I would have to report you to the authorities.

Grey

To: grevkeller0143@state.edu
From: calvin.m.thompson04@smu.il.edu
Subject: Naughty Nurse Keller? Yes please.

Grey. Wow, you would make the world's shittiest nurse. I'm sensing all your sympathy lies with Aaron, and I won't stand for it. We're not supposed to rough each other up in practice. I swear to fucking God he's pissed that I haven't gotten Melody's number for him. I don't know where he thinks I'd GET it from, because I haven't told anyone you and I have been talking. – Calvin

Grey: *So now I'm your dirty little secret?*

Cal: *No, that's not what I meant at all. You're more like…*

Grey: *More like…? Come on, tell me. Don't be shy.*

Cal: *Me, shy? Yeah, right.*

Grey: *Don't change the subject. If I'm not your dirty little secret, then what am I?*

Cal: *You're more like—this is going to sound really fucking dumb.*

Grey: *SAY IT OR I SWEAR TO GOD CALVIN I WILL COME FIND YOU.*

Cal: *Well, in that case I'm going to zip my lips shut.*

Grey: *Aww, you are so cute.*

Cal: *You're not my dirty little secret. You're my guilty pleasure.*

Cal: *Oh my god, that did sound fucking dumb.*

Grey: *Hold on. I'm going to pass out now from shock. That wasn't dumb—it was the sweetest thing I've ever heard.*

Cal: *And THAT'S ^^^ the reason I shouldn't have said anything.*

Grey: *I'm taking a screenshot of that and saving it for eternity so I can stare at it at night when I'm alone.*

Cal: *Wow. Spoken like a true stalker.*

Grey: *LOL.*

To: grevkeller0143@state.edu
From: calvin.m.thompson04@smu.il.edu
Subject: Worse than a bunch of women. No offense.

Greyson. My roommates are driving me fucking crazy. If they don't stop asking about you, I'm moving out. Mason checks his *Twatter* constantly, looking for my name in your feed, and mopes around like a sad puppy dog when he can't find one. It's annoying. Could you do me a favor and get him off my back by throwing the dog a small bone? – Calvin

---

@Grey_VKeller Tweeted: *The countdown to Gala continues. Thanks 4 dinner last night* @calthompson3192 *the poem & wine & roses & chocolates were 2 MUCH! Kisses to my big SWEETIE POOH* #bestboyfriend

---

Cal: *I hate you so hard right now.*

Grey: **blank stare* Was it something I said?? I tried to use every available character #140*

Cal: *That was really fucking rude. They are RIDING MY ASS right now. Calling me pussy whipped. Hope you're happy, you brat.*

Grey: *Oh, don't be a baby. You asked me to send the tweet.*

Cal: *You know damn well that's not what I meant. Who's moving out of state and changing their name? >> This guy <<*

Grey: *Changing your name? *claps happily* Ooh, ooh! Let me help you pick one!!!! What about Chet Montgomery? That sounds sporty and badass.*

Cal: *No.*

Grey: *Allan Thouroughgood*

Cal: *Oh my god.*

Grey: *Randolph Christian Kuttnauer*

Cal: *WHERE the HELL are you coming up with these?*

Grey: *Those don't sound regal to you? Or manly?*

Cal: *No.*

Grey: *I've got it!!! Dark Gray Keller.*

Cal: *LOLOL Okay. I'll admit, that one was funny.*

Grey: :) *I try. TRY. GET IT? GET IT???*

Cal: *Honestly, Grey. What am I going to do with you…*

Grey: *I might have some suggestions.*

Cal: *No comment.*

To: calvin.m.thompson04@smu.il.edu
From: grevkeller0143@state.edu
Subject: We're becoming THAT couple ;) haha

Calvin,

You're not still mad about the tweet, are you? Believe me—I got as much shit from my friends as you probably did. Apparently, when you publically call someone Sweetie Pooh, it makes people want to toss their cookies inside their preppy monogram tote bags. Or so I've been told. Multiple times. Jemma, your roommate's cousin, has been getting the scoop on you from Mason, and now she wants me to stay away from you. Says you're only going to break my heart because you don't "do" relationships. Oh, and you're a total dickhead. (Mason's words, not mine).

Oddly enough, I ended up defending you like this charade is real. What's THAT all about?!

Grey

To: grevkeller0143@state.edu
From: calvin.m.thompson04@smu.il.edu
Subject: Admit it. I'm growing on you.

Greyson. No, I'm not still mad. Actually, I wasn't mad to begin with, just surprised. Want to know the truth? I don't actually mind the teasing. What's THAT all about? – Calvin

To: calvin.m.thompson04@smu.il.edu
From: grevkeller0143@state.edu
Subject: Bats in the Belfry

Dear Calvin,

Do you realize we've been emailing and texting for over three weeks now? Every time I giggle at my phone—at something YOU said—my roommates and sisters give me the weirdest looks. At this point there is no doubt they think you're real. It's going to make things that much more awkward when Gala night arrives. I cannot wait for this thing to be over. Which reminds me, pretty soon I'm going to have to publicly break up with you. Don't worry, it will be mutual, even though having a real life boyfriend would have been handy last night. We had a BAT in our house. I swear to God, Calvin, the screaming coming from Melody… My eardrums shattered. WHAT? *Did you say something*? I CAN'T HEAR YOU! We must have called our landlord five times, and he never showed up. Finally, Beth, my other roommate, called one of the guys from our brother fraternity, and not one but THREE of them showed up—three of us, three of them. See how they planned that?—with tennis rackets, of course, like THAT was a smart idea. One of the brothers kept asking all these questions about you. His name is Dylan, and if he touched my leg once he touched it six times while grilling me about you. Or the Cal I made up. Anyway, he kept telling me about how long-distance relationships never work. I wanted to smack him.

Grey

PS: The bat is gone. FOR NOW.

To: grevkeller0143@state.edu
From: calvin.m.thompson04@smu.il.edu
Subject: RE: Bats in the Belfry

WHAT THE FUCK, GREYSON? I don't even know where to start. How does a fake boyfriend respond to an email like that? I can't come pound some dude's face in because he touched you just like I can't beat your landlord's ass for not showing up to kill a bat—and that infuriates me. I'm going to take a deep breath here and calm the fuck down for a second. – Calvin

To: calvin.m.thompson04@smu.il.edu
From: grevkeller0143@state.edu
Subject: There's only room for ONE (fake) boyfriend in my life.

Cal,

I'm sorry I upset you. It really wasn't that big of a deal. I mean, yes, Dylan kind of upset me, but he wasn't doing it intentionally. Well… okay. That's a lie because he was obviously hitting on me pretty hard and CLEARLY trying to badmouth you. Or the *OTHER* Cal. LOL. It makes me—I don't know—happy that you care enough to get mad. Who knew that we would become FRIENDS? Life is crazy, isn't it? Just in the middle of cooking dinner here, but I wanted to send you a quick note. What time is your match tomorrow?

Grey

To: greykeller0143@state.edu
From: calvin.m.thompson04@smu.il.edu
Subject: Wasted man meat.

Grey. What did you end up making for dinner? I bet it was better than what we had—or didn't have. We bought a few choice steak filets that Mason immediately burned the CRAP out of on the grill. Charred. Fifty bucks flushed down the shitter, and he kept blaming the charcoal. Our game tomorrow starts at 6pm, and it's 80 minutes—two 40-minute halves, obviously. Have you ever been to one? This match is going to set the tone for our entire season. Aaron has his sights set on a professional team in Ireland after graduation and has a good chance at being signed. We've been friends since middle school, so his level of play is surreal, even for me. I love the kid like a brother and I'm really proud of him. I swear to God, Grey, if you ever repeat that… – Cal

To: calvin.m.thompson04@smu.il.edu
From: greykeller0143@state.edu
Subject: Sisterhoods and Bromances

Calvin,

Who would I even TELL about your love for Aaron? My sorority sisters? The Twitterverse? Anyway, I don't get why guys never want to talk about their feelings for each other. It's really stupid if you ask me. A slap on the ass among men during a sporting event hardly a brotherhood makes. Wait. Did that even make sense??? Whatever, I'm not deleting it. Haha. You probably won't even see this because you're getting ready to rugby.

Grey

Cal: *Oh, I saw it.*

Grey: *You're there!!*

Cal: *Grey, it's only noon. Lol. Where else would I be?*

Cal: *And for your information, rugby players do NOT slap each other on the ass. Ever. I'd get punched in the face if I ever swatted another dude in the ass.*

Grey: *Want to test that theory? Swat someone on the ass and see what happens...*

Cal: *No.*

Grey: *Boo, hiss.*

Cal: *So. Got anything going on tomorrow afternoon?*

Grey: *Maybe. I don't have afternoon classes on Fridays, so the girls and I might take a short trip.*

Cal: *That sounds... terrible.*

Grey: *That's 'cause you're a party pooper.*

Grey: *Incidentally, if you had a drink of choice after your game, what would it be?*

Cal: *Um...??? That's really random.*

Grey: *Humor me.*

Cal: *Probably a green tea lemonade.*

Grey: *Ah, a Starbucks man.*

Cal: *GTG. Team meeting in twenty.*

Grey: :)

Four

Calvin

I'm pulling the slobbery mouth guard off my teeth when I see her.

I briskly shake my head side to side, beads of perspiration flying out of my damp hair, and squint up into the stands, convinced my eyes are playing tricks on me.

Under the stadium light, among the SMU and Notre Dame fans donning their navy and gold school colors, Grey stands, her long blonde hair whipping in the wind as she makes her way, one metal bleacher step at a time, down towards the rugby field.

I shake my head again. Holy fuck. What is she *doing* here?

My breath catches as I blink in her direction—not just

from being winded from the hard-fought game we just won. No. I'm suddenly winded from an adrenaline rush of another kind: Lust. Anticipation. Uncertainty.

I stand frozen on the sidelines, surrounded by my teammates packing up their gear. Another bead of sweat rolls down my neck and drips onto my already soaked jersey.

"Hottie approaching at three o'clock," the team's athletic trainer, Paul, announces. "Wow. She's… wow. "

"That's no ordinary hottie, Paul," Mason announces, slapping a hand down on my shoulder. "That's Tighthead's stalker. Steer clear."

Paul stares, captivated, at Greyson's encroaching figure. "Why would anyone want to steer clear of *that*?" Lucky for Paul, he just sounds fascinated, not perverted.

Aaron stuffs a towel and sweatshirt into his duffel before joining in the mocking. "Holy shit, man. It looks like your stalker really *is* a stalker! Were you full of shit when you said she wasn't stalking you?"

"Are you guys being serious?" Paul, armed with this new information, tilts his head and appraises her. "*She's* a stalker? No way."

"Stop being an asshole, Mason. And stop fucking using that word," I growl, shoving him out of my personal space. Grey's throng of friends lingers behind her, obediently up in the bleachers as she approaches me, her bright white smile lighting her stunning face.

A low whistle of appreciation escapes Paul's lips. "Damn, Tighthead, *that* girl is into *you*? No offense."

Shit. Fuck.

"She is way out of your league, bro," Mason charitably points out.

Don't I know it.

She's gorgeous, and I'm a mutt, and Mason's reminder pisses me off.

"Would you all just effing go away," I demand with another shove, and he laughs, giving Grey a little wave before hefting his equipment bag over his shoulder and retreating towards the university's field house.

"Come on, guys. Let's give Tighthead and his girlfriend here some *pri-va-cy*." The way he says it has everyone, including our coach, snickering.

"Fuck off, all of you," I sneer, embarrassed and irritated. Several of the guys are avidly checking out Greyson, and that's pissing me off too.

"Tsk, tsk. That's not a very nice way to talk to your friends," Grey calls out to me, and I hear several of my teammates laughing in the distance as Grey steps onto the playing field in those same wedge sandals she wore the day we met, her dark jean capris hugging her long legs. And are my eyes deceiving me, or is she eyeing me up with unconcealed appreciation?

"I didn't see you smacking anyone's ass during the match," she teases. "That's a tad disappointing. I thought maybe you were lying when you said you never did that." Her eyes roam to Mason, who keeps glancing back at us as he trudges to the building.

Greyson's keen eyes notice. "What'd he do to piss you off?"

She's thirty feet away.

I swallow the hard lump in my throat. "He was being an ass."

Fifteen.

"Well, never mind him."

Five feet.

She extends her hand, presenting me with a large green tea lemonade from Starbucks. "The ice melted because I couldn't give it to you sooner. Sorry." Perspiration slides off the plastic cup.

Shell shocked, I take it from her while she continues gushing.

"My gosh, Cal," she breathes when she's standing in front of me, her hands reaching up to hover over my hardened pecs like she's about to run them up-and-down my broad chest.

I hold my breath, but she drops them back to her side.

But then…

"You are amazing! You look so *incredible* out there, Cal. I swear, I couldn't take my eyes off you." Moving in closer, she actually goes up on her tiptoes and plants a kiss on my sweat-drenched cheek. As if she couldn't stop herself.

I watch, transfixed, when Grey licks her lips instead of wiping the sweat on her mouth off with her hand. "Wow, you smell good. Like a man."

Jesus H *Christ*.

"Um, hi?" I manage, fighting the urge to blurt out, *What the hell are you doing here?*

"Surprise!" Grey giggles, a delighted little twinkle that tinges the apples of her cheeks a pretty pink color. "I couldn't stay away. The temptation to show up unexpectedly was impossible to resist." She gives me a wink and shoves my bicep, her fingers sinking into my skin and lingering far too long to be accidental.

She prattles on. "Well, I mean I *could* have stayed away—but I didn't want to."

Down in my spandex rugby pants is the telltale twitching of an impending hard-on.

Fuck.

"Grey, uh…" I tip my head to our audience. My teammates are huddled on the far side of the field, avidly watching with interest, while her sorority sisters do the same from up in the bleachers.

She glances back over her shoulder and shrugs without a care. "My friends wanted to come down here, but of course I wouldn't let them. You're safe from the inquisition, if that's what you're worried about." Grey runs a hand through her highlighted wavy hair and gives it a shake.

It settles on her shoulder like a silky cloud, shining under the stadium lights like a halo.

Mesmerized, I stare down into her large, laughing hazel eyes, darkened with black eyeliner and coated with a heavy layer of mascara. She's wearing a simple white t-shirt, but it's tight, and my eyes are drawn to the smooth bronze skin in the deep V neck.

Her brown eyebrows are raised at me expectantly.

Oh shit. She wants me to say something.

"Hmm." Her hands settle on her narrow hips. "You were much chattier when you came to my house. Is everything okay?"

"Yeah, I'm just—you want the truth?"

"No, I want you to lie." Grey rolls those brilliant eyes with a smile. "Yes, of course I want the truth."

"I'm shocked to see you. It's one thing for me to ambush *you*, but another for you to ambush *me*."

"Well, if it makes you feel better, we can't stay long. I have to get that crew of misfit toys behind me back to campus. A few of them are running a 5k tomorrow, and they want to stuff themselves with pasta." She rolls her eyes again. "They think they're pro athletes now and want to carb load. By the way, this is one of those 5ks where you wear a fluffy tutu and get pelted with color bombs, so…"

Again with the raised eyebrow.

I can't stand it. "I know I'm being fucking awkward, okay? Just say it."

"You're a *little* awkward." She crosses her arms and taps her foot. "But I find you *very* charming."

"Stop looking at me like that," I mumble.

"How am I looking at you? I'm not doing anything." Greyson laughs. "I'm standing here *talking*."

She playfully gives my tricep another tap, the contact from her feather-light touch giving me goosebumps *and* a goddamn boner.

The tightening in my shorts has my jaw clenching and my nostrils flare. "Stop flirting."

"Why?"

Fuck it. "Because it's making me hard."

Instead of being offended by the lewd comment, Greys hazel eyes leisurely skim down my body to my spandex shorts, alive with interest. The air between us crackles and sizzles.

"Spoilsport," she whispers, the disappointment in her voice palpable.

At that moment, I'm certain of one thing: this girl is going to be the death of me.

She tips her chin thoughtfully at me when I frown. "Okay, okay. I'll leave. Tell Mason and Aaron your *stalker* says hi."

"You heard that?"

"Um, yeah—they were practically shouting."

"Sorry."

"Do I look like I care?" She flips her hair and shoots a flirty smile over to my group of teammates, wiggling her fingers in their direction. They stare back at the pretty girl, transfixed, before several meaty arms enthusiastically wave back. "Could they be any more obvious?" Greyson's laugh fills the night air. "They're nosier than a group of sorority girls. Look at them pretending to be busy instead of heading into the building."

"They're just staring because you're kind of nice looking." I sound disgruntled.

"Nice looking?" Grey laughs again and reaches up to touch my jaw, running a thumb along my busted up lip. "Aww, see? You can be sweet."

"Yeah, whatever." A smile curls my lips.

"Alright, well. I'm going to go now." She lets out a little puff of air and closes the space between us. "Can you do me a small favor, since my friends are watching?"

"That depends." I cross my arms, one hand fisting the Starbucks, noting with satisfaction that my biceps are bulging nicely. "What is it?"

Grey notices too.

"See, remember how I told you no one knows I made you up? Well, it wouldn't seem *natural* for me to just walk away right now. You know, without…" Her sentence trails off, and she stares me down.

I'm not following. "Without *what*?"

"A good-bye kiss, you idiot."

It takes me a few to realize she's being serious. She *actually* wants me to kiss her. This gorgeous, smart, funny girl wants *me* to kiss *her*.

"You're asking me to kiss you." It's a statement, not a question. "I have stiches in my lip."

"Do the stiches bother you? It doesn't have to be real—just one for show. If you can stand to put your lips near me."

Now it's my turn to roll my eyes. "Don't be so dramatic. I think I can manage."

Her eyes shine. "Put the cup down."

The air crackles around us like unharnessed electricity. Bending slowly, I do as I'm told, setting the green tea lemonade on the playing field.

"Well? Get closer, you shameless hussy. Unless you're afraid to get dirty."

"I'm not afraid to get dirty if you're not."

"Would you stop saying shit like that? Jesus." I grasp her arm, tugging her into my damp, mud-stained rugby jersey, trailing my calloused hands up her smooth arms. Grey sighs and leans into me, returning the favor. The tips of her fingers start at my wrists, tracing their way up the sensitive skin of my underarms. She flattens her palms and closes them around the corded muscles of my flexed biceps.

Her breasts press against my sweat-soaked chest.

My cock gets harder, and any intentions of a chaste good-bye kiss go up in smoke as my hormones rage inside me like a wildfire.

I gently cup her neck in my large palms, kneading the nape and cradling her jaw when her head lists to one side with a moan.

My fingers find themselves threaded through her thick, silk-spun hair.

Bodies drawn together as if by necessity, our hot lips press together, softly at first. Tentatively. I hesitate a few seconds, inhaling to harness my raging testosterone levels, and begin pulling away.

"Wait." Grey's delicate hands gently glide up my biceps to my shoulders, her index finger tracing my square jawline, then the lobe of an ear. "Don't back away yet. Please."

Without thinking, I grab her wrist and roll my head, bringing her palm to my mouth and planting a wet kiss there. I kiss the tips of her fingers and her palm, running my nose along the velvety skin of her wrist and inhaling the musky smell of her perfume.

Her lips part as she watches me, her pupils dilated.

"God, Grey."

Our foreheads touch. The tips of our noses follow.

A few millimeters closer and our lips part. Mouths touch. Tongues meet.

"Kiss me, Cal," Grey begs against my mouth, her voice a whisper in the breeze. "*Kiss* me."

Fuck it. I'm going all in.

I snake my arms around her waist and haul her in, so flush with her body that I'm cradled in between her legs. I groan. She moans, and her hands travel south, down over my firm ass, squeezing it through my thin shorts.

Holy shit, *yes*.

I lose half my brain cells in that moment—then the rest—when she sucks my tongue farther into her mouth, like she's actually enjoying herself. Her tongue darts out, licking along the deep cut on my lip.

I give her a few more kisses before I tighten my grip on her arms and, regretfully, give her a small push to create some space between us.

"Shit, Grey, we have to stop." My breathing is labored, but so is hers. "Jesus. This is nuts."

"I don't want to," she pouts against my lips.

"I don't either, but my dick is hard as a rock and I'm wearing fucking spandex. People are watching."

As if on cue, my teammates begin cat-calling from the field house. Assholes.

She huffs; it's adorable. "Okay, fine. But only because I don't want to be called any more nasty names 'cause I can't keep my hands to myself."

"Trust me, it's no hardship," I feebly joke, my voice catching when Grey runs her palms up the front of my jersey, tracing the outline of the team name screen printed there. I reach my hand between our bodies, adjusting my groin and jockstrap before capturing her hands to hold them still. "I'm going to be walking crooked for a week."

Grey takes a step back, giving me a once-over and pausing on the bulge in my shorts before averting her eyes and glancing up into the bleachers as her hands fall to her sides. She swallows hard and clears her throat. "You played great tonight, Cal. I'm proud of you."

"Grey, why…"

"Yes?"

"…are you here?"

We stare at one another, and I know by the expression on her face that she's doing what I'm doing: memorizing every line in my face, every curve of my body.

Just in case we… just in case this is the last time.

And there goes that crack and sizzle.

Grey closes the gap between us. Slowly, her soft lips press against my mouth, tenderly resting there. "You know why I'm here, Cal Thompson."

She turns reluctantly, glancing back at me at least a half dozen times as I watch her go.

I don't how long I stood there.

Cal: *I'm sorry I manhandled you tonight.*

Grey: *If I remember correctly, I did basically TELL you to kiss me, so in a way, I was doing the manhandling. For the sake of my friends, of course. And my charade.*

Cal: *Of course.*

Grey: *For the sake of science?*

Cal: *That sounds even less plausible.*

Grey: *Fine, don't believe me.*

Cal: *Fine, I won't.*

@Grey_VKeller Tweeted: @tightheadthompson *you sexy sexy beast*

Cal: *I know you did NOT just tweet that shit.*

Grey: *Are getting teased again by your friends? Come on, it can't be that bad.*

Cal: *Is this all just a joke to you? A sorority prank?*

Grey: *Is WHAT a joke???*

Cal: *Sexy sexy beast? Seriously, WHAT THE FUCK, GREYSON?*

Grey: *WHY ARE YOU SO PISSED OFF?! CALM DOWN*

Cal: *You can't say shit like that. It makes you sound like a goddamn…*

Grey: *A goddamn WHAT*

Cal: *Forget it. Just don't say shit like that.*

Grey: *I will NOT forget it. Tell me what your freaking problem is.*

Grey: *And for the record, you overreacting jackass, I MEANT IT.*

Cal: *Oh.*

Grey: *Oh?*

Grey: *Hello? You there?*

Grey: *Cal?*

Grey: *Okay then*

Greyson

"I don't understand. You tweeted that he was a sexy beast, and then he goes radio silence on you? That's so messed up."

I drum a number 2 pencil on the wooden table, and blow a puff of air at my bangs to move them out of my eyes. "I guess I don't get it. I thought that maybe, when he kissed me, we were… I don't know."

"Becoming more than pen pals?"

"Yes. Because I felt that kiss *everywhere*, Mel. Everywhere. That wasn't a kiss between two friends."

Melody speaks slowly then, choosing her words carefully. "I mean, I know it's a weird thing to ask, but do you think you scared him away?"

I give her a hard look. "What's that supposed to mean?"

"Nothing! I just wonder if he thought maybe you were… making fun of him? Lying?"

I ignore that she just called me a liar, but my mouth still gapes in indignation. "Making *fun* of him? Why would you even *say* that?"

"Well, jeez, Grey. Look at him. He isn't winning any beauty contests."

My mouth falls open even wider, and the rash on my chest shoots up my neck at a breakneck pace, coloring my cheeks, nose, and forehead. My face is flaming hot, which I bet it looks spectacular against my light blonde hair. "Melody! What the *hell*. I think he's gorgeous!"

"Well, yeah—*you* do. But you didn't think he was so hot when he showed up at the house. You think he's hot because you're finally getting to know him. That's why you think he's attractive; he's grown on you. Everyone else, erm, not so much."

"You—that's so mean." I stand abruptly, knocking a cup of pens over with a curse. Tears threaten to spill out of the corners of my eyes. I wipe them away angrily. "Not all of us want just want to date pretty frat boys."

Melody sighs, her eyes pleading with me. "I'm sorry. That's not… this is coming out all wrong."

My bottom lip trembles.

"Grey." Melody stands. "You're beautiful. And sweet. And funny. Of course everyone expects you to hook up with some GQ model. Not some… Not a busted-up *rugby* player from SMU. I'm just trying to be honest."

"I do *not* like you right now."

"Grey, you don't even know this guy."

"Yes I do." I cross my arms and stare out the window into the yard, tuning her out. Softly, I whisper, "I know enough."

To: calvin.m.thompson04@smu.il.edu
From: grevkeller0143@state.edu
Subject: Please talk to me.

Calvin,

It's been two days. Why are you shutting me out? I don't understand. I don't understand why you over reacted to the tweet, but I'm sorry if I embarrassed you in front of your friends. I called you sexy and I meant it. I wasn't making fun of you—how could you THINK that??? I thought we were becoming friends. I miss you. I miss my friend.

Grey

To: grevkeller0143@state.edu
From: calvin.m.thompson04@smu.il.edu
Subject: I'm an ass.

You're right. I overreacted. I don't know how to explain it without sounding like a complete douchenozzle, so can we just forget about it? I feel like a tool. And since we're friends and I'm being honest, this is exactly how I would treat you if you were a dude. I'd give you the silent treatment until I got over myself. So you should feel pretty good about that. – Cal

To: calvin.m.thompson04@smu.il.edu
From: grevkeller0143@state.edu
Subject: Best Friends 4Eva

Cal,

Yes, I'll forget about it, but... You know what, never mind—I'm just so relieved you emailed me back. I'll keep this light hearted. After all, we hardly know each other. As for you treating me like one of your guy friends, well—I'm flattered. Kind of? Have you ever had a girl that's a friend before? The distance between us certainly makes it easier to have that kind of relationship, yeah? I doubt I could manage to be *friends* friends if we were at the same school—if we were in the same town.

Grey

To: grevkeller0143@state.edu
From: calvin.m.thompson04@smu.il.edu
Subject: Huh?

Greyson, I'm not even sure what that's supposed to mean.

To: calvin.m.thompson04@smu.il.edu
From: grevkeller0143@state.edu
Subject: Seriously?

Read between the lines, Calvin. And why are you emailing me this? Wouldn't it be easier to text?

Grey

To: grevkeller0143@state.edu
From: calvin.m.thompson04@smu.il.edu
Subject: Still don't have a clue. Sorry.

Grey. I'm not texting because I had already composed the email. And last time I checked, I was a guy—and one that gets concussions on a regular basis. You need to spell it out for me. – Cal

To: calvin.m.thompson04@smu.il.edu
From: grevkeller0143@state.edu
Subject: Forget I said anything.

Cal,

I'm not in the mood to explain myself. Maybe some other time.

Cal: *This is going to get ridiculous if we don't talk.*

Grey: *What's going to get ridiculous?*

Cal: *You know what? Never mind. I'm not playing games with you.*

Grey: *Time. Out. Why are you being so stubborn about this? I don't know what flipped your switch, but you need to explain it. Answer me, Calvin.*

Cal: *You're right. I'm sorry. You're my friend, and it was an asshole thing to do, and I'm sorry.*

Grey: *I like you, Calvin. I think you're sexy and handsome and funny. Accept it and move on. And stop be-*

ing an ass.

Cal: *Have you always been this bossy?*

Grey: *Yes.*

Cal: *I like it.*

Grey: *I know you do. Why do you think I'm acting so bossy?*

To: grevkeller0143@state.edu
From: calvin.m.thompson04@smu.il.edu
Subject: Not that kind of trim work

Greyson. Going home this weekend to help my dad do some landscaping. My mom gets all weird about having all the shrubs and flower beds weeded and cut down before it gets cold out, so… just wanted to let you know. My folks get pissed when I'm constantly checking my phone. Disrespectful and all that shit. – Cal

To: calvin.m.thompson04@smu.il.edu
From: grevkeller0143@state.edu
Subject: TWO WHOLE DAYS?

Calvin,

So what you're saying is, you don't want me to feel bad when you're MIA for a few days? Aww, that's sweet. Very considerate to let me know. I will admit that I have gotten used to talking with you during the day. Well, not "talking," but you get my point. Does your sister have to

partake in this landscaping torture, too?
Grey

To: grevkeller0143@state.edu
From: calvin.m.thompson04@smu.il.edu
Subject: Evil Mastermind

Grey. Yes, everyone will be there. My parents are Equal Opportunity Sadists. But Tabby (aka: the smart one in this case) will throw a fit at some point and pick a fight so my mom yells and kicks her out of the yard. IT'S SO UNFAIR. She's a genius. – Cal

To: calvin.m.thompson04@smu.il.edu
From: grevkeller0143@state.edu
Subject: Why should Tabitha have all the fun?

Calvin,

Maybe you should beat her to it. Where are you from originally, anyway? I don't think we've ever talked about it. My parents moved this summer from Lake Walton to another little lake community just south called Six Rivers. It's also a resort town, but there's tons to do there, which is a nice change. Lake Walton was pretty small—the closest Target was a day trip.

Grey

Cal: *You did NOT say Six Rivers.*

Grey: *Yes, why?*

Cal: *Take a wild guess.*

Grey: *SHUT UP. No way.*

Cal: *Yes way. Well, next town over. 20 minutes on a bad day.*

Grey: *There is NO WAY you live near where I live.*

Grey: *You know what this means, don't you?!*

Cal: *That we can be best friends and do karate in the garage?*

Grey: **crickets* That made absolutely no sense.*

Cal: *Never mind. It's from a movie. LOL. Tell me what you were going to say before when you said, "You know what this means, don't you?" and I so rudely made a movie reference.*

Grey: *Well, besides you being hopelessly clueless, this means we can be buddies during summer and the holidays and hang out! We can have drinks at that bar near the lake.*

Cal: *Sully's on the Lake? It's not near the lake, it's ON the lake. LOL*

Grey: *See. This is why we need to hang out when we're home.*

Cal: *What are the odds?*

Grey: *It's fate.*

Cal: *Oh.... boy.*

Grey: *You can show me the sights. We can float on the lake.*

Cal: *Did you say FLOAT on the lake?*

Grey: *Yeah, you know, on rafts?*

Cal: *Ah, okay. So, literally floating. Will this floating require bathing suits?*

Grey: *Not necessarily.*

Cal: *Are you flirting with me?*

Grey: *I think it's really sad you can't tell when a girl is flirting with you. But since you asked, I wouldn't dare. Remember the last time I tried that? #epicfail #sexybeast #angrycalvin*

Cal: *Fine. But in my defense, no one has ever called me sexy. I thought you were being a bitch.*

Grey: *You are LYING. How is that possible?*

Cal: *Which part? The sexy part or the bitch part?*

Grey: *You are getting sexier and sexier by the day. Sorry, but it's true. Time to accept the facts.*

To: grevkeller0143@state.edu
From: calvin.m.thompson04@smu.il.edu
Subject: Warning! Warning!

Grey. As I suspected, my mom drove us nuts over the weekend with her demands. The woman is obsessed with mulching. And, as I predicted, Tabby picked a fight and Mom kicked her out of the yard. The brat winked at me as she fake stormed off. I can't freaking believe my mom still falls for that bullshit. The good news is, all I had to do was drive the bobcat while my dad raked leaves into the shovel. What can I say about Sunday? For starters, my damn sister tricked me into telling her about you. I don't know how she figured it out, but I must have been checking my phone about a hundred times—just in case you decided to send a message—and she caught me. When she tried stealing my phone and I pitched a bitch fit instead of letting her take it, she knew there was shit on here I didn't want her to see. Boy, was she a pain in my ass. The entire day she tried to steal my phone. Wanting to see pictures of you. Asking a shit ton of annoying questions. If you get a friend request from Tabitha Thompson, would you do me a huge favor and DELETE IT?

What did you do this weekend? – Cal

To: calvin.m.thompson04@smu.il.edu
From: grevkeller0143@state.edu
Subject: I consider creeping research.

Calvin,

In fact, I DID get a friend request from a Tabitha Thompson! LOL. No worries, I haven't decided what to do about it yet. I did sneak onto her page, though. She looks awesome. Very beautiful. My objective, of course, was to find pictures of you. Très stalkerish of me, wouldn't you say? Whatever. I got all giddy and girly over a few—the one of you in a tux for your senior prom? OMG. So handsome. And the one of you with your childhood dog? Must say, Calvin, I have something of a crush on you. I can admit that, right, now that we're pen pals?

Grey

To: grevkeller0143@state.edu
From: calvin.m.thompson04@smu.il.edu
Subject: Creeping, lurking = Same thing

Grey. Not surprised that you were lurking on my sister's pics. That picture of me with the dog? Brownie, his name was—he was the shit. Cried like a baby when my parents put him to sleep. I don't even want to know if you saw the picture of me snuggling Sparkles, the kitty cat I had when I was 3. Tabby posted that one last year for my birthday, that rude bitch. Shit. That was a joke. I would never call her that to her face; she'd scratch my eyes out. My sister, not the cat. – Cal

Cal: *By the way, I've decided I will allow you to have a crush on me.*

Grey: *How magnanimous of you.*

Cal: *You're welcome.*

Grey: *You ass.*

Cal: *Speaking of asses, yours is incredible.*

Grey: *Well, aren't you just full of compliments today! I've got one for you: I could stare at your firm, tight ass in those rugby spandex all day long.*

Cal: *Holy shit, that is NOT what I was expecting you to say.*

Grey: *Why?*

Cal: *Because you're classy.*

Grey: *Maybe, but I also have eyes. And hormones. I can't say you have a firm, tight ass? Okay, fine. Can we at least talk about your buff arms? DROOL.*

Cal: *NO! Maybe. Okay, fine.*

Grey: **pouting* I want to talk about your tattoos.*

Cal: *Thank god you're an hour away, because I can't spend the whole night jerking off—*

Cal: *Shit, I did NOT mean to send that.*

Cal: *Ugh. It didn't even make any sense.*

Cal: *Greyson, fucking say something*!

Grey: *Shush. Shhhh. Shhh. I'm not done visualizing you doing naughty, naughty things to yourself *closes eyes* Also, why did you TYPE it if you didn't mean to send it? WHAT THE HELL?? LOLOLOL*

Grey: *The WHOLE night jerking off? Wow. That's some stamina you must have...*

Cal: *Oh my god. This is my worst nightmare*

Grey: ^^^ *you sound like such a girl.*

Cal: *Wait. Did you just screenshot that shit????*

Grey: *No. Maybe. Okay, fine. Yes.*

Cal: *What are you up to right now*?

Grey: *I'm about to walk into work. But instead I'm sitting here in a chair by the door like a creeper, texting you.*

Cal: *Sorry.*

Grey: *Don't APOLOGIZE. Sheesh, Calvin. How could you have known I was at work? Besides, it's my choice. I'd rather sit and talk to you any day of the week. I work until 10 tonight, which—yuck.*

Cal: *That's a long shift.*

Grey: *Yeah, but it's the only day I work this week. I'm really grateful they're so flexible. Confession? I think the manager has a crush on me or something. It's kind of embarrassing, but it also works in my favor.*

Cal: *I don't blame the guy. Wait. It is a GUY, right*?

Grey: **rolling my eyes**giggle* Yeah, it's a guy. Not*

nearly as sexy as you ;)

Cal: *You did NOT just say that.*

Grey: *Oh boy, here we go again…*

Seven

Greyson

The espresso machine hisses, and I pour cold, clear water into the top of the machine's water chamber, checking quickly to make sure the boiler cap is secured. My co-worker Rebecca tosses me the filter holder that I'd forgotten to grab when I started to fill the machine with grounds, and I call out a hasty "Thanks" as I lightly brush the coffee debris off the counter that escaped when I changed it earlier.

I remove the glass carafe under the spout and flip the switch on the machine, humming to myself as the steam heats the water to an extra hot temperature—like the customer ordered—and almost don't notice when the coffee starts to overflow into the small carafe. Crap, how on earth did *that* happen?

"Shoot," I murmur as the brown liquid skims the top of the glass container, the foam now becoming white. I push back the lever and remove the cup, careful not to spill any of the precious nectar.

Nectar? Oh, brother, listen to me.

I add a shot of sugar-free vanilla, pour the espresso into the tiny to-go cup, pop the plastic lid on, and slide the beverage across the counter at my waiting customer with a smile.

"Anything else?" I ask.

"Nope!" She tosses her hair over her shoulder and a few pennies into the tip jar, giving me a backwards wave, and pushes her way out the front door.

I reach behind me and pull back on the ribbon securing my green apron, tighten it so it's not quite so loose, and begin wiping down the hard granite counter where we keep the flavor syrups.

As I'm adjusting the nozzle on the sanitizer spray bottle so it comes out in a steady stream, Rebecca scoots by me, giving me a sharp shove in the hip.

"What the hell, Becca?"

"Meathead, twelve o'clock," she mutters, rushing to the cash register. I hear her brightly call out, "Hi there! What can we make for *you* today!"

Wow, she sounds uncharacteristically cheerful.

Shaking my head with a chuckle, I begin spraying the sanitizer around the basin of the steel prep sink, but a deep baritone response from the other side of the cash counter has me stopping in my tracks.

"Grey working?"

I spin on my heel, tossing the rag in my hand to the

backsplash. "Cal!" I take a few surprised steps forward. "What are you doing here?"

"I've been doing a shit ton of studying today and needed a break. Grab some caffeine," he says, causally stuffing his hands in the pockets of low-slung sweat pants, then looking up at the menu board on the wall. "Anything good here?"

Delighted, I cannot contain my enthusiasm. "You're an hour away! Are you crazy?"

I'm positively giddy.

Cal looks embarrassed, his cheeks taking on a pinkish hue.

"Didn't we already establish we both have a touch of the crazy?"

A bubble of laughter escapes my lips. "Good point."

Beside me, Rebecca clears her throat loudly. "Uh *hem.*"

"Oh! Sorry, Becca. Cal, this is my co-worker Rebecca. She is required to put up with my atrocious barista skills. Becca, this is Cal, my friend. He goes to SMU."

"Cal? *The* Cal? *Boyfriend* Cal?"

Oh, crap, that's right. I give Becca an amused look. "You follow me on Twitter?"

"Uh, everyone follows you on Twitter," she snickers.

This is news to me. "Well, Becca, this is Cal."

"In the flesh," Cal adds gamely, giving her a cocky grin.

"Phew, is it hot in here?" Rebecca blushes down into her black collared shirt. "Okay, well. Since we have no other customers, why don't you go take a break? If it gets swamped—" she rolls her eyes "—I'll shout for you."

Have I mentioned lately how much I freaking *love,*

love, love Rebecca?

"Do you want to go sit for a bit?" I ask Cal. He gives a jerky nod. "Can I make something for you quick?"

"Um… how about a trenta green tea lemonade."

"Coming right—"

"—Actually, Grey, I got it," Becca says, cutting me off with a wink. "Go. Sit. The lull isn't going to last forever."

She doesn't have to tell me twice.

Calvin

"I can't believe you're here."

"I can't either," I deadpan. "I got in my truck to grab a coffee and kept driving until I ended up here."

"Just like that, huh?" Greyson is beaming at me, a megawatt smile so blinding it's like gazing at the sun, and I can hardly stand to look at her.

"Um, don't read too much into it," I force myself to say.

"Mmm hmm, okay." She's leaning back now in the stiff wooden chair, her shoe dangling from the foot crossed over her leg. She tilts her head to one side as she studies me, and her long, blonde ponytail—a stark contrast against her black shirt—cascades over her shoulder. "I won't. You just got in your car and drove. For an hour." Grey bats her eyelashes at me.

I blink then look away.

"Stop it," I finally say as Becca walks over, setting a large green tea lemonade on the table in front of me. She doesn't say anything, but I see her mouth *Oh my God* to Greyson before turning and hustling back to the counter.

"I must say, Calvin, if you're trying to dispel the rumors that I have a boyfriend, you're doing a terrible job by showing up here."

"I think you fueled the rumors yourself after that match last week."

"Alright, fair enough. But I wouldn't do anything differently because that kiss was... *phew*!" She props her elbow on the table, resting her chin in the palm of her hand. "My toes are still tingling."

I ignore her blissful sigh and clear my throat.

"I told you, I came here for a coffee."

Her hazel eyes zero in on my green tea lemonade, and she arches a perfect eyebrow.

"Fine, sexy barista, if you really must know, I don't drink coffee."

Greyson's eyes soften around the edges as she watches me fiddle with my straw. "Your bruises are fading," she remarks.

"Yeah, I know. It sucks, too. No one messes with me when I have double shiners."

Grey sits up and reaches across the table, wiggling her fingers in my direction. "Let me have your arm."

I lay a tan arm on the table. She rolls her eyes.

"Not that one. Your other arm."

Biting back a grin, I rest my tatted arm on the tabletop and sit back, watching as she leans forward, intently studying the sleeve on my right arm.

A dozen intricate, bright designs are interwoven on my skin, and she memorizes every single one. I can see the interest in her eyes, the questions. But unlike other girls, she doesn't ask. Her fingers curiously roam over the American eagle tattooed in honor of my grandfather's many years of military service that eventually took his life, the lotus flower tattooed in honor of my mother's winning battle with cancer, and the Celtic cross in honor of my

Scottish heritage.

I sit, ramrod straight, learning every expression as it crosses her face.

She glances up at me then, her finger continuing to trail along the sensitive skin on my arm, and there's a fire in her eyes that damn near takes my breath away.

No way is she looking at *me* like that.

Greyson

We sit for twenty minutes before Becca comes to get me, talking and teasing and flirting. Well, I flirted; he complained about it.

"Let me walk you out," I say, stalling for more time with him.

I start untying the green apron strings around my waist, but Cal stops me.

"Leave the apron. It's cute."

I preen with pleasure as he pushes through the glass door of the coffee shop and holds it open for me, giving me an opportunity to train my eyes on that gloriously tattooed bicep beneath his shirtsleeve as I pass in front of him.

His red truck is parked out front, but instead of walking to it, I lead him to a partition under the overhang, conveniently located in the shadows of the strip mall.

I lean against the brick wall, facing him, and cut to the chase. "Tell me the real reason you're here."

He moves into the dark recesses of the building, propping a hand against the partition next to my face, the dim lighting hardening the angles of his face, slashing it in half by shadows. A band of light cuts across his eyes, and they burn bright blue. "I told you. I wanted a study break."

"Okay…"

His face might be cloaked in darkness, but even so, I can tell his eyes are dancing. "Okay what?"

I wish he'd cut the crap. "So, you're here because you were thirsty. And what else?"

He's quiet, watchful, when a dark SUV pulls up with tinted windows. For a few seconds, as it idles, his stance hardens and he moves to stand in front of me protectively. He relaxes when the engine cuts off and a young couple steps down, heading towards the coffee shop.

Finally, in a low murmur, his voice resonates close to my ear in a husky drawl. "You know why I'm here."

"Yes," I agree quietly with a shiver. "But I want to hear you say it."

Cal groans miserably.

"Why won't you just admit you drove all the way here to see me?" I ask gently.

"If you already know the answer, why are you trying to make me say it?"

"Because I'm a girl, and that's what we *do*." My head tips back against the brick wall, and I watch him from under my long lashes. "Hurry up and spit it out. I have coffee to brew."

Minutes on the clock tick by.

"You're a brat."

I push off the building and straighten to my full height as I start towards the door, throwing in a theatrical eye roll to illustrate just how *over* this conversation I am. "I'm going inside. Thanks for stopping by."

I know he's not going to let me go, and two seconds later I'm proven right when my back is pressed flat up against the cold, brick wall.

Greyson 1: Cal 0

Smugly, I let him struggle for the words I crave from him, but this time I don't goad him into talking, even though I know Becca is going to be pissed when I walk back inside after leaving her alone behind the counter for so long.

"You're right." His deep voice whispers next to my ear, and I get chills when he braces those sexy, muscular arms on either side of my face, his breath caressing my cheek. "I drove an hour to see you, and I would have driven three."

God, that is so sexy and romantic.

"Say that again."

He pauses before his palms slide down my shoulders, and his large hands span my waist. "I drove an hour to see you," he repeats, his full lips grazing the soft spot behind my ear. "And I would have driven three."

Oh *yeah.*

My head tilts to the side, my eyes flutter shut, and I almost forget to breath. "Why?"

"Because I can't stop thinking about you."

Cal's lips drag slowly across my jaw, his abrasive beard stubble sending shocks of pleasure up my spine.

God, I love his facial hair. "Say that again."

"I can't stop thinking about you."

My lips curve up into a sly smile. "Good."

World around us forgotten, I exaggerate my pucker, inviting him in. I *ache* with need for him.

We ache with need for each other.

Our lips press together, and for a moment we do nothing but breath in and out, the same air. The same breath. Cal's full mouth covers mine, deep and…

Tentatively, our tongues touch. Deliberately. So agonizingly unhurried.

I'm breathless now, my knees shaking.

Painful. Arousing. Exciting.

It's wet, and delicious, and incredible.

Grey: *I still can't believe you just showed up tonight. I hate to be the one to say it, but... it was really romantic.*

Cal: *You're not mad, are you?*

Grey: *NO! Why on earth would I be?*

Cal: *Just checking.*

Grey: *That kiss was... indescribable.*

Cal: *Yeah, it was pretty incredible.*

Grey: *I don't know how I made it back into work, my legs were all wobbly. I could hardly walk straight.*

Grey: *You showing up was off the charts sexy and romantic—albeit a tad stalker-ish. Totally something I would do if I were one. Which I'm not. But YOU are.*

Cal: *Stop.*

Grey: *IF I did have a stalker, I would want it to be you.*

Cal: *Ditto.*

Grey: *Soooo... Becca thought you were cute... *avoids eye contact and checks nails**

Cal: *What? Cute? Ugh, nooo! Anything but cute! A wise woman once said that CUTE was the "kiss of death" and for grandmas and kittens.*

Grey: *LOL. I did say that, didn't I? But it's true. Because when she said you were cute, I wanted to tackle her to the ground. Haha, kidding.*

Cal: *Are you trying to tell me it made you jealous?*
Grey: *What? Me jealous? Pffft.*
Grey: *Okay, yes. I was jealous.*

Cal: *Morning sunshine.*

Grey: **groans* I can already tell this is going to be a loooong day.*

Cal: *Why is that?*

Grey: *It's only 8:00 in the morning and I've already gotten 3 panic texts from one of my sisters.*

Cal: *Chin up, sweetheart. Text me after your next class, and I'll cheer you up.*

Grey: *You do realize you just called me sweet-heart….*

Cal: *I did? Shit, I did.*

Cal: *Sorry?*

Grey: *Did you mean it?*

Cal: *That depends. Did you mind?*

Grey: *No. I liked it. Loved it actually.*

Cal: *Then yes. I meant it.*

Grey: *Awwww *blushes prettily and giggles**

Cal: *Has your day gotten any better?*

Grey: *Much better, thanks to you. Starting my day with a text from Calvin seems to always help. But enough about me—how was YOUR day?*

Cal: *It would have been better if my friends weren't such sick sonsabitches. I won't get into details, but let's just say it involved naked ass cracks, lunges, and MY boxer shorts. And the boxer shorts were not on me, but on Mason.*

Grey: *I just laughed out loud, and now my friends all want to know why I'm giggling.*

Cal: *Where are you?*

Grey: *Sitting in the dining hall, having a group lunch on campus.*

Cal: *What did you tell them you were laughing at?*

Grey: *The truth. I told them the truth: that you made me laugh and that you make me happy.*

Grey: **yawn* My gosh, why am I so tired?!*

Cal: *You already in bed?*

Grey: *Yes. The pillows were calling my name. You?*

Cal: *Yeah. Reading a book.*

Grey: *Which one?*

Cal: *American Sniper. Have you seen the movie?*

Grey: *Not yet.*

Cal: *We should definitely go see it. I mean—if you want.*

Grey: *Yeah, we should. I'll go anywhere that serves popcorn in a gallon-sized bucket. Do you read a lot?*

Cal: *Yes. I'll read just about anything—except maybe textbooks. Ha ha.*

Grey: *Likes to read: add that to the list of things I like about you.*

Grey: **yawn* Hey Cal?*

Cal: *Yeah, Greyson?*

Cal: *Grey?*

Cal: *Did you fall asleep on me?*

Cal: *Guess so.*

Cal: *Sweet dreams, sweetheart.*

Grey: *Morning! I am so sorry I passed out on you last night. Your messages were nice to wake up to, though. Although, somehow I can't picture you calling me sweetheart to my face. Don't tough guys hate that kind of mushy stuff?*

Cal: *Hold that thought, baby cakes. Ha ha. Just got in from my jog. Give me a few to jump in the shower. I'll text you in a bit.*

Cal: *Really needed that shower. I did a quick 5 miles. You don't happen to jog, do you? Six Rivers has some sweet trails.*

Grey: *Honestly, no. But I'm willing to try anything once that won't kill me.*

Cal: *Seriously?*

Grey: *Yes. I'll just make sure to run behind you so I can stare at your superb ass #motivation*

Cal: *Hey. You stole my line.*

Cal: *Hey Grey?*

Grey: *Yeah?*

Cal: *I'm starting to miss you.*

Grey: *Me too.*

Cal: *You miss you too?*

Grey: *Stop it, you're killing the mood.*

Cal: *Sorry. But I do miss you. Is that weird?*

Grey: *Everything about us is weird.*

Grey: *Tell me something about yourself that no one else knows.*

Cal: *Oh brother, that's horrible. Did you steal that line from a movie?*

Grey: *JUST DO IT*

Cal: *So feisty in the morning—I like it. Okay, fine.*

But I'm only doing this because although you're small, you're scary. Let's see, something no one else knows. Um. Okay. I have one: everyone thinks I broke my nose playing football, but in reality, it got broken when I was in a fight with my sister.

Cal: *She was chasing me, and I smashed into a door trying to get away from her. I was 15.*

Grey: *LOLOL >tear< you're so adorable.*

Cal: **rolls eyes* your turn.*

Grey: *Alright, um…I broke up with my last boyfriend, but I let him tell people he broke up with me.*

Cal: *You must have really wanted to get rid of him. When was this?*

Grey: *Freshman year. So, two years ago.*

Cal: *And that's the last guy you dated?*

Grey: *Pretty much. What about you?*

Cal: *I haven't dated any guys in the last two years either.*

Grey: *Would you KNOCK IT OFF?*

Cal: *Why do you keep yelling at me in all caps?*

Grey: *Just answer the question.*

Cal: *Fine. My last "real" girlfriend was a girl I dated in high school. Kid shit, nothing serious. I didn't even take a date to prom; I only went to that because I was on court and my mom made me go.*

Cal: *So, going back to what you said before: if it's been two years since you dated anyone, does that mean…*

Grey: *Does that mean… what? *blank stare**

Cal: *It's a personal question. You don't have to answer.*

Grey: *Go. Spit it out already.*

Cal: *How long has it been? Since.*

Grey: *Ah, now we're getting down to the nitty gritty... How long have you been dying to ask me about sex?*

Cal: *Long enough, smart-ass.*

Grey: *LOL. Okay, so how long has it been since I've had sex—2 long-ass years. Sorry, but I'm not the kind of girl that sleeps around. I'm a committed-relationship kind of person. Does that satisfy your curiosity?*

Cal: *Yes. I like that about you.*

Grey: *Yeah, yeah, yeah. That's what all guys say until they want to have sex with me but refuse to commit. Then they get pissed and never call back. Some guys are so delusional. They think buying a girl one cheap beer is enough to get them into bed. Please, don't make me laugh.*

Grey: *Besides, if you were trying to have sex with me, you wouldn't like it so much either.*

Cal: *I can't like the fact that you don't sleep around? And trust me, I don't need to pressure anyone to sleep with me.*

Grey: *You only like the fact I don't sleep around because it would make you jealous if I did. Let's be honest. ;)*

Cal: *Are you a mind reader?*

Grey: *See, I knew it. Okay. Now you have to answer the same question: How long has it been? Since.*

Cal: *Uh, let me think... Honestly? Maybe 4 months?*

Grey: *Ugh, maybe I shouldn't have asked.*

Cal: *Why?*

Grey: *Because I would have felt much better if you would have said 2 years. LOL. Or lied and said you were a virgin.*

Cal: *Sorry :(It was a one-night stand. I can't even remember her name. Wait. Now I do. I think her name was—*

Grey: *STOP! NO DETAILS! My ears will bleed.*

Cal: *Or maybe her name was…*

Grey: *Haha, very funny.*

Cal: *I thought so.*

Cal: *Have you crawled into bed for the night yet?*

Grey: *Just. So snuggly. You?*

Cal: *Yeah. Reading and not at all tired. But I miss your face.*

Grey: *You miss my FACE? LOL. Oh my god, you're so cute.*

Cal: *Yup, that's what they call me. Cute.*

Grey: *Want to... Um. FaceTime?*

Cal: *Yeah. Let's do it.*

Grey: *Well, THERE'S a loaded statement. *snickers**

Cal: *I think you might be a bigger pervert than I am.*

Grey: *It's a definite possibility…*

FACETIME

Calvin

I lean back against the headboard of my queen-sized bed and pound my pillows to get more comfortable as my phone pings with an incoming FaceTime notification. Nervously, I wipe my clammy palms across my navy comforter before clicking ACCEPT.

Greyson's beautiful face stares back at me from the small screen. She's lying down, blonde hair fanned out on a white pillow.

"Hi." She gives me a cute little wave, blonde tendrils brushing her cheeks, and she brushes them away, tucking them behind an ear.

"I was beginning to forget what you look like," I tease, eyes devouring her tan, bare shoulders and pink tank top.

"Well, now you won't."

"You know, I don't really do…" I'm momentarily sidetracked by Grey slowly running her index finger along the thin band of her sleep top, adjusting the straps. My eyes are drawn to her lips, then her long, mussed hair. Is she trying to drive me to distraction on purpose?

Her voice interrupts my salivating. "Don't really do what?"

"Huh?"

Her light, lilt-y chuckle fills my room. "What don't you really do?"

"What was I gonna say?" I ask. She shrugs, biting her lower lip. I narrow my eyes. "Knock that cutesy shit off."

"I'm not doing anything!" she shouts with a laugh.

"Stop being irresistible. It's rude."

She rolls her sparkling eyes. "You think *everything* is rude. And why is that?"

"Because I'm here and you're not," I blurt out. "I meant that it's rude you're being cute when I can't touch you. Shit. I didn't mean that if you were here, you'd want me to touch you. Or even want us to be together."

Why am I still talking? Shit.

"Maybe I would, maybe I wouldn't." Greyson lowers her phone so it's hovering just above her face, giving me an extreme close-up. She wiggles her brows. "Are you a cuddler, Calvin," she whispers into the screen.

"Uh, *no*." Her bottom lip juts out in a mock pout. "Yes. Yes I am."

She studies me through the camera on her phone, hazel eyes seemingly raking the planes of my face. "I wish I could touch you. I love your face."

Fuck it. I'm going for broke. "Not as much as I love your face," I announce in a lovey-dovey tone of voice. Seriously, what the hell has gotten into me?

I glance over at my door and make sure it's locked. I so do not need anyone busting in here right now.

"Wanna bet?" Grey teases. She's gazing back at me with doe eyes and an adoring smile, and it's fucking killing me that she's so far away. Well, theoretically speaking, of course. Realistically, it's less than an hour.

"Sweetheart, don't mess with the bull or you'll get the

horns," I throw out lamely, trying to be clever but sounding like a complete horse's ass instead. I hold back a whiney groan.

"Horns? That sounds exciting." She wiggles her eyebrows at me.

"Are we flirting?" I ask, to be sure.

"You're hopeless." Greyson laughs. "I don't know about you, but I certainly am." She lolls her head on her pillow and bats her lashes at me through her phone. "You could step it up a notch. You're a little rusty."

"Well, to be honest, I don't usually bother."

"So, what is it you *usually* do?"

"Nothing. I do nothing."

Her pert little nose wrinkles in thought. "Alright, but what if you're trying to… *you know*."

"Get someone to sleep with me?"

She nods, and I let out a deep bark of laughter. Greyson's blonde hair billows out around her head, and she looks like an angel.

"What, like it's hard?" I clear my throat before continuing. "Well. Okay, honestly? Ugh, how do I put this?" I scratch my head. "Girls are easy, okay? All we have to do is show up to a party, and…" I pause for a second. "Yada, yada, yada."

Grey gasps back a surprised laugh, dropping the phone and rolling over on her bed. The phone falls on the bed, camera facing the ceiling—I can't see her, but I can hear her wheezing, "Yada, yada, yada? God, Cal… That was priceless… I love it…"

I wait her out. When she's finally done giggling, she sits up, propping herself up against her headboard, and wipes a tear from the corner of her eye.

"It's good seeing your face," she says quietly. "I haven't seen you in forever."

I feel my expression soften, and I think my goddamn heart just fluttered in my chest. God, I've turned in to a sap.

"It's because we're not, you know—a thing." Why is that so painful to say? Why would I *say* that? Get a grip, dude.

"I know," she says softly. Sadly.

We regard each other silently then, the mood changing from carefree and teasing to serious. Greyson's hazel eyes question me from the small screen on my phone. She tucks her hair behind her ears, almost self-consciously, and we both smile stupidly.

I take a deep breath, gathering up my courage. "Greyson, I—"

Someone bangs on my bedroom door, and just like that, the spell is broken. *Fuck*, fuck, fuck.

"Shit. I should…"

"You should…

"Get that," we both say.

"Talk to you later?" Grey asks into the camera.

Yes. Later.

"Night, Grey."

"Night, Calvin." The quiet, gentle way she says my name, and how she's watching me as I end the call, has me awake all night.

Nine

Cal: *Morning, sunshine.*

Grey: :)

Cal: *I think my roommates were on to me last night. I think they knew it was you.*

Grey: *How so?*

Cal: *Must have looked guilty after FaceTiming when I opened the door. They heard your voice on speaker phone but were convinced I had a girl in my room. What pains in my ass.*

Grey: *Note to self—if I'm ever in your room, hide in closet?*

Cal: *Like I'd ever want to hide YOU.*

Grey: *You are so perfect. Adorable.*

Cal: *Well, you're gorgeous. Does that make us even?*

Grey: *I swear, I want to smush you.*

Cal: *Smush me? God, I hope that's not all?*

Grey: *Well... no.*

Cal: *Shit, we have to stop this. I'm about to walk into a team meeting. I can't be all freaking smiley. I'll get sacked in the nuts.*

Grey: *You are such a prude.*

Cal: *Me, a prude? Hardly. Your plans today?*

Grey: *Meeting with the sisters on my committee to put together donation baskets at the sorority house. It will probably take most of the afternoon. How bout you?*

Cal: *You know, if you weren't busy, I would*—

Grey: *???*

Cal: *I would have come to see you?*

Grey: *I would have loved that if I wasn't so busy today...*

Cal: *Me too.*

Grey: *Sigh.*

Cal: *Sleepy?*

Grey: *The sleepiest. I'm glad you texted me though. FINALLY! Why didn't you text me this afternoon? I checked my phone so many times during our meeting that Jemma snatched it away.*

Cal: *I knew you were busy. Didn't want to bother you.*

Grey: *You're the highlight of my day, Calvin. You can text me any time you want *blushes**

Cal: *Ditto, babe.*

Greyson

To: calvin.m.thompson04@smu.il.edu
From: greykeller0143@state.edu
Subject: You are cordially invited…

Dear Calvin,

As you know, the Theta Rho Theta Gala, which I've worked so hard to plan, is right around the corner. Two weeks away, actually. Friday the 9th, 6:00 pm at the Crown Hotel ballroom. I've given this a tremendous amount of thought, and I know it's a lot to ask, but the thing is. The thing *is,* Cal, there is absolutely no one I would rather go with than you. I'm asking you to stand by my side, as my date. Nothing would make me prouder than walking in on your arm.

Yours, Greyson

I stare at the message, my finger hovering about the SEND button, before I take a deep breath and push down.

Calvin

I'm asking you to stand by my side, as my date. Nothing would make me prouder than walking in on your arm.

Yours, Greyson.

Yours.

Surely she didn't mean it like *that*.

But what if she did?

Shit. I stare at that signature line for what seems like an eternity, reading and rereading her message at least five times before closing out the email app and tapping open my calendar.

And there it is: Friday the 9th. SMU vs. UCONN

It's a huge game for us. Top three match of the entire season, and our season has only just begun. If I miss it, I could very well kiss my Captain's position goodbye, along with my starting position, and say hello to being a second-string bench warmer.

I close the calendar with a curse, and I let my head fall against my bedroom wall with a loud thud.

"Goddammit."

Greyson

"I did something stupid," I say to Melody as she putters around our kitchen, prepping her beloved macaroni and cheese. My arms are braced on the small round table near the stove, and she gives me a quick glance as she measures out milk in a measuring cup.

"I'm listening."

"I invited Cal to the Gala, and he hasn't responded to my message."

"How long ago did you send it?"

"Um, two days ago?"

"So?"

"So, we've been texting and emailing every day for a while."

Melody looks over at me in surprise. "Like *every* day?"

"Pretty much. All day, every day," I clarify with a nod.

"Wow, how did I not know this? Why didn't you say anything?" She asks, ripping open the bag of powdered cheese and tapping it into the pot of noodles.

I shrug. "No reason. Maybe I got carried away with the idea of him. We've been talking for weeks, Mel. *Weeks*. He and I..."

When I look up, she's staring expectantly but says

nothing.

"I'm not going to put a label on what I feel for him, but my feelings are real. And they're strong."

That's a lie. I know what to label my feelings for Cal, and those feelings go well beyond strong.

My roommate taps the wooden spoon on the side of the metal pot, sets it on the stovetop away from the burner, and walks over, enveloping me from behind in her arms. "I'm sorry, then, Grey. Sorry that he hasn't gotten back to you. Why don't you send him another note?"

Her chin is resting on my shoulder, and I raise my arm to pat her on the head.

Melody clears her throat. "Alright. Would… would it make you feel better if I sent Mason a note to find out what was going on with him?" she asks bashfully, as if embarrassed to be confessing a secret. "We've kind of been talking. Jemma gave him my digits."

I want to tell her no, but that would be a lie. Another one.

"Could you?"

She squeezes my shoulders. "Sure. You know I'd do anything for you."

Melody: *Heard back from Mason. The guys have a match on Friday the 9th and it's a BIG one. I'll forward you his message.*

Melody: [FWD: Mason Gille] *Hey hot stuff. All I can tell you is that Cal's been a real asshole for the past few days. Bitchier than usual. We have a game the same night* *as your thing and it's a big one. No way would he miss it. Sorry bae.*

Melody: :(*I'm so sorry, Grey. Do you want me to ask Brandon Bauer if any of the Tau Kaps would be your date?*

Grey: *No thanks. It's fine. I'll be fine. Love you for thinking of me though* xxx

To: calvin.m.thompson04@smu.il.edu
From: greykeller0143@state.edu
Subject: Put me out of my misery

Cal,

It's been a few days since my last email, and I'm just writing to tell you that I know you have a match that night. The 9th. I obviously didn't know about it when I asked you to be my date, so I'm sorry if I put any pressure on you by asking. I feel horrible. But why haven't you emailed me back? Why haven't you texted me? It's making me feel really shitty. I thought we were friends, and I thought… Never mind what I thought. Just send me a note back. Because I'm bossy and I say so. And because I miss you so much.

Yours, Grey

Cal: *You know what?*
Cal: *Fuck it. I'm coming.*
Cal: *What time should I pick you up?*

To: grevkeller0143@state.edu
From: calvin.m.thompson04@smu.il.edu
Subject: Douchebaggery

Grey. I don't think you can begin to comprehend the level to which I'm getting harassed over here for missing this match to come to a dance. Some bastard put tampons in my locker yesterday, and today the ugliest prom dress was hanging from the wakeboard rack on top of my truck, blowing in the wind like a flag. – Cal

To: calvin.m.thompson04@smu.il.edu
From: grevkeller0143@state.edu
Subject: Squeals of delight.

Calvin,

Oh no! That sounds… hilarious, actually. But don't mind me. I'm just delirious with excitement that you're coming. I would love to have seen your face when you opened your locker to tampons. What brand are they? I'd hate to waste a new box. KIDDING. Kidding. Sort of.

I'm not even going to pretend I'm not happy dancing my way around the house. I'm not going to send you "*Oh, Cal! You HAVE to go to your game! Don't miss it on my account*!" notes. Because the truth is, when you texted that you were escorting me to the gala, I squealed so loud Melody burst into my room with a baseball bat. She thought I was being attacked. So, I CANNOT WAIT to see you. I can't wait for you to see my dress. I can't wait to dance with you. And I guess I should mention now that the evening is going to run really, really late. I know SMU is only an hour away, but…

Greyson

Cal: *Why, Miss Keller, are you propositioning me for an overnight?*

Grey: *Hmmm. Am I? I just meant I know you'll be tired. I have to stay afterwards with my committee and remove some of the sorority insignia and stuff. The hotel staff will do the rest, but there will be a short lag before I can leave.*

Cal: *This is at a fancy hotel, right?*

Grey: *Yup. The Crown Hotel. It's 5 stars.*

Cal: *Wouldn't it just be easier to book a room?*

Grey: *Well, yes, but…*

Cal: *Let me take care of it.*

Ten

Greyson

I have a thousand things to do but can only focus on one thing: Cal. Cal, who's skipping his game for me and is surely going to pay the consequences. Cal, who's driving an hour out of his way to be with me. Cal, who calls me sweetheart.

Four times in fact.

I counted.

Sigh.

I scoured online for hours to find this, the perfect dress, and as I stand in front of the mirror, nervously adjusting the invisible neckline with trembling fingers, I stare, trying to imagine how Cal will feel when he first sees me in it.

I didn't just choose the dress with him in mind; I chose it *for* him.

Flesh-colored netting hugs my shoulders so they appear bare, while an intricate white lace overlay creates a cap sleeve and bodice. White embroidered flowers cover the tapered waist, the skirt flaring in a bell at my hips. The dress is both ridiculously sexy and modest at the same time. Rhinestone stud earrings complete the elaborately elegant ensemble.

I run a hand over my hair. The intricately loose fish braid is nestled in a cascade of loose hair and adorned with a vintage white floweret clip. I sat patiently in a salon chair two hours, and the outcome is messy and complex and exquisite.

I love it.

My minimal eye makeup was expertly applied. Dramatic false eyelashes, the darkest mascara, nude shadow. Flushed skin. Bright plum matte lips that are a contrast to my white dress and blonde hair.

I take a deep breath, running a hand over my nervous stomach.

"Whoa! I mean—wow! Seriously, Grey, you look freaking amazing!" Melody floats into the room, her soft pink gown drifting airily around her tall frame. "You look like Blake Lively on the red carpet. Holy wow. Just *stunning.*"

"Me? Look at you! Let me see the back," I say, twirling her around to peek at the back of her dress. Or lack of it. "Seriously, Mel, Sam is going to crap himself."

She runs a hand down a front pleat and sighs. "Well, I'm hoping to get a few good pictures taken so I can snap them to Mason. Who is, by the way, totally pissed off at

Cal for bailing on their game. Or match. Or whatever they call it."

"What's he been saying?"

Melody smoothes a hand over her sleek chignon. "That Cal is pussy whipped."

I try to hide a smile behind my long braid, but the dark plum lipstick gives away my pleased smirk.

"I see that smile, Greyson Keller! Brat." She lets out a wistful sigh. "It's so romantic. He's going to end up on the bench, but Mason says he doesn't even give a shit."

My eyes widen, riveted.

"Yup. Benched. For three games or something like that."

"What else did this endless wealth of knowledge tell you?"

"That he's making a huge sacrifice for someone who hasn't even, uh…"

"Hasn't even… what?"

"You're seriously going to make me say it?"

"I don't even know what *it* is!" I laugh.

"Ugh, fine. He said that Cal is making a huge sacrifice for a guy who hasn't even *fucked you* yet and doesn't even know if the pussy is worth the price tag."

"*What*?" I'm convinced my eyes bug out of my head. "He said that to *you*? What a pig!"

Melody blushes. "Yeah, it was harsh, but all his teammates are seriously pissed. It's blowing up on him; I mean, he's their Captain. Plus Cal didn't tell the guys until after he'd told their coach—who, by the way, was furious. That being said, I'm glad."

Melody walks over and grabs one of my nude colored high heels out of the shoebox, unbuckles it, and squats down so I can slide my foot in. She glances up as she fits the leather ankle strap through the gold clasp. "For the record, it's about time you found a guy with balls big enough to go after what he wants. He basically gave his entire team the proverbial middle finger so he could be with you tonight."

I get warm and tingly all over.

"Anyway, I wish I could be here when he picks you up, but I better skedaddle if I'm going to get the shit done on that list you made me so you could meet Cal here instead of at the hotel. You owe me big time for this, you know. Oh, shoot, I almost forgot. Hand me your overnight bag. I'll take it now so you don't look awkward hauling it out in your fancy dress. Not classy."

"Not classy," I agree, and I wheel the small lavender carry-on suitcase over to the door.

She grabs it, leans to peck me on the cheek, and starts back towards the door. I call her back. "Hey Mel?"

Turning, she regards me. "Yeah?"

"I love you."

"Love you too."

Cal: *Just about to leave. I'll see you in an hour. Sooner if I push the gas.*

Grey: *Don't do that! Be safe. Two hands on the wheel. Melody and Jemma are picking up my slack, so there's no rush.*

Cal: *Alright. Be there in an hour.*

Grey: *I can't wait to see you.*

Cal: *Me either.*

Calvin

I pull at my necktie as I take the steps to Grey's front door, tugging it back and forth to tighten the knot I'd loosened on the way over so I could breathe.

It's a white silk tie with white embroidered flowers, a tie my sister picked out when I told her what I was doing, and who I was doing it with. It's also the color of Greyson's dress.

Maybe the guys are right; I am fucking pussy whipped.

But I swear, when Grey finally opens that door, I don't give one shit what anyone says. They can bench me or filet me alive or kick me off the team, for all the fucks I care.

Because Greyson is stunning.

And the look she's giving me right now has me standing twenty feet tall.

Greyson

For a moment, we just stare at one another.

It's me who moves first, opening the door wide enough for Cal to step through, up into the living room.

He looks so handsome. Black pleated dress pants, crisp black shirt, tailored black jacket, and a glaringly white embroidered tie that matches my dress perfectly.

I want to touch him.

"Jesus, babe, let me look at you," he says with a strained voice, stepping farther into the room. "You are so *beautiful*."

"I *feel* beautiful." I give a pleased little twirl, and my skirt flares up around my hips. His eyes go to my bare legs, and I bite back a smile as I say, "I need a hug or something."

Or *something*.

Cal smiles, shrugs off his suit coat, lays it neatly over a kitchen chair, and wraps his arms around my waist after I step into his outstretched arms. I lean into the embrace, mindful not to get makeup on his shirt.

My lips graze his jaw, tattooing his skin with plum lip prints, and I draw back, fingering his tie. It matches my dress.

I gasp with delight. "Wherever did you find this?"

"Tabitha." He rolls his eyes. "She literally lost her shit when I asked for her help. It made her whole year. But then my mom got all weird because I didn't call her first. It was a whole *thing* I'd rather not talk about," he jokes. "Tabitha had it rush shipped to school. She can't believe I'm going to a sorority formal and wants to meet the girl putting up with my bullshit for an entire night—her words, not mine."

"Well, thank your sister for me because you look… Is it possible that you got more handsome since the last time I saw you? How am I going to keep my hands to myself?"

"You don't have to keep your hands to yourself," he jokes.

"Okay. I won't."

"In that case, I guess I'll have to send my sister a bouquet to thank her for making me irresistible."

"Maybe you should."

We stare at each other until I'm itching to run my fingers down his chest. Instead, I flex them and state the obvious. "We should go. Melody is covering for me, and I can't leave her hanging or she'll *kill* me. I promised I'd be there by five thirty."

Calvin

When she's not leaning in to hug or shake someone's hand, Greyson's arm is looped through mine, her hand clasping my tricep as we stand at the head of a receiving line, enthusiastically greeting the Gala's arriving guests: sorority alumnae, her sorority sisters, and their dates.

I cannot stop giving her sidelong glances, for she is truly a vision.

It's over an hour before we're "alone" and Greyson can take a break from her hostess duties. I set my beer glass on a nearby table, and we wordlessly move out onto the hardwood dance floor. I pull her in close, and her fingers snake under my suit jacket, clasping at the small of my back.

I want to kiss her so badly right now, but it's not the time or place. I settle for resting my lips on her neck, just below the white flower she has pinned there, running my hands up and down her spine.

We dance like this through one song, then another. I've never been more grateful to hear a bunch of cheesy slow songs in my life.

Because somehow... we just *fit*.

And fuck if it doesn't feel amazing.

Greyson

At this point, I don't even think we're moving. Cal's nose is buried in my hair, his fingers are stroking my back, and when the chords from the next slow ballad begin, I don't even care that I have responsibilities to see to.

Just one more song, and I'll go pull the silent auction bid cards.

One more.

Or two. I can afford two more songs.

My hands find their way up the front of his shirt, resisting the urge to pop open the row of black onyx buttons one at a time. Those same hands wrap around his neck, resting there so my delicate fingers can rake through the curly hair just above his starched black collar.

Cal kisses my temple and tightens his hold, his hot breath on my neck throughout the song.

I continue stroking his hair. He rubs my back in a light caress.

I'm sure we look ridiculous just standing here, barely dancing, but I still feel like I'm floating on air.

"I don't know if I mentioned it, but thank you for coming tonight," I aimlessly twirl a piece of his hair around my finger.

His voice is a hum next to my ear. "You've only mentioned it four or five times. But for the record, there's no other place I'd rather be."

I whisper against his skin. "I won't ever take you for granted, Cal. I know the sacrifice you made to be here tonight."

"I know."

I arch back and cock my head at him. "Is your sister horrified you're at a sorority formal?"

His mouth curls up into a smirk. "I wouldn't say horrified; I'd call it shocked. I mean, I'm not really the type to, you know…"

I nod. "I know." We sway to the music, and his hands rest on my hips. "Speaking of types, what is yours?"

"Oh, gee, let me think," he laughs. "Blonde hair, hazel eyes, infectious smile…"

I nuzzle our noses.

Sick, I know.

"You think I have an infectious smile?" I smile at him.

"And kissable lips."

"Ooh! Now *that* I like the sound of." I release my fingers from his silky mop of hair, trail them over his shoulders and down over his firm pecs, and give them a squeeze. He puckers his lips, and I touch my trout pout to his—briefly, so I don't smear my lipstick.

Cal rolls his head to the side and groans. Loudly. "I want to, *ugh*. So bad."

Laughing, I press my lips to his for another quick kiss. "Want to what?"

"Never mind. I'll sound like a dog in heat if I say it."

My heartbeat quickens. "Say it anyway," I plead.

He hesitates. "I want to stick my fucking tongue

down your throat."

"I want that too," I murmur, leaning in to flick his ear with my tongue. "I want to lick you from head to toe."

"Fuck. Um, okay. You win." He gives a strangled laugh and buries his face in my neck. "I cannot believe you just said that."

"Why?"

"Because. You look so sweet. And you're classy."

"Hmm," I hum in his ear as we sway, enjoying the power of my femininity when his whole body stiffens at the simplest inflection of my tone. "Well, you know what they say about the classy ones."

"No." His voice squeaks slightly. "What do they say?"

I raise one eyebrow suggestively.

His head shoots up, eyebrows in his hairline. "My dick is so hard right now." He groans. "Shit. Sorry, I shouldn't have said that out loud."

"Hard? Ya *think*? It's been digging into my thigh this entire time. Trust me, it's taking every last effort for me not to grind on it."

"Jesus, Grey!" Our bodies are flush, and Cal is pushing his hips into me slightly. Not enough to be obvious to an onlooker, but enough that I notice. "I'm trying really, really hard to be polite."

"Polite boys deserve a reward." My warm breath flirts with his square jawline, his dark blonde hair tickling my nose. "You know what that means, don't you?"

He gives his head a jerky shake. "No. What does that mean?" The Adam's apple in his throat bobs up and down when he swallows.

"Thompson, it means you're getting *lucky* tonight."

"Um… You were seriously steaming up the dance floor. For a fake boyfriend, it sure did look real." Melody sidles up to me by the cake table, whispering around a stack of dessert plates and nodding politely at each passing guest. "Jeez, sexual tension much?"

"Tell me about it. And I don't think there's anything fake about it anymore," I whisper back, smiling broadly at a new member of our sisterhood when she comes up for a slice of the marble cake Mel and I are cutting.

We make small talk with her and serve several more pieces of cake before we're able to speak alone again. "Grey, you two look like you're…" She hesitates, and the cake knife she's wielding pauses mid-slice. "You know—in *lurve*."

I consider this, glance across the room where Cal stands with a group of some older gentleman—alumnae dates and husbands—gesturing wildly and causing everyone to die laughing uproarishly.

I wonder what's so funny.

He raises a drink to his lips just then and glances over, watching me above the rim of his glass. I blush furiously before looking away.

A knot forms in the pit of my stomach. Oh God, I'm actually jealous that I'm stuck on the opposite side of the room serving stupid, dumb cake.

"Geez Grey, look at you, all flustered and a*dork*able."

"I can't help it. He makes me positively giddy. I'm head over heels."

"Yeah, I can tell. And I think the feeling is mutual.

That boy hasn't stopped watching you all night. But I mean—who could blame him. You're clearly the babeliest babe in the room." The cake knife is thrust my way. "And I'm not just saying that because you're my best friend."

"Yes you are, but I'll permit it."

"What are your plans for later? You check in to your room yet?"

"Yeah, Cal took care of it while I was helping Carly and Jemma with raffle tickets."

"Nervous?"

"No. We've been building to this point for over seven weeks. *Seven.* I want to kick everyone out and drag him upstairs, caveman style. Like, by his beautiful hairs." I sigh wistfully and hand her a stack of napkins. "Lick."

Melody covers her laugh with a cake plate. "Oh gawd, if only he knew how dirty your mind was, he wouldn't be so content chatting it up over there with Stella's husband Ryan."

"Well, he kind of *does* know. I may have whispered some naughty, dirty things to him while we were dancing."

"Such as…?"

"Such as, 'I want to lick you from head to toe.' I think he almost wet himself."

"Why are you let loose to roam around in public?"

"It's not like I say things like that to just anyone. Besides, I just wanted to see the look on his face. It's totally different."

"Yeah, yeah, whatever you say, Keller. Now keep handing me plates."

Eleven

Calvin

By midnight, we begin making our way back to our room. It's late, but my body crackles with electricity, buzzing with seven weeks' worth of anticipation. A burst of pure adrenaline zips through my body, fueled by Greyson's words as they play on a loop through my mind.

It means you're getting lucky tonight, it means you're getting lucky tonight, it means you're getting lucky to-night...

Arms wrapped around each other's waists, we walk side-by-side in companionable silence and pent-up sexual tension to our hotel suite, taking the elevator to the eighth floor from the Grand Ballroom.

Grey relaxes against me as we watch the numbers

climb from one floor to the next.

The elevator dings, having reached its destination, and we step out, make a right turn, and quickly arrive at our door. Grey rests her back against the wall, watching as I dig the room key out of my suit coat and slide the keycard through the card reader.

She leans forward as I turn the doorknob, and I pause, pressing against her gently for a quick kiss. The door eases open, and she sweeps inside, reaching up to pull the flower clip out of her hair and laying it on the dresser. Next to the dresser is the suitcase I placed there earlier.

"I should probably get out of this dress before taking my make-up off," she says from the other side of the room, clicking on a lamp.

My nerve endings strum high on vibrate.

It means you're getting lucky tonight, it means you're getting lucky tonight, it means you're getting lucky tonight...

"Help with my buttons?" Grey turns towards me, presenting her back, holding her lustrous blonde hair aside, and glancing at me over her shoulder.

It means you're getting lucky tonight, it means you're getting lucky tonight, it means you're getting lucky tonight...

In two long strides, I'm reaching for the pearl buttons at the top of her dress, the gentle illusion collar at the nape of her neck a stark distinction to my large, battered calloused hands, and I briefly pause to regard the juxtaposition of them against her dress.

One by one, I pluck the buttons free, and when I'm done, I splay my hands over her smooth back, running them up her spine before brushing her hair aside and pressing my mouth against her skin. Pushing the sleeves of the sheer fabric down her arms, my lips kiss a trail down the tantalizing column of her neck.

Grey shivers, lolling her head to the side with a loud, labored moan as her dress lands in a pile of crinoline and lace at her feet. I take her hand, and she steps out of it, leaving it in a lacy puddle.

Her hazy eyes watch me intensely as I kneel and bend her knee. Unbuckling the straps of her sexy nude heels, I slip them off one at a time, then run my hands up her smooth leg, planting a kiss on the inside of her arched thigh.

I trace a path of kisses up her leg, running my hands up her lean torso. She's standing in only a white pair of lacy underwear and a strapless white bra; one that pushes her sexy tits together until they threaten to spill over the edge of the cups.

It pains me, but I stand, releasing her so she can use the bathroom.

She cups my chin in her palm. "Be right back. Don't go anywhere."

"Not in a million fucking years."

This earns me another kiss, and a second later I get to watch her retreating, toned ass sashaying towards the bathroom.

Sexy as hell.

Biting back a groan, I set to removing my own shoes, followed by my socks, tie, and belt, draping them over the single chair in the room. I untuck my black dress shirt, plucking the buttons opens and letting it hang open.

I heft Greyson's small suitcase up onto the dresser so she won't have to struggle with it later, before removing the cell phone from my pocket and checking it for messages.

There are four text notifications.

Mason: *Thunder cunt. I sure-as-shit hope this chick is worth the shit storm coming your way. We got our asses handed to us tonight, no thanks to you.*

Aaron: *Hey condom breath, you're fucking your stalker right now, aren't you, asshole? I want all the nasty dirty details.*

Aaron: *Sorry. That was really out of line. Don't listen to me. I'm totally shit-faced and probably a little jealous.*

Tabitha: *Hey little brother. How's it going so far? Did Greyson like the tie? GOOD LUCK TONIGHT! She is one lucky girl*!

The text from my sister is the only one that makes me smile—the others make me scowl—so I shoot Tabitha a reply.

Me: *Night went great. You were right about the tie. She loved it. Says to thank you.*

Then, knowing there's only one way to get her to leave me alone, I add more.

Me: *Stop texting. Speaking of lucky, I'm about to get laid—her words, not mine.*

My sister immediately replies.

Tabitha: *You're disgusting.*
Me: *Whatever.*

I smirk, hitting SEND before powering my phone down and tossing it on the dresser next to my wallet and car keys.

I'm standing in the middle of the hotel room when the bathroom door opens, and Grey emerges wrapped in a fluffy white hotel robe, fresh-faced and glowing, her face free of makeup. Her lips are still stained from her deeply pigmented lipstick. She's removed the pins from her hair; it cascades down her back in loose waves created by the braid.

She's so un-fucking-believably gorgeous.

I try to say something, but no words come out. I'm crazy for this girl.

Grey's hazel eyes widen as she purposefully strides towards me on a mission, eyes on the exposed skin under my unbuttoned shirt. My body goes ramrod straight, and I inhale sharply with breathless anticipation as her smooth palms connect with the planes of my bare chest, fanning out over my pec muscles under my open dress shirt. Unable to prevent myself from flexing, my pecs contract beneath her roaming fingers, and I watch her face, transfixed as her pupil's dilate.

"Your turn. Go clean up and… come to bed," she whispers huskily as her fingertips skim, feather light, over my shoulders and push the black shirt down my arms, over my biceps, until it joins her dress.

Greyson parts her lips.

Her tongue darts out to moisten them.

The shirt drifts silently to the floor. My nipples harden under her soothing touch, and I fight the urge to moan.

Come to bed. Come to bed. Come to bed. Jesus. Do three sexier words even exist in the English language? If so, I sure as shit haven't heard them.

I nod incoherently, my head dipping up and down like a bobble head, putty in her hands. Right now I would literally do *anything* this girl asked me to.

Anything.

Once inside the bathroom, I make quick work of taking a piss, washing my face, and brushing my teeth. Several sexy, dark burgundy lip prints line my jaw.

I leave them.

Taking a deep breath, I open the bathroom door with a shaking hand.

Greyson

I'm not nervous.

Nope, not one bit.

I hear the sink running in the bathroom, and I glance at myself in the mirror above the dresser before unzipping the purple suitcase Cal has thoughtfully removed from the floor for me.

Loosening the belt of the hotel robe, I slide it low on my shoulders and take a few deep cleansing breaths to compose myself and calm my racing heart as I continue to study my reflection; color high, my eyes are bright and slightly wild. Aroused.

I finger a pink sleep shirt in my suitcase, rubbing it while I debate: on one hand, if I don't put a shirt on, I might look cheap and easy. On the other, I did already tell him he was getting lucky, so why bother putting on clothes?

Ugh, crap. I'm *crap* at this.

It's been two years since I've had sex. Two. Years. And quite honestly, I don't ever recall those experiences being particularly memorable.

The robe peels open farther, and the lacy white g-string undies and pristine white bra peek through.

Maybe I'll just…

…let it fall open. Like this?

No, like *this*.

Just then, Cal emerges from the bathroom, and I watch, spellbound, as his hard body advances to the center of the room, clad only in a pair of loose-hung gray sweatpants. You know the ones; they dip low on a guy's hipbones and hug him in all the *right* places.

I can't see it, but I know they're emphasizing his fine, round, athletic ass….

Every firm muscle on his body, every jaded scar, every line of his colorful tattoos are there for my perusal, and boy do I look my fill. He moves closer, watching me through hooded, lust-filled eyes before turning and depositing his folded suit pants on the dresser.

His eyes grow wide at the sight of me standing next to the dresser, first with total shock, then with desire. Hunger.

Want.

Need.

But that's not all I see there.

This guy wants to let himself love me; I can see it in the way he's looking down at me. Like I'm a precious, cherished thing.

I'm not nervous.

Nope, not one bit.

Calvin

I don't know what I did to deserve this girl, but…

Fuck.

Rugby.

Rooted in spot next to the dresser, Greyson faces me, the white robe a contrast to her tan skin, its gaping sliver baring her white bra and panties. She reaches to loosen the knot on her belt farther, the terrycloth falling completely open.

I stare.

I stare at her beautiful body, her waterfall of blonde hair, her high, round breasts and curvy hips. She's not perfect, but she's perfect to me.

"Cal," she entreats quietly, her voice filled with desire. Hunger.

Want.

Need.

For me. For fucking *me*.

I don't know who moved first, but our mouths meet, and my hands span her waist, kneading her bare, warm skin. Provocative. Achingly slow, our hot tongues mingle, wet and wanting.

Wet kisses. Open-mouthed kisses. Lips, tongue and teeth.

Grey's robe falls to the floor, and she breaks the kiss

to skim my abs with the tips of her fingers and the waistband of my pants, untying the white knot holding them around my hips.

My dick throbs so hard I can feel it beating in my pants.

Fuck.

I walk her backwards to the bed, the back of her knees hitting the mattress. She lies down, the gold comforter providing a backdrop for her magnificent blonde hair that pools around her fresh, flushed face.

The look she gives me invites me to look. To taste.

To touch.

I crawl on top of her then, dragging an open palm and my tongue up her stomach, over her breasts.

She pants when I lick her cleavage, my wet tongue flicking the groove between her blessedly plump tits. My fingers briefly toy with the small white clasp in front of her bra, and without preamble, I pop it open.

My mouth covers her then, and she moans loudly, her hips wiggling impatiently beneath me. I grind my erection into the apex of her spread thighs. Grind into her hard.

It's torture.

She grabs a handful of my disheveled hair and tugs.

"Lights on or off," I ask between sucking on her flawless skin.

"On. I want to watch you."

"I'm going to make you feel so fucking good, Grey."

"You already have, baby." She gasps into my mouth. "So fucking good."

Baby. Jesus Christ, it sounds good spilling from her lips. The dirty talk. I bite my cheek to stop the litany of endearments threatening to spill off the tip of my tongue, wanting to call her every goddamn mushy name I can think of: baby, sweetheart, sweetie, honey, babe, cutie pie, darling.

Shit. My friends were right; I am pussy whipped.

But only a spineless dickhead would give a shit what his friends thought.

"God, you're fucking sexy as shit," I whisper, caressing her hip. "I love your skin. I love your tits." To illustrate my point, I lick them both, sucking on the dusky nipples.

"Keep talking. What else," she asks, panting in a long, drawn out breath. "You feel so good." It sounds like she's sulking.

"I love how funny you are." Grey tips her head back as I suck on her neck gently, palming her breasts with my now trembling hand, kissing my way down her collarbone. "I love how smart and clever you are."

"You feel so good, Cal. Did I say that already? I'm losing my mind."

"You make me crazy." I moan, totally losing control of the situation. "Do I make you crazy?"

Our incoherent, sex-induced babble fills the room.

"Oh yeah, so crazy." Her hands push frantically at the waistband of my pants, and together, we slide them down my hips, then set to tearing off her underwear in a heated frenzy.

"God, just give it to me, Cal. I don't want to wait anymore; I want you so bad," she implores, reaching for my hard erection, stroking it up and down with her talented fingers. "Don't you want this inside me? I do. I want it bad."

Holy hell. Holy shit, the dirty mouth on her.

"Stop. Don't, baby," I beg through clenched teeth. "Or I'm gonna come."

"Come inside me," she moans, grabbing my ass and pulling me down. My dick brushes the slit of her pussy, pre-cum making it slick. "Please. I'm on the pill. Honey, please. I want this with you so bad."

Pill. *Honey*. Please.

I try to make sense of the words in my brain, but I've lost the function of reasoning.

Shit. *Shit, shit, shit.* I've never had sex without a condom—then again, I've never been serious about anyone before. Ever. Not even close.

But I am now—and whatever she wants I'm going to give her: Commitment. A relationship. Date nights. My cock inside her without a condom.

I swallow the lump in my throat and my balls tighten, eager and twitching with greedy anticipation.

"If we fuck without a condom, Greyson, you're mine. Do you understand?" My plea is hoarse, raw and full of emotions I didn't know I was feeling. "The only person I'd ever consider screwing without protection would be a steady girlfriend."

Or future wife, but I keep *that* shit to myself.

"Silly boy." Greyson cups my cheek in her palm tenderly, even as her rotating hips work the tip of my dick. "I decided I was keeping you the day you showed up at my door. You're *mine*."

Greyson

He feels so good.

So unbelievably good.

Words spill out of his lips. My lips. Incoherent rambling. Babbling. Endearments.

Begging.

Cal slides in and out of me and, "Oh God." I moan, spreading my legs wider as his hips pump, giving it to me good. So, so good. "Deeper, Cal, *push*. Yeah, yes, right there."

My head rolls to the side and I lie like a rag doll as he drives into me, the sensation of his bare flesh against mine almost unbearable. *Ooohhh yeahhh. Uuhhh.* Cal.

"Shit, oh shit. God, this feels amazing. Fucking incredible, baby. I… I… You're my best friend, baby," he confesses in an emotional, choked whisper. "I think I love you." He blurts out this sentiment as a choke gets stuck in his throat.

"I know, I know," I chant. My mouth finds his earlobe and I suck. "I love you too."

Love. What a word. We can't stop saying it.

Can't stop.

"I am. I'm fucking in *love* with you, Greyson." He swivels his pelvis and grinds me down into the mattress.

"I love you, Cal. So much." The words spill out of my

mouth in a sob before I can analyze the consequences of our slurred confessions.

Cal's giant hands reach under me, and he grasps my ass, pushing deep.

Our mouths meet then, and we burn for each other. *Burn.* With each kiss and every touch, we worship as only two people who've just declared their love for each other can—with passion and restraint and tenderness.

And once you've said those three little words, a floodgate opens, and you never want to stop saying them. So we don't. We say them again and again, in whispers and whimpers and groans and throaty sighs.

It's raw and deep and *real.*

It would be nauseating if it weren't us.

"I love you," Cal groans again as his hips pump and he slides slowly in and out of me. "Fuck, you feel good, Greyson. So *fuuuu…* sexy. Shit. *Uh*, Grey, I love you, baby."

He's way too gentle. He's way too slow.

My fingers move down his sweaty spine and squeeze his firm ass. "Harder, Cal. I said *harder.* Yes, right there, baby. Don't stop. I love you, I love you. Oh God, *deeper.* Harder. Cal."

Our lips and bodies tell a story, one we've been writing for the past seven weeks… a story of our friendship, bond, and love.

Calvin

Holy shit.

My girl loves me.

My girl loves it deep and hard and dirty and loud. And that's how I give it to her.

Greyson

We don't stop until we're both panting and sweaty and exhausted.

And then we do it again.

Twelve

@Grey_VKeller Tweeted: *I'm officially someone's* #girlfriend *and off the market* #facebookofficial

@tightheadthompson Tweeted: @grey_vkeller *damn straight*

@Grey_VKeller Tweeted: @tightheadthompson *I love you*

@tightheadthompson Tweeted: @grey_vkeller *I love you too, baby*

@JemmaGemini Tweeted: @tightheadthompson @grey_vkeller

Gross. Stop. NO ONE wants to see this crap. NO ONE #tmi #gag #wordvom

@MasonGille32 Tweeted: @tightheadthompson *Hey* #jerkoff *did we NOT just talk about keeping this #shit to yourself? TMI dude* #hornybastard

@Grey_VKeller Tweeted: @JemmaGemini *WHAT THE HECK JEMMA – we're literally sitting across from each other at the same table* #LOL

@JemmaGemini Tweeted: @grey_vkeller *Exactly! GET BACK TO WORK* stop #daydreaming

---

Cal: *You miss me already, don't you?*

Grey: *Yes. Remind me again why you had to leave so early this morning?*

Cal: *Post-game team meeting from last night's match. Of course I got my ass chewed out by at least four people. It wasn't pretty. Coach called me a 'cocksucking little prick' at least twice.*

Grey: *That's so horrible! What did you do???*

Cal: *He flew off the handle when I told him I didn't play because I was getting my priorities straight.*

Grey: *Aww, Cal!*

Cal: *It also didn't help that they got their asses handed to them, which of course is my fault because I wasn't there.*

Grey: :(*My poor baby. Is now the time I say I'm sorry?*

Cal: *You're worth the ball busting. Trust me.*

Grey: *You say the sweetest things!!! What are you*

doing now?

Cal: *Waiting for the guys. Short practice, the gym, then they want to grab pizza and beer or some shit. You?*

Grey: *Boxing up all the table decorations. Taking everything back to the sorority house for storage. Probably grab dinner and a movie with a few of my sisters. Saturday night, so they'll want to go out.*

Cal: *Stay away from the ass grabbers.*

Grey: *There's only one guy I want touching my backside, but he's got plans tonight. I'll do my best to stay away from the rest of them*

Cal: *You should probably wear a plastic garbage bag over your outfit. And a big hat. Ugly yourself up a bit.*

Grey: *LOL. Now who sounds jealous?*

Cal: *Me, dammit. I am.*

Grey: *Baby, haven't you figured it out yet? I love you. You have nothing to be jealous of…*

Grey: *You downtown yet?*

Cal: *Not yet. Sitting here on the couch playing Xbox. Aaron and Tom are both in the bathroom bathing in the same cheap cologne.*

Grey: *Speaking of cologne, have I mentioned lately how good you smell?*

Cal: *No. Tell me again.*

Grey: *Amazing. You smell amazing. Like a clean, woodsy, sexy boyfriend. Mmm. Seriously yummy boyfriend.*

Cal: *I can't fucking believe I have a girlfriend.*

Grey: *It has its benefits.*

Grey: *This bar is packed. Not even fun.*

Cal: *What are you wearing?*

Grey: *A plastic garbage bag and a large floppy hat. I look really ugly. You?*

Cal: *Sunglasses, a baseball hat, and an old winter coat.*

Grey: *Perfect.*

Cal: *Remind me again why I'm out with these dipshits and not with you? Why are you there and not here? With me?*

Grey: *Because you're a dumb boy.*

Cal: *Sounds about right.*

Grey: *Let's play a game?*

Cal: *Fine. Beats watching these putzes make asses of themselves. I'm pulling up a barstool. Pick your poison.*

Grey: *20 Questions. You start.*

Cal: *Hmmm. Um. Okay. Favorite Color*

Grey: *That's your question? My favorite color is yellow. Yours? Also, next question: boxers or briefs?*

Cal: *My favorite color is—duh—grey. I prefer boxer briefs. Next question: Favorite spot to be kissed.*

Grey: *Thong. Favorite spot to be kissed: on the neck.*

Next question: Last thing you licked.

Cal: *What the fuck, Grey*!

Grey: *LOL. Answer the question.*

Cal: *Oh my God, woman, you're killing me. Fine. My favorite spot to be kissed besides my *pointing down there* would be my chest. Last thing I licked? Beer foam.*

Cal: *Question 5. Um. Favorite spot for a first date*?

Grey: *Was that a hint? Cause if it was…*

Grey: *Wait. I have to play catch-up here. Last thing I licked: cupcake earlier today at the sorority house. Delicious. But not as delicious as you. Favorite spot for a first date? Out on the lake. Question: Last thing you WISH you'd licked.*

Cal: *Okay, that's not fighting fair. You wanna play dirty, little girl? Fine. Last thing I wish I licked? You. All over. Tits, ass, everywhere.*

Grey: *Are you trying to shock me? Because it won't work. You'll have to do better than that.*

Grey: *Crap. Some guy just spilled beer all over my shoes. Running to wipe them off. BRB.*

Cal: *Seriously? NOW? Dammit.*

Cal: …

Cal: ??? *UGH*!!

Grey: *Okay, I'm back. Sorry, I know that was a total buzzkill. Last think I wish I'd licked? Your tattoo looks like I want my tongue on it. Next question is yours, slacker.*

Cal: *Alright. Favorite body part on the opposite sex (and I'm going to ignore the tongue on my tattoo comment because if I don't, I'll get hard.*)

Grey: *Question amended. Favorite body part on YOU. Your tight ass, specifically in those gray pants you wore to bed last night. I mean. Orgasmic. Seriously. Your* *abs are insane.*

Cal: *STOP. Just stop. You're making me hard.*

Grey: *Yeah, well. I guess SOMEONE should have invited me to join him tonight and we could have taken care of that problem. Let's call your hard-on a punishment for being too wussy to ask me out.*

Cal: *That's hitting below the belt.*

Grey: *Below the belt. Mmm mmm... yum.*

Cal: *Knock that shit off. I'm in public. One of my teammates has been trying to steal my phone for the last ten minutes. Says I'm looking down at it like a horny bastard.*

Grey: *Are you?*

Cal: *Yes.*

Cal: *We never did finish that game of 20 Questions. Are you still up?*

Grey: *Yeah, we got home about 30 minutes ago.*

Cal: *Sober?*

Grey: *Yes. You?*

Cal: *Yup. FaceTime?*

Epilogue

Tabitha

I trail in the wake behind my brother and his new girlfriend, the three of us paddling in kayaks across the surface of Lake Walton, slicing our oars through the dark water at a leisurely pace.

The day is calm, sunny, and perfect.

I adjust the brim of my straw sunhat so it completely covers my face, and push the sunglasses up higher on the bridge of my nose before maneuvering my kayak closer to my brother, Cal, and his girlfriend, Greyson.

They're ahead of me, rowing side by side in companionable silence, and I trail after them, in no hurry to partake in their love-fest.

I try to avert my eyes when they steal glances at each other every couple feet as they paddle, trying to be sly about it but failing miserably. They cannot keep their eyes off each other, and if I weren't so damn happy for my brother, I would be completely repulsed.

Nonetheless, as a single female, I feel it's my duty to give an eye-roll towards the cloudless blue sky.

"Babe, let's check out that sand bar over there." My brother's low voice carries back to me. He twists his lean torso and looks back at me. "Tab, we're gonna stop at the island."

"Hey, I know that place!" Greyson exclaims, excited. "You showed me a picture of it once."

Cal grins at her, obviously pleased that she remembered, and we all paddle deftly towards the little island. It's actually more of a peninsula jutting out into the water, with a white sand beach, picnic tables, and a campfire site.

As we get closer, I can see a small smokestack where the last campers had their bonfire, the faint, smoldering gray cloud rising into the canopy of trees from the dying embers.

My brother continues talking. "I've always wanted to stop, but stopping by myself always just seemed depressing."

Greyson blushes at him prettily. "Well, now you never have to."

My brother's steely gaze lands on the cleavage appearing from beneath the zipper of her life jacket. "Kayaking with you is almost worse."

Her large hazel eyes widen. "What! Why?"

"Because I just keep wanting to lean over and pull you into the water. Get us both wet."

Gross. I want to splash them both with my paddle. "Alright, you two, stop. Just stop. You're making me sick."

My brother, who I never in a million years thought would so freely give PDA, leans his muscular, tattooed arm out to draw Greyson's kayak closer, and he bends over the side of his, puckering his lips.

Their eyes close behind their sunglasses and their lips meet, pressing together over the water.

They both sigh.

Greyson lays her paddle across her red kayak, the delicate fingers of one hand reaching up to gently stroke the new gash under my brother's left eye. "I have to put some Neosporin on this." Her voice drifts over the water, soothing. "I'm worried."

My annoying younger brother nods into her palm like a puppy dog. "Okay."

What the…

Seriously, could this get any worse?

"I brought us a picnic."

Never mind. It just did.

Greyson gasps in delight. "Oh my god, Cal, sweetie—could you be any more perfect?"

"I don't know. Could you?"

"I love you."

"I love *you*."

They're disgusting. Just disgusting.

Greyson sighs.

I sigh too, and with a jealous little huff, keep paddling.

Our kayaks hit the sandy bank of the island, and Cal hops out first, dragging Greyson's up onto the shore with ease, and holding his hand out to steady her while she steps out onto the beach.

I hold back a groan when his hands go around her waist and their lips meet for another quick kiss. He gives her butt a swat when she starts up the bank towards the campsite.

My brother turns, wading in a few feet, and grabs the rope at the front of mine, pulling my kayak alongside Greyson's and extending his hand to me the same way he did for her. Only instead of graciously accepting his help, I narrow my eyes at him from my spot on the water.

"What's the look for?" he asks, glaring down at me.

"I don't trust you," I say.

Cal snorts. "What—you think I'm going to dump you in the water? What are we, thirteen?"

"Oh *please*. I know how you operate. Don't tell me you aren't thinking about it right now," I tease, but extend my hand.

He takes it, pulling me up so I can step out. When my feet are on the shore, I'm ankle deep in water and my brother crosses his arms indignantly.

"You give me no credit at all. I would never shove you in the water."

Now I'm laughing as I stand. "You are such a liar."

"What kind of an asshole shoves his sister in the water with his girlfriend watching?" He leans over as he bends to steady my kayak, busying himself by pulling them onto the shore farther so they don't float away. "You know—" he looks slyly over at me "—you're right. I did think about shoving your ass in the water."

"I knew it!" My foot gives a kick, and I splash him.

"Yeah, well, you deserve it. I still owe you from the time you laid under my bed hiding while I changed my clothes, then scared the shit out of me once I turned off the lights and climbed into bed."

I throw my hands up, exasperated. "That was three years ago!"

"Whatever—you're sick. Watch your back, that's all I'm saying."

"Shut up," I scoff, glancing up to where Greyson is walking around the picnic area, alone, while we bicker like children. "And why are you bothering me when your girlfriend is waiting? I love you to death, but the two of you make me sick."

And I already love *her* to death—like a sister.

I love them both.

They have formed an unbreakable bond, an incredible friendship.

And I want them to continue being happy.

Things *Liars* Hide

For those who *dare* to follow

the *path* less taken.

One

Collin

"I don't understand why you're not getting this one. It's perfect!" My sister nags beside me, pulling the lavender shower curtain off the hook and tossing it in the cart. "I think it's so cute."

I reach into the cart and snatch it up, replacing it on the display. "I'm not putting this in my new condo. It's purple. And floral."

My little sister *tsks*. "More like a grayish lavender. Girls will love this."

"Greyson, I don't plan on parading a string of girls through my condo, and I am not going to look at this ugly-ass shower curtain every damn morning before work."

She sighs loudly, relenting. "Fine, have it your way. I'm just trying to make your place a babe magnet."

I laugh and grab hold of the cart. "Let's just grab towels and everything else on the list, and then we can come back to this aisle. Right now, I'm over picking out shower curtains. Agreed?"

Greyson nods, her pale blonde ponytail swinging jauntily and settling on her shoulders. With tan skin from perpetually being out in the sun, pert nose, and large hazel eyes, my younger sister by five years is beautiful—inside and out.

Not to mention *kind*, sweet, and funny.

We are nothing alike.

Where she is all sunshine and light, I am stormy and dark. Greyson is five-foot-five and delicate; I am six-foot-two and imposing.

Unyielding.

I stand brooding beside her, leaning my elbows against the handle of the red cart as we trail aimlessly through the center aisle of her favorite supermarket chain. She lets me push the cart of household items and cleaning supplies I'll need for my new condo, chatting next to me about her new boyfriend, Cal.

We arrive at the lighting department, and Greyson halts the cart, nudging me. "Didn't you say you needed a lamp for your living room?"

I shrug, pausing to adjust the sunglasses perched on top of my head. "Yeah, but I was planning on just stealing one of Mom's."

Greyson tips her head back and laughs. "And you don't think she'll notice?"

I shrug again. "Maybe. But by the time she notices her lamp missing, I'll be long gone. It's a solid plan."

"But she'll see it at your housewarming party next weekend." My sister knocks me with her hip. "Just go pick out a lamp, tightwad, and spare us all the drama."

"Fine," I grumble. "But explain to me why I have to pay thirty bucks for a lamp, then another twenty for the shade? That's highway robbery. All I *really* need is a light bulb and a switch."

But I comply, knowing it's a losing argument. She's going to make me buy a lamp no matter how long we stand here disagreeing. Striding with purpose down the lighting aisle, I eyeball them all and reach impulsively for a silver base with sleek lines.

There. This will do.

Now for a shade to coordinate; something simple with clean lines would work.

Sleek. Clean lines.

What the hell is wrong with me? *I sound like a goddamn interior decorator.*

"That one's actually really nice!" Grey exclaims excitedly, helping me rearrange the shopping cart contents to make room for the lamp and shade among all my other crap.

"Gee, don't sound so surprised," I deadpan. "I'm not a total Neanderthal."

"Well, I mean… not *totally.* Although your usual decoration of choice is Star Wars posters and The Incredible Hulk."

I scoff loudly, crossing my muscular arms over my broad chest resentfully. The navy-blue tee shirt I shrunk doing my own laundry strains across my shoulders. "I'll have you know, my condo in Seattle had none of those things, smartass."

"I'm only teasing… Mom packed all that away when you moved after college. But I'm sure the boxes are in the basement somewhere if you're interested."

“I’m not,” I insist with a scowl.

Well. Maybe I am, a little. But only because I don’t have any artwork to hang on my white condo walls.

Dammit. There I go again, sounding like a goddamn decorator.

“Can we just grab what I need and get the hell out of here?”

“Yeah, yeah, yeah, hold your horses.” Greyson holds up the handwritten list I brought, consulting it like it’s a treasure map. “We still have to grab you a rug for your kitchen, and some gadgets. You need a wine bottle opener —” She’s skeptical. “Really? A wine bottle opener? That’s necessary?”

“I like wine sometimes. I need a new bottle opener.” If sighing sarcastically were a thing, I would do it right now. But since it’s not, I just do it loudly.

My sister relents, holding her hands up, one still clutching the list. “Okay, okay, calm down.” She checks the list again. “*Wine* bottle opener,” the brat emphasizes with an eye-roll. “Can opener. Water glasses. Garbage bags.”

Greyson’s voice fades out as I stare absentmindedly up the center aisle, the repetitive elevator music from Target’s sound system lulling me into a zombie-like state. A leggy blonde up ahead wearing a hot-pink baseball hat peaks my curiosity—long, tan legs in white shorts and a light gray shirt. I perk up considerably at the sight of her.

She stops in the middle of the aisle and gapes, arms laden with shampoo and hairspray and shit, and the pink lips I’m admiring part in a surprised *O*. I can see from here that her eyes are bright blue, set off by the color of her cap. Without hesitating, I scan that body from the long blonde hair falling loosely under her hat, to the round breasts beneath her simple shirt, up to the shocked expression on her face.

No. That's not right—she looks spooked.

Like she's seen a ghost.

When she darts quickly behind a display up ahead, abandoning her cart, I crane my neck, hoping to catch another glimpse.

Fail.

Dammit, where the hell did she go?

"Are you even listening to me?" my sister asks, threading her arm through mine to recapture my attention. Knowing me like she does, she takes pity on me. "Tell you what. Let's quickly run over to the cleaning supplies, grab some detergent, and call it a day. Then we can grab lunch. Your treat, of course."

Her head hits my shoulder, and she gives my arm an affectionate, sisterly squeeze.

"Of course."

Tabitha

I put a trembling hand to my chest to calm this racing heart inside me. It's going positively wild, and I place my other hand on the shopping cart for support. Somewhere in the next aisle over, I hear the tinkling laugh—one that I recognize. One that I'm all too familiar with, and I know it's her.

Greyson Keller.

My brother's girlfriend…

…grasping the arm of a guy I don't recognize, pulling him towards a display of bed spreads, holding his tan, muscular arm firmly with one hand, and pointing to a quilt display with the other.

"You said you *just* wanted to quickly grab some more cleaning supplies," I hear his deep voice grumble.

"I know what I said. But since we're near the bedding, wouldn't it be nice to roll around on crisp, clean sheets?"

The guy's hesitation is followed by more grumbling. "I *guess* so…"

This is not happening right now.

I am not witnessing Cal's girlfriend cheating on him with another guy. I can't be.

I refuse to believe it. Squeezing my blue eyes shut, I lean my limp body against the metal rack of pillows behind me, and I use the rack to support myself. My legs are weak, wobbly, and I lower my palms to steady my knees, taking a few deep breaths.

I'm physically shaking.

I am *not* seeing this. *I'm not, I'm not, I'm not.*

I can't be.

Cal loves her. I love her, too—she's the sister I never had.

I can't even conjure up any nasty or unkind thoughts about her right now, even with the truth before me. One aisle over. The truth that's *laughing* and simpering and giggling like a flirty teenager. I love Greyson so much that I don't have the heart to storm over and confront her for being a lying, cheating, backstabbing…

Ugh.

I stare up at the ceiling of the store at the fluorescent bulbs now blinding my eyes, and I pull the brim of my hot-pink hat down to shield my eyes, debating my options.

I can't even think about her being a cheater.

Horrible.

I think I'm going to retch all over the floor in this aisle.

Oh sweet baby Jesus.

I inhale and exhale slowly, trying to catch my breath—the way I did in college after I'd had too much to drink and was trying to stop myself from barfing. I stand like this until my queasy stomach subsides, and the pukey feeling passes.

My lids flutter open.

What do I do? *What the hell do I do*? This is my brother's girlfriend, the center of his whole world, the love of his life. I cannot tell him she's cheating on him. I cannot tell him what I just saw—but at the same time, I can't unsee it.

I also can't stand here all day, hiding behind the bean bag chairs and pillows with a cart full of unpaid toiletries, as Greyson and *that hot guy* idly stroll, aisle after aisle, laughing and flirting and touching each other with familiarity.

There goes his laugh again. Deep and rich and amused.

Happy.

I thought *Greyson* was happy—happy with Cal.

Shit.

And suddenly, here they are. A million uncharitable thoughts race through my brain as I hide, concealed from their view. How dare she? How long has this been going on? How can she so brazenly flaunt this guy in public, where anyone could bump into them? *What do I tell my brother*?

My brother, who has never been in love until now. My brother, who has never let anyone into his heart. He will be *crushed*. Devastated won't even begin to cover it.

Cal will never trust anyone again.

My chest tightening and heart breaking, I take another deep, stabilizing breath and try to recall some of the breathing techniques I learned in yoga class. And… I got nothin'.

Crap.

Why don't I ever pay attention in that dumb class? *In through the nose, out through the mouth... in through the nose, out through the mouth.*

I peek my head around the corner to catch a glimpse of them.

Greyson and that dark-haired hottie.

Shit, he's deliciously attractive.

He's tall and broad with thick, dark brown hair and sexy black sunglasses propped on top of his head. Greyson has her blonde head resting against his wide shoulder. A large hand slides around my brother's girlfriend's waist, giving her an affectionate squeeze.

I hate it. I hate how comfortable they obviously are with each other.

How the hell can my brother compete with a guy as handsome as *that?*

I glare at them, sick to my stomach and wanting to vom, then plaster myself back up against the shelf with a shaking breath. A sharp price tag stabs me in the back, jolting me out of my angry stupor.

Why the hell am I the one hiding? I'm not the one doing anything wrong!

Another rich laugh fills the air, coming from the next aisle over, and I steady myself. Straighten my spine. Count down from three.

Two.

One.

I step out into the main aisle, plastering on a wide smile when I come face to face with Greyson and this homewrecking asshole.

"Greyson! Hi!" My voice comes out saccharine sweet, sounding hollow, fake, and robotic as I try my best to act surprised to see them. Surprised but cheerful. Definitely cheerful.

Gag.

"Oh my gosh! Tabitha!" Greyson gasps, delighted, and steps out from behind the cart, coming around it to embrace me. "It's so good to see you!"

Hmm, she sounds suspiciously joyful. *For a lying, backstabbing cheater*.

"Hey." My body is stiff, arms clutching the toiletries that haven't yet made it into my cart. I glance between the two of them bitterly from under the brim of my cap. "What are you doing in town? So far from school?"

She and my brother are in college three hours away, but coincidentally, our parents only live twenty minutes apart from each other.

Imagine that.

Greyson's painfully attractive date's eyes linger on me with rapt interest, his hazel irises checking me out from head to toe, landing on my chest a heartbeat too long, his high cheekbones taking on a rosy glow before jerking his gaze away.

Of all the nerve!

What. An. *Asshole*.

"We're getting odds and ends for his condo," Greyson replies slowly, stepping out of our embrace and narrowing her eyes as she studies me. My brother's girlfriend might be stupidly gorgeous, but she's definitely not stupid. "Tabitha, what's wrong?"

"Nothing," I lie, shaking out of her grasp. "Who's your *friend*?" Agitated, I begin tapping my foot on the hard tile, biting my tongue.

Greyson's lip's part, and I brace myself for her lie.

"You mean Collin?" Confused, she looks back and forth between him and me, apprehension marring her beautiful face. "Tabitha, I'm not sure—"

"How *could* you?" I hiss in a whisper.

Her expressive eyes get wide. "How could I what?"

"Oh my god, seriously?" I raise my palms in frustration, the deodorant, hairspray, and toothpaste falling to the ground with noisy, hollow clangs. The metal hairspray can bounces, rolls, and hits the adjacent metal shelf, but I don't even care.

"How could you *do* this to my brother? He loves you!" It takes every ounce of my self-control not to have an outburst, but based on the shrill sound coming out of my mouth, I'm not successful.

"Tabitha, tell me what's wrong, *please*. You're scaring me," Greyson implores, reaching for my arm.

I jerk it away.

Upset and near hysterics, I turn to leave, bending with a sob to snatch my purchases off the ground. "Whatever you're going to say, save it, okay? Enjoy your *ridiculously* good-looking boy toy. I'll be there to pick up my brother's broken pieces after you break his heart into a million little shards."

I turn to stalk away.

"What!" Greyson gasps from behind me. "Oh my god—"

"Hey!" the dark-haired Adonis bellows after me, taking several long strides and cuffing his large, warm hand over my bicep. "Get your bony ass back here for a second."

Bony ass? *Bony*. Ass?

"H-how dare you!" I sputter furiously; whether it's from the manhandling or name calling, I'm not entirely sure.

"How dare *I*? You're the one that sounds like a mental person. That's my *sister*. Greyson is my sister."

Okay.

Yeah.

So this is the part where I stand there dumbfounded, staring at both of them with my mouth agape. Yup, that's what I do. I stand there, gaping. Embarrassed. Face flushed. Horrified. Mortified.

As far as misunderstandings go, this is one of the worst.

"I… oh."

"Yeah, *oh*. What the hell is wrong with you?"

"I didn't… I didn't think."

"You didn't think? I can see that." He runs a tan hand through his dark, mussy hair. "Nice to meet you, by the way. I'm Collin Keller. Greyson's *brother*."

Collin Keller extends his hand, and I gawk dumbly at it, still sheepish. He leaves it there, hanging between us, waiting for me to shake it.

"I… Hi." My hand slides into his and I shiver. Our eyes connect.

They're hazel.

His eyes are hazel, just like Greyson's.

Exactly. Like. Greyson's.

As we take each other in, the hard set of his mouth transforms; the corners of his beautifully sculpted lips tip into an awkward smile, framed by the shadow of a beard playing along his strong jawline and defined chin.

He's *so*… male.

"You don't have any pictures of him on Facebook," I blurt out, releasing Collin's hand and wiping any traces of him off on my white shorts.

He studies me then, awareness prickling the back of my neck. We regard each other intently before he turns towards his sister, his eyebrows going up quizzically.

"You don't have any pictures of me on Facebook? Why the hell not?"

She laughs and smacks him in the arm. "You said you *hate* when I tag you in pictures. Besides, you haven't even been in town the last two years. So I have almost no recent pictures of you. Unless you count the ones where our whole family's wearing matching Christmas pajamas."

He chuckles then, deep and low and manly. God, his voice is sexy. His hazel eyes shine and my breath hitches for the second time today. "Fair enough." He regards me then with another grin. "She's right, I *do* hate when she tags me in pictures."

I shake my head, miserable. "I'm sorry, Grey. I can't believe I thought…"

She nods, understanding. "I know what you thought, and I don't blame you."

I'd feel so much better if she called me an asshole. Or an overreacting jackass.

I deserve it.

"Yeah, it's just. When I saw you touching him…" I let my judgment trail off suggestively, glancing back and forth between the two of them with raised eyebrows to emphasize my point. "You and him, my imagination ran a little wild."

If only she knew how wild my imagination really was.

"Ya think?" Collin deadpans beside her.

Greyson ignores him, shaking her head before reaching over, pulling me in for a hug. "Collin just accepted a job offer," she murmurs into my hair. "He just moved back to the city from Seattle. I'm helping him buy a bunch of stuff for his new condo."

All I can muster is a weak, "Oh," when she pulls

away. Then meekly, I say, "In my defense, except for the eyes, you two look nothing alike."

"Thank *God*," Collin jokes, and Greyson playfully smacks him again.

"Hey!"

"Sorry, but you're the least attractive of mom's three children."

Greyson rolls her large hazel eyes. "Anyway, I feel horrible you thought that me and him... I mean. Look at him—*so* not my type."

Oh, I'm looking alright. As if I could stop myself.

I fidget with the toiletries in my arms awkwardly, speaking cautiously. "Grey, could we… can we *not* tell anyone about this?"

She hangs her head and shakes it ruefully, patting me on the arm. "No can do, Tabby. This one is just *too* too good to keep a secret."

Two

Tabitha

Blare Wellborn wasn't always this guarded; she was fun and outgoing and loud. But she had a secret, one she was hiding from everyone she cared about—the one thing that brought her the most joy, was the one thing she couldn't tell to anyone.

Blare freezes in the aisle of the store, not sure which direction to head in first. She didn't come for cosmetics, but the glittery display of mascara beckoned her. Man, was she a sucker for new products, and she loved getting dressed up. These days, though, there wasn't much opportunity, and she heaved a loud sigh when she snatched up a hot-pink mascara tube and tossed it in her basket.

Biting down on her lower lip, she studied her choices, not paying any attention when someone brushed past her and bumped into her shoulder, causing her to drop her purse. "Oh!" She gasped, startled. "I'm sorry." Blare was always apologizing, and mentally kicked herself for doing it now. After all, she wasn't the one who had smacked into her.

They both bent down, grabbing at her bag. Hands touching. Fingers grasping. Then, "Oh..." Hazel eyes stared back at her, a tuft of shockingly dark brown locks brushed away by a masculine hand. "Don't apologize. I bumped into you." His voice. His lips. That ruggedly handsome face, those kind eyes. They regarded each other then, something passing between them: recognition. Attraction. Definitely *attraction....*

Leaning back in the high-back chair, satisfied, I hit SAVE on my laptop, pleased with the progress on my second novel.

My. *Second*. Novel.

Two novels that *I* wrote, all by my freaking self.

Me!

A romance writer.

I can hardly believe it, and if someone had told me a year ago that I'd be publishing a book—let alone two—well, I wouldn't have believed them. I might have even laughed in their face. Not very ladylike, I know, but there you have it.

My parents would be shocked. And horrified—not because I've written a book, but because they're fifty shades of smut. I don't even want to imagine what I'd say to my grandparents.

And if Cal found out? I would never live it down.

I grin, imagining the tasteless jokes and innuendos my brother would throw down if he discovered my secret, but also saddened by the knowledge that I'm hiding it from him, because I know he would support me. Be proud.

My biggest fan.

Ironically, despite his rough exterior and grumpy disposition, Cal has always been my biggest cheerleader. When I was a teenager and became obsessed with animals—stray dogs at the pound in particular—he helped me raise money to donate to the shelter. Together we went to buy pet supplies the shelter needed with the cash I'd raised.

When I went through my boy band phase, it was Cal who went with me to stand in line at the radio station, overnight, to enter a contest for a chance to win tickets.

And every spring when we mulch our parents' landscaping, I always weasel my way out of working in the yard by faking an injury, and he's never *once* ratted me out.

Heaving a loud sigh at the memories, I reach over the side of my chair to root around the tote next to my table for a pen, feeling around inside the bag blindly with one hand and coming up empty. I lean over farther to yank it open and peer inside.

Ah-ha, there it is.

I pop the pen cap off with my teeth and admire the paperback proof for my *first* book—which hasn't even been officially released yet—resting on the table next to my soy latte, trailing my fingers across its sleek cover and glossy design. I turn the paperback this way and that, admiring the two entwined, *naked* bodies in the heat of passion, the shocking red title, and my name in bold letters splashed across the front.

My name!

Well, my pen name, anyway.

A pair of blue ear buds dangle from my lobes and down the front of my white tee shirt, and I reset my music playlist before flipping open the proof copy of my book, pen poised and ready for edits.

Disappointed, the first page—the title page—is pixelated, so I circle it and add a note in the margin for my formatter. Thirty pages in I find a typo, and a few chapters further, too many spaces between paragraphs, a sentence that's meant to be italicized. There are narrow margins in the epilogue.

I circle them all.

I forgo acknowledgements in this book because, well, who am I going to thank?

No one knows I wrote it.

And if none of my family or friends know I wrote it, who's even going to read it? Probably no one. But I didn't write it for them or for strangers; I wrote it for me.

It's something I've always wanted to do; it's always been my passion. My career goals never included working for my parents. Don't get me wrong—I love them to death and I like my job, but…

…the construction company is *their* passion. *Their* vision. *Their* dream.

Not mine.

But my parents count on me—always have—trusting that Cal and I will take ownership of their company when they retire. They have confidence in us, put us through Business School at Ivy League colleges, and rely on us to continue their legacy.

Lately though, for the first time in my life, the thought of living someone else's dream is stifling me. Suffocating. It might be what my brother wants, but it's holding me back.

I rest my back against the soft cushion, my pen hovering above the cream pages of my novel—all three hundred and eighty pages of it. Setting the blue felt-tip pen down, I trace the title on the cover with my hand, letting my fingers run up and down the glossy surface.

I lift it with both hands and lift it to my nose, inhaling the smell of freshly printed paper and sighing before clutching it to my chest.

This book is my baby. My labor of love. The best thing that's happened to me in years.

And I have no one to tell.

With a sigh, I continue to write.

***B**lare closed her eyes and tried to remember him. What he looked like, how he sounded, what it felt like when he handed her the discarded mascara that had fallen on the cold tile of the store. He felt familiar to her, like someone she'd known all her life. Like they were connected somehow, and it made her heart beat faster.*

Oh well. She wasn't going to see him again. What would be the odds? A million to one? Serendipity only happened in fairy tales, and Blare's life was anything but. With her eyes open and reality surrounding her, the fast-paced beating of her heart gradually returned to normal. But her memory of him never would...

Collin

The pink hat gives her away.

I spot it as soon as I push through the door at Blooming Grounds, a coffee shop in the heart of the city, sandwiched between a hotel chain and insurance brokerage firm. It's surprisingly cozy.

Hefting my black leather laptop bag up and bending at the neck to move the strap over my head, I sling it around my torso, resting the cross-body strap diagonally against my chest.

I hold it steady while I… *study* her.

I hone in on Tabitha Thompson, the brightest spot in the room. It can't be anyone but her—I would recognize that ball cap anywhere. She was wearing it during that embarrassing display she put on last week when she accused my sister of cheating on her brother. With me.

Not that I blame her; my sister and I look nothing alike and Greyson was far from college, home for an impromptu visit.

With her back to me, Tabitha's spine is bent over a glowing laptop monitor, blonde hair in a ponytail she's pulled through the back of her hat.

Baseball caps and ponytails; man, I love that shit.

Cautiously, I approach her from behind, my eyes raking her back. Her bra is visible through her thin white tee, faded cut-up jeans, and navy flip-flops—she looks casual and relaxed. As her fingers fly across her keyboard, the *tap tap tapping* sound resonates, filling the gap of space around the small square table she occupies in the center of the room.

I observe her for a few minutes from across the room until she leans back in her chair, digs in her bag to produce a pen, and eventually begins scribbling in a paperback book.

Inching closer, I watch as she sets the pen down and closes the book to run a hand over its surface, her fingers stroking the cover before raising it to her nose and giving it a whiff. Yeah, you heard me—she's smelling the book.

Who does that?

Then, as if *that* wasn't weird enough, Tabitha grasps the book tightly, clutches it to her chest, and… hugs it?

Uh, okay.

She might be weird, but my looming over her is just as creepy. The soft, dull light from Tabitha's monitor draws me in, and curiously, I hover closely behind her, scanning the paragraph she'd undoubtedly been pounding away on earlier.

Wait. Does that sentence say, *Blare could not stop thinking about him, the guy from the store. His hazel eyes burned holes into her soul and made her center quake. She was experiencing want and desire like nothing...* nothing *she'd ever felt before. She wanted to strip them both naked right there, drag him into a dressing room, and let him—*

Holy shit.

I *feel* my eyes widen in shock. Bugging out of my fucking skull is probably more accurate, because—holy shit—Tabitha Thompson is writing a sex book in the middle of a public coffee shop.

Smut. A bodice ripper.

Whatever the hell you wanna call it.

In disbelief, I give my hair a shake before pushing the black sunglasses up so they rest atop my head. My eyes hit her monitor again, seeking, reading word after suggestive word.

I've seen what I've seen and I can't un-see it.

Drawing even closer, my intention isn't to scare the *shit* out of her, but that's exactly what happens when I let out a surprised gasp. Yeah, I fucking gasp. Like a god-damn girl.

Startled, Tabitha turns.

Her eyes hit my legs first, climb leisurely up my body, pausing on my broad chest, and widen with surprise, then recognition.

Dismay.

The book falls from her hands, landing on the floor with a soft thud on the carpet, and when I bend to scoop it up, her hand darts out and grips my wrist.

"Don't touch it!" Her voice is filled with panic. "Please just leave it."

I rear my hand back and straighten, my eyes flitting to her glowing screen before she glares at me for gawking, and twists in her chair to close the top with a resounding snap.

She tidies up her workspace then spins to face me.

Well, well, well, someone doesn't want me learning any of her dirty little secrets. My eyes dart to the discarded paperback lying facedown on the floor, and for now she's too flustered to pick it up. What's in that damn book that she doesn't want me to see?

"Collin Keller." Tabitha flashes me a fake smile, her

lips pulled tight across her white teeth. "What on earth are you doing here?"

"You don't have to sound so thrilled to see me."

A blush creeps up her neck, and the hot-pink bill of her ball cap creates an unflattering fuchsia shadow on her skin. She has the decency to look embarrassed by her lack of manners.

"I'm sorry, that was rude. It's just that you startled me." Tabitha bites down on her lower lip, takes a steadying breath, and then asks, "So… what *are* you doing here?"

A laugh explodes out of me. "Just can't help yourself, can you? I work in the financial district. It's four blocks up, actually, but I like it in here better than Starbucks. Much warmer and definitely more quiet. I get more work done here." I motion to the laptop draped across my body, giving the canvas bag a pat. "What about you? What brings you to this neck of the woods?"

"I actually live nearby. I… come here often, usually after work, but I didn't have a lot going on at the office today, so… here I am. Earlier than usual." Her shoulders give an apologetic shrug, and she nervously reaches up to adjust the bill of her pink ball cap.

While she's doing that, my eyes flit to the laptop.

A sly smile curls my lips. "What are you working on?"

Tabitha's hands stop, still holding her brim as her bright blue eyes narrow suspiciously for a few seconds, assessing, as if trying to gauge my sincerity.

Like she doesn't quite trust me.

Like she's looking for any clue that I've seen what's written on her screen.

Why yes, Tabitha. *Yes I have*.

I've seen words like *tremble, breathless, stroke*, and *panting* flash across her monitor, burning themselves in my brain—forever. I'll not likely forget them anytime soon, not only because they were sexy, but because *she* was writing them.

Those sexy words came out of *that* sexy girl, and it has me wondering what other thoughts are going through her obviously dirty mind—because I'm a guy and I wonder about shit like that.

And now look how agitated she is.

She suspects I've seen something; it's written all over her beautiful face.

I try not to snicker. "What was it you said you were working on?"

"What am I working on?" she parrots, her brows furrowed in confusion.

"Yeah, it looks like I interrupted something."

Something *smutty*.

Tabitha bites her bottom lip and looks away guiltily. "Um. Work stuff, I guess."

"What kind of work stuff?" This time I *do* snicker.

She closes the notebook in front of her with a scowl and crosses her arms defensively over her chest. "What's with all the questions?"

"Just curious, that's all." I shoulder the weight of my laptop, laying it on the floor next to her table, and lean my elbow on the back of her chair.

I'm so close now I can smell the sweetness of her hair when she fidgets in her chair, kicking up the air around her.

A nervous giggle escapes her lips—her very nicely

shaped, pink, pouty lips. Some people would call them glossy; I'm calling them *juicy.*

Juicy lips I want to suck on.

"Are you coming?" asks my lazy drawl.

"Ex*cuse* me?" Tabitha's mouth gapes in an *O* of surprise and I suppress the urge to say, *Speaking of coming, weren't you just writing about that very same thing only moments ago*?

But I don't. Instead, I say, "Are you coming to my housewarming party?"

"I didn't know you were having one."

Liar, liar, pants on fire.

"Oh, really? Because I'm pretty sure Greyson told me she invited you. Personally."

"She did?"

I study her, the large blue eyes lined in black, the clear, smooth skin flushed from frustration and embarrassment, and the full lips. Letting my gaze linger until she gets uncomfortable with my scrutiny, she finally breaks contact and turns her face towards the bank of windows on the far side of the coffee shop.

I give my chin a scratch. "Yeah. I'm pretty sure she said you were coming."

Tabitha shakes her head in denial, her blonde ponytail swinging back and forth. "I never said that. I said I had to check my calendar."

Gotcha.

"*Ah*, so she *did* invite you to come."

"Please stop doing that."

"Doing what?"

"You *know* what. Using the word..." Tabitha turns back to stare at me, her eyes bright but guarded. "Stop pushing. You're pushing."

"I'm not pushing." I smile. "I just want you to come."

Yeah. You bet your sweet ass I meant for that to sound dirty, and from the look on her face right now, she knows it.

She hesitates before responding, furrowing her brows and eyeing me from under her flirty cap before sliding her notebook off the table and stuffing it into her bag.

Tabitha lifts her laptop, unplugs the earbuds, winding them up along with the power cord, and rises. "I have to go."

My eyes flick to the book on the floor, but morbid curiosity keeps me silent.

She grabs at her phone charger, stepping on it and stumbling when she yanks it up, trying to coil it around her hand. As she abandons tidiness, the black cord gets shoved haphazardly into her brown leather tote, and she shoulders it before grabbing an uncovered, steaming coffee off the table top.

It spills, wetting her hand and soaking the hem of her white shirt.

Her cheeks are beet red when she faces me, barely able to look me in the eye. "It was nice seeing you again."

Tabitha turns, stalks away.

Doesn't look back.

Doesn't see me bend and snap the thick paperback novel up, discarded on the floor.

Doesn't see the expression on my face when I flip it over and crack the cover, or the grin that spreads across my face.

I look up, watching her hurriedly retreating form through the glass, her ass in those ripped up jeans. Tabitha stops at the corner, glancing both ways before crossing to the other side of the street.

Within seconds, she's out of sight.

Gone.

Three

Collin

A few hours later, my solitary dinner plate washed and put away, I step into the kitchen to wipe down the cold granite countertop, pausing at the sink to rest my hip against the cabinet.

"The book," as I've started calling it, rests on the kitchen table, cover-side up, the erotic silhouette of a naked couple in all their bare-assed glory for my viewing pleasure. I stride over, gaping down before gingerly lifting it, intently fixating on the suggestive embrace, the full-on kiss, the sweaty bare skin, and the sexy shot of side boob.

Overturning it to read the blurb on the back—studying it for the third time since jamming it into my laptop bag at Blooming Grounds and bringing it home—my eyebrows still shoot damn near into my hairline as I read:

On the Brink, a debut novel by TE Thomas.

Rachel Neumann is a virgin on the brink... on the

brink of want, on the brink of curiosity, on the brink of her twenty-first birthday. Rachel wishes for one thing and one thing only: to be ruined. To lose it all in one night of passion... With seduction in mind, there's only one person who can cure her aching body: Devon Parker. He's the only person who has always stood by her, and he's the one person who stirs all her lust-filled desires. Will friends become lovers, or will Rachel always be a virgin on the brink?

Whoa.

Holy shit.

I flip the book over to the front, and I scan the cover again before flicking it open to look inside. Bold, black handwriting and notations are scrawled across the first few title pages in pen:

Too pixelated. Must be 300 dpi, not 199. Change font.

There's no doubt this has to be what she was working on at the coffee shop. I flip the book back over to stare at the author name on the cover:

TE Thomas

It's quite conceivably the *least* creative pen name I've seen. And I've seen—okay fine, I've seen *none.*

But TE Thomas isn't clever at all, especially if she's trying to be covert about it. I mean, come on, TE Thomas? I might be going out on a wild limb here, but it's safe to say her middle name is Elizabeth. If I was a betting man, I would win.

So, this is what she's been hiding.

She's an author.

I take the book into the living room and flop into an overstuffed leather chair, propping my feet up on the coffee table Greyson made me buy. Settling in for the long haul, I crack the novel open to the first chapter and read: *Rachel Neumann was hot, sticky, and panting—and it wasn't from the heat…*

A grin crosses my face as I devour page after page.

Tabitha Thompson, you secretive little sneak.

Four

Tabitha

I can *feel* Collin Keller surveilling me from across his living room, his scrutiny so penetrating that sweat begins to dampen my spine.

Great. *Just* what I need.

It's not like I've never had attractive guys notice me before; I've dated my fair share of handsome men. In fact, my last boyfriend was a Minor League Baseball player on his way to the pros, and a total babe.

Hilarious. Smart.

Constantly surrounded by groupies…

Jared would have been perfect if it hadn't been for those damn baseball groupies. No woman wants to listen to their date's phone blow up the entire time they're trying to eat dinner, and no woman wants to see their date's lips tip into a knowing smirk every time he checks a text.

Shady.

But the thing is, Jared never witnessed me on the verge of a public meltdown, never saw me screech like a banshee and react without getting the facts, never saw me stutter out an apology. Never saw me panic and flee from a coffee shop like I had something to hide.

Never caught me writing erotica.

Collin Keller has.

And I'm humiliated.

My gaze swings to him, now that he's *finally* turned his back on me, and trails down the corded column of his long neck—the most erotic part of a man's body, in my opinion—and rests on the silky hair that could use a trim.

Or my fingers running through it.

The solid muscles of his back are outlined by the worn cotton of his clingy tee, and my trajectory aims for his spine. Down. Down to the tapered waist. His ass… *Jesus*. His ass.

Collin Keller is all hard lines and smooth edges.

My mouth waters a little, not gonna lie.

Momentarily, I forget myself and want to see the rich hazel eyes and lopsided grin that made my insides go melty the *second* I found out he was Greyson's brother, and *not* her new boyfriend.

Melty like warm, liquid chocolate.

I bet he tastes just as good.

God, he's so effing handsome.

Still, I made a complete and utter *fool* of myself in front of him two weeks ago, and again last week when we bumped into each other at Blooming Grounds.

When I totally lost my cool... slammed my computer shut… spilled my coffee… dropped my book… tripped over my power cord.

Ran out on him without saying good-bye. *Who does that?*

I can hardly look the guy in the eye now—and he seems so nice.

Looks so nice.

Nice and yummy.

Guh!

And let us not forget how ridiculously attractive he is.

If only he'd stop looking over here, like he knows a secret. Like I'm… captivating. Like I amuse him. Well, okay, I *am* captivating and amusing, and not without my charms, but he doesn't need to keep *staring* at me like that. It's making me extremely uncomfortable. Not to mention *tingly* in all the right places.

Yeah, *those* tingles.

It's one thing for *me* to gawk at someone, completely another for them to gawk at me. I at least do it from a corner when no one's watching.

Oh. Wait…

I'm going to classify his heated stares as figments of my *very* vivid imagination, which has gotten increasingly more colorful since I started writing my books. *Every* guy, young or old, is a potential character or potential muse. I can now turn everyday occurrences into romance, innocent sentences and questions into innuendo.

Take our run-in at Blooming Grounds, for example, when Collin asked if I was going to be at his housewarming party. He said 'coming,' and immediately my thoughts went to *sex*—lots and lots of sex. Sweaty, sticky, loud sex.

How sick and wrong is that? My deliberately tawdry mind *went* there willingly, and all the poor guy did was ask an innocent question.

I am a horrible person.

Heat rises in my neck, and I can feel my face get bright red. My only option is to turn and face the snack table, staring down the guacamole dip and willing my heart rate to slow down. I'm not hungry, but I busy myself, grabbing a plastic plate from the stack and piling tortilla chips—*lots* of tortilla chips—then carrots, cucumbers, and celery onto the plate until I run out of room.

I glance down at the bending plate. *Shoot, maybe I overdid it a tad.* Biting down on my lower lip, I stare at the wall—at the artwork he has hanging above the snack table, shifting my attention to his bookshelf.

Curious, I meander over, balancing my plate with one hand and trailing the other along the shelves. Surprised by the diversity of titles, I finger a vintage copy of To Kill a Mockingbird, which is sandwiched in between a biography on John F. Kennedy and the Maze Runner series. There's a colorful row of the same children's Encyclopedias I had growing up, and I crack a nostalgic smile.

I loiter a bit longer and sigh, knowing I should rejoin the group I came here with: Greyson, Cal, and their friend Aaron. The fact that I'm hiding in a corner is absolutely ludicrous; I'm a grown woman.

Nonetheless, I glance over my shoulder.

Yup. Still staring.

Dammit!

Why is he still staring? What is his *deal*?

Rattled by his attention, I stare at my plate, the hairs on the back of my neck prickle, and a tiny, nervous knot takes root in my stomach. When I inhale a deep breath and count to three, raising my head again to meet Collin's eyes, that knot turns into a flutter.

A flutter of excitement.

He doesn't even have the decency to pretend not to be watching me, hoisting his beer glass up in a silent toast, nodding his head towards me in a friendly greeting.

It's his eyes, however, that give him away.

They're perceptive. Insightful. *Kind* but also… shrewd. And he was acting weird at Blooming Grounds. I mean, how many times did the guy say *come* in a sixty-second period? Five? Six?

He *knows* something. I can feel it.

Collin

I lean against my shiny stainless steel oven, arms crossed as I blatantly stare at Cal's sister from across the kitchen of my new condo. I'm half listening to something my childhood friend Dex is saying, and my narrowed eyes bore into Tabitha Thompson as she tucks a loose, dark blonde strand of hair behind her ear, then tips her head back to laugh.

Her throat is tan and graceful and smooth.

Just how I remember it.

Damn, I bet she smells good, too.

Casual in jeans and a plain black tee shirt, there is no mistaking the resemblance between Tabitha and her brother now that they're in the same room together. Both tall with dirty blonde hair, they share the same bright blue eyes and height; but where Cal is hard and rugged—rough around the edges—sporting a perpetual black eye and scarred lip from rugby, Tabitha is all feminine curves and delicate features.

When I said she had a bony ass two weeks ago, I was full of shit.

She's the most fascinating thing I've ever seen.

She writes sleazy romance novels and works for a construction company.

She called me ridiculously good looking—*ridiculously* good looking. What does that even mean?

I continue observing her, waiting for her attraction towards me to manifest itself in some way—a flirty glance in my direction, a coy smile. Shit, I'll settle for *eye* contact.

She's giving me nothing.

If Tabitha Thompson is attracted to me, she sure as shit hides it better than most; she's been avoiding me like the plague since stepping her high-heeled feet through the front door of my condo.

I have to give her props; she's stealthy, that one. I'm talking expert-level evasion. My condo isn't large, but somehow she's managed to elude me like the fiercest competitor in a game of Mortal Kombat.

Not to brag, but I'm fucking *great* at that video game. I will Level 300 that shit against any thirteen-year-old and kick their tech-savvy ass. Oh, Mortal Kombat doesn't have levels, you say? Tough shit. It does when *I* play—I'm so badass I *make* levels.

It's been one week since I bumped into her writing at Blooming Grounds, and two weeks since Grey and I ran into her shopping. But since her arrival at my housewarming party, she's been dodging me, pretending not to be affected by my presence.

Like right now, for example, Tabitha is bearing down on the snack table, staring at the sandwiches and loading up on nachos like she's a waitress in a bar, and it's her job. She's probably not even going to eat any of it; she just doesn't want to turn around and acknowledge me.

As if I wouldn't notice her reluctance to be in the same room. I enter a room, she exits. I move through a room, she crosses to the other side. Cat and mouse.

In my own damn house.

Shit, now she has me rhyming.

This little game of hide and seek is driving me fucking nuts.

"Are you even listening?" An elbow meets my ribcage, jarring me momentarily. Finally nodding at something Dex is saying beside me, I turn towards Cal and rejoin their conversation.

"I'm sorry, what were you saying?"

My sister's boyfriend tracks my movement, looking over at his sister and then at me. He briefly pauses before responding. "I asked Dex if he was coming with you to my match against Purdue in two weeks. He said no."

Dex pulls at the preppy bowtie around his throat. "Can't. My sisters have a thing."

He has sixteen-year-old twin sisters.

"High school musical opening night," he explains. "Shouldn't be too bad. This year they're doing..."

Nodding absentmindedly, I stop listening to watch Tabitha out of the corner of my eye. She leans against the far wall of my living room, balancing a monster plate of chips and veggies while smiling at something my aunt Cindy and cousin Stella are saying. At that moment, her tongue darts out between cherry-red lips to lick the corner of her mouth.

My eyes are riveted.

"Alright, let's cut the crap," Cal's deep voice interrupts, along with another quick jab to my ribcage. "What's going on between you and my sister?"

"Nothing."

He doesn't mince words. "Bullshit. I've been watching you watch her try to get away from you all night."

Strangely enough, I understand every word he just

said. And since he brought it up, I might as well ask. "Yeah, what is *up* with that?"

I cross my arms over my chest resentfully, still staring at Tabitha.

"Okay, I get it now." Cal tips back his beer and swallows hard. "No wonder she didn't want to come."

My head whips around. "What the hell does that mean?"

The bastard laughs drolly. "Grey had to practically *force* her."

"Why?"

He shrugs his broad shoulders. "Because. I guess she's still embarrassed about accusing Greyson of cheating on me with you or some shit. We had to pull out the big guns to get her here."

For fuck's sake. "What's *that* supposed to mean?"

"It means we had to fucking bribe her to come. We knew at some point you'd have to see each other again, and figured she might as well get it over with. Grey swore she'd come home for a girls' night out with Tab's friends. Oh—we also promised her she didn't have to talk to you tonight." He tenderly traces two fingers over his left eye, which is blackened by a fresh bruise and stitched up with black thread. "Still, we literally had to shove her into my truck. I felt like a goddamn kidnapper, minus a disturbing lurker van."

Lovely.

But can I point something out? Two weeks ago she called me ridiculously *good looking*—not to mention, *s*he was totally checking me out at Target. Damn straight she was. Which means she's attracted to me.

Like I'm going to forget *that* little factoid anytime

soon. Not a chance.

Cal taunts, "I mean—just look at her trying to avoid you and shit."

He's right. Tabitha skulks from the snack table to the bookshelf on the far wall of my living room, balancing her loaded plate in one hand and running the other along the wooden shelves. She trails the tips of her fingers across a leather-bound volume of Walt Whitman, then all the way over to a copy of Divergent.

She pops a chip in her mouth, chewing slowly, and stands rigidly, studying the contents of my collection—which isn't that extensive. I'm not a big reader or anything, but I have a few good ones, most of them gifts from my mom, who's always tried to get me to read more. And play Sudoku. Improve my "brain function," like I have all the time in the world for word puzzles and shit.

Also propped on the bookshelf, dead center on the middle shelf not far from where Tabitha is lingering, is her novel, faced out and eye level. All she has to do is take three dainty steps to her left. Three tiny steps or one hundred and sixty degrees to her left, and she'd see it.

Right there, in front of her beautiful face.

I raise the beer bottle in my hand to my lips, sipping with a wide smirk when Tabitha turns her back to the books. Yup, I'm confident she doesn't know I have her paperback proof. Her naughty, *naughty* little novel, all marked up with edits and comments.

I can hardly wait to finish reading the damn thing.

Then tell her about it.

Man, she is going to be *pissed*.

A sick part of me is disappointed, wanting her to turn back around and notice the book; it would force her to confront me. And yeah, it's kind of a dick move to keep it and display it out in the open where anyone could see it, put two and two together—but what are the odds of that happening? Slim to none.

It must be important. And yes, I realize I have to eventually return it, but seriously, what fun would it be to just hand it over?

No. I'm going to make her work for it.

Does that make me a sick bastard, or what?

***B**lare could hardly believe she was seeing him again. She actually wanted to crawl under a rock and hide. Unfortunately for her, she was trapped in this condo with a group full of people, her ride home no closer to being ready to leave than she had been ten minutes earlier.*

She turned, grasping for a fancy bookend she'd managed to knock loose. It fell to the ground with a heavy clang, and when she bent to pick it up, there he was, devouring her with his penetrating stare.

He was staring, watching her from across the room. How had he even ended up here, in this condo?

Wishing she had something to occupy her hands, Blare made a beeline for the food, his image filling her mind as she filled her plate. He was so painfully handsome she could barely stare at him for too long. Why couldn't he have been a jerk at the store? She moved then, closer to the windows, looking down into the bustling city traffic, wishing she were anywhere but here... away from him.

Because he scared the shit out of her.

Why was she avoiding him? Because in a crazy, bizarre twist of fate, the good-looking stranger with the gorgeous, seductive eyes is her best friend's step-brother and completely off-limits. Cheeks flaming hot, Blare plucked a wine glass off a nearby table, and chugged it....

Collin: *I have something here that belongs to Tabitha. Can you give me her cell?*

Greyson: *You haven't texted me in days, and now it's only because you want my friend's number?! Rude.*

Collin: *Please? I'll go buy that ugly-ass shower curtain you picked out.*

Greyson: *Fine. Deal. But I'm not giving you her cell—she won't want you having that. You can have her email address instead.*

Collin: *What the hell, Grey? Why not?*

Greyson: *She's still embarrassed about what happened at Target.*

Collin: *So?*

Greyson: *loud sigh You just don't understand women at all, do you...*

Collin: *That's never been up for debate.*

Greyson: *Do you want her info or not?*

Collin: *Fine. Yes.*

Greyson: *I know you're pouting, you big baby.*

Greyson: *Ready? Here it is…*

Greyson: *Don't abuse it. Tell her what you need to tell her, then leave her alone.*

Collin: *Me? Abuse it? It pains me that you would say that. Like I would abuse her privacy like that…*

Greyson: *You WOULD do that.*

Collin: *Yeah, I totally would, but only because I have no boundaries—but not in a weird way.*

Greyson: *I'm confused. What other way is there?*

Collin: *Oh gee, let me think—inventing a fake boyfriend and blasting it on Twitter like some "other people" I know. That's the other way.*

Greyson: *Sometimes I wish I was an only child.*

To: tabtomcat@tthompsoninc.gm
From: CollinKell59@ztindustries.corp
Subject: Thank You

Tabitha, thanks for coming with Cal and Greyson to my housewarming party last night. I hope you enjoyed yourself. Thank you for the bottle of wine. Just a quick note: I have a book that I think belongs to you. Actually, I *know* it does because you left it at Blooming Grounds and I'm just now getting around to letting you know. Let me know how best to return it to you.

CK

To: CollinKell59@ztindustries.corp
From: tabtomcat@tthompsoninc.gm

Subject: ??

Collin. I'm confused. How did you end up with it? I knew I misplaced it, but it never would have occurred to me that you had it since I was just at your house. So now I'm wondering, why didn't you give it back to me then??? I'm sure you've guessed by now that it's important. Would it be an inconvenience for you to pop it in the mail as soon as possible?

Tabitha Thompson

To: tabtomcat@tthompsoninc.gm
From: CollinKell59@ztindustries.corp
Subject: No can do.

Tabitha, to answer your question, you dropped the book at Blooming Grounds. During your tizzy. And unfortunately, mailing the book won't work for me. Want to meet somewhere? I don't mind getting it to you in person.

CK

To: CollinKell59@ztindustries.corp
From: tabtomcat@tthompsoninc.gm
Subject: I wouldn't want to impose.

Collin. That's a very generous offer, but to save you trouble, again, why not just pop it in the mail? I'll gladly pay the shipping.

Tabitha Thompson

To: tabtomcat@tthompsoninc.gm
From: CollinKell59@ztindustries.corp

Subject: No big deal

Tabitha, I can assure you, it would be no imposition. How does 5:30 on Thursday night sound? After work? Does Finches Tap House sound good to you? It's on the corner of Rayburn and Division. CK

To: CollinKell59@ztindustries.corp
From: tabtomcat@tthompsoninc.gm
Subject: Sounds good

Collin. Yes, I know where that is.
You're going to force me to see you… aren't you?

To: tabtomcat@tthompsoninc.gm
From: CollinKell59@ztindustries.corp
Subject: It's a date.

We're on for 5:30. Can't wait.
CK

To: CollinKell59@ztindustries.corp
From: tabtomcat@tthompsoninc.gm
Subject: Fine.

It's not a date.

Tabitha: *Collin, it's Tabitha Thompson. I hope it's okay that I asked Greyson for your cell. I wanted to let you know that I'm no longer available to meet Thursday.*

Collin: *Not to be rude, but you are full of shit.*

Tabitha: *Why on earth would I lie?*

Collin: *I can think of a couple reasons. 1) because you're embarrassed I witnessed your tantrum at the store, and 2) because you write dirty, dirty books...*

Tabitha: *They are NOT dirty books!*

Collin: *Not dirty? What about this part: "And when he stroked my inner thigh, my body quivered and started on fire, igniting my core." What the hell is a core, by the way?*

Tabitha: *STOP! Just stop. I get the picture. Fine, they're dirty books. Big deal. And anyway, I have a work thing on Thursday I forgot about.*

Collin: *"A work thing." Has anyone told you you're a terrible liar?*

Tabitha: *I honestly CANNOT meet with you on Thursday. Can you just send my book in the mail? Please.*

Collin: *That makes no sense. We live in the same city. Besides, how is that any fun?*

Tabitha: *Fun? I'm not looking for fun. I just want my book back! I'm sure you've noticed it contains notes. It's valuable. The sooner you send it back the better.*

Collin: *Too bad. I'm not sending it in the mail. You have to meet me, or you'll never hold it in your greedy hands again.*

Tabitha: *That's blackmail!*

Collin: *No, it's extortion.*

Tabitha: *Um no... it's blackmail.*

Collin: *Semantics. Text me when you're ready to ne-*

gotiate.

Tabitha: *That will NEVER happen. NEVER!!!!*

Tabitha: *Okay, fine. What's it going to take?*

Collin: *Wow, you held out an entire twenty minutes. I expected more resistance from you, quite honestly. This must be driving you crazy, huh?*

Tabitha: *You have no idea.*

Collin: *Oh, I have an idea.*

Tabitha: *Could you please just mail it? Please. I'm asking nicely.*

Collin: *Actually, that sounds more like begging.*

Tabitha: *You're bordering on obnoxious.*

Collin: *Calling me names isn't going to convince me.*

Tabitha: *...and by 'obnoxious' I meant adorable*?

Collin: *Fine, I'll think about it.*

Tabitha: *Really?!*

Collin: *No.*

To: CollinKell59@ztindustries.corp
From: tabtomcat@tthompsoninc.gm
Subject: Clearing the air.
Collin. So, I've been wanting to clear the air since we last met, but have been too nervous. And embarrassed. I never did apologize for what happened when I saw you and

Greyson at the store and jumped to conclusions. And for being weird at the coffee shop. And avoiding you at your housewarming party. Wow. Putting it into words really looks… terrible. Yikes! It was all very childish. I'm sorry.
Tabitha

To: tabtomcat@tthompsoninc.gm
From: CollinKell59@ztindustries.corp
Subject: Possession is 9/10th of the Law

If you're trying to get me to change my mind by apologizing, it won't work. Nice try though. Seriously, your mild effort only mildly warms my heart. This reminds me of the time I nailed my sister in the face with a football and the force knocked her flat on the ass. I apologized, but only because my parents made me. And Greyson knew I only said sorry to get myself out of trouble. It worked on my parents, but it won't work on me. You can sweet-talk me *all you want*, but this book is now in a hostage situation. I shall enjoy reading it *again and again and again,* while thinking of you the entire time.

CK

To: CollinKell59@ztindustries.corp
From: tabtomcat@tthompsoninc.gm
Subject: Thinking of me the entire time?

Collin, dear God, please don't—I don't want you thinking of me AT ALL, let alone the *entire* time you're reading my book. Alright. You've worn me down. Since the book is valuable to me, I agree to meet you Thursday.

But just so you know, it's under EXTREME duress. Tabitha

Collin: *TE Thomas, I will see you Thursday.*

Six

Collin

If a glower could kill, I would be a *dead* man.

We're sitting across from each other at a booth at Finches Tap, a slightly grimy sports bar in a rougher part of town, but what Finches lacks in cleanliness it makes up for in atmosphere.

Dimly lit leather booths line the walls, loud music masks chatter from surrounding patrons, and beer is served ice cold. The wait staff is experienced and knows when to disappear.

Like now.

Left alone to our own devices in the seclusion of our giant corner booth, Tabitha and I each have our arms crossed defensively, regarding each other across the marred tabletop like the worthiest adversaries, spoiling for a showdown. Under the hazy overhead light and flickering candle in front of us, Tabitha's glossy lips gleam as her eyes do their best to spear me into silence.

Unsuccessfully, I might add.

I refuse to let her spoil my good mood.

"You know what my favorite part of your *whole* book was—besides the part where Rachel finally loses her virginity? This part here." I poke the open page with my forefinger and slide the book nearer to Tabitha across the table. "This part here, where she asks Devon to be her love coach." I lower my voice to a whisper, conspiratorially. "Did you know by *love*, Rachel actually means…" I look to my left, then to my right, acting covertly like I don't want anyone to overhear me. "*Sex*?"

I do my best to sound appalled.

"I am well aware." Tabitha glares at me from across the booth, holding her hand out, palm up. She's not smiling, but her gorgeous eyes dance with mischief. "Are you done having fun at my expense?" She wiggles her fingers. "Please hand it over."

"Whoa there, grabby hands." I tsk and wriggle my index finger at her, hesitating to hand her book over. "Just hold your horses a minute. I'd like to read out loud from it first, if you don't mind."

"Actually, I do mind."

"Yeah, but the part where he takes her to his family picnic, and they almost kiss behind the shed? Brilliant sexual tension. Now, drawing your attention to chapter ten—"

"I know what chapter ten says, you ass." Her hand flies across the booth to deftly snatch her novel out of my evil clutches, and defensively she cradles the book to her chest like a newborn baby.

I watch as she relaxes and begins fanning out the pages, thoroughly examining them for damage. Her lithe fingers run over the cover, stroking it like the paperback is actually precious cargo.

What a weirdo.

"What the hell are you inspecting it for?"

"You dog-eared the pages!" She accuses me with another pissed-off scowl, her blue eyes squinting at me. Opening a black messenger bag, she carefully digs through it, clears a spot, and strategically places the book inside. "*Why* would you do that?"

"You *wrote* in it!" I pick up a menu that's lying in the center of the table and give her a carefree shrug. "Besides, I didn't have a bookmark."

"You read it?" She gasps, horrified. "You *read* my romance novel?"

"Well, yeah. I like to read, so…" I shrug my broad shoulders again, defensively. "It's not a big deal."

"But it's my proof copy! I mean, the author's copy. For editing," she screeches. The woman in the next booth shushes us. Frustrated, Tabitha lowers her voice. "You don't just *read* a proof copy."

"*You* were reading it," I point out, grabbing a hunk of bread out of the communal bread basket, then peeling the tabs back on two tiny pats of butter. I spread them on before shoving the hunk in my mouth, chewing slowly.

"But it's *mine*. I—" Tabitha clamps her mouth shut.

I swallow before responding. "Wrote it? Yeah, I know." Her mouth falls open. "And you don't trust me with it."

"Look, we could sit here all night—"

"Excellent." I lay down the butter knife and sit back, crossing my arms. Noticing with satisfaction, her eyes follow my movements, up the length of my ripped arms, landing on the hard muscles of my biceps.

I flex.

She rolls her eyes.

"Jeez, would you knock it off? I'm not falling for that." Tabitha gives her head an agitated shake, her silky blonde hair floating around her shoulders in waves. "And stop trying to bait me into an argument."

"Bait you? *Bait* you? What the…" Realization sets in. "*Ahhhh*, a slutty romance book word. I like it."

Her forehead lands with a thud onto the tabletop. She lets out a loud, tortured groan. "Oh my god."

"Don't be embarrassed," I soothe. "It's a really good book. Sort of." I lift the menu, scanning the appetizers. "I mean, it's not winning any Pulitzer Prizes for literature, but I *did* particularly like the part where Rachel finally loses her virginity. It took long enough though—more than halfway into the book? Come *on,* Rachel, show some hustle."

"We are *not* having this conversation."

She's so cute.

"Look, all I'm saying is, Rachel could have shown more sense of urgency. Wasn't the whole point of the book for her to get laid?"

Tabitha lifts her head and wrinkles her nose—her adorable, pert little nose. "No, that wasn't the point of the book, and you do *not* get to give feedback on the plot. It's bad enough that you know I wrote it. I don't even know how you knew."

"Seriously, Tab? I would think that was pretty obvious. I mean, your pen name is basically your name, so…"

"It is not!"

"Tabitha Elizabeth Thompson. TE Thomas? *Really*? What kind of a moron do you think I am?"

"No one is supposed to know." She says it in such a small voice I have to strain to hear her across the noisy din of Finches.

"What do you mean no one is supposed to know? Does your family know?" I lay my palms flat on the table. "It's awesome that you wrote a book. Tabitha—you *wrote* a *book*."

She's silent, so I continue. "Help me understand why someone beautiful, intelligent, and so obviously clever would hide the fact that she wrote a novel. Why won't you tell people?"

She hides her face in her palms and mumbles, "Because. It's embarrassing."

As if that explains everything.

"What is?"

She sits up straighter then and blows out a frustrated little puff of air, causing delicate wisps of light blonde hair to float around her face. She tilts her head back, and it hits the red leather back of the booth. After staring at the ceiling for a few heartbeats, Tabitha raises her head and looks me directly in the eye. "If I hadn't written a romance, I would probably tell people. Maybe if the book wasn't as explicit as it is. But I don't want my parents to know I wrote something so…"

Her hands come up and do this little lilty thing in the air that girls do when they can't find the right words to finish a sentence.

I decide to help her out. "Porn-ish?"

"No! It's not porn, it's…" Again with the hand waves.

"Whore-ish?"

"No! Collin, stop." A smile teases her lips and her eyes, well—those are gazing at me all wide and sparkly. Laughing. Fucking intense is what those gorgeous eyes are, and they're directed at me. "It's… it's…"

"Literotica?"

This stops her train of thought and she looks at me, her face twisted up in obvious confusion. "Wait. *What*?"

"What? You've never heard of Literotica and you *write* it?" She shakes her head slowly. "Don't worry, I hadn't either. It popped up in the search results when I Googled your pen name."

I pick up the water glass and calmly slurp through the straw. The sound makes Tabitha scowl. "Anyway, it's basically written to turn people on. Like porn. But you know—in writing."

"I was going to say that my writing is risqué." Tabitha rolls her eyes; they appear even bluer on her blushing, bright red face. "My book is *not* erotica. That's not what it's about and you know it. Stop making fun of me. It has an actual *plot*, and a storyline, and a climax."

A snort escapes my nose.

"Without trying to get myself into *deeper* trouble, can I just point something out?" I lift the menu again to study the entrées, casually perusing it before coolly pointing out the obvious. "You just said climax."

Her arms go up in defeat. "See? This is why I can't tell my family! Put that menu down!"

Holding the menu *higher*, I block out the glacial stare I know is being directed my way. Her exasperated voice drifts over the top with a huff, and she gives the plastic menu a poke with her finger to regain my attention.

"Would you put down that menu? Collin Keller, we are *not* staying for dinner."

Shit. I kind of like it when she says my name like that, all pissed off and agitated. *Collin Keller, we are not staying for dinner*! So fucking cute.

I put down the menu and pretend to be confused. "But it's dinner time. Aren't you hungry?"

She rolls those gorgeous, baby blues again. "I had a late lunch. On *purpose*."

What a fiery little hothead she is.

I like it.

My fingers drum the tabletop in thought. "So I've been thinking, I know you said you don't consider this a date, but—"

"Hold it right there." Her palm goes up to stop me from finishing my sentence. "This is not a date. A date is getting dressed up, going somewhere nice, and getting to know someone."

"Kind of like what we're doing right now?"

"That is *not* what we're doing right now. Right now we are making an *exchange*."

I disagree and it shows on my face. "What do I get in return?"

"Nothing. I get my book and you get nothing."

"Well, gee, when you put it that way… my end of the deal sounds shitty."

We're interrupted at that moment by the waiter, who steps forward with his pad of paper, pen hovering at the ready. "Have you decided on anything yet, or do you need a few minutes?"

I expect Tabitha to grab her messenger bag and slide her sexy self out of the booth, but instead, she surprises me by grabbing her menu with a resigned huff, scanning it briefly, and saying, "I'll have the black angus cheeseburger, medium rare, with a side of fries. Extra pickles. Oh, and an iced tea please."

She sighs and hands the waiter back his menu. "You made me come here. This is what you get in exchange."

"A non-date date?"

She folds her arms across her fantastic breasts. "*Exactly*. I'm just not sure dating you would be a good decision for *either* of us."

I watch her the entire time I give my order to the waiter. "Double cheeseburger medium rare, cheese curds, ranch on the side." I hand the menu over, Tabitha's earlier agitation making me chuckle. "Why isn't dating me a good decision? And why do you have to say it with that look of disgust on your face. I'm kind of insulted."

"Several reasons, and I'll gladly list them off for you. First, you're Greyson's brother—you don't think that's weird?"

"I refuse to discuss it. *Next*." I watch the kitchen's service door swing back and forth, willing the food to come out though we just placed our orders.

I'm fucking starving.

And not just for food.

Tabitha prattles on across from me. "Second, we got off on the wrong foot. I freaked out at the coffee shop, and now this dating thing could be awkward for us."

"Quit bringing that shit up. Trust, me, you'll get over it. I did. *Next*."

Now she's ticking items off on her fingers, bobbing her cute little head as she counts. "Third, you just moved back into the area. Don't you want to see what's on the market? There are a lot of attractive women in this city."

"Been there, done that. *Next!*" Shit, maybe I said that one a little too loudly—the couple at the neighboring table crane their necks in our direction.

"You're really annoying."

I ignore her complaining. "Are you looking forward to dinner? I'm *ravenous*." I chuckle, delighted with my own wit. "How's that for smut romance lingo?"

"Meh." She gives me a flirty little wink. "Not bad."

I take that as a good sign. "How bout a glass of wine?"

She sighs, defeated. "I guess I could use some alcohol to calm my nerves, but wine doesn't really go with a burger. How 'bout a beer?" Tabitha reaches for her water, taking a dainty sip before continuing. "You don't want to play the field? Casually date?"

"What am I, nineteen? No." I reach for her hand across the table and pull it towards me. She lets me. "Look, we could do this all night, Tabitha. But I'd rather just enjoy your company." She bites down on her plump lower lip. It's driving me crazy. "God, I can't even look at you without wanting to put my mouth on you."

"Oh my god, you can't just say things like that!" she hisses, mortified.

"You're kidding me, right? You write *sex* books for a living."

"Shh! No one is supposed to know that." Her hand settles into mine and her thumb begins distractedly stroking my palm. "And that's not what I do for a living."

"But that is what you *want* to be doing, right?"

She frowns. "What I want and what's best for me are two totally different things. I can't leave my dad's business until Cal is ready to take on more responsibility."

"Is that what your parents told you?"

"Well, no—"

"And you don't think they want you to be happy, Tabitha?"

When I say her name, she looks up from our joined hands. "Have you always just done what you wanted? As if it were easy?"

"Honestly? Yes."

She bites down on her lip again and gives her head a gloomy little shake. "I thought working for my parents was what I always wanted. It's the only thing I knew." She scoffs. "Hell, my degree is in Business with an emphasis on Construction Management, for crying out loud. It's the only thing I'm qualified for. How sad is that?"

"You're incredible. I am actually in awe of you right now."

"Collin, stop." She tugs her hand out of my grip and sets it in her lap.

"Why should I? You need to hear it."

"I do hear it. My family tells me they love me all the time."

I disagree. Being told you're loved and being given the chance to make your own choices are *not* the same thing, but I keep that opinion to myself, choosing my next words wisely. "Then why are you hiding yourself from them?"

For a while, I don't think she's going to respond. Instead, her forlorn frown studies her hands, where she's clasped them in her lap. Opening her palms, she spreads them wide, appearing, for the first time since I met her, young and vulnerable. "It's because I'm scared."

"Of what?" My words come out above a whisper.

"Of everything."

I pause. "Well, that's horseshit."

Surprised laughter bursts from her lips. "You're ridiculous," she says, shaking her blonde hair. "And kind of an ass."

"You'll get used to it."

And when she does, she'll like it.

Tabitha

I'll be the first one to admit I'm actually enjoying myself on this non-date. Of course, I won't be admitting that to anyone out loud anytime soon. Or in writing.

Well, okay—*maybe* in writing. After all, I still need a storyline for my second book, and Collin makes the perfect muse for the hero: strong, handsome, charming…

Tenacious. Disarming. Alluring.

I sip this disgusting beer and sigh, watching him retreat to the men's room, my rapt gaze trailing after and landing on his tight, firm, denim-clad ass. He's been incredibly attentive, respectful (sort of, for the most part), and funny. Intelligent. Not to mention really, really ridiculously good looking.

Crap.

Now I sound like freaking Derek Zoolander.

And I mentioned he's funny, right? It's a pretty lethal combination, and if he weren't Greyson's brother… and I hadn't acted like a complete bitch when we first met, well…

There might be a slight chance I'd date him.

Oh, who am I trying to kid? I'd date the *shit* out of him in a heartbeat because nice, funny, respectful guys aren't easy to find. In fact, they've become more of an urban legend than a reality.

However, the fact remains: he *is* Grey's brother, and for whatever reason, I find the thought of dating him a bit strange. Weird. Creepy, even.

For me, it feels like fishing for a boyfriend in the family pond.

You just don't do it.

I give myself a pep talk, reminding myself to quit gushing. This thing with Collin Keller is not happening...

I will say this though: he's going to be hard to resist.

Fortunately, I deal with impossible, sometimes arrogant, men at work on a daily basis, so his persistence should be a piece of cake.

Theoretically.

I'll just enjoy his company tonight, and in the future we can causally bump into each other at family functions. This attraction thing is no big deal; I can handle it. I am a fortress of feminine willpower. I've taken all the feminist classes in college. Women's Studies. How to be an Independent Woman 101.

I'll plop Collin deftly into the Friend Zone category, right where he belongs, and that will be that.

It won't be weird at all.

Yup, *that's what I'll keep telling myself.*

The waiter comes with our food and refills while Collin is in the bathroom, and to busy myself, I prep my burger, adding the garnishes and extra pickles. Dipping the burger in ketchup, I take a huge bite and chew.

It's so delicious I actually whimper into my next bite.

My thoughts stray to Collin, and I shake my head. *Get a grip, Tabitha. He is not the guy for you. If you get close to him, the carefully erected wall you built will come crashing down around you...*

I'm so committed to *not* falling under his spell, I avoid looking directly at him when he re-approaches the booth and drops himself down with a cheeky grin. A grin full of white teeth. I don't look away quick enough and can't help but notice one of his bottom teeth is just a tad bit crooked.

Irresistible.

So irresistible that my stomach does that fluttering thing again, followed by my annoying, rapidly beating heart.

Sweaty palms.

A nervous giggle, and I slap a palm over my mouth, horrified. My traitorous body apparently belongs to a hormonal teenage girl.

It has terrible timing.

***Blare** twisted a lock of her brown hair and regarded Adam from across the booth, her eyes riveted on his full lips and five o'clock shadow. His words sent shivers down her spine every time he opened his mouth to talk—a mouth she wanted all over her body. Of course, she couldn't admit this out loud—not until she knew how he really felt. He smiled again and laid his palms flat on the table. "Stop teasing me," Blare said, giving her brunette locks an agitated shake, her silky hair floating around her shoulders in waves. "You're trying to bait me into an argument, Adam, and it won't work."*

"Bait *you? What the hell does that even mean?" The dawning of realization sets in and Adam laughs, rich and deep and throaty. A laugh that makes Blare want to climb across the table on all fours and straddle his lap. "Ah, a word from one of those slutty romances you're always reading. I like it." He winks at her and she drops her head onto the tabletop with a loud thump, letting out a groan. How humiliating. "Oh my god.".*

Seven

To: CollinKell59@ztindustries.corp
From: tabtomcat@tthompsoninc.gm
Subject: Thank you. Again.

Collin, thank you for bringing my book back, and for dinner last night. I'm sorry the check ripped in half when I grabbed it, trying to split the bill with you. If I'd known you had the world's strongest vise grip, I wouldn't have bothered.

Tabitha

To: tabtomcat@tthompsoninc.gm
From: CollinKell59@ztindustries.corp
Subject: You're welcome. Again.

Tabitha, don't worry about it. I'm sure the waiter enjoyed taping the whole thing back together after we left. Know what he probably enjoyed even more? Seeing you slap my hand away when I tried helping you out of the booth. The expression on his face was priceless.

CK

To: CollinKell59@ztindustries.corp
From: tabtomcat@tthompsoninc.gm
Subject: Helped me out of the booth?

I think you're remembering it wrong. You weren't trying to HELP me out of the booth. You were trying to touch my ass—the SAME ass you called BONY only two weeks prior. *Now* what do you have to say for yourself?

Tabitha

To: tabtomcat@tthompsoninc.gm
From: CollinKell59@ztindustries.corp
Subject: Your ass?

I'll admit, I was hasty in my judgment of your ASSets. Your rear is in no way bony. Especially in those black yoga pants you had on last night. I realize it was your attempt to appear dowdy and less attractive, but you failed miserably. Those pants did nothing but showcase your second best feature.

CK

Collin: *You're adorable when you're nervous.*

Tabitha: *What are you talking about? When was I*

nervous?

Collin: *I'm thinking about dinner the other night, when I came back from the bathroom. When you tried to mask your laugh. You shouldn't have covered it up.*

Tabitha: *I wish you wouldn't say things like that.*

Collin: *What things?*

Tabitha: *Charming things that make me question my resolve.*

Collin: *You're thinking way too much. Why can't you just act like a big girl and do what you want? Or better yet, act like a guy and straight up don't give a shit.*

Tabitha: *Because you're Greyson's brother.*

Collin: *What the hell does that have to do with anything? I'm a grown man. I started living for myself years ago.*

Tabitha: *Do I have to spell it out for you????*

Collin: *Yes. And while you're at it, spell out a few naughty words too. I know you know lots of those.*

Tabitha: *Knock it off. I am not sexting you.*

Collin: *That's disappointing. For a sex book author, you're kind of a prude.*

Eight

Tabitha

"So you think he's into you?" my best friend Daphne asks, propping the popcorn bucket on her legs and balancing it when she reaches to grab her soda off the sofa table.

Tonight is movie night at her place, and I grab the remote for the Blu-ray player, pointing it at the big screen hanging on her living room wall. Skillfully, I click through the menu, find Netflix, and choose How I Met Your Mother. (Does anyone besides me still watch this show?)

"Definitely. We literally argued about why it's a bad idea to date."

"I don't understand how the two of you ended up having dinner together in the first place. Didn't you say you just bumped into him at Target? How'd you end up at Finches Tap? I don't get it."

So here's the thing. I haven't exactly told any of my friends about the books, either. Especially not Daphne. Don't get me wrong—I love her to death, and we've been friends almost our entire lives, but she wouldn't be able to keep this secret to save her soul. She'd be way too proud and want to tell the entire world!

Daphne is an incredible, loyal friend—but I know eventually she'd spill the beans, and I need my secret to stay hidden.

I hate the lying, but I do it anyway. "Greyson left a textbook at Collin's new condo during his housewarming party, and we met so he could give it to me. Cal's coming home tonight and he's swinging by my place on his way back."

Daphne nods, popping a kernel into her mouth.

In front of me, my cell phone—set on vibrate—begins a jaunty little dance across the wooden coffee table, the buzzing sound oddly shrill in my friend's tiny apartment. The LED lights up.

Collin Keller's name flashes across the screen.

Holy. Moly.

I stare at it, stunned. Why is he calling me? Why. Is. He. Calling. *Me*?

Popcorn spills onto the carpet when my best friend dives off the couch like a rocket, snatching my phone. "Shitballs, is that him? He's calling! No one makes phone calls anymore!" Her hands fly out to stop me from grabbing the phone, but then she tosses it at my chest. I barely catch it, fumbling as Daphne continues shouting at me. "Don't answer it. Wait, answer it! Hurry!"

I smack her hand away. "Shh, would you be quiet!" Laughing, I answer the phone.

"Hello?"

I hear heavy breathing, followed by a tentative, "Tabitha? Hi. It's Collin. Uh, Collin Keller."

I point to the phone, mouthing, *Oh my god! It's him!* to Daphne, who's now bouncing up and down on the couch like a child, popcorn spilling everywhere. And by everywhere, I mean everywhere—the cushions, the carpet, the table—all littered with fluffy, buttery kernels.

What a flipping mess.

Daphne bounces and looks exactly how I feel—like a teenager, bubbly and giddy and ridiculous.

"I know who this is, you goof." I smack a palm to my forehead. Goof? Ugh. Unsexiest word ever. Daphne titters and tosses a kernel of popcorn into her open mouth, sitting back on the couch and watching me like a television show.

"I hope I'm not interrupting anything?" Surprisingly, he sounds self-conscious.

I glance down at my gray sweatpants, maroon Ivy sweatshirt, and polka-dot fuzzy socks. "Uh, no. It's fine. You caught me just as I was about to climb into a bubble bath."

Daphne raises her eyebrows and snorts. *What*? I shrug. *I'm just giving him a visual of me climbing into the tub. Naked.* Everybody knows that's basic How To Drive a Guy Wild 101: Give him a visual.

"Really?" Is it just my imagination, or did his voice just crack a little?

"Yeah, but don't worry. I'll just take the phone in the tub." Daphne rolls her green eyes towards the ceiling then makes the universal *you're insane* gesture with her hands.

"What are you doing the rest of the night?"

"Um, I'll probably have a glass of wine and sit out on the deck with my laptop." Now my best friend is shaking her head back and forth at me, clearly disgusted. *I'm sorry!* I mouth, while pantomiming, *I can't tell him I'm chilling in sweatpants!*

She sticks her tongue out, sitting cross-legged on the couch. I find my manners and ask him about himself. "What about you? What are you up to?"

Collin thinks about it for a second, static filling the silence. "Not much. There's a How I Met Your Mother marathon on that I'll probably watch."

I freaking love that show.

"You do?"

Shit, did I say that out loud? "Yes. Love, love, love."

"*Say love one more freaking time*," Daphne whispers. I swat my arm towards her. *Shut up, Daph!*

"Do you…" Collin clears his throat. "Wanna come over and watch it with me? You can sit on one side of the sofa and I'll sit on the other. I'll even let you put your stinky feet on my new coffee table."

Ugh, he is so sweet. I make an *aw* face at Daphne.

"I'd love to, but I really need to stay in tonight." I glance over at my best friend, who's watching me intently. Lowering my voice, I walk towards the kitchen, away from her intense eavesdropping. Peering over my shoulder, I check to make sure she's not listening. "Um, remember I told you I started a second book? I should probably get some of that done since I'm on a roll lately."

"Ah, because I'm your muse." He says it so confidently, like he knows. Damn him. "Bring your laptop over and I'll let you follow me around, observing me in my wild habitat."

I laugh softly, biting my bottom lip to stop the grin spreading across my face. "Collin Keller, you're becoming a real pain in my backside."

He hums through the phone. "You're a breath of fresh air. With a lovely backside."

I shiver. "Collin, don't make this hard."

"Um..." His low hum trails off suggestively. "Too late."

"Oh my god. No."

"Come on, Tabitha, admit it—your mind went there, too."

His voice when he says my name, though... *Ugh.* I love it. I can't resist flirting with him just a little, and if this phone had a cord I'd be twirling it around my finger. "Yours went there first. Besides, it's a hazard of the trade. I can't help playing out scenes in my head."

His laughter is filled with humor. "Just admit it; you have a filthy mind."

"Filthy? That might be a bit of a stretch. I prefer to call it *imaginative*."

"That brings me to the actual reason I'm calling. Let me take you and your imagination out on one date." He's quiet. "Just one."

Daphne is perched on the edge of the couch, spell-bound, mouth agape. I point to the phone, mouthing, *He just asked me out*! Then I shoo her to be quiet when she loudly hisses, "*You freaking better say yes*!"

Feigning indifference, I relent. "You know what? Okay. Fine. I give up."

Collin's low chuckle on the other end sends another shiver up my spine. "Okay fine? I give up? Calm down, Thompson, or I might think you actually like me."

"It sounds like you're pouting. Are you pouting, Collin?"

"No comment."

Before I can stop myself, I say, "Aw, you're kind of adorable. Did you know that?"

This cheers him up and I can virtually *hear* him smiling. "Two dates."

"Don't push your luck. Let's just start with one…"

"Can't blame a guy for trying."

Collin: *Hey blondie. Write anything good last night?*

Tabitha: *Actually, yes! A few more chapters in the new book. Plus I'm done editing the proof for On the Brink, book one.*

Collin: *Be honest. You ARE using me as a muse. For real.*

Tabitha: *Why would I do a thing like that?*

Collin: *Because I'm charming and ridiculously good looking. Besides, I noticed you're not denying it.*

Tabitha: *LOL knock it off. I can't get anything done with my phone blowing up every ten seconds.*

Collin: *Give me one line from your new book and we can both get back to work. Promise.*

Tabitha: *Fine. Here it is: "The quiet way she spoke was louder than the words she could have shouted."*

Collin: *Holy shit, that's amazing! You're amazing!*

Tabitha: *blushes Now go back to work.*

Collin: *Fine, but I'm going to be thinking of you all day. I hope you're satisfied.*

Tabitha: *Alright, well—I guess I'll see you soon?*
Collin: *Tomorrow night. Six o'clock?*
Tabitha: *Yes. 6:00.*

Nine

Tabitha

What was so wrong with him knowing? Blare mulled the question over in her mind at least a few dozen times as she sat in her apartment, wondering what it meant for him to know her secret.

It wasn't like he was going to tell anyone. She liked him—really liked him. Trusted him. Longed for him. Blare finally admitted to herself that it felt good that someone finally knew; the burden of her secret had been lifted off her shoulders, and she didn't have to keep lying anymore. Well, she did, but not to everyone. *Not to him. Blare felt freer than she had in years now that someone else knew. And now he was taking her out. On a date. For Blare, the future seemed infinite…*

Deftly, my fingers fly across the keyboard on my laptop, and I hesitate. Should I delete any of those few sentences? Will any of them give me away if someone I know reads it? Oh, who am I trying to kid—the only person reading my work is Collin, and he's not saying anything to anyone.

Is he?

I scoff at this notion, deeming it absurd. Quickly, I make myself a note in the margin of my book document, hit SAVE, close my laptop, and stand.

Walking to my closet, I throw open the door and brace my hands on both sides of the doorway, wearing only a nude colored bra and matching underwear. I study my selection of clothes before going in, and head right for the dresses.

Pulling out a gorgeous emerald-green wrap dress, I hold it against my body, running a hand down the length of the fabric and deciding it's the perfect dress for this date.

The color is rich and jewel toned, and sets off the flush of my skin and the blonde of my hair. I've never worn it—never had an occasion—so the tags still hang, dangling from the sleeve. I carefully tug them off and toss them in the garbage under my bathroom sink.

And I might be lying to my family and my friends about what I do in my free time after work, but I won't lie to myself about this date.

I am excited.

No.

No, there has to be a better word for it than *that…*

Euphoric. Nervous? Elated. My body is positively humming with anticipation.

I flatten one hand on my stomach, putting pressure there to quell the nerves taking root, inhale, steadying my breath, and hang the green dress on a hook by the shower. Deep breath, Tabitha. *In through the nose, out through the mouth.*

Why am I so nervous? My hands go to my face; my cheeks are burning. Positively on *fire*.

God, I'm burning up—for *him*.

I feel like…

I feel like this is the start of something momentous. Like the minute I walk out that door, my life is going to change.

Is that weird? Crazy? Melodramatic much?

Who cares! I'm twenty-four years old, for crying out loud. Old enough to be facing this date more logically—instead of like a ditzy sixteen-year-old headed out on her first date.

First date.

First kiss.

First… everything.

With Collin Keller, of all people.

After flipping on the light switches surrounding the vanity at the sink, one by one until the whole room is ablaze, I pull out the stool usually kept under the counter, and sit.

Studying myself in the mirror, I debate how to make over my face. Dramatic look or simple? Dewy or matte?

Smoky or—guh! What the hell am I even saying?

Yes, now I do sound crazy!

My blonde hair is up in giant rollers, and I leave them to cool while applying makeup, my nervous hands shaking when I try to brush on my mascara, careful not to clump it up, and I just barely manage not to stab myself in the retinae. *Barely*.

I brace my hands against the counter, take a few steadying breaths, and stare at my reflection before tackling the mop of thick hair piled on my head.

The rollers come out one at a time, and the blonde waves loosely fall down around my shoulders. I add styling cream to eliminate the flyaways, and set it.

Once that chore is done, I fish around my makeup drawer for the dark plum matte lipstick Greyson gave me for my birthday—she calls it her "lucky gala lipstick"—swipe a few times across my pout, and then give them pucker.

Transformed, I stare.

Give my locks a shake.

Inhale, exhale.

Decision made: I won't resist him anymore if he wants to keep taking me out. If he wants to email and text and talk on the phone. If he wants to take me to bed. I won't resist him at *all*. Doing so would be foolish, and I am no fool. Yes, the lying needs to stop.

I'm going to start by admitting how Collin Keller *really* makes me feel.

He makes me feel clever and funny.

He makes me feel desirable.

He makes me hopeful.

Ugh. How annoying.

Collin

I cannot physically make myself stop staring.

Tabitha is gorgeous.

I give her another sidelong glimpse across my car, my eyes appreciatively scanning her silky legs, demurely crossed at the ankles. The slit in her dress slides open at that exact moment to reveal a sliver of tan thigh.

Focus on the fucking road, Collin, *Jesus*.

Clearly I've completely given up playing it cool.

I'm nervous as hell.

As I white-knuckle the steering wheel, my palms actually begin *sweating*, not just because Tabitha and she's stunning, but because of what I have planned. She's either going to love it or… never want to see me again.

Or slap me across the face, which, to be honest, would be hot as hell.

She's given me one date. One chance. The last thing I want to do is fuck it up. However, I wanted to pull out all the stops without having to ask my sister for advice, and this was the only way I knew how.

Life imitating art.

Her first book.

The chapter I used as inspiration for tonight's date burns, imprinted in my brain.

God, those eyes. Those shoulders. That ass. Would

she ever get sick of watching it walk away? Not in this lifetime... Rachel tried to hide the smile threatening to escape, raising her Chardonnay and studying it. She swirled it then watched as the clear gold liquid crept down the side of the glass, clinging to life. Rachel lowered it then returned it to the table, and watched as Devon reapproached. The butterflies in her stomach flitted and danced carelessly, unaware of the turmoil they caused. These feelings—they weren't part of the plan; she wasn't supposed to fall for him this way... she wasn't supposed to fall for him at all. *The room he'd reserved was intimate, down a narrow hall in the back of the dimly lit Italian restaurant, meant for private parties. Three roses sat in a thin vase in the center of their table: red, yellow, and peach. Roses that Devon had placed there himself. The chardonnay. The way he'd found out and ordered her favorite foods... It was all so perfect. But what did it mean? Rachel was both anxious—and scared—to find out...*

I push her written words out of my mind. What's done is done.

Love it or hate it, there's no turning back now.

Having reached our destination, I easily find a parking spot, pull in, and shift my black sports car into park. I throw open my door and hop out hurriedly, bending at the waist and sticking my head back inside the car to peer in at her. "Don't. Move."

I jog around to the passenger seat and pull the passenger side door open. Tabitha's long, smooth legs appear first, nude high heels hitting the pavement with a tap. My hand reaches for her, and she grasps it, allowing me to assist her out of the car.

The wind throws up a gentle breeze, lifting her hair at the nape of her graceful neck and parting the hem of her dark green dress, à la Marilyn Monroe.

Thank you, wind gods, for that complimentary peep show, although not enough peep to glimpse the goods.

Damn, no such luck.

Tabitha tucks a small purse—handbag, I think girls call it—under the crook of her arm, then runs her hands down her dress, flattening out the wrinkles caused by the wind. She adjusts the sash around her narrow waist, and I notice her flowy dress has a blessedly plunging neckline, exposing an entire eyeful of cleavage that makes my fingers itch.

Of course, I can't help but admire her amazing tits.

Sorry, I mean *breasts*. But come on: They. Are. Right. *There*. The low-cut neckline is an invitation for my eyes to ogle away.

To be completely honest, I'm shocked she's wearing this dress. This dress means she considers this a real date; this is not a dress you wear when you're Friend Zoning a guy. It's a sexy-ass dress you're able to untie with only a gentle tug to the sash. One you drop to the floor at the end of your date.

The kind of dress you wear when you want him undressing you with his eyes all night.

And tonight, it's damn good to be Collin Keller.

The fabric is flirty, silky, and light—touchable *everywhere.* My eyes wander, my hands impatient to shove her back in my car, drive her back to my place, and screw her brains out until she can't remember a single reason we shouldn't be here together—and give her a million screaming reasons why we should.

As my eyes rake over her cleavage, again, I wonder if she's wearing lingerie underneath and what it looks like. My hand settles at the small of her back to guide her towards the restaurant—and hell if it doesn't graze her ass while I'm checking it out.

Damn fine ass.

Makes me wanna slap it, too.

Mind out of the gutter, Keller.

Inside, we're greeted by the hostess.

"Hi," I start, clearing my throat. Here goes nothing. "Party of two for Neumann. That's N-E-U-M-A-N-N. Not to be confused with New Man."

Sadly, the hostess's features remain stoic, not getting my joke and ruining all my fun. Nodding, she motions for us to follow, leading us to the back corner of the restaurant, taking a left to steer us down a hallway. Tabitha glances at me over her shoulder, puzzled, so I feign a shrug, pleading ignorance.

Shit. I hope this wasn't a mistake.

"Here you go, sir. The private room you requested." A door opens and the room we enter can only be described as opulent. Lavish. In the center of the secluded dining room, beneath an ornamental crystal chandelier, is a single set table. Draped white linens cover the surface. Candles and a crystal vase of four long-stem roses occupy the center: red, peach, yellow, and lavender. Several steaming plates of Tabitha's favorite foods have already been served.

The hostess hangs back. "Your sommelier will be back shortly with the Chardonnay."

Tabitha's head rears towards me and her smoky eyes widen, appearing a shocking shade of blue. "Collin, what on earth…"

"Now, Rachel, before you say anything, don't overreact."

"Why are you calling me Rachel? What… Oh, sweet Jesus." She looks around, confused. "Did you..? Wait. Is this what I think it is?"

"No?"

Her eyebrows shoot up into her hairline, skepticism written all over her face. I can't tell if she wants to smack me or not. "Collin Keller, what is going on? Is this the date scene from the paperback proof you stole?" She whispers this last part. "Be honest."

"Okay, yes. This is what it looks like. Are you mad?"

She gives pause, sets her purse down on the table, and then rewards me with a smile when I pull the chair out for her, a gentlemanly gesture that has her blue eyes softening.

I know I've got her.

Score one for Team Collin.

Nervously, she pushes a few strands of hair behind her ear. Sparkling green emeralds shine in her lobes. "I don't even know *how* to be furious with you right now. I'm speechless. Later it might be possible that I'll want to kill you, but right now… I can't even believe you did this."

This is the recreation of the first date scene from her very first book.

This is me romancing a girl who's making it damn near impossible to romance her.

But I'm sure going to fucking try.

Ten

Tabitha

"Give me your best line." Collin watches me from across the table, taking a forkful of steak and chewing slowly. "Tell me something you've only put on paper. In one of your books."

"It's only the *one* book, remember? Well, two. But the second one is just… me playing around."

He rolls his eyes, still chewing. "Let's assume there will be more."

It's right then that my chest swells and my heart begins beating wildly. Becomes huge. His words release a spark of affection inside me that I can feel—actually *feel*—blossoming into something bigger.

Something wonderful.

Collin believes in my dream.

Collin believes in… *me*.

I could leap across the table and kiss him all over his

beautiful, sexy, freshly shaven face.

I bet he smells good. All sexy and mannish.

Collin breaks the silence. "Well? If you can't think of one, I can supply one for you. Confession time: I read your proof *three* times before giving it back to you. I've got a few good zingers locked away up here." He taps his skull with a forefinger, saying it so casually I have to replay it in my mind a few times.

"*Three times*!" I sputter ineloquently. "Why?"

"Because it was good?" He lays his fork on his dinner plate and leans forward, resting his elbows on the table. "Mostly I just thought it was nuts that *you* wrote it. You. That's what went through my head while I was reading. *Holy shit, Tabitha wrote this*. I'm in awe of you." He says it so matter-of-factly, his voice a low purr. "I couldn't stop picturing you at your laptop in that sexy little baseball hat, pen tucked behind your ear, dreaming up that shit. You're so fucking smart."

Tilting my head a little, I gaze at him with doe eyes. I *know* they're doe eyes because my entire face softens and my whole body gives a blissful, dreamy sigh.

Collin straightens in his seat. "What's that look you're giving me right now?"

I quietly exhale. "What look?" Even *that* comes out sounding breathless and wistful.

His lips curve into a knowing smile. "Don't deny it. You're looking at me like this." He puckers his mouth and flutters his dark, sexy eyelashes. Lowering his voice, he arches one perfect, masculine brow. "You're totally thinking about climbing into my lap right now, aren't you?"

Yes. "No."

He relaxes in his seat and crosses his arms.

God, those arms.

"Pfft. That is *not* how I'm looking at you." My lying eyes go to his lips—his full and soft and pliant lips. Well, I don't know for *sure* that they're soft, but right now there's nothing I'd love more than to find out.

I almost groan out loud at the wayward ideas running rampant through my mind that have nothing to do with enjoying the rest of our four-course meal: Unbuttoning his dress shirt, one button at a time to expose his warm skin. Climbing into his lap. Kissing his neck. Finding out how *happy* his trail actually is, all the way down to his…

I take a sip of wine to occupy my hands and my tongue, guiltily glancing away.

Collin laughs. "You *dirty*, dirty pervert."

"What?" It's on the tip of my tongue to point out that, as a romance writer, it's practically my job to picture him naked. "If you must know, my thoughts weren't dirty. I was—" I clear my throat so I can lie with a straight face. "I was just…" God, this is torture. "I was just thinking about how *soft* your lips look."

"Soft. My lips?" If a man has ever looked disappointed by a pronouncement, it would be Collin Keller right in this moment. Actually, disappointed doesn't even cover it; the man stares at me, crestfallen. "That's it? You weren't undressing me in your mind?"

"Pretty much."

"Not my muscles or my… cash and prizes?" He raises his eyebrows again. "Soft lips don't sound sexy. Soft lips sound like a snooze-fest."

"Are you *sure* about that?"

The table we're at is square. Small.

Intimate.

Just enough room for the two of us, a few plates, and not much else. Which means with very minimal effort I can prod. "Lean towards me for a second."

I remove the napkin from my lap and brace my elbows on either side of our table. I watch, fascinated, as Collin's hazel eyes run down the length of my neck, over my collarbone, and land on my exposed skin. On the smooth skin of my cleavage.

My breasts.

Lifting myself off the chair gets me closer still, my laser-like focus directed entirely on his mouth. He chooses that moment to slide his tongue over his lips. "Should I pop in a breath mint?"

He sounds so hopeful I almost giggle.

"Shhh." My whisper is centimeters away, so close we're sharing the same breath. Parting my lips ever so slightly, I kiss *just* his bottom lip. Softly, I rest my lips there before teasing him with one small suck. A tender pull. I was right: warm, tender, and so, so soft.

His large hands grab fistfuls of white linen table cloth and clench when I brush my mouth against the irresistible divot above his chiseled chin. Back and forth, back and forth, taking the opportunity to inhale the masculine smell of him. Fresh. Woodsy. Delicious. Virile.

I could have the Big O just from the *smell* of him.

My kiss lands in the corner of his lips. Left side… right side.

His lips part a fraction and holy mother of… it feels so good.

Eyes quivering closed, his body shivers on an inaudible moan. Collin sits utterly still when the flick of my tongue meets his cupid's bow, and I press my entire mouth firmly against his one last time before pulling away.

Mmmmm, mmm, mmm.

Satisfied, I plop back down, settling into my cushy dinner seat. Silently, I calmly lay the napkin across my lap and sink back into my chair, trying to get comfortable. I shoot Collin a long, meaningful look across the table.

He looks about as dazed as I feel.

I grasp my wine glass with unsteady fingers and take a casual sip. "Was that a snooze-fest?"

"*Uh…*" Collin un-fists the tablecloth and smooths out the creases. "I don't know. We should probably do it again to make sure."

I tsk, giving my head a shake. "Let's save some of that mystery for later, shall we?"

"I thought you'd be more like Rachel," he huffs with a pout but gives me a wink. "If I start calling you Rachel, will you start acting like her?"

"In my book, Rachel and Devon had *sex* on the table during one of their dates, remember?" I point out. "No offense, but I think I'd rather sit and eat this sourdough bread." I set down my glass and pull a slice of bread from the loaf. "Wait. Having sex on the table tonight wasn't part of your plan, was it?"

A loud, obnoxious snort fills the room. "No! God no—I was trying to surprise you by doing something romantic. I mean… unless you *want* me to bend you over the table. Shit, sorry, that was…" Chagrined, he blushes and starts over. "You know, this date is the best idea I've ever come up with. And *you're* the one that came up with it. The details were easy to recreate. Wine. Food. Flowers."

Speaking of flowers… "Do you even know what any of these colors mean?"

"The color of the roses? Yeah, I Googled it." Collin takes a drink of Chardonnay. "Red means love, or in this case, passion. Yellow means friendship—or a new beginning." My face reddens as he prattles on. "And peach means closing the deal."

"What about the purple one? That's not in the book." I already know what it means because I had researched their meanings too, but I ask anyway. Just to see if he'll say it.

He hesitates. "Promise you won't freak out?"

I roll my eyes and tease. "Nothing you do would surprise me at this point; you're like a loose cannon. Besides, I'm destined to be a famous writer of smutty romance—it's impossible to shock me."

Hair flip.

He gives a jerky nod, steeling up his courage. Him. This handsome hunk of man, nervous. Imagine that. "Alright, smartass. Lavender means enchantment." His voice deepens. "Tabitha Thompson, I'm without a doubt *enchanted* by you."

Lavender roses also mean *love at first sight*, but I don't say it. Can't say it.

He must know it, too.

Must.

The blush creeps from my cheeks then lower to my chest, over my body, down to my legs. I'm blushing everywhere—from the roots of my hair to the tips of my red painted toenails.

My lips part and I muster a feeble, "Do you Google everything?"

He's not fooled by my casual countenance—not one bit. His beautiful hazel eyes wrinkle at the corners in amusement. "Pretty much."

"Maybe you should stay off the internet," I suggest quietly.

"Maybe I should." He leans back in his dinner seat and crosses his arms, the blue dress shirt stretching and straining over his muscles. "But then again, maybe I shouldn't. I'm always amazed at what I find."

His underlying meaning makes me shiver—and not from the cool air being pumped into the room. Oh boy. Is it hot in here? Waiter! Oh, waiter! Could someone bring me a fan, or a pitcher of water to pour down my pants?

Or maybe that's his line.

"And what did you find when you Googled *me*?"

"Well, Tabitha Thompson—did you know if you google Tabitha Thompson, a whole history of accomplishments pop up? Track and Field scholarship. Summa Cum Laude. A random picture from a Greek Formal you went to." He reaches forward and picks a small baby carrot off his plate, popping it in his mouth. "Sexy dress, by the way."

I look down at my outfit, my eyes hitting my generous cleavage. "This one, or the one I wore to Greek formal?"

"Both." His eyes do a leisurely, appreciative scan of my exposed clavicle and the swell of my breasts.

I stab blindly at the plate in front of me with my fork, spearing a hunk of seafood and stuffing it in my mouth so I don't have to reply.

Classy, right?

I swallow and say, "How did you know these were my favorite foods?"

"Easy." Collin smiles. "Your brother through my sister. And the best part is, they're my favorite foods, too."

We continue eating in silence, giving each other furtive glances over wine and steak and lobster. When dessert comes—crème brûlée and banana cream pie, more of my favorites—we share, wordlessly passing the plates and spoons back and forth between us like we've been dating for years.

Heaven. Every mouthwatering bite. Every delicious time our eyes meet.

We sip wine, falling into easy conversation. So easy. Natural. Relaxed. Collin grabs my hand and finds my knee under the table with his other, giving my smooth skin slow, gentle strokes until I'm biting my lip and looking away.

Then we're leaning into each other across the tiny table, our knees touching, our lips pressing together. My eyes flutter closed as Collin's hand finds my inner thigh, the other finding the nape of my neck, pulling me in closer. Sweetly. Hungrily.

Aroused.

Our mouths part and our tongues touch, exploring deliberately. An unhurried pleasure that sends a shockwave of desire between my legs and surging through my body.

This isn't just a kiss; this is an unspoken invitation for something more. More meaningful. Full of surrender.

I will worship you, the kiss whispers.

I will be good to you, the kiss promises.

It doesn't last long. Collin pulls away first, resting his forehead against mine, stroking the underside of my jaw with his thumb.

He's breathing hard.

I'm breathing hard.

"Tabitha." His voice is a low, gravelly plead. "Tabitha, come home with me."

I will worship you...

I will be good to you…

I know I shouldn't. I know it's too soon to be intimate. But I know if I don't…

I'll regret it.

I give a barely perceivable nod. "Yes."

Yes.

***B**lare Wellborn did not sleep around. Didn't do one-night stands. Didn't sleep with men on the first date. But as she looked across the table at him, the only sensible thought running through her mind was... nothing. There were no sensible thoughts, only need and want and desperation. For him. For Collin Adam.*

He slid his hand across her knee. "Blare, come home with me." All she could do was nod, the words lost in her throat. When he got her home she would see to it that he worshipped the column of the smooth skin there—her favorite spot to be kissed.

"You want me to come home with you? I want to, but... I barely know you. We've only known each other, what—three weeks?"

He leans in and presses a kiss to her chin. "Blare Wellborn, I am enchanted by you." With those seven words, all her fears melted away...

Greyson: *What's going on? Hello! I haven't heard from you in days…*

Tabitha: *Sorry! I'm sorry. Work has been so busy.*

Greyson: *Busy? I hate when people say that. Busy is just an excuse.*

Tabitha: *You're right—I haven't been THAT busy, but I do have a confession to make.*

Greyson: *A confession?! I like the sound of that!*

Tabitha: *The truth is, I've been spending some time with your, um.*

Greyson: *My, um... what?*

Tabitha: *I've been spending time with Collin. Your brother.*

Greyson: *WHAT? Since when? What kind of time?! How! What? LOL. I mean—WOW! In a good way!!!!!!!*

Tabitha: *Phew. I was kind of worried.*

Greyson: *Are you kidding me? You're amazing. He's awesome (most of the time)! My second and third favorite people. Cal is obviously my FIRST favorite... dating! Love it.*

Tabitha: *Not dating, just thinking about it?*

Greyson: *So where are you right now? What are you doing tonight?*

Tabitha: *We just went to dinner and now we're... uh... heading to his condo?*

Greyson: *RIGHT NOW???? This very second??? Is he there with you?*

Tabitha: *Yes? Is that bad? I'm so nervous my hands are shaking.*

Greyson: *Tabitha Elizabeth Thompson, you'd better be "dating" if you're HEADED TO HIS CONDO at eleven o'clock on a Saturday night!!!! Do I need to Mom lecture you about "safety"? cough cough*

Tabitha: *Oh god, please don't.*

Greyson: *I'm not ready for nieces and nephews yet, just so you know. Even if he is 26. Nevermind—I'll take a niece...*

Tabitha: *NO. Just no!*

Greyson: *Alright, I'll stop, but only on one condition: you tell me everything later. Well, not EVERYTHING...*

Tabitha: *It's a deal. <3 you*

Greyson: *<3*

Eleven

Collin

We don't go through the pretense of wanting after-dinner drinks when we arrive at my condo, don't make small talk in my living room, don't loiter in the kitchen.

I bypass a tour entirely, assuming she took one during my housewarming party, and lead her by the hand up the stairs to the master bedroom. I give it a squeeze when I push open the double doors, and she steps over the threshold first, walking to the bed, sitting, and crossing her legs.

Flushed, she rests back, bracing herself up by the elbows on my soft mattress, and I stroll in after her, flipping on a newly acquired table lamp from Target. I give my shirt collar a tug, loosening the top button and leisurely sliding it through the hole. One. Two. Two buttons undone.

Those hypnotic blue eyes never leave my face.

Three buttons.

The pads of Tabitha's fingertips lightly caress my white duvet cover, stroking it softly. "Are these the crisp, clean sheets that Greyson said would be nice to roll around on that day I found you shopping?"

"Hell yeah." A chuckle escapes my throat.

She swallows and licks those juicy lips. "Good choice."

My fingers pull a fourth button unfastened. Five. "You impressed? I got me a new wine bottle opener, too."

"Oh, fancy." Her voice is throaty and breathless.

"You like the sheets, Tabitha?"

"Oh *yeah.*"

Six.

"You should see yourself. Hair all over, skin all hot. I couldn't be more turned on. You're so fucking sexy."

Her hooded eyes leave my face to rake me up and down, searing, as I pluck button number seven free. "So are you."

"You know what would make us even sexier?"

Eight.

"What?" she says in the barest hint of a whisper.

Her legs part voluntarily when I kneel… go down on bended knee… unbuckle the thin straps on her high-heeled shoes, each one the same color as her flesh and sexy as shit. I remove them both and kiss the top of her foot before tossing both heels off to the side. They hit the closet door with a loud thud. I ignore them, running my palms up her silky thighs, letting them roam up and under the skirt of her dress, parting the seam in the process.

I watch, transfixed, as Tabitha's eyes flutter shut, losing herself in the feel of my hands gliding across her skin.

Still on my knees, I inch forward to settle myself between her legs and wrap my arms around her waist. I trail kisses along her collarbone, the glowing skin where her shoulder and neck meet.

Tabitha tips her head back to give my greedy-as-fuck lips access, her long blonde hair falling to the comforter, cascading like a waterfall. Stunning. I take a few strands, rubbing them between two fingers, then lift them to my nose.

"Your hair smells amazing." I drop the locks and my lips speak into the hollow of her neck. "You smell like I want to do *this*."

This is my tongue trailing the length of her collarbone.

Tabitha moans, stiffening slightly.

"What are we doing, Collin? What are we doing," she pants. "This isn't me. I don't d-do one-night stands." She releases another moan when my tongue licks the hollow between her breasts. "I'm a… *mmm*... relationship kind of girl."

"So am I," I respond dumbly, my mouth nipping her bare skin, hands pushing aside the soft fabric of her dress, lips grazing her bare shoulder.

Tabitha gives her head a little shake.

"I would never bring this up, but… *oh god, that feels good…* we're stuck with each other no matter what. Cal and Grey are going to end up married and… *mmmm…* we're going to be in each other's lives whether… *your tongue is amazing...* or not."

Tabitha threads her fingers through my hair, roughly raking her nails along my scalp. Her back is arched with pleasure, and my large hands move up and down her spine, kneading. I wet the pulse in her neck with my tongue, too. "Good. I want you to be stuck with me. You're so goddamn sexy."

I wonder if she knows what a turn-on her brain is, her *mind.*

No lie.

"What will our parents say?" she asks with bated breath into my hair as my fingers splay across her middle, enjoying the feel of her silky dress beneath my fingers. But not for long: she needs to be naked. "All their kids dating each other. Collin, it's not normal."

"Who gives a shit? I don't." My mouth finds purchase on the swells of her breasts and my fingers deftly work the belt on her dress. Swiftly. *Done*. "You're beautiful."

Her fingers continue their savage plunge through my—

"I love your thick hair."

I'm close to purring like a goddamn jungle cat when she massages my scalp. "I love your hands."

"I love *your* hands."

These hands are going to make her feel even better. I nuzzle her cleavage again with my nose and inhale the musk of her perfume.

"I fucking love your boobs." I palm one through her dress. "Definitely love these boobs."

Tabitha tips her head back and laughs through a gasp. "Take off your shirt."

Oh, now she's giving orders? "Take off your dress."

But I stand to pull the last few pearl buttons through their holes. She stops me.

"Wait, let me do it."

I watch, mesmerized, as her nimble fingers fly down the seam of my shirt. She spreads her hands on my bare chest when she succeeds in releasing the remaining button. Her palms span flat over my washboard abs.

Her breath hitches in wonderment. “I was right.”

“About?”

“This is one of the *happiest* trails I’ve ever seen.” Still sitting on the edge of my bed, the tip of her finger leisurely traces the narrow path of hair that runs from my belly button, and disappears into the waistband of my pants.

I swallow. “When… when were you thinking about my happy trail?” She stands, both palms traveling flat over my abs, roaming the length of my stomach, pecs, and up, over my shoulders. Unhurriedly, they descend again towards my belt buckle in such a slow, deliberate pace it almost makes my leg twitch with urgency.

Like a dog in heat.

“When was I thinking about all *this*? *Hmm…*” Tabitha hums. The sound of metal coming unfastened, leather sliding, and a thud on the ground are the only sounds filling the air. “The minute I found out you *weren’t* Greyson’s new boyfriend, my mind went there. And stayed there.”

Her talented fingers work the fly of my pants, then the zipper.

Jesus.

I bite my lip and deeply inhale towards the ceiling, count to… to… *shit yes…* to control my breathing as my large body begins to vibrate, strumming high with eagerness.

Tabitha’s fingers skim my waistband, tormenting. Grasping my black slacks, she *finally* fucking pushes them down my hips. I step out of the legs, kicking them aside like a Neanderthal so they land in a heap near her shoes, out of the way. It wouldn't be cool to trip on that shit once we're frantically stumbling around bare-ass naked.

And we will be naked *soon*.

Guaranteed.

She teases, stroking me with a feather-light touch. "You really do have the best hands," I damn near whimper. It sounds like I'm whining as goosebumps cover my skin.

Fucking goosebumps—and she hasn't even stroked my cock yet.

"That's what *all* the boys say." She giggles then at my sullen expression. "What? I've always wanted to use that line out loud."

"Maybe you should use it in your next book."

"Maybe I should."

Impatiently, I begin working the sash on her dress, yanking it free and letting it limply fall to the side. My fingers, of their own accord, pursue her skin like a heat-seeking missile. Tabitha bites her lower lip when I push her dress all the way open, permitting the pads of my hands to roam her body, the flat planes of her stomach, the plump breasts pressed together by a sheer, nearly transparent push-up bra.

Barely there, flesh-toned G-string.

If I didn't know any better, I'd think... "Were you *planning* on getting naked tonight?"

With a single shrug, off comes the dress. It cascades to the floor. "You'll never know, will you? And I'll never tell."

Tabitha Thompson, you secretive little sneak.

My hands reach out, grab on, and toss her on the waiting bed.

It wants to get laid, too.

Tabitha

When our clothes fall to the carpet and the pile of fabric is discarded, I waste no time scooting to the center of Collin's bed in my bra and panties. It's been who knows how many months since anyone has touched me intimately, and my body is alive with *everything* for Collin.

He follows on all fours, crawling towards me from the foot of the bed, kissing his way up my leg, starting at my ankles, dusting kisses on the insides of my thighs that leave me trembling almost uncontrollably.

I spread my legs desperately, affording him easier access to all my sensitive spots, because let's face it—it feels ah-freaking-mazing and my inner slut has apparently been unleashed.

I want it so bad.

I do everything but thrash my head around on the pillow as Collin's mouth grazes my stomach at the same time his forefinger hooks itself under the seam of my sheer underwear. The rude asshole teases with a tug, releasing the elastic with a snap and leaves them on.

I touch his shoulders, urging him upward till he stops, his mouth latching onto my nipple through my bra, sucking and sucking and swirling his tongue until the mesh is soaked through.

"Oh *j-jesus* that f-feels…" Yeah. *That* good.

When our mouths finally meet, we're tortured and aroused at the same time, noisily groaning our relief. His large, hard body is smooth and firm, and I can feel every inch of him.

Every *solid* inch.

He's so hard.

His dick is so *hard.*

It feels s-so… so… *oh god...*

But I'm not relieved—not *nearly*—and won't be until he gives me what we both want. Lord, listen to me, using words I've written in my own books—chapter seven, as a matter of fact.

Thank god I didn't blurt it out loud. Then again, as I get to know him better, it would probably turn him on hearing me talk all smutty and dirty.

His skin is sweaty and warm and I want to lick him all over.

I want him to lick *me* all over. All. Over.

And then, as if reading my mind… he does.

Yes! Shit *yes*.

"Do you like that, baby?" he murmurs as his hot lips follow a path from my stomach to my clavicle. Normally I can't stand tallking during sex—and I can't stand the word *baby*—but coming from Collin? He can call me anything he wants. I am putty in his large, capable hands.

My overactive imagination kicks into overdrive as the sound of our panting and kissing fills the air. I do nothing but lie like a limp rag doll beneath him, raising my arms above my head and grabbing hold of the fluffy pillow.

"I knew it was you the moment I saw you." His praises reach my soul, even as his mammoth hands worship my breasts. "You're all I think about. Jesus, Tabitha, stop rocking your hips like that."

But I don't stop. I release the pillow, reaching my hands between our bodies to stroke him up and down through his boxer briefs. He's long and ready and throbbing. "Why are we still wearing fucking clothes? Take these off."

The wait is unbearable.

Agonizing.

I'm begging now. "Please, Collin, take them off."

"You don't have to fucking tell me twice." He rolls off me to swiftly strip himself bare, and I do the same, fumbling to unclasp my bra and peel off my underwear, dropping them to the floor.

"I don't know if I can wait." Collin licks my ear lobe as he settles himself between my thighs, stiff in all the right places. I moan my appreciation—loudly—into the hollow of his neck when he rotates his pelvis, grinding into me, and press a kiss to his Adam's apple. "I'm gonna make you come so hard.""

I want more.

He gives it to me.

Yes... *Yes,* Collin. *More*.

Twelve

Collin

A distraction: that's what she's been for the past several weeks. I wanted her blonde, beautiful, and beneath me.

And now she's here.

Her neck thrown back as my mouth eagerly imprints the smooth, bare skin of her shoulder, Tabitha's golden hair spills across my pillow. I brush the hair out of her face, cupping her jawline with my palm.

My thumb strokes her bottom lip and I lower my chin until our lips meld together. Brush back and forth. Once. Twice.

I savor the feel of our naked bodies pressed together, impatient to feel her around my hardened cock, the pulsing between my legs almost *un*-fucking-*bearable,* wanting to dig in deep.

I don't want to rush her, but—

"Condom, now. Collin, Collin," she chants my name. "Enough playing around. I need it *now*."

I give it to her then, sliding in and nailing her slow and fast and… *motherfucker…* Soft and hard and… *fuck, Tabitha, right fucking there…* Slick with sweat, the air thick with urgency, we move in sync, whispering. Demanding. Coaxing.

Gasping.

The fucking moaning never ends.

"Yes… oh, mmm, *God*, Collin… Collin… *Uh! Oh god…*"

"...Hold on tight to the headboard, baby... Fuck me, Tabitha, just like that…"

"…Right there… p-please don't stop, *don't stop, don't... stop…*"

We're raw. We're tender.

We're a walking, talking cliché.

Fuck. *Yeah.*

Tabitha

We settle into a pattern after our night together—meeting at Blooming Grounds during the work week; he works and I write. Laughing, talking. Dinners. Hiking.

Movies at his place.

Our feelings for each other grow; we ache.

We *burn*.

We hold hands, talk, kiss constantly. Cuddle.

Touch.

And have sex. Lots and lots of hot, incredible sex.

We make love, too.

Collin Keller is everything I've ever wanted—everything I've only fantasized about in writing.

***Blare** watched Adam from across the bedroom as he pulled off his shirt, stalked over, and pulled back the covers on his side of her bed. Sliding in, he reached over, trailing a hand down her bare stomach. "Tired?" he asked, kissing her shoulder.*

"Yes and no," she said, stretching like a feline alley cat, satisfied and content. "It was a long day." Blare might have worked for her parents during the day, but she

had a side project she worked on at night. Moonlighting as an artist was taking its toll.

Adam went further down her body, disappearing under the covers. "Sweetie, don't you think it's time to tell someone besides me?" His voice was tentative and unsure. He'd suggested it before, but... "I'm not ready. Give me time."

"When will it be time, Blare? It's been over a year."

Blare stiffened under his inquisition, but softened immediately when his fingers... did that thing... right... there...in that *spot... "Yes. I know. I will, but I have to be the one to tell, okay? Promise you won't say anything."*

He kissed her neck. Nipped at her breasts. Licked in that spot that drove her absolutely wild.

"Baby, I promise." Adam kissed her abs. Her belly button. "You can trust me. I won't tell a soul...."

Blare lost herself in him then as he worshiped her body. Loving him.

Trusting him...

Thirteen

Collin

"Greyson tells me you've been spending shit tons of time with my sister. That's a big change from her avoiding you at your party." That's something I've always respected about Cal since he started dating Greyson; he doesn't fuck around. When he wants to know something, he asks—he doesn't beat around the bush, and he's not passive aggressive.

But that doesn't mean I have to give him a full shake-down of my personal business.

I glance over my shoulder in the direction of the restrooms, where the girls have disappeared to. We're at a bar in Calumet, the city where Cal attends an Ivy League university, and coordinated the trip for a weekend Greyson happened to be staying with him.

Win-win for all of us.

For Tabitha and me, it was like killing two birds with

one stone, getting to visit them both at once. It's also the first time our siblings will see us acting like an actual couple.

"Dude. Are you listening to me?" Cal prods me in the ribs.

"We're having fun."

Lot of sex. *Lots* of fun.

"We're having fun?" He snorts, resting his elbows on the counter in the bar we're sitting in. "Humor me and define *fun*, would you, because you say *fun* and all I hear is *I'm banging your sister*."

Cal uses air quotes when he sarcastically intones the word fun.

He's perceptive. Calculating. And clearly not amused.

I look him in the eye, tapping the bottom of the beer bottle in my hand against the counter. "Without getting into detail, Tabitha and I are friends—"

"It better not be friends with fucking benefits."

"Would you let me finish?" Okay, initially I assumed he was going to be cool with me dating his sister, but now I'm not so sure. I tread lightly, choosing my next words carefully. Don't get me wrong—Cal is cool guy and he's perfect for Greyson, but he's also built like a tank, has about thirty pounds on me, and I've literally watched him suckerpunch a guy between the eyes during a rugby match. So yeah. Pissing him off is not on the itinerary.

"Tabitha and I are friends. I'm not *just* physically attracted to her; I respect the shit out of her. Do you even know how amazing she is?" I take a swig of beer. "The minute I saw her, I just kn—why the fuck are you staring at me like that? Am I starting to sound like a goddamn pansy?"

Cal rolls his eyes. "The minute you saw her at your housewarming party?"

"No, man, the minute I saw her hiding behind a rack of chairs at Target, working herself up into a tizzy, wearing that cute pink hat. So fucking adorable." I chuckle when Cal looks back at me, his brows scrunched into a confused scowl.

"My sister is not adorable. She overreacts to *everything* and is a giant pain in the…" He stops short when I cock an eyebrow.

He shakes his head, regathering his thoughts. "Look, I'm not going to start an argument with you. All I'm saying is you better not be playing around. She's dated enough assholes; she doesn't need to date another one."

"Have you ever *met* your sister? Pretty sure she'd have my balls in a vise if I screwed her over." Cal nods in agreement. I swallow what's left in my beer bottle before waxing poetic. "So sweet I can barely stand it. Last night she surprised me with a—"

"Keller, *stop*." My sister's boyfriend curls his lips, disgusted. "You've obviously never seen her throw a hissy fit about having to chop fire wood on the weekends at our parents' house."

I scoff, unimpressed. "*Puh-lease*. You think that's bad? I'll counter a wood-chopping hissy fit and raise you one *you've obviously never seen Greyson stuff eighteen marshmallows in her mouth at one time*. Ask her to play Chubby Bunny with you once."

Cal's blue eyes widen. "Seriously? Eighteen marshmallows? Dude, what the fuck."

"Yes, seriously. It's a game they used to play at sleepaway camp. Then she'd come home and play it with her friends. It's freakishly disturbing." I grimace at the memory of my dainty, blonde-haired and bright-eyed little sister—my parents' pride and joy—cramming white puff after white puff of fluffy marshmallow into her mouth as a teenager.

Like a boss.

My sister's boyfriend snickers. "Well, being able to fit large objects in her mouth is a skill that comes in handy for us both—where can I send my thank-you letter?"

"Ha ha, *real* funny, asshole."

Cal's booming laughter echoes loudly, sounding unpracticed and rusty as the girls re-approach, Greyson taking the lead with Tabitha nipping at her heels.

She eyes us skeptically.

"What are you two laughing at?" Greyson asks, automatically shimmying up to Cal, her body contouring to his—like two puzzle pieces that were made to fit together. Her arm slips around his waist while narrowing those light hazel eyes at me.

My sister unattractively purses her lips.

"What? What did *I* do?" I ask. "What's with the stink-eye?"

Those slits of hazel get thinner. "What did you tell him?"

I immediately grab a square white cocktail napkin from the center of the table, wad it up, and shove it in my mouth. "Chubby bunny."

"Oh my god!" Greyson laughs and smacks me in the arm. Hard. "You shithead!"

I wad up another one. It joins the first. "Chubby. Bunny."

"Stop it, Collin, or you'll choke. I don't want to have

to call Mom and Dad from the hospital because you're jamming napkins down your throat."

"Hey, I was forced into it—we were comparing bratty sister stories." My voice is muffled around the two napkins packed in my mouth. A white corner sticks out from between my lips as I continue. "He didn't leave me any choice."

I can't tell by Tabitha's neutral expression if she's amused or appalled by my childish antics.

My sister grabs a cocktail napkin, balls it up in her fist, and throws it at me, laughing. "On second thought, here. Shove this one in your face, too. Maybe it'll shut you up." Greyson turns to Tabitha and rolls her eyes. "Honestly, I don't know what you see in him, and now I have to question your taste in men. For a grown man, sometimes he is *so* immature."

Tabitha giggles.

Cal glances back and forth between his sister and me. "Wait. For real, you're seeing each other? I thought you were full of shit before."

"No. Why would you think I was full of shit?"

He glances at his sister. "I mean, I love you, Tabby, so no offense—I'm just not used to seeing you dating anyone. I was already in college when you were dating that douchebag baseball player, and even *I* knew he didn't deserve you."

I move closer to Tabitha, pull her in, and relax my hand on her hip. "Damn right he didn't deserve her," I add, even though I have no idea what baseball player he's talking about. I make a mental note to ask about it later. "Your sister is incredible."

"I *know* that, Collin. I'm just saying she's dated some

real dickshitters."

"Not on purpose," Tabitha points out, resting her head on my shoulder. I give her a squeeze. "Remember Bryan Rickman? *He* wasn't completely horrible."

Cal laughs. "Correct me if I'm wrong, but didn't you date him in *ninth* grade?"

"What's your point?"

"That doesn't count. You were fourteen."

She narrows her bright blue eyes. "How do you even remember all this?"

Cal blushes, the gash on his face appearing even more severe. Chagrined, he mutters, "I may or may not have read your diary." Tabitha hauls off and whacks him with her purse. "Ouch! I said I *may* have! Jeez! There's no tangible proof that I actually did."

"Okay, break it up you two," Greyson referees, stepping in. "Go to your rooms."

But Cal is on a roll and brings the conversation full circle. "Really though, I'm just curious—how *did* you end up hooking up in the first place?" He grimaces. "I didn't mean hooking up. I meant *talking*."

"Dating?" Tabitha clears her throat. "Well, coincidentally, we ran into each other one afternoon doing out-of-office work stuff. Sometimes I take everything to a coffee shop, sit with my laptop, and drink coffee."

I agree. "Same. And that's what we were doing when we bumped into each other before the housewarming—"

"He scared the crap out of me—" Tabitha interrupts.

"She had the most adorable panic attack and spilled coffee all over herself. All over her white shirt. I was hoping it would turn into a wet tee-shirt contest—"

"Shut up, you were making me nervous!"

"I was making *you* nervous? *Pretty* sure it was the other way around."

"Oh my god, you are so sweet." She pecks my cheek, excited, then speaks to her brother. "So he's just standing there staring, right, which was weirding me out. I end up knocking everything off the table, including the proof of my book—"

"It just lands under the table," I add with a knowing smirk.

Tabitha throws her arms in the air. "And what does he do? Nothing! Doesn't say a word about it, the shithead."

We entertain Greyson and Cal, volleying barbs.

"What was I supposed to do? I had to get your attention somehow. Pocketing the book you wrote was the best way to do it…"

"Well, you didn't have to steal it and hold it hostage so I'd go out with you." She slaps my arm playfully, squeezing my bicep in the process. I flex. "It was so rude. He used it to blackmail me into going on our first date."

"Puh-*lease*, don't even act like you were going to say no—"

"I was going to say no! You were so annoying." She punctuates this pronouncement with a kiss to my jawline before enthusiastically prattling on. "He was purposely trying to embarrass me. He even read out loud from chapter ten when we met up. I finally agreed to meet him because I *really* needed it back."

Lost in our own stream of babbling nonsense, neither of us realizes why Calvin and Greyson are staring at us, slack-jawed.

Wait.

Why the fuck *are* they staring at us like that?

Was it something we said? Did we….

Oh shit.

Oh. Fucking. *Shit.*

I squeeze Tabitha's waist, prodding her to stop talking. In her excitement, she doesn't even realize we blurted out her secret. That with her rambling, she's giving away her secret, too.

Cal holds his palm up to stop us. "Back up. Did you guys just say the book she wrote? What book? Who wrote it?"

I feign ignorance. "Did we say that?"

"Yes, jackhole, you did." He looks point blank at his sister, a dark cloud descending on his expression. "Tabby, did you write a *novel*?"

"Uh…" She stands frozen, rooted to the floor, stunned. "Oh my god. I told, didn't I? Collin, please tell me I didn't just…"

Silence.

Followed by the inevitable.

Tabitha pulls away, unfolding herself from my body. I try to stop her by grabbing her upper arm, but she surprises me by giving me a shove so hard I stumble back a few steps. "Tabitha, it just slipped out. Babe, calm down —"

"Just slipped out! Just slipped out? Oh my god, I was going on and on about it! I'm such an *idiot*. An idiot!" She throws her arms in the air, defeated, and turns to confront me, poking me in the chest with the tip of an index finger, ignoring her brother and my sister. Angry. Frustrated. "One year, Collin. *One. Year*. Twelve months. Fifty-two weeks. That's how long I've kept my novel a secret." She stomps away, huffing and muttering to herself before stomping back. "Everyone is going to hate me for lying! How am I going to look my parents in the eye, and see my grandma on the weekend after they find out? They're going to think I'm a… a… Collin, I just told everyone the secret I've been keeping from them for an entire year!"

"Well, not *every*one. Mom and Dad aren't here," her brother interjects, trying to be helpful.

"Shut *up*, Calvin. This is between me and Collin," Tabitha admonishes with a loud shriek. Okay, maybe it's not a shriek, exactly, but it's definitely a cross between a scream and a whine.

Whoa, nelly, calm down.

She seriously needs to chill.

I'm not a *complete* idiot, so I compress my mouth shut, determined to power through her tirade.

"This was my well-guarded secret. How could I have been so stupid? What was I thinking! God, why didn't I just tell you *no* when you asked me out the first time? This never would have happened. I'm such an idiot."

Wait. Is she blaming *me*?

"Tab, please. Calm down, sweetie, be reasonable. This is a *good* thing, can't you see it? I'm sorry, but maybe your brother knowing—"

"No. Forget it, Collin. This isn't for you to decide. You don't get to tell me to calm down." She grabs her purse off the table.

"Tabitha, stop. Where the hell are you going?"

"I need time to think about what I'm gonna do. Alone."

Except, we're in a college town, staying with her brother for Christ's sake, not back home where she can hitch a cab and go back to her place.

"Take me back to your apartment, Cal. I can't sit in a car with him for three whole hours right now. Not just yet." Tabitha drags her brother towards the door by the upper arm. "I just have to get out of here. Think."

He's powerless to fight her, instead launching an inquisition.

"What novel?" I hear Cal asks as he's physically being led away. "Did you write a book, Tabby? Will someone please tell me what's going on?"

"No."

She's so angry. At herself. At me.

Irrational.

From beside me, my sister places a caring hand gently on my forearm, reminding me of her presence. "So, I take it Tabitha wrote a novel and didn't want to tell anyone?"

My head gives a jerky nod. "Yeah."

"Wow." Pause. "That is so… *cool.*"

"Yeah."

"Why would she keep it a secret?"

My broad shoulders shrug feebly. "Because it's romance. The slutty kind."

"Wow," Greyson repeats. "That is so… *awesome.*"

Tell me about it.

Grey rests her palm on my shoulder and gives it a squeeze. "This will blow over. You'll see." My sister's words are quiet and slightly skeptical.

"Yeah."

But even I don't believe it.

Collin: *Tabitha, would you please answer my calls? You barely spoke on the car ride home and you're not responding to my texts. We need to talk.*

Collin: *Please. I'm so fucking sorry they found out that way, but it was bound to come out eventually.*

Collin: *Greyson told me that your brother told your parents. What did they say? Please call me back.*

Collin: *Did you get the roses I sent to your office? I didn't want to be cheesy and I know you're pissed, but the red, yellow, lavender, and peach roses say everything—please, Tabitha. Let me tell you in person how I feel about you. Please.*

Tabitha's Notes for Book THREE, title to be determined. Titles I'm considering: THE BETRAYAL. Back cover blurb: Tarran felt betrayed by the world. By the one man she loved. Handsome and clever, the quick-witted devil had become her downfall. Because of him, the walls she'd so carefully erected around herself didn't just fall; they imploded...

Fourteen

Tabitha

"Honey, can I come in?" A few short knocks at my office door interrupt my thoughts, and quickly, I close the expanded document on my laptop screen when my dad sticks his head in.

Ironically, building up walls has become my specialty lately.

"Sure, Dad. Of course."

It's his company and his building; the man hardly needs permission.

His distinguished salt-and-pepper gray hair appears in the doorway, leading the way inside my office, the permanent smile he's never without pasted across his face. Around his eyes, weathered from the elements and years of working outdoors, are well-earned wrinkles and laugh lines.

We get our humor from him, Cal and I.

"Come in. Want to sit?" I indicate a spare chair in the corner.

Plopping himself unceremoniously in the chair that has been around this office longer than I've been alive, my father, Hodge Thompson, stretches, crosses his arms, and looks around.

"I haven't been in here for quite a while." He inches forward, plucking a framed photograph of me and my college roommate Savannah off my mahogany desk, studies it wordlessly, then sets it back in its place. "Your mom will be joining us shortly."

My mom and dad sitting in here together?

Oh crap, this can only mean one thing: an ambush.

I give a stiff laugh. "Is this an intervention?"

He raises a gray brow. "Why, do you need one?"

"Good one, Dad." I feign ignorance, forcing out a fake laugh. "Are the two of you taking me to lunch or something?"

He raises his other eyebrow and gives me "the look." You know the one your parents give you when *they* know *you* know *they* think you're full of shit.

Did that even make sense? For an author, I can't even string a few words together today.

Wait. Did I just call myself an author?

Crap. I did, didn't I?

I've never had that thought before—that I'm an author. A writer. And now I can't help but wonder why it suddenly crossed my mind, now of all times, with my parents about to lecture me about… who knows what.

Nope, that's a lie. I know exactly what they're going to lecture me about, thanks to Collin and my loud-mouth brother.

My writing. My book.

My *novel.*

I slump down in my desk chair a little, swiveling towards the window to avoid my mother's gaze when she swoops into the room, sophisticated, blonde haired, and blue eyed.

"Sorry I'm late! Did I miss anything?" She bends and kisses my dad on the top of his head, then lowers herself into the chair beside him, dropping her purse on the floor. Her hands go to her hair, and she fluffs. "Ugh, how gorgeous is it outside? Too bad we're stuck inside."

Mom, who does the accounting for the company, looks pointedly in my direction. "Take a break, both of you, and make some time to sit outside for a few. Get some fresh air."

I grab the nearest pencil and anxiously tap it on the surface of my desk. "I'll try." I scan their faces. "So..?"

My dad starts, and, having no patience for bullshit, cuts right to the chase. "So. You wrote a book."

He states it as a fact, not as a question.

Denying it would be futile, so I nod. "But it didn't interfere with my work, I swear. I didn't use company time to write, and I used my own laptop."

My mom instantly looks deflated. "Honey, that's not what he meant." She reaches towards the desk and nabs the pencil from my nervous hands. "We want to know why you didn't tell us."

Because.

Because.

I have a million reasons why, but when I open my mouth to give them, no words spill out. Then I say, "What did Calvin tell you?"

Dad shakes his head, shrugging his broad shoulders. "Nothing. Just that you wrote a book. And that no one knew about it."

"It's a novel, actually," I blurt out, unable to stop myself, and then I regret it when they both raise their eyebrows in surprise. "Sorry."

Dad clears his throat. "He also said you've been seeing the Keller boy." Unable to resist, I roll my eyes at that. The Keller boy. "He's the one you were with when you spilled the proverbial beans, I assume?"

Only my dad would use air quotes when he said 'proverbial beans,' like it was a *thing.*

"*Sort of* seeing him. Yes."

My mom, who can't resist meddling in my love life, chooses her next words carefully. "Honey, why are you taking this whole thing out on this nice young man? Cal says you walked out on him. How is any of this his fault?"

Because I'm stubborn and willful and embarrassed. But of course, I don't say any of this. Instead, I shrug, gazing out my office window for the answers.

"Tabitha." My mother's voice holds a sharp edge. "Did you hear what I said?"

God, I hate it when she talks to me like this, like I'm a child. I feel my chin start to wobble a little when I open my mouth to say, "Why did I take it out on Collin? Because it was easier to get mad at him rather than myself. Because I knew I was wrong. I needed someone to blame and he was there."

Mom leans back in her seat and waits for me to continue.

"God, I acted so juvenile." A tear slips down my cheek, and I swipe at it with my shirtsleeve, refusing to stare into the faces of my disappointed parents. "He's so great, Mom. I hope… I hope you get the chance to meet him."

"If he's anything like his sister, I'm sure we're going to love him."

"He is. You will."

Silence fills the room then, and when my dad doesn't continue where my mom left off, she sniffs impatiently. "Your father and I aren't here to talk about your relationship, although we were concerned about it when we heard." She shoots a pointed look at my dad, to get him on board with the discussion. "The real reason we wanted to sit you down was to tell you that we're *proud* of you, honey. Of course we were shocked! But not for the reason you'd think. Tabitha, sweetie, you wrote a novel!"

"God damn right my girl did!" my dad booms, accompanying his decree with a bang of his fist to my desktop. "My daughter wrote a book. A goddamn book!"

"Hodge," my mom scolds him for cursing, and rolls her eyes impatiently. "Anyway. The thing we're disappointed in, is that you were afraid to tell us. The thought that you kept that *secret* from your father and me for a year makes me… so *sad* for you, sweetie. It breaks my heart that you'd even think we wouldn't support you."

"I…" I look down at my folded hands, clasped together on my desk. "I know you depend on me. I went to college for this, for freaking construction. Do you know how many women were in my classes? Hardly any. Then I had to go to an Ivy League school. Who does that? Why didn't I just go to State, for crying out loud?" I'm on a roll now that the floodgates have opened. Cathartic, I forage on, mindless of the consequences my words might have.

"This is the only job I've ever had since I was in middle school, working in the office—why would I leave to be a writer? Talk about a bad decision."

"Honey, your dad and I—"

"And then there's Cal," I blurt out. "He's counting on me to be here when you and Dad retire, which is when? Eight more years? Seven? Then what? He'll hardly be qualified to take over by himself. I'm not either, but at least I have a few more years of management under my belt."

My parents glance at each other, worried that I've lost my damn mind, then back at me. "Tabitha Elizabeth, haven't we always told you, you can be anything you want to be?"

Where is Mom going with this? "Well… *yes*."

"Then why are you working here?"

My head snaps up. "What?"

What does that even mean?

"If you want to be a writer, why are you working here?"

"I just told you. Weren't you listening?" My voice is meek. Weak. Pitiful.

For a strong, independent woman, I sound *pitiful*.

I suck.

"You do not suck, sweetie."

Oh shit, did I say that out loud?

"There you go again. Do you always mutter to yourself?" my dad asks. "I hope you don't do that around our clients." He chuckles. "It's bad for business."

My mom smacks him in the arm. "*Hodge*."

"What your mom and I are trying to tell you is we want you to follow your dreams. We never meant for you to be imprisoned here."

"Dad, that's not it at all!"

He ignores me. "If you need to stay working here while you get on your feet—until your books take off and you can earn a living—then you're welcome to stay. If you want to take some time off, we'll help you do that."

"Help me do… what?"

"Well, you're twenty-four years old, but if you want to move back home to save money—"

Ew.

"I am not moving back in with you. No offense, guys."

"We're just giving you options. You're not stuck here. I know you've always thought you were responsible for holding down the fort until your brother was old enough to take on more responsibility, but give me some credit. That's what Dale and Roger are for."

Dale and Roger are my dad's Vice President of Operations and General Manager.

"But… they're not family. I thought you wanted this to remain a family business."

"Sweetie," my mom puts in sharply. "Now you're just being ridiculous. Maybe that would have been possible twenty years ago, but times are changing." She pats my dad on the hand. "Do you hear your daughter, Hodge? She thinks we're not with the times."

They both laugh. "I bet she doesn't think we know all about them Timber and the Tweeter Apps. Please, we're down with that."

My mom makes a gesture with her hands that looks surprisingly thug. Gangster even.

"Please stop throwing hands signs," I plead.

She does it again.

"Don't do that. Please stop."

Mom laughs. "Greyson showed me that Bumble site last time Cal brought her home. You should see some of the young hunks online these days."

"It's an app mom, not a website."

She waves her hand in the air. "Same thing."

No, it's not the same thing. I beg the universe for patience. *Breathe in through the nose, out through the mouth...*

And then she asks the question I've been dreading: "So, your dad and I were wondering, what is your book about?"

I groan into my hands as my head thumps down onto my desk. My mother ignores my obvious discomfort and chatters. "Is it one of those murder mystery novels? I was just telling Donna Standish you have *such* a flare for drama, and that of *course* she could have a signed copy of your paperback."

One thought—and one thought only—flashes through my mind as my parents ramble on like I'm not even in the room.

I am going to *kill* Collin Keller.

If I don't kiss him first.

Tabitha: *So in the end, Mom and Dad were really supportive...*

Calvin: *I can't believe for a second you thought they wouldn't be.*

Tabitha: *I know, but you have to understand, I was really embarrassed.*

Calvin: *Why? It's not like any of us are going to read it.*

Tabitha: *YOU JERK! Greyson's gonna read it. COLLIN read it!*

Calvin: *But Collin only read it because he has a boner for you. That's totally different. No dude reads a romance novel unless he really likes a girl. Or wants to bang her. Just saying.*

Tabitha: *You're revolting.*

Greyson: *He's right about one thing, Tab. Collin genuinely likes you. Would you please put my brother out of his misery and call him. Or text him? He feels terrible.*

Tabitha: *God, I love these Group Chats [heavy on the sarcasm]*

Greyson: *Do what you want, but keep this in mind—it was an honest mistake. He cares about you, so much. He's a great guy, Tabby. Don't let your PRIDE get in the way of a great relationship.*

Calvin: *You and your damn Keller pride.*

Greyson: *^^^^ Hey, smart-ass. I seem to remember you flipping out over a certain tweet before we started dating. You refused to talk to me for days #sexybeast*

Calvin: *Oh yeah, I totally forgot about that. Thanks for reminding me. Not.*

Greyson: *Aww, baby, but that's when I fell in love with you.*

Calvin: *I can't wait until tomorrow when I get to kiss those sexy lips of yours.*

Greyson: *YOUR lips are sexy. Rawr*

Calvin: *I love you*

Greyson: *I love YOU*

Tabitha: *HELLO! GROUP CHAT! Stop. Do NOT start sexting. OMG. How the hell do I take myself out of here? SOMEONE HELP ME. bangs on glass*

Fifteen

Collin

I've been waiting close to two hours at a table in the far corner, waiting to see if she'll walk through that front door. Tuesday and Wednesday she was a no-show, and yesterday I arrived a second too late, only to catch the tail-lights of her car pulling away.

But still, I wait.

Like clockwork for the past four days, hoping luck will be on my side.

The lukewarm mug on my table stopped steaming over an hour ago, the soy congealing at the bottom. I stir it to keep my hands occupied, but don't take a sip.

As fidgety and anxious as a crack whore, I tap the spoon on the saucer until a young woman at a nearby table brings a finger to her lips to shush me, shooting me a dirty look in the process.

Noted.

My legs bounces beneath the table restlessly.

Dammit, where is she?

Digging into the interior pocket of my jacket, I pull out the envelope tucked inside and smooth the wrinkles out with my palm, using the surface of the flat tabletop. I look up when the coffee shop door opens with a whoosh, a small cluster of leaves blowing in along with the brisk wind.

Holy shit, it's her.

She's here.

I fucking swear my heart skips a beat at the sight of her. It's only been a few days, but man, she's a sight for these hungry eyes.

I stand, moving towards her, and then double back because, shit, I forgot my envelope. It gets stuffed into the back pocket of my jeans before I call her name.

"Tabitha."

She places her bag at a table near a bank of windows and stills at the sound of my voice, her movements halted. Turning, just like in the movies—or a romance novel—her eyes widen at the sight of me. And she looks how I feel: tired. Weary. Desperate to stop the instant replay of what happened between us over and over in my mind and just wanting… something. Anything.

A resolution. A conversation.

Closure.

That's a damn lie; I don't want closure—I want her.

"Collin." Why doesn't she look surprised to see me?

"Hey," I say, approaching. My eyes drop to her laptop bag, and I cautiously let my lips curl into a tentative smile. "What are you working on?"

She bites down on her lower lip, amused by the déjà vu. "Work stuff."

I can't get enough of this beautiful girl and her laidback sense of humor. Thank God she hasn't told me to fuck off.

Yet.

Relief sags my shoulders.

"What kind of work stuff?" I raise my hands and do air quotes, because I know she hates when people do that. I'm rewarded with a cheeky grin for my efforts.

Her hand goes to her hip. "What's with all the questions?"

"Just curious, that's all."

"Remember what happened the last time you were curious?" she asks, leaning against the large, overstuffed chair next to her table.

"Yeah. But I'm willing to take my chances." I pull the envelope out of my back pocket and extend it towards her. "This is for you. Could—would you read it? Please."

"Now?" She glances down at it, then at my face, studying it a few moments before reaching out to take the envelope. Our fingers meet when she does, and I'd like to think it was intentional on her part. Or maybe I'm delusional.

She shivers.

Nope. Not delusional.

My pulse quickens when she pulls out her chair and sits.

Awkwardly, I stand there, not sure…

"Would you sit down?" she demands. "You're making me nervous."

I sit, watching intently as she breaks the seal on the envelope, removes the thick cream paper from inside, unfolds it, and begins to read.

Tabitha

No man has ever written me a love letter before—not unless you count the time in seventh grade when Tim Bachman passed me a note in class describing how he wanted to feel my boobs. Did I want him touching me under my sweater after the soccer game? Yes or No. (Firm no on that one, by the way).

Unfolding a piece of cream stationary paper that looks like it's been read and refolded a few dozen times, my breath catches in my throat, because there in black ink and masculine script is a handwritten letter.

I bend my head and read.

Dear Tabitha,

I've never written a woman a letter before—not unless you count the time in eighth grade when I asked Melissa Spellman if she'd make out with me under the bleachers after the football game. She said no, by the way, so I guess we can't count that. So please, bear with me…

I don't know where to start, except to say that you're all I can think about, from the minute my eyes open in the morning—until I climb into bed at night. I would say I think about you when I close my eyes to sleep, but the truth is, I lie awake most nights staring up at the ceiling, trying to picture your face and remember the sound of your voice. Is that weird?

The other day When we argued and you walked out that door, it went against every one of my instincts not to chase you down. I panicked. I thought you were walking out of my life before our relationship had a real chance, and it scared the shit out of me. I can't say I'm sorry for what I said because you shouldn't have to hide how incredible. You know how I feel about you; I haven't played any head games and it kills me that people don't fucking know you've created something incredible. On your own, standing on your talent. Maybe to you it doesn't feel big. Maybe to you it doesn't feel remarkable.

But it is, holy shit, it is.

Is this the worst love letter you've ever received? Because that's what this is, so sorry about the swearing. It was hard for me to articulate how I feel—I don't have a way with words the way you obviously do. Numbers, yes. Words, no. I'm trying not to fuck this up. Is it working?

If you'll let me, I'll stand by and support you, whether you choose management for your parents' company or you want to write. I won't say another word about it.

I miss you. Let's start over.

Sincerely Love, Collin

I continue staring down at the letter, scanning it at least a dozen times, reading and rereading each word, over and over, devouring it, memorizing every line. Each and every beautiful, ineloquent word. Not because they're the most poetic words I've ever read, but because *he* wrote them.

He's the most fascinating man I've ever met.

He writes me sort-of love letters and works for a stock brokerage firm.

He's funny and smart and ridiculously good looking. He thinks I'm beautiful, smart, clever, and funny.

Collin believes in my dream.

Collin believes in… *me*.

And that's more than enough.

I bite down on my lower lip to stop the stupid grin spreading there, and raise my head, our gazes colliding. Tears moisten the corners of my eyes and I wipe them away, embarrassed.

"I'm sorry," I say, folding up the sheet of paper, lovingly tucking it into my laptop bag where it's safe and sound. Standing, I push back my chair and inch closer to where he stands regarding me.

I take a deep breath. "I overreacted—as usual—and I'm sorry. I might write romance novels, but the truth is, in reality… I'm complete shit at relationships."

His hand lovingly brushes some wispy stray tendrils of hair away from my jawline. "So am I."

"You're just saying that to make me feel better." I tilt my head into his palm, letting him cradle my cheek. "You've done nothing but try to win me over while I ran scared. For what? To push you away because I was lying to my entire family? This letter just proves what a fool I've been. Collin, this letter… it was…"

"*Don't* say sweet." He frames my face and plants a kiss on my nose before his hands glide down my ribcage to grip my hips, tugging me in, pulling our bodies flush. Mine gives a shuddering sigh.

It missed him, melts into him like a pile of magic sand. Like it belongs there.

"Fine, I won't." I lay my head on his chest, listening to his heartbeat, and wrap my arms around his waist with a whisper. "But it was. It was sweet *and* beautiful, Collin. The most beautiful thing anyone's ever written me."

"*You're* beautiful." His warm breath flirts with the shell of my ear. "I can't wait to get you home. I'll let you show me your gratitude then."

Oh, I just bet he does.

I wince. "Hey, Collin?"

"Yeah?"

"People are starting to stare."

"So? Let them."

So we do.

Taking Chances, a Novel by TE Thomas
Acknowledgements [re-edited]

This book means a lot to me, not only because it's my second novel but because along the journey, I think I might have found myself. But I didn't do it alone. I had the support of my family, my parents, my friends, and someone else.

To Collin: who discovered my writing all these months ago, before anyone else, and who believed in me when I didn't want to tell a soul about it. The past six months with you have been.... indescribable.

You love my writing, you love my wacky sense of humor, you love my pink "thinking" baseball cap. But most of all, I'm pretty sure you loved me at first sight. I can see it in your eyes when you look at me, and hear it in your voice when you whisper my name in the dark. You're my best friend.

I love you, too.

Epilogue

Daphne

"Everyone raise your glasses in a toast," I announce around the high-top bar table, hoisting my wine glass in the air and encouraging the friends we have gathered to do the same. Clearing my throat, I begin. "To Tabitha: the author friend we're here to celebrate! She worked her ass off for many years to get to this point. She took a risk and left her job to write full-time and is proudly publishing her *second—yes second!* romance novel." I put a hand next to my mouth and address our small group in a hushed tone as if I'm telling them a naughty bit of gossip. "And even though she kept it a secret from us at the beginning, we're all so proud of her."

Beside me, Tabitha groans loudly among the laughter.

I continue. "Her first book has been in the top 100 for

nine weeks and we expect the second to do just as well because my best friend is a wordsmithing genius."

"We are so proud of you!" our friend Samantha shouts.

"So proud!" Greyson—who is dating Tabitha's brother—echoes, raising her glass higher. "Seriously Tab, we're so excited for you… even though you used my *brother* as a muse for your second novel, which I cannot get past." Grey gives a shudder. "Especially where the characters finally do the deed. Did it have to be so descriptive? All I could do was picture my brother and you—horrifying. I will never be able to un-read that scene, and for that I will forever be ungrateful."

My best friend Tabitha, laughs, her blue eyes sparkling with mischief. "Yeah, but we all know the best ideas imitate real life."

I roll my eyes and lower my glass. "But do we have to *know* about it? Honestly. The visuals we could have lived without." Even though her boyfriend Collin is a complete hottie with a hot bod and killer smile whom none of us, if forced, would mind picturing naked in the sack. But of course, I can't say that shit out loud.

That would be tacky.

Tabitha has the decency to blush. Her hands go up in defeat. "I swear I only used Collin to form the male character! I didn't use our *relationship* to plot the book!"

She can't even look us in the eye when she says it, the liar.

We all stare and Samantha's expression clearly asks '*who are you trying to kid right now*?' "You expect people to believe that? The entire second book is about two people who meet at a store; that's you. Then they bump into each other at a party. You. Then he finds out her secret. Also you. You, you, and you. *Your* story. Just admit it so we can finish toasting your success."

A dreamy smile crosses Tabitha's face. "Fine. I admit it. I was falling in love with him, so yes—I might not have done it on *purpose*, but it *is* our story."

"*Finally*. Now, as we were saying: here's to Tabitha, who we all knew would do something spectacular. Thank you for proving us right. We love you and are so proud. Cheers!"

"Cheers to Tabby!"

"Hey," Bridget—an old college roommate in town for the weekend—cuts in. "When do we get to *see* this famous love letter we keep hearing about?"

She's referring to the love letter that my best friend's boyfriend wrote her during a rough patch while they were dating. Tabitha has never shown it to anyone, but did reference it in her new book.

Which, of course, made us all curious.

Tabitha throws her head back, and face palms herself. "Oh crap. I forgot I put that in my book." She laughs the kind of laugh that makes a guy like Collin fall in love with you and write you love letters. Light and airy and full of humor. "Sorry, ladies. The contents of said letter are private."

"Is it dirty?" Greyson wrinkles her nose. "Please say no."

"No! It's sweet. Ugh, just the sweetest. Maybe someday I'll let you read it, but for now I'm keeping it to myself."

"Damn you and your secrets!" I complain. "I showed you the poem Kyle Hammond wrote me last year."

Half the table groans out loud, and Bridget smirks. "Are you *kidding* me right now? First of all, Kyle Hammond is a stalker that works in your office. Secondly, he plagiarized that poem off the internet. Third, it wasn't a love poem; it was a poem about a man's love affair with a married woman."

I scoff indignantly. "It's the thought that counts."

"He's just so adorable I can hardly stand it," Tabitha sighs into her wine glass.

"Who, Kyle?"

"Collin," my best friend sighs again in a daydream, resting her elbows on the bar table.

"Collin? Adorable?" Greyson laughs. "Okay, yeah—my brother is somewhat good looking. But I also remember he and his friends back in high school doing some pretty stupid crap, like toilet papering their friend's houses and leaving dead animals on the front porch that they found on the side of the road. Gross."

"What!" Samantha sputters, pausing with a wine glass halfway to her lips. "Wait. *What*?"

Greyson nods with authority. "Yup, Road Kill Cafe. He and his hockey buddies would use it as their calling card when they'd go TP someone's house. Anything they found on the side of the road, they'd take and put on someone's porch."

"That's so totally disgusting I need to chug this," Bridget adds, lifting her wine glass and pointing it in Tabitha's direction. "You kiss that mouth."

Greyson continues. "Skunks, opossums, squirrels; basically anything dead on the side of the road. Like, who *does* that?"

"I don't even know if I can drink any more of this,"

Bridget wrinkles her nose and stares down into her wine glass. "I think I just lost my appetite."

"Don't say you've lost your appetite, because I'm starving." Tabitha successfully changes the subject, head swiveling around in search of a menu. "I think this place serves food. We should order something."

My stomach and I grumble at the same time. "It probably only serves bird food to go with this wine. Like cheese and dry fruit and crap."

"Whatever it is, we'll just order double."

Not seeing a menu, I hop down off my stool and dash to the bar to fetch one, returning with a few and setting them in the middle of the table. "Have at it ladies."

I crack one open. "Okay, this looks good: brie wedge and warm raspberry compote."

"Let's also do the artichoke dip, and the bruschetta."

Bridget rubs her hands together gleefully. "Yes and yes. And look, they have crab cakes, but you only get three, so we'll have to order two."

"We're going to look like slobs," I say, closing the menu and signaling the bartender with the flick of a wrist in the air, eying our round table dubiously. "Is this table big enough for all this food?"

"Do you care?"

I shrug, the pretty lavender scoop neck sweater I'm wearing falling down off my shoulder. "Well, *no…*"

Samantha pokes me with the corner of a menu. "Because I don't see any guys here about to sweep you off your single feet. We're free to do as we please. This is girl's night."

Disgruntled, I wrinkle my nose. "You're all either engaged or in serious relationships. Being single sucks. Must you point out my deficiencies?"

"I'm sorry, that wasn't my point! I'm just saying…"

Bridget throws her hands up to stop our banter. "Hold that thought. Rewind! A group of guys just entered the building, three o'clock." We all crane our necks to get a good look, Bridget—the only one of us who's engaged—straining the hardest to catch a peek. "One of them is pretty hot."

"Um… what are you doing?" Greyson asks, shaking her pretty blonde head with a grin on her face.

Bridget winks and tosses her long, brown hair with a flip. "I'm scoping them out, of course. For *Daphne*."

The bartender walks over with her stylus poised above her tablet to take our order and Greyson rattles off our selections, adding two more appetizers, along with another round of drinks.

"That should hold us over for a little bit," she says, handing back the menus. "Thanks." The bartender taps away on her tablet before nodding and walking off.

Bridget's eyes are glued across the room, her wineglass poised at her cherry red lips. "What do you think those guys would say if they saw a shit ton of food show up at this tiny table?"

"What guys? Those guys?" Greyson's hazel eyes widen with surprise, and she cranes her head to look around the dimly lit club. "Why are you staring over there so hard? You're engaged."

If anyone should be ogling that hard, it should be *me*.

"Jeez, don't everyone look!" Samantha demands. "Yes, the guys who walked in before. They're at the bar now and totally checking us out."

Surreptitiously, we covertly sneak glances towards

the front of the wine bar. Sure enough, on the far side of the room, seated along the rails, a small group of guys is in fact checking us out, doing nothing to conceal their interest.

One of them even points.

I do a quick count of the math: four of them. Five of us. Unfortunately for them, I'm the only single one in this group. Well, I suppose we could technically count Samantha as single because she broke up with her boyfriend just days ago; her status might be single, but emotionally she's in no place to be picking up guys at a bar, sophisticated clientele or not.

We figured dragging her out tonight and plying her with alcohol would take her mind off Ben & Jerry.

"Crap, they look like they're going to come over." Greyson groans miserably; if there's one thing I've learned about Grey, it's that she might be outgoing and friendly, but despite her stunning beauty, she's modest, private—and hates getting hit on.

I however, do not. And apparently neither does—

"Samantha keeps staring!" Bridget accuses with a scowl. "You're going to give them false hope if you don't knock it off."

"I wasn't staring!" She huffs. "Alright, so what if I was? There's no harm in window shopping."

While they argue back-and-forth, not gonna lie; my ardent green eyes wander, seeking out the group of young men seated at the bar. They're not a large group, but they're loud and boisterous, with several flights of wine lining the counter like shots.

In my age range.

Several of them gather up their stem less wine glasses, their course of action to head in our direction. I stand taller, assessing.

The leader is a few paces ahead of the rest, his laser-like focus hell bent to reach us first. Undoubtedly so he can control the situation, or have first pick. Or both. I know his type—cocky swagger, lopsided grin meant to be captivating, tight white tee, and straining muscles that can only be obtained with hour-upon-hour at the gym. If that weren't enough, a visible tattoo snakes up the side of his neck and disappears into his hairline. An arrogant grin with blaring white teeth complete the unappealing package.

Wow. This guy thinks he's the shit.

The other three, well they trail along after him like afterthoughts. The 'yes' men, donning the official uniform of "Mr. One-Night Stand:" tight shirts, bleached teeth, and matching shit-eating grins. I bet two out of three of them have rib tats.

Except the straggler.

I eyeball the guy shuffling behind them, my green gaze *fixating* on him, latching on with fascination; not only is he deliberately lagging behind, he looks damn uncomfortable. This one… he's a complete paradox.

Dark, tousled hair, The Straggler effortlessly dons a gingham plaid shirt, neatly tucked under a preppy blue sweater vest, and a belted pair of navy khakis. His only concession to casual: rolled shirt sleeves pushed to his elbows.

All he's missing is a bow tie.

Honestly? The poor guy looks like he's just arrived from the office; a tax attorney's office, I speculate. Or a cubicle at a technology company. Yeah, definitely computer programming.

Or insurance sales.

Wait, no. The internal revenue service.

I bet he's an auditor; that sounds boring.

I'm not trying to be being mean, but the guy is wearing *khakis* and a sweater vest in a bar on a *weekend*, for heaven's sake. He's practically begging me to judge him.

To the upwardly mobile, wearing a plaid shirt to a bar during the workweek would be just fine; but not on a Saturday. Unless of course, he happens to be from the deep south—maybe Georgia or South Carolina? Don't they wear bow ties down there? Yeah. They do.

I study him further and after some serious contemplation, concede that The Straggler pulls off the stuffy look *just* fine.

And did I mention his glasses?

Kind of adorkable.

He pushes those tortoise shell rims up the bridge of a straight nose on an average face, crosses his average arms across an average chest, and I watch as he tips his head towards the ceiling and murmurs to himself.

Adam's apple bobbing, I read his lips: *I'm in hell.*

Nope. I'm not eyeballing the guy because I'm interested; I'm eyeballing him because he's so *obviously* miserable.

Is it sick that I'm enjoying his discomfort? Ugh, what is wrong with me?

Smirking, I bring the bowl of my wineglass to my lips, concealing the smile growing there as the guys approach, confidently, like a pack of vultures. Swallowing a chuckle, I gulp my wine.

"Hey, I think I recognize that guy," Tabitha says, her

eyes squinting at The Straggler, then snapping her fingers. "*Ha*! Yes, I do. I'm pretty sure that's Collin's friend Dex. Dexter Ryan? I think."

Dexter.

I turn the name around inside my head, testing it out.

How nerdy.

But it fits.

And I like it.

Things *Liars* Fake

Daphne

All my friends are falling in love and it sucks.

Don't get me wrong; I love them all and I'm happy for them, but sometimes it would be nice to call them up and have them be readily available. Up for anything, including an impromptu night out.

Or a night in.

These days, it takes days—if not weeks, to coordinate the simplest get together. Why? Because none of my friends can plan something without asking their significant other. "Let me check with Collin…" or "I think we have plans, but let me ask…" or "Collin's coming home that night from his business trip and I want to be here when he gets back…"

If I wasn't so damn happy for my friends, I would feel sorry for myself.

Okay, fine. I *do* feel sorry for myself.

And how will I rectify that? By drowning my self-wallowing emotions in the form of buttery popcorn and movie theater chocolate, of course.

Trust me: it works every time. It's foolproof, if not fleeting, but at the moment, I don't care.

Alone in the lobby, I clutch my movie stub and stand patiently in line at the concession stand, staring up at the glowing menu board, debating between adding butter to my popcorn. Do I want SnowCaps or Bunch of Crunch? Twenty ounces of soda, or thirty?

Unhurriedly, since I'm a good fifteen minutes early, I watch as the teenagers behind the glass counters avoid smashing into each other as they grab treats, food, and fill beverage cups. Ring customers up.

I cringe as a young man with spiky hair drops a card-board tray of freshly nuked White Castle burgers to the tile floor, his shoulders slumping in dismay at his error.

Poor kid.

Reaching the front of the line, I tap my folded twenty-dollar bill on the glass counter, watching as he quickly fills a new box with the tiny burgers for the guy in the next line over, as a manager swoops in with a broom to sweep up the mess behind him.

Already having mentally placed my order, I absent-mindedly cast a sidelong glance around the concession stand lines, taking in the people. Couple after couple. Small groups of teenagers. Families. Sci-Fi nerds coming to see a re-mastered version of a classic. Customer after customer steps up to the counter to order munchies and drinks, and I'm ready to repeat my order when a lone figure in an expensive blue coat catches my wandering eyes.

I do a double take.

Wait. I think I recognize that guy. Is that…

It is.

Dexter.

Dexter Ryan.

Collin Keller's good friend from the other night.

We hardly spoke that night at Ripley's Wine Bar, but I'm good with faces and would recognize him anywhere. I mean, seriously, who could forget the guy wearing a sweater vest at a bar on a Saturday night?

I watch him now, inwardly cringing.

Fine. *Out*wardly cringing, sinking deeper into my puffer vest; of course I'd bump into someone I knew—even in passing—while I was at the movies alone.

Completely.

Alone.

What were the freaking odds?

Covertly, I watch him from under my long dark lashes, thankful I'm somewhat cleverly disguised in a knit winter hat and non-prescription glasses, and barely distinguishable. At least, I hope so.

Dexter, for his part, looks polished and geeky and smart and oddly kind of…

Sexy.

In a very geeky way.

Ugh.

"Ma'am?"

A voice interrupts my thoughts.

"Ma'am, are you ready to order?" A teenage girl behind the concession counter stares back at me like I'm an oddity. "*Ma'am*?"

Ma'am? Oh shit, she's talking to *me*.

Sporting a bright, azure blue baseball cap with the movie theater logo embroidered on it in white, the girl's black hair sticks out the bottom in a frizzy, messy bun, tips dyed a shocking yellow. Six earrings line her left ear, one of them a hot pink barbell. Her dull gray eyes are rimmed in heavy black kohl, and she regards me impatiently.

Like I'm a mental person.

"Sorry, I thought you were talking to someone else."

Black eyebrows raised, her pointer finger hovers above the cash register buttons, ready to strike.

Rattling off my order—the same order every time I come to the movies—it's not long before another teen behind the booth assists her, dropping a big tub of fluffy, buttery popcorn unceremoniously on the counter.

Each and every kernel for me, and me alone.

Chocolate.

Soda.

As I'm pondering more bad choices, like adding licorice or Swedish Fish, the teenage girl interrupts. "If you order *another* drink for your friend, you get a discount on both beverages of fifty cents. Your total would be $23.11 instead of $24.11"

Her monotone voice offers me the discount deal; her eyes say she doesn't give a shit if I take it.

I give a tight lipped smile, tapping my debit card on the glass counter; no way is a twenty-dollar bill going to cover all this food. "There is no friend. It's just little 'ol me, thanks."

Her eyes troll to the colossal popcorn bucket, chocolate and drink. "It's just *you*?" She damn near shouts. "Sorry, I mean—just the one beverage?"

Could she be any louder? Could we *not* broadcast to

everyone I'm flying solo at the movies?

I nod, affirmative, wishing she'd lower her voice a few decibels. "Yes, just the one beverage. Wait. I'll take a bottle of water, too, please."

Of course, it's my fault she thought I was part of a couple when I ordered the large with extra butter, box of Snowcaps on the side, and a soda.

I pay, trying to scurry undetected to the condiments, putting both my beverages into a cardboard snack tray, awkwardly juggling it as I pluck a few napkins from the metallic holder. One, two… five napkins.

That should be enough, right?

For good measure, I pluck out two more from the holder because sometimes my butter hands get out of control. I hate having buttery fingerprints.

Still clutching my ticket stub, I attempt to lift it to see which theater my movie is playing in, but fail miserably and have to set everyth—

"Daphne?"

I freeze.

Look up.

Pivot.

Standing behind me in his navy blue pea coat, Dexter Ryan smiles crookedly down at me.

He smoothes his hands down the front of his dark pressed jeans—or is he wiping sweat off his palms?—and pushes his tortoiseshell glasses up the bridge of his nose.

I take it all in—every inch of him—from the preppy jacket, the glasses, the slight cleft in his chin, up to the black cable knit winter hat when he suddenly removes it. Instead of his hair being flattened by the hat, it's unruly and a bit tousled. A rich brown, his locks are wavy, shaggy and desperately need a trim.

He finger combs it out of his face.

"It *is* Daphne, right?" He asks, unsure of himself.

It's hard to hold back my groan of dismay at being spotted, but I muster up a cheerful, "Yeah. Hi. Dexter?"

He smiles then, his eyes shining behind his dark, tortoiseshell lenses. I mean—I *think* his eyes are shining. Maybe it's just the reflection of his glasses?

Those dark eyes dart down to my snacks, the ticket stub grasped between two fingers on my right hand. His brows go up. "Do you need help with anything? Sorry, I'm an idiot; it's obvious you're waiting for someone."

A nervous giggle escapes my lips, only I can't smack a hand over my mouth to stop it. "Gosh thank you. I don't need help," I hurriedly say. "I just have to see which theater I'm in, but I'm having a hard time with…"

All my food.

"It's just you?" His head cranes around, confused. "I'm sorry, that was rude. Of course it's not just you. Why would it be?" His deep voice gives a forced, nervous chuckle.

Wow, this is about to get awkward. "Nope, it *is* just me," I barely manage to get the words out. "I'm here alone."

Dexter's eyes go wide, sending his brows straight into his hairline. His mouth even falls open a little but no sound comes out.

"Great," I joke, more for my benefit than his. "I've rendered you speechless."

I follow the line of his jacket, down to the hand tightly gripping his winter hat.

"No! Shit, sorry. I didn't mean… I don't know what I

mean." Deep breath. "I'm here alone, too."

Suddenly, his mouth twitches into a goofy grin, and my green eyes make a beeline to his lips as they form the words, "Which movie are you here to see?"

Those lips.

Huh?

Instead of formulating a response, I find myself trying not to stare at a perfectly sculpted upper lip and a full mouth surrounded by a days' worth of five o'clock shadow. Strong jawline. Straight, white teeth. And is that line in his cheek a dimple?

Dexter clears his throat, and I watch transfixed as the chords in his neck flex when he reprises, "Which movie are you here to see?"

Huh?

"Huh?"

Jesus, I have some serious issues. And if Dexter thinks I've gone space cadet on him, he doesn't let on; his brown eyes are kind. Friendly. Sincere without a trace of egotism. "What movie?"

Oh god. Could this be any more humiliating? The guy's asked me the same question three times.

"Uh… StarGate?"

Don't judge me! *Don't judge me, Dexter!* I want to shout. I want to hide behind my massive bucket of popcorn. *Yes, it's true! I am at a nine o'clock screening of StarGate, the twenty-year-old movie turned nerd cult classic of all time.*

By myself.

As in: alone.

On a Saturday night.

A pleased grin quirks, his thick brows shoot up for a

second time in surprise before he clears his throat. "Me too."

Dexter briefly glances down at his ticket stub, pushing his glasses back up the bridge of his nose with a forefinger. God, it's such a sweet gesture I actually cock my head and stare.

Truth be told, I could probably stare at him all night.

It's been all of three minutes and I find him charming, adorable, and unassumingly handsome. The kind of handsome that sneaks up on you.

He clears his throat again. "It's, uh, in theater twelve. Let me just…" He reaches around me then to grab a few napkins for himself, though he's only carrying a medium soda.

No popcorn. No candy. No snacks.

Wait. *No snacks*?

Who doesn't get *snacks* at the movies? Who?

Self-conscious of my gluttony, I back away, wielding my embarrassing armload of junk food, face flaming hot. "I guess I should go find myself a seat. Yeah. I should go do that. The previews have probably already started and those are my favorite part…"

Stop talking Daphne!

Dexter nods and grapples for a few more napkins.

Oh brother; between the two of us, we have enough napkins to last us through Armageddon.

"Alright, well…" We both move gracelessly at the same time, in the same direction, doing that awkward sidestepping dance you do when you're trying to get around someone, but failing miserably.

"Here, let me at least carry something for you," Dexter offers, reaching to take the beverage tray out of my hands.

"Thank you." I laugh nervously, a horrible hot, furious blush creeping up my neck. "We go this way, I guess."

Walking towards the same hallway, it's obvious neither of us knows what the proper etiquette is when you run into someone at the movie theater when you're flying solo, and seeing the same movie. I'm aware of his every movement; every sidelong glance he surreptitiously gives me along the way.

Without speaking, we lumber down the endless, empty hallway, kernels from my popcorn bucket occasionally falling weightlessly to the carpet below. I look behind me down at the trail; I'm *such* a Gretel.

When we reach theater twelve, Dexter beats me to the door, his arm shooting out to grab the door handle, pulling it open, and waiting for me to walk through first. It's such a gentlemanly thing to do.

Something a date would do, I can't help but muse with longing.

The theater is packed, dark and—dammit, the previews have started! Disappointed, my eyes scan row after occupied row, seeking out in the dim one empty spot—*any* empty spot *not* near the front. I would rather poke my eye out with a stick than sit in the front row, and luckily, I find several halfway up.

I *feel* Dexter hesitate on the steps as he approaches me from behind, just as I sense him internally debating his options; should he say good-bye and go in search of his own seat? Or should he tag along and sit with me, not knowing if he'll be welcome?

How do I know he's thinking this? Easy. Because I'm feeling it, too. Should I invite him to sit next to me?

Would that be awkward? Probably, but wouldn't it be worse knowing he's a few seats behind me, staring at the back of my head?

Slowly, guided by the illuminated track lighting on the stairs, I climb step after step. Ascending to the middle row, eyes seeking—scanning in the dark, until…

There, three rows up, are two seats.

Together.

What were the odds?

Over my shoulder I softly whisper, "Those?"

"Sure."

Together we shimmy our way towards the empty seats, making apologies, sidestepping purses, popcorn buckets, and legs in the dimly lit space.

Once we're seated, settled in, Dexter removes his pea coat, and I watch him unhook each double toggle button from the corner of my eye. His heavy coat comes off and the woodsy, male smell of him reaches my sensitive nose.

Good lord he smells freaking fantastic. Like a fresh shower and fresh air and wintergreen toothpaste.

The truth blindsides me: I'm *insanely* attracted to this guy.

He's such a dork.

But *so*, so cute.

I stuff a handful of popcorn in my mouth to occupy myself—it weighs down my tongue like sandpaper—and when I crunch down, the speakers in the theater choose *that* moment to go dead silent, filling the silence around us with the sound of my chewing.

Mortified, I pause.

Chew.

Pause.

Oh my god, I'm so loud.

Chew.

I give Dexter a weak, popcorn-filled smile before my head falls back on the headrest and I smother a groan by shoving more popcorn in my face.

I hate myself right now.

Dexter

Daphne Winthrop.

The woman I spent half my weekend stalking on social media after meeting her at Ripley's Wine Bar because—let's face it—she is beautiful.

She's also way out of my league.

Outgoing, charismatic and sweet, I try not to watch as she nervously shovels handful after handful of buttered popcorn into her gullet from that giant bucket, and ignore the sidelong glances from her piercing green eyes.

The brightest green eyes I've ever seen in person.

God, she must think I'm a freaking loser.

I mean—coming to a movie alone, on a Saturday night? And StarGate of all things.

Christ.

Why couldn't it have been something cool, like Star Wars or Planet of the Apes?

For a split second I want to lean over and ask Daphne what *she's* doing here alone, but think better of it; she looked mortified when I approached her at the condiments counter, but really—I *did* need those napkins.

In front of us, the movie previews roll on. Holiday, comedy and zombie Coming Attractions quickly flash on the two-story mega screen below but I'm not paying one goddamn bit of attention. Nope. Instead of being riveted on the digital display, my traitorous eyes spend their time stealthily sneaking peeks at Daphne.

They trail her movements when she finally sets the large tub of popcorn on the hard, concrete floor at our feet. They watch as she unzips her puffer vest, shrugging out of it then twisting her body to drape the vest over the back of her seat. Even in the shadowy theater, I notice her breasts strain against the fabric of her fuzzy lavender sweater when she arches her back.

Her breasts, her breasts.

Shit, what am I doing staring at her breasts?

Getting turned on, that's what.

I haven't gotten laid since I broke it off with my ex-girlfriend Charlotte eighteen months ago, and haven't had a real date in over ten months; in case anyone wanted to fact check the math, that's roughly three hundred and four days of missed opportunities. Give or take.

And yes—I counted.

Daphne leaves her gray winter hat on, her long brown hair frames one of the prettiest fucking heart-shaped faces I've ever seen, and shines glossy beneath the changing lights of the big screen.

Black framed glasses she hadn't had on the other night lend a stark contrast to the sexy, confident Daphne who was out with her friends at Ripley's Wine Bar. Don't get me wrong; she was nice enough—but that Daphne wouldn't ordinarily give me the time of day.

This Daphne… she's better.

Casual. *Soft*. Approachable.

Plus, she came to fucking StarGate alone on a Saturday night. Who does that?

I mean—besides nerds like me.

Not beautiful girls like Daphne, with full social calendars. Girls with *great* bodies and better personalities. Fun loving. Girls who have guys lined up for their phone numbers—and I would know, because I saw it with my own eyes last weekend.

I give her another curious glance, wondering why someone like her isn't on a date tonight. Me? That one is easy: I'm perpetually put in the Friend Zone because I'm *nice*. Easy going. A commitment kind of guy that doesn't take the time to date around, I'm more likely to be found chaperoning my kid sisters school dance than asking someone on a date.

So, I get why *I'm* here alone—but why is she?

Her head turns and our eyes meet when she bends to grab her popcorn bucket off the floor. In the dark, I see her mouth curve into a friendly smile; Daphne's eyes rest on me a few steady heartbeats before she turns her attention back to the movie screen. Her hand digs in the giant tub of popcorn like she's rooting around for buried treasure.

She pops a kernel in her open mouth.

Chews.

Swallows.

"Want some?" She offers in a whisper, holding the tub between us.

I don't—but I'm also smart enough to know that when a pretty girl offers you something—*you take it.* "Sure, thanks."

She beams at me in the dark. A friendly, *platonic* smile.

Platonic: story of my life.

However, I'm not complaining twenty-minutes later when Daphne is frantically seizing my upper arm as an enemy ship onscreen (an enemy of Planet Dakara) launches an attack against Colonel O'Neil. In the distance, explosives go off, and a spacecraft is blasted into smithereens.

It's loud, bloody, and pretty fucking intense.

Daphne gasps when someone onscreen is violently shot, her fingers wrapping tighter around my bicep. Another blast and she buries her face in the shoulder of my plaid, flannel shirt.

A tad melodramatic?

Yes.

Do I give a shit?

Hell no.

Without hesitating, my neck dips down and I inhale, giving her a quick whiff. She smells like heaven; I mean, if heaven smelt like butter and chocolate.

"Can I look now?" Comes her muffled voice. She peeks up at the screen with one eye. "Is it safe to come out?"

"Yeah, it's safe," my chest rumbles with laughter.

Daphne sits up then, still holding my forearm.

"Sorry about that. Sometimes I get a little…" Her hand unnecessarily presses down the sleeve of my shirt to smooth out wrinkles that don't exist, and then—is it my imagination, or are her fingers running the length of my forearm? I swear she just gave it a squeeze.

Biting her lower lip, she shoots me an innocent smile in the dark, causing my heart to do some weird shit inside my chest.

Not to mention the stirring of *other things* in my pants.

If I was a girl, I might sigh.

Daphne Winthrop may just be the girl of my dreams.

Two

Daphne

Not going to lie: I barely saw *a single minute* of that movie.

Why?

Obviously I was distracted by Dexter.

Judging by the way he sniffed my hat when I had my head buried in his shoulder, I suspect he didn't see much of the movie, either.

In fact, I suspect a great *many* things about Dexter: such as his need for punctuality. He *looks* like he's always on time. I know you shouldn't judge a book by its cover, but his wearing a sweater vest and dress shirt to the bar last weekend lends me to believe he's no stranger to buttoned up and slightly stuffy.

I suspect he thrives on structure and order.

I suspect he probably takes life a bit *too* seriously.

A little too lanky, a little too quiet, and tad too aloof, he's hardly the kind of guy a girl writes home about. Dexter is definitely not the kind of guy that inspires fantasies in a young woman—sexual or otherwise.

And yet…

When the credits roll at the end, we stay seated, watching name after name scroll across the giant screen down in front. I turn my head towards Dexter and ask, "What'd you think about the part when they found the interstellar teleportation device?"

I'm such a nerd sometimes.

"Uh, hello. Not gonna lie; I kind of *want* one of those now and I'm not ashamed to admit it," he says as the wall sconces in the room illuminate the cavernous room, the people around us rising and heading towards the exits.

"We could battle if we both had light sabers."

"That's Stars Wars," he points out.

"So?"

"You can't mix Universes," He says in a *duh* kind of tone. Like I should know better.

I let out a long, dramatic sigh. "True. But you're probably just saying that because you don't want me to Princess Leia your ass. I would *destroy* you."

Dexter laughs, tipping his head back against the cushioned seat. "Are you shitting me? I'd *pay* to see you dressed as Princess Leia."

My eyes must get wide because he clamps his lips shut and looks away, embarrassed.

We sit in compatible silence a few seconds before I break it. "Isn't it crazy how twenty years ago, the technology in this movie was cutting edge?"

This perks him up. "Right? Imagine how incredible the movie would be if they remade it."

"I was thinking the same thing!"

"Don't judge me, but I have a small army of Star Wars Storm Troopers on my desktop at work. My sisters gave them to me for Christmas a few years ago. They look so bad ass on my computer."

I sit up straighter in my seat, interested. "Where do you work?"

"I'm in wealth management at a firm downtown. Right on Michigan Avenue. What about you?" Dexter asks as he removes the plastic lid from his soda, shakes the ice around, and tips his head back for a drink. A small bead of liquid glistens, wet, on his bottom lip, and I stare.

Oblivious to my ogling, he licks it off, daring my eyes not to follow the movement of his tongue.

"Daphne?" He waves a hand in front of my face. "Hello?"

"I'm sorry, you were asking where I work?"

He replaces the lid on his soda and laughs around the straw. "Yeah, where do you work?"

What I want to say is, "At the corner of *Get Inside My Pants and Let's Make Out…*" but what I *actually say* is: "I'm about ten minutes from here, at a boutique PR firm; Dorser & Kohl Marketing. I've been with them since I graduated and absolutely love it."

God, I am so boring.

We stare at each other then, two matching stupid grins on our faces. Dexter's smile gets wider when my teeth bite down on my bottom lip to stop the nervous giggle bubbling up from inside me.

Just then, overhead lights flood the theater, and a teenage crew comes in to clean, bustling in loudly with brooms and dustpans. One teenager noisily drags a garbage can behind him, so Dexter and I have no choice but to grudgingly remove our butts from the cushiony theater chairs and rise to our feet, collect our jackets and garbage, and make towards the exit.

Well, mostly *my* garbage since I was the only one stuffing my face with snacks.

"This was fun," he says as we trudge down the bright hallway, into the crowded lobby. "I'm glad I ran into you."

I feel my face heat. "Yeah, me too." I pause in front of the bathroom, gesturing. "Would you mind waiting? I have to…"

Pee.

"Here, let me hold these for you." Dexter takes the tub of popcorn out of my hands, my water bottle, purse, and candy wrappers. "Do you wanna toss any of this in the trash?"

He is *so* sweet and nice.

"Sure. If you don't mind. Wait! Maybe keep the popcorn?"

I'll munch on that in the car.

A few minutes later, I'm washing my hands and rejoining Dexter, who holds my puffer vest out and open to assist me into it, and I pivot so I can slide my arms through the holes.

Sweet and nice and a *gentleman.*

A trifecta.

"This was fun," he repeats when I turn to face him. I look him up and down, watching as he slips into his heavy wool coat. His shoulders might not be wide and athletic, but I can tell they're lean and fit. I watch, riveted, as his masculine fingers deftly work the toggle buttons. They're long, strong, and male.

Unexpectedly, in my mind, I'm picturing them running slowly under the hem of my sweater, over my bare stomach, and up my—

Crap. And here I thought Tabitha was the one with a vivid, sexy imagination. Or maybe I need to go reread her sexy romance novel. Again. For the fifth time.

Glancing away, I try to keep my dirty thoughts at bay. I mean, *Jesus*! What the hell am I *doing*, goggling the poor guy's hands like they're sexual objects?

If only he knew.

Raising my hands to my cheeks, I find them flaming hot: a common theme tonight.

My eyes continue tracking his movements; he pulls the winter hat out of his pocket, drawing it down over his mop of hair. His nose twitches, shifting his glasses into place; a move I find incredibly adorable, if not a tad dorky.

Swallowing hard, I smile. "It really was fun. It was nice having company for a change. I usually…" I draw in a breath. "Normally I come watch these old Sci-Fi movies, um. Alone."

Dexter shifts his feet, and I look down at the brown dress shoes more suited for the office than a casual night at the cinema.

"Uh, so." Dexter takes a deep breath, stuffing his hands into the pockets of his coat. Exhales out. "So maybe…" He pauses to push up those tortoiseshell frames with the tip of his finger.

This is it. He's going to ask me on a date.

I lean towards him, bucket of popcorn tipping, anticipation making my body hum. "Yes?"

Does my voice sound breathy? Over eager? Shoot. Cool it Daphne; bring the desperation down a notch.

Dexter hesitates, rocking back on his heels. "So maybe—"

"Dex, sweetie, is that *you*?" A shrill female voice interrupts his entreaty, causing us both to twist around, surprised at the woman approaching us at a hastened pace. Short with sandy blonde hair, the woman looks around my mother's age and is sporting a wide, toothy grin. "I thought that was you! What a pleasant surprise."

She envelopes him in a full contact hug, her arms squeezing.

"Aunt Bethany." He sounds pained when she finally peels herself away. "I'm surprised to see you. Who are you here with so late?"

"Late?" She laughs, loud and tinkly, and checks her watch. "It's only eleven forty-five on a Saturday night! I'm old but not *that* old." Aunt Bethany's eyebrows raise when focusing her attention on me, intense gaze alive.

Mischievous.

Her pink lips form an 'O' of glee.

"I don't mean to intrude on your *date*. I just wanted to come over and say hello." Aunt Bethany scrutinizes me with wide, interested brown eyes; not in a negative way. No. Quite the opposite—she's so excited she almost looks euphoric. Ready to burst. "Dexter sweetie, are you going to introduce me to your *friend*?"

She says the word friend innocuously enough, but what she really means is: *friend*-friend. As in: girlfriend.

Dexter sticks his hands back into the pockets of his thick coat. "Aunt B, this is my friend Daphne. Daphne, this is my mom's youngest sister. My Aunt B."

Bethany wastes no time extending her open arms towards me and pulling me in for a hug, which is super awkward since I'm still clutching my popcorn. Her embrace pins my arms to the side before she squeezes the life out of me, thereby crushing my bucket.

I'm positive a few kernels fall to the ground.

"So good to meet you," I croak into her curly hair, gasping for air. Sneaking a glance over her shoulder at Dexter's stricken face, I try desperately not to laugh.

I fail.

Aunt B gives me one more squeeze before releasing me, then steps back to look me up and down with a sigh. "You are gorgeous. Those green eyes are stunning. Dex, she's gorgeous."

Dexter blushes furiously, removing a hand from his pocket to adjust his glasses while his Aunt continues fussing, oblivious to his obvious discomfort.

"Where has he been *hiding* you! Never mind, don't answer that; it's none of my business. The real question is, are you bringing her to Grace's engagement party next weekend? Wait, don't answer that!"

I don't want to embarrass Dexter further by reminding his Aunt we're just friends; one's who have only met twice—not that the first time at Ripley's Wine Bar counts since we hardly spoke.

So instead, I go with, "Um."

"Has his *mother* met you yet?" Bethany asks, eyes sparkling. She is completely giddy.

I cast a helpless look at Dexter; he shakes his head, so I answer truthfully. “No ma’am.”

“No ma’am.” She parrots. “*Ugh,* I love that. You sound positively southern. Say something else. Say *y’all.*”

Laughing, I fake a southern accent (which I happen to be really good at) for his eccentric Aunt, whom I’ll never see again in my life. I put a hand on my hip for added effect and wave my other hand about airily.

“How y’all doin’? When life hands you lemons, put them in your sweet tea and thank Gawd you’re from the South.” I fan myself, channeling my inner Scarlet O’Hara and getting into the role. “*Fiddle dee-dee*!”

Beside me, Dexter groans, throwing his head back and staring at the ceiling. *Oh my God*, he mouths toward Heaven, running a hand down his face. “Please don’t encourage her.”

My eyes fly to the cords of his lean neck. His jawline. His Adam’s apple. I remove them swiftly when Aunt B follows my line of vision. A knowing smirk crosses her lips.

Crap.

Busted.

His aunt titters gleefully, speaking to her nephew. “Wait until I rub it in your mother’s face that I met your girlfriend before she did! She’s going to have a cow from the jealously. A *cow.*”

“Aunt Bethany, we’re not dating. Daphne is *not* my girlfriend.” The look he shoots me is apologetic. “Sorry Daphne, I didn’t mean to say it like that.”

Another blush warms my cheeks.

Bethany brushes him off. “*Ach*, you kids today and your secrecy. Why hide it? Why are you all so afraid of commitment? Please don't tell me you're on The Tinder? That's a trolling site for hook-ups and, you know."

She clucks her tongue, lecturing us on the downsides of dating in the 21st Century. "All you kids do is put everything on-the-line, but you don't want to commit to a relationship."

We *must* look horrified, because she takes one look at us and busts out laughing.

"Fine, fine, I won't say anything if you're trying to keep it a secret. Shhhh, my lips are sealed." She makes another shushing sound, those brown eyes fixated on me. "I don't know if Dex *told* you, but our family tree is full of nuts. I don't blame him for keeping you a secret. Once the family finds out, it's Good night Eileen."

Good night, Eileen? I'm not… What the hell does that even mean?

She jabbers on. "Anywho, I better get going; my friend Brenda ran to the bathroom and she'll have a hissy fit if I'm not standing where she left me when she walks out. Goodness, I can't wait to tell Little Erik I bumped into you."

Dexter snorts and turns to me with a grin. "*Little* Erik is my younger cousin. He kind of idolizes me," he bashfully informs me. "He's named after my Uncle Erik—Big Erik and Little Erik, get it? He's also over six feet tall."

"We like the irony of calling him *little*," Bethany snickers. "It's my favorite joke. Everyone is always expecting a toddler. My poor Sadie inherited all the short genes." She gives her theater soda a shake, back and forth, swirling around the ice inside the cup.

"Sadie is your daughter?" I inquire politely, but genuinely interested.

His Aunt chatters on with great enthusiasm. "Yes! Nineteen going on forty-five; she'd rather stay home and *read* than go out with her friends. You'll meet her at Grace's party if she comes home from school that weekend."

"Aunt B—"

"Oh, don't worry, I'm not gonna tell a soul. Just pretend you never bumped into me." She leans in close, like we're conspiring. "Can you just give me a little nibble of the details though? Where did you two meet? One of those dating sites? MySpace?"

"MySpace isn't a thing anymore, Aunt B."

"Oh. Bumble App?"

Dexter shakes his head. "How do you know about—you know what? Forget I asked."

His composed exterior fading, I put my hand on his forearm to calm him, and he glances down at it before looking into my eyes.

"It's fine," I intone to him quietly. To Bethany I say, "Aunt B, while we're *not* a couple, Dexter and I did meet last weekend when we were both out with friends."

"I was out with Elliot's friends." He supplies reluctantly. "Elliot is a cousin."

Aunt Bethany scrunches up her face. "Elliot? Is he single again? I thought he was dating Kara."

"Nope. Single."

"Good. Kara can do better."

Dexter chuckles, a smile finally tipping his lips. "Yeah, that's probably true."

"Well," Aunt B sighs. "Like I said, I better run." She gives me a once over, eyes shining. "Hold on tight to this one, young lady. He's a keeper."

Daphne: *You're never going to believe who I ran into at the movie last night.*

Tabitha: *Hold up. First tell me who you went to the movies with, and what did you see?*

Daphne: *StarGate. And I went alone, but that's not my point.*

Tabitha: *You went to another movie alone? I told you to call if you did that! I would have met you there. No man left behind and all that.*

Daphne: *You were on a date. Plus, I repeat: it was Stargate—you hate SciFi.*

Tabitha: *Like that matters. I hate when you go to the movies alone. Plus, I would have sacrificed Collin. He loves that crap.*

Daphne: *I do love you for that offer <3 Anyway... the news is that I ran into Dexter Ryan. He was alone, too, so.... (dot dot dot)*

Tabitha: *Shut. Up. He is such a dork.*

Daphne: *Don't call him a dork! He's really sweet and he saved me from myself. And my giant bucket of pop-corn.*

Tabitha: *What is it with you and popcorn? I can nev-er figure it out...*

Daphne: *It's delicious.*

Tabitha: *Alright, so you saw Dexter. I take it you sat with him? Was he as dull as he looks? He's nice and all, but kind of boring, don't you think?*

Daphne: *No. He wasn't dull. He was sweet and adorkable.*

Tabitha: *You know, I should write a book about a hot nerd with a dirty mouth and a hot bod. Would you read it?*

Daphne: *Shut. Up.*

Daphne: *And yes. Yes I would read it...*

Three

Dexter

"Halyard Capitol Investments and Securities, Dexter Ryan speaking." My brisk voice is clear, crisp, and to the point.

"Dexter Ryan, why are you answering your own phone?" My mother's demand shouts at me from the other end of the line. "Where's your secretary?"

For some reason, my mom loves boasting the fact that my firm appointed me my own secretary. Drives me crazy.

I sigh, swiveling in my desk chair towards the window and stare outside at the pond. "She's at lunch, Mom. Occasionally I unchain her from the desk so she can eat."

"I'm going to ignore your sarcasm young man, because I know you're at work and don't have time for a lecture."

I know there's a reason she's calling…

"Who's Daphne?"

And there it is.

"She's a friend."

Just a friend; a beautiful, vibrant, and funny friend.

"That's not what your Aunt Bethany said. She said you had a *girl*friend. Why haven't we met her yet? Quite frankly, when she told us she ran into you, my feelings were hurt."

Another thing my mother loves? Guilt trips.

"Your feelings were hurt? Come on, Mom. Bethany was totally over exaggerating to get a rise out of you." I pick up a pencil and start doodling circles on a notepad. "Wait. Who's this *we*? What *we* are you talking about? Who did Aunt B tell?"

My mom hesitates a heartbeat, then drives home the kill. "Your sisters and I, Aunt Donna and Aunt Tory. We all happened to be together when B called."

The Gossip Network of Ryan Women: once those five catch a whiff of chatter, you might as well rent a billboard in Times Square to broadcast your secrets.

Fuck.

Exasperated, I run a hand through my hair, tugging at the thick strands and releasing a loud puff of air. I can feel the ends sticking up in several places, but I'll worry about that later.

"Mom. I'm sorry you're upset, but I'm telling the truth. Daphne is just my friend. In fact—we've only met twice. I don't know what B told you, but we're not dating."

My mom makes a sniveling sound, and I know she's digging deep for a tear. "Dexter Phillip, don't lie to me. It hurts my feelings."

I lean back in my desk chair, balancing on the back wheels, and stare up at the ceiling. Breathe in and out. "Mom, what reason would I have to lie?"

Another sniffling sound, followed by a scoff. "You tell me."

Drama, drama, drama.

"I—"

"B tells us you're bringing her to Grace's engagement party; she was *rather* pleased to rub the news in. You know I hate when she finds things out first; and about my own son?"

"Mom—"

"It would have been nice if I'd meet your girlfriend first, don't you think?"

Resigned, another long puff of air leaves my throat, and I blow it out into the receiver. "Technically, yeah."

"Bethany said she's just stunning. A petite thing with the sweetest little Southern accent."

A Southern accent? *Jesus Christ*.

My mom continues. "I'm not pleased you kept this from us and I had to find out from B, but Daphne *does* sound lovely."

"She is," slips out before I can stop myself.

Mom sighs one of those wistful, breathless sighs woman breathe when they're overcome with joy. I roll my eyes and watch as the landscapers outside walk back-and-forth across the parking lot with leaf blowers. Another drives a riding lawn mower so fast through the grass it's like he's vying to race Danica Patrick's NASCAR.

Grass flies everywhere.

"Come a little early, please, so she can meet us before we head into the party. I won't get the chance to talk to her when we're there. Gracie's invited over a hundred people. Tory told me it's turned into quite the circus."

My cousin Grace has always been high-maintenance, so this news doesn't surprise me in the least. Her brother, Elliot, is the dickhead who stood me up at the Wine Bar last weekend.

"Come early? Uh… that might be hard to swing. I'm pulling extra hours next Saturday."

Mom sighs loudly, long-suffering.

"Just make sure you tell her it's formal. I assume you're wearing a suit?"

Silence.

"Dexter, are you listening?"

I glance down at the Blue Chip stock portfolios stacked on my desk. The three million plus dollar contract, open to its annual shareholder's report, sits atop another one point five-million-dollar portfolio I manage.

Millions of dollars, dividends, and reserves; all whose investment future earnings rest in *my* capable hands while my *mother* lectures me on the phone about a girlfriend I don't even have.

This irony is not lost on me.

"Yes, I'm listening."

"Formal attire." Pause. "And Dexter?"

"Yeah?" The pen in my hand stops drawing circles, and I flick it across the desk. It hits the hard surface of the wall, ricochets then falls off the far edge with a satisfying clatter.

"We're happy for you honey."

I can only grunt out a reply.

This is ridiculous.

I've been staring at my phone for the better half of an hour, debating my options about whether or not to call Daphne.

I mean, other than the fact that this is a horrible fucking idea, why not pick up the phone and call?

So:

I hunt her number down online and call her at work to propose this ridiculous scheme.

Or.

I can *not* call Daphne, inventing an elaborate explanation for her absence to appease my meddlesome family.

Or.

I can do the honorable thing and show up to the engagement party alone; tell everyone the truth. There would be no shame in that, simple misunderstanding that it was.

But if I'm being honest…

I want to see her again.

Not gonna lie.

Fucked up as it sounds, I'm willing to concoct an elaborate charade and look like an ass just to see her again.

I think about my mom and my sisters, then my dickhead cousin Elliot, whose guaran-goddamn-tee'd to have his ex-girlfriend Kara at the party hanging all over him, even though he's broken up with her a few times.

See, Elliot subscribes to the motto *man-kind isn't meant for monogamy.* His past girlfriends, historically, eventually find issue with this motto, and once they do—they typically begin the process of trying to change him (ie. get him to be faithful). Immediately getting themselves dumped.

Elliot has dumped Kara twice, once at a family function, and once before Valentine's Day just so he wouldn't have to pay for a fancy dinner on the 14th.

They got back together on the 15th.

Kara, who has huge surgically enhanced tits, bleach blonde hair, and applies her make up with a painter's palette knife. Kara, who has the IQ of a plastic Barbie doll—maybe even lower. Kara, who giggles like an eight-year-old. My point is: Elliot thinks he's *hot shit* because he's dating a woman that looks like a Playboy centerfold.

Kara's elevator might not go all the way to the top floor, but Elliot thinks she's smoking hot and his opinion is the only one that counts.

I guess I'd feel like hot shit too if I liked parading around cheap looking woman.

Which I do not.

My last girlfriend, Charlotte, was a paralegal at a law firm whose offices occupy the top floor in our building. Classy and serious, we both ultimately wanted the same things out a relationship—marriage, kids, and a house outside of the city.

But there was always something missing; something exciting.

Everything with Char was… *fine*. Predictable.

Vanilla.

Boring?

Missionary sex, buttoned-up cardigan sweaters—even on the weekends—unless she was wearing her Northwestern sweatshirt to do her gardening. Yawn.

Char was cute, if not a little… plain. Straight brown

bob trimmed exactly every six weeks, serious brown eyes, she reserved her mega-watt smiles for the partners in her law firm, her close friends, and occasionally—me.

Bottom line: the sight of her entering a room didn't get my dick hard.

The staid climate of our relationship wasn't doing it for me anymore. There was never any anticipation. Never any spontaneity.

Never any fun.

Sure, I've been on a few dates since breaking it off with Charlotte; with more quiet, serious girls. Girls who sipped wine and stopped at one glass. Girls who counted networking as a hobby, drank three double shot Starbucks a day so they could work late, and gave tight smiles instead of laughing.

Fucking depressing.

And for whatever reason, my asshole cousin finds it *hilarious* to bring up my relationship status at every opportunity. No idea why. Like having a date is supposed to define my character. Like having a date makes me more masculine.

Honestly, I'd rather be completely alone and a decent guy, than a douchebag with a shitty date.

Elliot is a dickhole.

My thoughts stray to Daphne, her long silky hair and green eyes. The black framed glasses. Her glossy pink lips tipped up into a sly smile. Her sexy, easy, musical laugh.

I palm the computer mouse, scrolling it around its pad, waiting for my Dundler Mifflin screensaver to disappear, and pull up Google.

Type in Dorser & Kohl Marketing.

The firm's website pops up in the search results, and I

click on the link, scrolling through the site for employee profiles until I find hers.

Daphne Winthrop: Junior Vice President of Public Relations.

Buttoned to the collar in a blouse, she's leaning against a stone building, arms crossed. Black blazer and pressed slacks, profile shot is classy, conservative and professional.

I read her bio; Age, 26. Graduated from State with a BA in Business. Alum of two professional fraternity organizations. Volunteer coordinator for a women's shelter. Hobbies: travel, skiing and reading.

It says nothing about StarGate, alternative Universes, or fangirling over vintage Sci-Fi movies. In fact, everything about her bio reads as 'my usual type.'

Exactly my type.

Only I know differently.

My hand hovers over the mouse, and I scroll until I find her contact information. Eight seconds later I'm staring, in color, at her phone number. Should I call? Text? Or send an email?

What the hell am I going to say? *Hi Daphne, this is Dexter Ryan. Remember me from last night? I'm going to need you at that engagement party my aunt was yammering on-and-on about. Turns out my family is riding my ass. They're driving me crazy, and you'd be doing me a huge favor if you pretended to be my girlfriend for an evening…*

Right; because that doesn't sound fucked up.

And yet, I don't abandon the idea entirely—not with my buddy Collin running around in my head shouting 'Balls to the wall, Dex. Balls to the fucking walls!' Collin, who pursued his girlfriend relentlessly, and who doesn't give a shit what people think of him.

He'd call her without hesitating and expect me to do the same. Shit, he'd dial the phone for me.

But unlike Collin's girlfriend Tabitha, *this* gorgeous girl is not going to want me to call her.

No way.

I palm the phone in my hand and push the glasses up the bridge of my nose, leaning back in my desk chair and swiveling it around a few times before setting the phone back down. My computer pings with an email notification and I rotate my chair back towards the desktop, click open the message, scanning it absentmindedly.

Noting that it's just a follow up on an account I just picked up from a competitor's firm, I flag it as priority, but close the window.

I can't focus.

Frustrated, I raise both hands and run my fingers through my thick brown hair, shake my head and let out a loud groan.

"Dammit!" I curse loudly.

Loud enough that my secretary Vanessa sticks her head in my office door.

Shit.

"Is everything okay in here, Sir?" Worry is etched across her face, but that's nothing new. A few weeks ago, Vanessa fucked up some client files and almost lost us a major account; these days her paranoia with the risk of being fired is at an all-time high—despite my constant re-assurances that her job is secure.

For the moment, anyway.

"No. Sorry about that. Everything is fine."

Vanessa stands idly for a few seconds, her heavily

mascaraed lashes sticking together briefly as she blinks rapidly at me from the doorway. Tapping the steel doorframe with the palm her hand, so nods slowly. "Sir, do you need anything while I'm up?"

My lips compress in a thin line; I hate when she calls me Sir. It makes me feel like an old man. "Nope. I'm good."

Her coal rimmed eyes narrow. "Alright, if you say so…"

Grabbing my phone, I click open the NEW MESSAGE tab and hit COMPOSE. Then I stare at the small screen, thumbs hovering above the touch screen keypad far too long.

Me: *Daphne, this is Dexter. This might seem really random, but I was hoping you'd be available this week at some point for a quick lunch or coffee?*

Before second-guessing myself, I hit SEND, tap out more messages to random co-workers, switch the ringer to 'vibrate,' and push the phone to the corner of my desk in an attempt to forget about it. It lays there, unmoving for the next six minutes.

I flip it over to check the display screen.

Nothing.

Three seconds later, I check it again.

Still nothing.

This is ridiculous—what the hell am I doing? Not only is this sudden onslaught of nerves uncharacteristic, I have shit tons of work to do with little time to waste. Stacks of paperwork with *millions* of dollars at stake, and here I sit, staring at my goddamn cell phone as if I'm expecting it to sprout wings and fly.

Frustrated by my own insecurities, I pull the top drawer of my desk open and toss the phone in, slamming it shut with resounding bang.

Another four minutes go by and I've accomplished nothing but listening in the silence for my phone's telltale rumble.

Another three, and I've manage to wad up eight pieces of printer paper and basketball toss them to the corner trash can.

Five of them land on the carpet.

I'm about to stand and toss them in the garbage when a low buzzing inside the drawer halts my actions, the vibrating sends my phone thumping spastically inside the hollow wooden interior.

Dammit. I forgot to silence it.

My pulse accelerates.

I lean back in my desk chair, looking into the hall for Vanessa, paranoid— like I'm about to do something criminal and don't want to get caught—before pulling the drawer open and retrieving my sleek phone.

One new message.

It's her.

A bead of sweat actually forms on my brow, and I wipe it with the sleeve of my white dress shirt before swiping open the message center.

Daphne: *Will today work?*

My eyes damn near bug out of my skull. Today?

She wants to meet *today*?

I recall a lecture given to me by my twin, fifteen-year

old sisters about the hazards of responding to a text message immediately: *you just, like, don't do it unless you're a loser*.

I disregard their instructions.

It's stupid advice.

Me: *Yeah, today is great. What time and place work best for you?*

Her reply, too, is almost immediate.

I grin stupidly.

Daphne: *I can probably cut out of work early and bring some things home. So how does two o'clock sound? Do you know where Blooming Grounds is*?

Blooming Grounds is the coffee shop where my childhood friend, Collin, and his girlfriend Tabitha, first began their relationship. It also happens to be less than a block from the offices of Halyard Capitol Investments & Securities.

It will take me five minutes to walk there.

Me: *Two works fine. I will see you at Blooming Grounds.*

Me: *Wait. What can I have waiting for you when you get there?*

Daphne: *How about an iced latte and a blueberry scone?*

Me: *Will do. See you at 2*

Daphne: *LOL*

I stare at that last message from Daphne: LOL.

LOL?

What the hell is that supposed to mean? Is she laughing at something I said? Does she not want me to meet her at two? How the hell am I supposed to interpret *L-O-freaking-L*?

Shit.

I'm twenty-six fucking years old and I need a goddamn girl translator. A nervous knot forms in my stomach; she's either going to laugh in my face when she hears my proposal and tell me to fuck off, or…

I don't even want to think about the alternative.

Four

Daphne

I can’t stop watching the clock and counting down the minutes.

One o’clock.

One fifteen.

One twenty-three.

At one forty-five, I shut down my computer. Gathering my belongings, I stuff them in the leather tote I use as a briefcase, and head out to meet Dexter.

There’s a carefree little spring in my step as I walk out to my car—a pep that only intensifies with my heart beat when I make the quick drive to the coffee shop, sliding into a tight little parallel parking spot like a champ.

Nervously, I run a hand over my hair, smoothing down the fly-aways. Staring at my reflection in the mirrored sun visor, I wonder what it is about me that had Dexter hesitating to ask me out after the movie—I don't usually get push back from men when I want them to take me out; quite the opposite in fact.

I snap the mirrored sun visor down and grab my purse—a few brisk steps later I'm stepping through the door of Blooming Grounds. The funky interior assails my senses as I take in the eclectic vibe; miss-matched couches line the walls, large green velvet wing back chairs flank the fireplace that's the focal point of the room, and small intimate tables take up the rest of the space.

It's warm. Cozy.

I brush a few tendrils of my long, brown hair out of my face; it's pulled back in a loose chignon, an old-fashioned style that's messy yet sophisticated. Classy yet fun. It looks a whole hell of a lot more complicated than it actually is, and looks amazing.

I pat the back of it confidently letting my green eyes scan the coffee shop, easily finding Dexter seated at a sofa in the corner. Our eyes connect.

He rises.

I take him in from head to toe; a starched, white button down shirt is tucked into slate gray slacks, a slim blue/black and white necktie falling crisply to his waistline. He rakes a hand down that silk tie before adjusting a pair of black glasses; a move I've come to recognize as a nervous habit.

His lips tip into a crooked smile at my approach, and I weave through empty tables towards him.

"Hi," comes my breathless salutation.

"Thanks for coming." Dexter shoves both his hands in the pockets of his pants, then removes them—fidgeting as if he doesn't quite know what to do with himself. I find a spot on the sofa and sit, resting my purse on the worn, patchwork cushions.

Comfy.

He sits in the overstuffed chair across from me, spreading his legs wide and leaning forward with his elbows resting on his knees. He steeples his fingertips.

I try *not* to look between his legs—I really, *really* do—but I'm not gonna lie to you; I sneak a covert peek at his crotch, my face engulfed in flames when my eyes land on the outline of his… junk.

Holy shit, I can actually *see* it through the fabric of his pleated, conservative dress pants; the telltale bulge of his… *Oh my god.*

I am the absolute worst.

The. Worst.

A horrible, perverted human being.

Yup, it's official: Tabitha isn't the only one with a dirty mind.

Although… I am a single, warm-blooded female—one that likes guys and relationships and sex. Definitely sex.

Shooting Dexter a guilty smile, I busy myself, taking large sips from the straw in my latte, mentally chastising myself for having such a depraved mind.

I give the ice in my plastic cup a shake, unable to look him in the eye.

Poor guy doesn't have a clue.

"I'm just going to put this out there to save us time." Dexter takes a deep breath, and exhales. "I told my mom that you'd be at my cousin Grace's engagement party."

Before I can respond, he continues. "You met my Aunt Bethany—did she look like someone who was going to keep our little meeting at the theater a secret? No. The first thing she did from her car in the parking lot was call my mom, who was with my sisters and aunts. So. Yeah."

When he rakes his fingers through his hair, the ends stick up haphazardly.

"Normally I wouldn't commit you to something like that—I mean, we just met and who am I, right? A virtual stranger. Not someone you'd want to spend your weekend with, I get that."

My mouth opens to disagree, but he interrupts.

"I have this cousin Elliot who is a complete douche." My eyebrows go up—not from the word douche; but from *his* use of it. Dexter looks too clean cut and proper to be hurling out vulgarities. "It's getting really fucking old. When my mom called and put me on the spot, I didn't tell her no. So there you have it. I'm in something of a bind, and you're the only one who can help me out of it."

He unsteeples his hands, clasping them instead. "What do you say? Can you stand to spend the night with me as my fake date?"

Wait. Did Dexter just ask me out on a date? My heart skips a beat and I grin so hard my cheeks begin to ache.

"A date?"

Date? Date!

Oh!

"A fake date," he clarifies.

Oh.

"A *fake* date." I repeat.

"Precisely." He nods definitively. "Totally fake. Just drinks, dinner, and if I know my cousin Grace, probably some dancing—but nothing romantic on my end." His hands go up in surrender with a chuckle. "Promise."

Something inside of me deflates. That flare of excitement distinguishes.

I muster up a weak smile.

Oblivious, Dexter grins. "If you could just do me this *one* favor, it would be huge. I would owe you a favor. Maybe even manage your retirement account," he laughs again. "I could probably double your savings in under seven years."

He peers at me hopefully. Naively.

What idiots.

Him. Me. Both of us.

"So? What do you think?"

What do I think? What do I *think*?

I think it's a horrible, stupid, insulting idea. I'm hurt. Pissed. Confused.

So utterly disappointed.

I want to smack him.

He watches me expectantly, his eyes detailing the play of emotions across my face, pushing those black framed glasses up the bridge of his nose.

He looks so… pleased with his idea that my shoulders sag and I feel myself breaking down and giving in.

God, I'm such a sucker.

I make a show of checking the calendar on my phone, poke randomly at the keypad on my phone, and paste a *fake* grin on my face before announcing, "I don't have anything going on this weekend, so yeah. That would work."

He leans forward. "Really?"

"Sure. I'll do it." My brows furrow at his reaction. "Why do you look so surprised?"

The glasses get pushed up again. "I just assumed a girl like you would have plans. A date maybe."

"Like a *real* date as opposed to this *fake* one?" The dig makes those big, chocolate brown eyes widen, so I shrug it off with a joke. "Naw, unless you count me rooted to my couch Netflix and Chilling with my bad self." I recline back on the sofa and cross my legs. "Okay, we're doing this. So what's the plan?"

Dexter

My palms are sweating.

I glance over at Daphne in the passenger seat of my silver Audi, her eyes scanning the landscape as we roll past; houses and businesses becoming further and further apart as I navigate my way out of the city. The long column of her graceful neck is illuminated by the dim glow of street lights.

It's on the cooler side this evening, but Daphne's creamy shoulders are bare beneath a simple, baby blue halter-top thing with a pearl neckline. Tucked into a black, knee-length pencil skirt, the top has a bow at the collar, cream colored ribbons tail down her bare back.

Simple, black strappy heels. Toes painted a shiny dark red I couldn't help noticing when I picked her up, it's almost as if she put real effort into getting ready. The kind of effort a woman puts into a real date; a real date she's nervous and excited about.

That she anticipated.

I don't know what I was expecting to find when she eagerly swung the door open to her condo earlier, but it's safe to assume: this wasn't it.

She looks incredible. Sweet. Undeniably sexy.

Unattainable yet approachable.

My eyes drop to her tan legs. I want to call them glowing—but that's not right, is it? Glowing? Shit, I don't fucking know. They look freshly shaved and must feel *smooth* if the way she's running her palms around her knees is any indication; up and down her knees in slow circular motions, probably to torture me for coming up with this dumbass idea in the first place.

I give those legs another sidelong glance, trying to erase the desire I feel for her from altering my expression. It remains pleasant. Passive.

Another quick glance as Daphne idly traces her knee cap with the tip of a forefinger has me hoarsely clearing my throat because, *dammit, stop touching your legs.*

Tightening my grip on the steering column, I focus on the road and pull onto the highway, blowing out a pent up puff of air.

I should have just told my mom I wasn't bringing a date. Or been more firm in my resolve that Daphne is just a friend. But can someone be your friend when you've only met twice? I might not be a rocket scientist in the female department, but somehow, even I doubt it.

And yet here we are, on the way to an engagement party.

Where I'll no doubt make an ass of myself.

Her voice jolts me out of my contemplations. "Do you want to go over any details before we get there? Just in case anyone decides to grill us about how we met."

I stare out the windshield, nodding. "Sure. Great idea."

"Alright. I'll start." She pauses with a secret smile. "Let's say we met at a wine bar through mutual friends? That part at least is true… and our first date was the movies."

"StarGate?"

"Yes! Exactly. StarGate." Daphne is quiet for a few seconds, and I can tell that she's thinking. Can see it on her face when I chance a glance her way in the dark cab of my car. Biting down on her lower lip, she hums to herself before asking, "Where should our second date be?" Her head gives a shake, her long, loose brown hair swaying. "Wait. I meant, where should we *say* it was?"

I might be wicked smart, but I'm a guy, so I say, "Uh…"

Daphne laughs and her hand hits my thigh with a teasing tap. It lingers there before returning to her lap. "*Uh*? You're hopeless, do you know that?"

I stare down at my pants, at the thigh that's now singing beneath my dark gray slacks from her touch.

"Do you really think anyone is going to ask where we had our second date? I mean, a continuous line of questioning is kind of rude, don't you think?"

I snort. "That's not going to stop my cousin Elliot from asking shit tons of inappropriate questions. He has no boundaries."

Daphne tilts her head and studies me back in the dark. The lights from the center median on the highway illuminate the cab, her glossy lips shining—and like beacons in the night, my eyes are drawn to them. She licks them.

"Elliot sounds charming."

"He's not a bad guy—not really. He just has no filter."

"What about your other family. I'm kind of nervous to meet your mom and sisters. I'm going to feel horrible lying to them."

"Sorry about dragging you into this. I just think my mom wasn't in the frame of mind to believe me, and instead of arguing with her about having a girlfriend, it's seriously just easier to bring you. My mom hears what she wants to hear. As awkward as it's going to be for you, this is the story of my life."

"Awkward for me?"

"Yeah." I glance at her. "Faking it. Pretending to like me. Pretending to be attracted to me." With a self-deprecating chuckle, my finger pushes my black glasses up the bridge of my nose. "Let's see how good an actress you are."

I find the exit ramp.

Take a right at the light.

Pretend not to be affected by the downturn of her lips.

Daphne

Stupid boy.

I should tell him I don't *have* to pretend.

That I *am* attracted to him.

That I do like him.

That if he'd only asked me on a real date, I would have said yes.

Yes, Dexter, I'd love to go to dinner with you!

Yes, Dexter, I'd love to see another movie.

Yes, Dexter, I'd love to…

But instead, he asked me to be his fake girlfriend for one night. Nothing really but an escort—and an unpaid one at that.

I scoff miserably, wondering if he's thought of it that way at all.

Probably not.

I sigh, glancing over at him, the reflection from the street lights whizzing past us reflecting off his glasses, taking note of the way he's concentrating on the road. How he keeps checking his blind spots. How he turns his blinker on every time he changes lanes. How he steals glances at me when he thinks I'm not paying attention.

But that's where he's wrong.

I *am* paying attention.

Have been since I swung open the door of my apartment earlier, eyes damn near bugging out of my head at the sight of him standing there. Preppy. Professional. Nervous.

Wanting to rip his clothes off, beginning with his buttoned up blue dress shirt, I'd start by running my hands up under the rolled up cuffs of his shirt—over his pale but toned forearms.

Tucked into a pair of black pressed slacks, nothing has ever made me hotter than the site of a guy in…

Suspenders.

Yeah. *Suspenders* for God's sake.

I want to snap them.

Run my hands up his chest, under the length of them.

Slowly unbutton his shirt and push the suspenders down his arms—just to see the look on his face.

I train my lecherous eyes back out the window. "What did you tell your mom about me?"

His deep voice fills the cab of his spotlessly clean car. "Nothing much, to be honest. She was too busy chastising me for keeping you my dirty little secret—she didn't ask for specific details. All she knows is what my Aunt told her."

A dirty little secret sounds… delightful.

I sigh, wishing I had one.

In the quiet cab of his fancy car, I hear Dexter shrug. Turning so my head faces him, I brush a lock of hair out of my face. Beneath the lamplights on the street, his eyes follow the motion when my hand caresses the side of my face, swiping at my long curls. "Which is what? What did your aunt tell her?"

"Just the facts—that you were polite." Dexter hesitates. "That you're beautiful."

Beautiful; the word lodges itself in my brain and takes root there at the same time my stomach does a summersault; an unexpected, pleased, little flip-flop.

Beautiful. No one has ever called me that before.

Cute? Yes.

Wholesome? Yes.

Girl-next-door adorable? *Unfortunately.*

Does *Dexter* think I'm beautiful, too? I'm not asking to sound conceited, but it crossed my mind after he didn't ask me out that perhaps… he's not attracted to me. Maybe I'm not his type. Maybe he does truly just want to be friends. Play the doting boyfriend for one night—and one night only.

"And head's up—they all think you're Southern, so good luck with that."

"Trust me, I can manage to throw a few *y'alls* into the conversations. Give Aunt Bethany a cheap thrill."

"Oh, I'm sure you can." His grin is lopsided and amused.

"Sugar, y'all are in for a treat."

Dexter clears his throat. "So she knows that, but not much else. And of course, she thinks we've been dating awhile. Which… I apologize for."

I find myself saying, "It's okay," as we pull into the parking lot of a country club. Find myself nervously fussing with the hem of my skirt as he purposefully strides around to my side of the car after we park. Find myself go a little weak in the knees when his hand presses politely into the small of my back, guiding me towards the crowd of people inside.

And when I remove my jacket and he passes it to the coat check, that hand wraps itself around my waist.

I stiffen; but not from displeasure.

From the opposite.

Dexter notices.

"Is this okay? I think it would be weird if I didn't touch you, don't you?"

I do my best to nod, swallowing the lump in my throat. "It's fine. You're right, it would be weird. I mean, if I was your… *girl*friend you would touch me. Act familiar."

He blows out a puff of air—like he's psyching himself up. "Yes. Alright. Good." He babbles. "Just so we're on the same page."

"Dexter, it's fine. I don't mind you touching me." It's going to drive my hormones absolutely ca-ray-zy but, "Truly. I don't mind."

Hell no I don't mind. Not at all—quite the opposite actually.

My eyes roam back to the suspenders.

Ugh.

Excited with this new development, Dexter's stiff arm relaxes, his hand resting on my hip. "You can call me Dex if you want. That's what my friends and family call me."

Nope. Not gonna do it; not when the name Dexter rolls off the tip of my tongue like the last drop of wine from a glass, and gets me hot and bothered in all the wrong places.

I shoot him a cheeky grin. "Maybe. We'll see."

"Is our brother romantic?" One of Dexter's twin sisters asks, leaning on her elbows towards me as dinner plates are set in front of us by the servers. We arrived casually late and were immediately seated at a table for ten, except the rest of his family hasn't joined us yet; it's just myself, Dexter, and his enthusiastic little sisters.

"Tell us the truth." The twins request at the same time, in the same playful voice.

The twins—Lucy and Amelia—are mirror image identical and almost indistinguishable; dark blonde hair, cut into jaunty, matching bobs. Identical almond-shaped eyes. Freckles across the bridge of their noses. Identical smirks with identical dimples.

You get the picture.

Tonight they're wearing the same dress, in different colors, and watching me across the table with such intensity I squirm in my seat. It's disconcerting and a tad bit creepy.

Especially since there's two of them.

"Is he romantic?" I exaggerate a blissful sigh. "Yes. So romantic, aren't you babe?" I pat his hand.

Dexter visibly swallows. "Totally."

"Mom is right." Lucy says. Then, at the same time, they both enthuse, "You're much prettier than Charlotte was."

Charlotte? Was?

"*Was*? Does that mean she's…" Dead? I can't bring myself to finish the sentence.

I'm guessing it's Lucy who laughs. "His ex-girlfriend, silly. She was—"

"—Awful." Amelia finishes.

"Boring." Both twins roll their brown eyes.

"Do you like Star Wars?" Amelia asks at the same time Lucy says, "Dex likes Star Wars."

"Charlotte hated it," they parrot.

Dexter meets my inquisitive gaze, before silencing them. "Guys, stop with all the questions. You're being rude."

To their credit, both twins blush. "Sorry Daphne. We meant it as a—"

"—Compliment." Lucy pokes at the chicken on her dinner plate before shoving it aside and crossing her arms on the tabletop. "So how is our brother romantic? Tell us. He works so much he hardly comes around."

Amelia sets her napkin on the table and scoots her chair closer to mine. "Tell us."

Crap. They're like a tiny twin mafia; they're not playing around. I'm going to have to make something up. "He, well. Dexter is…"

Amelia interrupts with a gasp. "Oh my god, did you hear that? She calls him—"

"—Dexter."

"So cute." They're like an echo.

It's freaky.

A smile tips my lips, and I'm honest. "Your brother is so sweet, and… such a gentleman. One of the nicest guys I've ever met."

Beside me, Dexter lets out a painful groan. "Sweet? *Nice*? That's horrible."

I nudge him with my knee. "Oh stop. It's a compliment."

He's not convinced. "Sweet and nice—exactly what every warm-blooded American guy wants to be called. Haven't you ever heard the phrase 'nice guys finish last?'

Story of my freaking life."

His sisters are watching us now, wide eyed. The one in pink take a long sip from her water glass, while the other one pokes at the chicken on her plate. For once, they're silent.

"Nice guys finish last? That's not true," I argue. "If they finish last, then what am I doing here?"

Dexter's lips purse. I can tell exactly what he's thinking: *you're here because you're doing me a favor.*

I give my head a tiny shake. *That's not true—not true at all.*

He raises an eyebrow skeptically.

I raise mine.

"Someone outgoing and beautiful doesn't do dull and predictable." His voice is low.

"How are you dull?"

Across the table, the twins lean forward in their chairs, hanging on our every word. Every syllable.

Dexter crosses his arms. "I work a lot."

Pfft. "Big deal, so do I."

It's then that Dexter removes his glasses… Transfixed, I watch as he wipes under his eyes before he meets my wide-eyed stare, his gaze boring into me. Long inky black lashes that should be outlawed on a man. Deep brown irises surrounded by tiny flecks of amber.

With his glasses he's adorkable.

Without them, Dexter is… is…

Holy. Hot.

I gaze.

I stare.

I gape at him stupidly.

One of the twins coughs to cover a snicker.

The other titters.

My date uses a linen napkin to wipe the lenses, oblivious to my enamored gawking, gives his head a shake, the moment fleeting when he places the glasses back on the bridge of his nose.

"So Daphne, where did my brother take you on your first date?"

I take a sip of wine then to occupy my hands, and buy myself a few extra seconds before responding. "We went to see StarGate," I say truthfully. "Sat in the theater after it was over talking until they kicked us out, didn't we?"

Dexter nods, glasses firmly back in place.

Amelia scrunches up her nose. His sisters are not impressed. "You took her to see *Star*Gate? Lame!"

With a laugh, I add, "Yes, but I happen to be a huge Sci-Fi junkie. So I wasn't horrified—not like you are right now."

The twins peer at us warily, giving each other sidelong glances. "What about your second date."

"Our second date?"

Shoot, Dexter and I discussed this in the car on the way here, didn't we? Crap, where did we say we went on our second date? With his sisters aiming their focus on me with laser beam accuracy, suddenly I can't remember. Or we hadn't thought this far ahead.

"We… our second date?"

Lucy's eyes are definitely narrowed doubtfully. "You *can't* remember where your second date was?"

Dexter pushes out a laugh. "Was it so boring that you've already forgotten?" His hand brushes my palm affectionately—the way a real boyfriend would do. "We went to a wine bar."

The twins scrunch up their noses. "You said you *met* at a wine bar. So did you meet there, or take her there on your second date?"

They wait.

"You know what? I'm twenty-six years old—you don't get to cross-examine me, questioning my motives. You're fifteen."

"Sixteen in less than three weeks," they clarify.

"That's not my point—"

"Aww Dex, you should see yourself, all flustered." Amelia cuts him off, preening happily before whipping out her cell and snapping a duck face selfie. "You're—"

"—So adorable."

"Dex, are you going to dance with her after dinner?" Amelia asks at the same time Lucy says, "They're setting up now and starting after dinner."

They both sigh. "Before dessert is served."

They sigh again. "Cake."

I can hardly keep up with their conversation.

Lucy pulls out *her* phone, checks the time, and then gestures us closer together. "Okay you little lovebirds. Scootch so I can get a picture."

"Can we post this on our Instagram?" Amelia asks.

"Hashtag *our brother's hot new girlfriend.*" Lucy adds while Amelia chastises, "Nobody uses hashtags anymore, Lucy. Nobody."

Lucy ignores her. "But can we?"

"Scoot closer," the voices probe.

We do. We scoot closer, Dexter extending his arm and resting it on my chair back. I lean back, into the crux of his elbow, the heat from his body brushing the skin of my exposed back.

I shiver.

My hand finds his upper thigh—like it would if I was his real girlfriend—and without hesitating, I rest it there and fight the impulse to give it a good squeeze. It would be tacky to feel him up at the dinner table, wouldn't it?

Especially since this isn't a real date.

Right?

I sigh, disappointed, as the flash from the cell goes off.

"Aren't you going to touch her?" His sisters ask him skeptically, clearly disgusted by our lack of PDA.

A look passes between the two of them; a knowing, secretive glance that's slightly disturbing and has me narrowing my green eyes.

"I *am* touching her," Dexter deadpans, flopping his hand near my shoulder. *Near* but not on. "See?"

"Dex," they coax. "This picture is gonna suck if you don't get your faces closer together."

"Oh, God forbid." Sarcasm becomes him.

"Maybe kiss her cheek," one twin suggests playfully with a simper, holding her phone out. They snap a few more selfies before aiming the cell back towards us. "Ready?"

"Closer."

Dexter's chest presses into my back and his hand comes down off the back of my seat. It covers my bare shoulder, solid and big and warm. His thumb caresses back and forth against my skin before he catches himself doing it and stops. Once.

Twice.

I shiver, catching Lucy's knowing grin.

She winks at me above her iPhone.

Why, that sneaky little…

"Smile!"

"Say cheese!"

I beam until my face hurts. Turn my face. Inhale the woodsy, fresh scent of Dexter's freshly shaven neck with no shame. I mean—since it's *right* freaking there. His jaw is so strong and defined it's just *begging* to be sniffed. Begging.

And it smells so…

So.

Good.

Down girl. He's not into you like that.

From the corner of my eye, I catch Lucy nudge Amelia with her elbow, and the pair of them do another series of head nods and eyebrow raises that I've decided must be some weird Twin Speak.

Those two are trouble.

Double trouble.

Dexter

So far, so good.

My parents haven't completely embarrassed me; but then again, not wanting to scare Daphne away, they've given us a wide berth, twins notwithstanding.

Been on their best behavior.

No questions being fired off at a missile-launching pace. No intrusively personal questions. No uncomfortable or inappropriate statements containing the words *marriage, babies, or give me grandbabies.*

Well, unless you count my Aunt Tory telling Daphne the reception hall where her daughter Grace is having her wedding has an opening nineteen months from now—if we hurry, we can still book it.

Only three of every ten statements have been intrusive; I consider those *very* good statistics.

I've managed to shuffle my faux date to the dance floor, away from the inquisition but not the prying eyes; if anything, I've made us more vulnerable to speculation by hauling Daphne to the middle of the ballroom.

Under the dim lights of the crystal chandelier, joy radiates off her. Or maybe it's just the reflection from the hundreds of prisms; either way, Daphne lets me hold her close and twirl her around, giggling at my tragic attempts at humor and grinning up at me at the appropriate times.

The urge to touch her intimately and pull her flush against my body is unbearable.

Either she's truly enjoying herself, or she's a terrific actress.

My cousin Gracie has hired some fancy cover-band from the city, and they're belting out some low-rent version of Photograph by Ed Sheeran. Daphne and I sway in synch along to the beat—her hands lock around my neck in a definitively girlfriendy way.

Contemplating me affectionately, she's acting like she *adores* me. A pink flush on her cheeks and fresh coat of gloss swiped across her lips. The look makes me—

Stop it Dex, this isn't real.

The look *isn't* real.

Because if it was, I would most definitely be dipping my neck and covering her mouth with mine to discover what flavor those glossy lips are.

But I won't.

I won't because that's not what this is—because I didn't have the balls to ask her on a real date.

And that's the pisser of it all.

I scan the room, groaning inwardly at the sight of my Cousin Elliot casually resting his elbows against the wooden counter of the bar. He tips his highball glass and chin as a greeting, his assessment of my date evident all the way across the room. Elliot begins at her feet, his brows raising the longer he studies her perfect figure—her waist, her firm backside. I know the exact moment his perusal reaches her perfect breasts because his lascivious grin widens, dammit.

Our eyes meet.

My cousin gives me another cocky nod as my hands skim Daphne's bare back, his mouth tipping into a toothy grin as he pushes himself away from the bar top. Turning towards the bartender, he throws down a few singles, says a few parting words, smacks our Uncle Dave on the back, and grabs his glass, weaving his way through the crowded reception room.

Towards us.

Determined.

Shit.

I knew he wouldn't be able to resist.

Now, if Daphne was plain and unattractive this would be a different story.

But she's not.

She's gorgeous and sexy and out of my league. What's worse, Elliot fucking knows it; he plans to take full advantage.

"My cousin is on his way over." I grumble, impulsively raising my hand to smooth it down Daphne's long, wavy hair. It feels like I imagine spun silk to feel— like warm water cascading in a languid, steady stream through my fingers—and smells a whole hellova lot better. Like shampoo and honey and baby powder.

So good.

So *not* mine.

Daphne

Elliot is a total douche.

I know it's not fair to run comparisons—particularly on someone I haven't met—but it's obvious Dexter and his cousin fell off different branches of the family tree: they are the complete opposites. Where Dexter is kind, caring and approachably handsome, Elliot is *in your face* good-looking. Cocky. Spray tanned. Manwhore with a heart of gold. A schmoozer used to gaining anything he wants from women.

Used to getting *in* anyone and *every*one's panties.

Gross, did I just say panties?

Ew.

I've met a hundred Elliot Ryan's in my short lifetime and I've no doubt I'll meet more; he is certainly no novelty.

Not to me, anyways.

He's sizing me up as a potential prospect even as he walks towards us, a knowing glint in his arrogant eye—he thinks I'm going to be charmed by his bullshit. His body.

His face.

He's so conceited and full of himself he thinks I'll ditch Dexter and leave here with him. Unfortunately for Elliot, I am immune and speak *fluent* douche.

Our dance near an end, Dexter relaxes his grip as his

cousin approaches with a swagger, and I mournfully unclasp my hands from their spot around his neck. Standing steadfastly beside him, I reach between our bodies to grapple for his hand, lacing our fingers together in a show of solidarity.

Plus, I *really* want to touch him.

He looks down at our joined hands surprised when I give them a flirty little squeeze.

"Hey cuz, pardon the interruption." Elliot is so full of shit I want to burst out laughing. He's not one bit sorry—he's rude. "Aunt Bethany said you brought a new girlfriend tonight, but I had to see it myself."

His mouth is speaking to Dexter, but his interest clearly lies with me. "And you must be…?"

"Elliot, this is Daphne. Daff, this is my cousin, Elliot."

Daff? Oh brother, he's pulling out the pet names?

"Hi, pleased to meet you. I'd shake your hand, but as you can see, it's otherwise occupied." I slouch on my heel, leaning on Dexter for support. He immediately releases my hand to slide his arm around my waist, pulling me flush into his body. Shamelessly, I return the favor, hugging my date's trim waist, letting my other palm rest on the flat of his abs.

I feel them flex under my fingers, and give them a playful little tickle.

"Dexter and Daphne. The Double D's, get it?" Elliot jokes, pasting a megawatt grin across his handsome face. So good-looking. So pleasant. *So fake*. "Hey man—sorry about standing you up at the wine bar the other weekend after the golf tournament. I didn't mean to leave you hanging."

His eyes never leave my face.

"No worries. It all worked out." Dexter's hand gives me a squeeze. "Besides, I wasn't there entirely alone."

Elliot cocks his head thoughtfully to study us. I can almost hear the cogs in his brain working overtime. Almost. "Yeah, I heard that's where the two of you met."

"Yup, I'm a lucky guy." Dexter kisses the top of my head.

Elliot squints at us. "Seriously though. The two of you are dating?"

Seriously though? Could he be any less subtle?

Dickhead.

"Well, the sparks *really* flew when we bumped into each other a few days later." I look up into Dexter's kind eyes. "Remember? You came to my rescue at the movie theater?"

"Was he wearing a bow tie?" Elliot laughs—a booming, obnoxious, and patronizing snort, revealing the dark side of his personality.

Asshole.

There was only one way to wipe that smirk off his face.

"Wearing a bow tie?" I ask purposefully. Slowly. "Well… he *was* wearing one at the *beginning* of the night. But I had it on in the morning." I push out a giggle. "Sometimes all I have on are his glasses, isn't that right babe?"

Bashfully in Elliot's direction, I demure. "I love his glasses, don't you?"

Unable to control myself, I rise onto my tip-toes and kiss the underside of Dexter's chin. My lips linger, the tip of my nose giving his jaw a little nudge.

Mmm. He smells heavenly. Divine.

"Wait." Elliot looks confused. "Hey man, am I seriously interrupting something? You're not fucking around?"

A laugh escapes my lips. "We were dancing! Of course you're interrupting something."

Idiot.

"Yeah *man*, we'll catch you later at the bar for a round, Ellie. Your treat." Dexter nuzzles my hair before spinning me around. "Right now I'm going to finish out this set with my gorgeous date."

"Sorry Elliot." Breathlessly, I don't take my eyes off Dexter's face. "You're gonna have to excuse us—I just want to be alone with these sexy suspenders. I've been *dying* to run my hands under them all night."

I shoot my date a pointed look. "*All* night."

To emphasize my point, the arms wrapped around his waist snake up the front of his button-down shirt, the pads of my palms slowly move up and under his blue paisley suspenders.

"I-I.." he stutters, pushing up his glasses with the tip of his forefinger. "You *like* these?"

He's genuinely shocked.

"No, I *love* them." I confess, biting down on my lower lip. "Why did you wear them if not to drive me insane?"

His mouth opens but no sound comes out. We're the only two people on the dance floor *not* dancing; the only two people on the dance floor, surrounded by his family and cousin Grace's good friends.

The only two people that matter; right here.

Right now.

Or maybe it's just me.

My fake date is kind of hard to read; he's spent more time being chivalrous and gentlemanly than flirty. He hasn't made one single overture. Not one single advance. Hasn't touched me in a way that was anything but friendly.

Unfortunately.

And yet…

It's his eyes that give him away. They're interested.

Intrigued.

Something in his eyes…

He *longs* for me.

I can see it.

But.

There's something else I see reflected in his dark, brown eyes; doubt. For himself and my attraction to him.

So that *longing*?

He won't do anything about it.

"You know how ridiculous the whole thing is, right?" I'm in my apartment, make-up removed, sitting cross-legged in the center of my big, fluffy bed. I couldn't resist a phone call to Tabitha with a recap of the past several days; the movie. The meeting at the coffee shop where Dexter propositioned me.

The engagement party.

"I don't understand why he didn't just ask you to be his date. It makes *no* sense." I can hear Tabitha shuffling around her kitchen, a pan going into the sink followed by running water.

I throw myself back, sinking into my pillows and staring up at the ceiling. "Right? The whole fake date thing was dumb. All it managed to do was fire up my imagination. It's running wild. You know how I always want what I can't have? Ugh, his lack of interest is driving me crazy."

"I wouldn't call it lack of interest; I'd call it a lack of cojones."

I ignore her flippant remark and prattle on. "Besides, what is this—a Made for TV movie? What are we, in high school?"

On the other end of the line, she's speaking around her toothbrush. "Yeah, it was pretty immature." She takes it out of her mouth to say, "But maybe…"

My best friend's voice trails off.

"Maybe *what*? I'm hanging on your every word here."

"Well, maybe—just maybe—he's intimidated by you and doesn't want to be rejected. That's Collin's theory, and I happen to agree with him. You can be pretty intimidating, Daphne."

I consider this.

I'm not shy or reserved, and if I'm being brutally honest, I haven't broken any mirrors lately.

"Okay, yes. That's a possibility." I pause before adding more information. "But I'm *pretty* sure he was going to ask me out after the movie. I'd bet my favorite yoga pants on it."

"He was spooked by his aunt," Tabitha declares with authority. I can picture her nodding in agreement. "And now he's too chicken shit—" She stops mid-sentence. "Tell the truth; do you *really* want to date a guy like that, though? Not enough balls to ask you on a real date? It's kind of *wimpy*."

I've debated this a million times in my head so I immediately jump to his defense. "Jeez Tabitha, just because he's not humping my leg or sending me dick pics doesn't make him a wimp."

She huffs indignantly. "Please don't call him *sensitive*. That's way worse."

I chuckle. "No, he's not *that* nice. I mean—he is, but he also has a smart mouth on him, too; it's sexy."

His smart mouth.

Those lips.

"Sexy Dexy," Tabitha croons into the receiver. "You know, I bet he's got a lot of pent-up sexual repression."

My ears perk up. "Ya think?"

"Oh *yeah,* definitely." Tabitha breaths seductively. "You said yourself he's a thinker—he's probably *thinking* of all the ways to *do* you."

God I hope so.

"No doubt he's got himself convinced you're out of his league."

I scoff at this. "He couldn't be more wrong."

"Then prove it. Show him he's wrong."

"I can't," I whine like a baby. "He put me in the Friend-Zone."

Tabitha sighs impatiently. "No, he put *him*self there. Now *you* need to take him out."

"Hmmm, we'll see…"

"I'm sorry, what was that? You need. To take. Him. Out."

"Have you always been this bossy?"

"No, it's something new I'm trying out." I can practically hear her rolling her blue eyes.

"Wow, sarcastic, too. Collin's one lucky guy."

Tabitha releases a breathy laugh. “Sweetie. If you like him, just do it; make a move. Don’t wait until your ovaries dry up.”

Seven

Daphne

It turns out, I don't have to make the first move. Instead, the opportunity to see Dexter falls into my lap in the form of two brown haired, mischievous teenage twins.

Who apparently *really,* really like me.

A lot.

Enough to *steal* my number out of Dexter's phone during the engagement party and message me on the sly behind his back, bless their heartless, black little souls. Was it inappropriate for them to text me without telling their brother? Without a doubt—*so* inappropriate.

Was it inappropriate for them to invite me to their Mom's house for their annual birthday cookie bake? *So* inappropriate.

Do I care?

Um, no.

Why? Because I want to see him again—and if Dexter Ryan isn't going to make a move on me, I'm not above resorting to my own brand of passive aggressive man-hunting.

Besides, *I was invited.*

Sure, I'll probably regret the decision to randomly show up at his mom's house, but as I reach behind my waist to tie the dainty, yellow polka dot apron strings in a bow, all I can think is the possibility that Dexter will walk through that front door.

I know the twins said they hadn't told him I was coming, but… a girl can dream. Plus, I'm no expert on twins, but these girls are pretty shady; I'm pretty sure they plan sketchy plots like this on a regular basis.

Mrs. Ryan—Georgia—has all the ingredients set on the counter by the time I arrive; everything pre-measured, eggs counted out, bowls at the ready. She's even separated the buttercream frosting into three metal mixing bowls, in the twins' three favorite colors: pink, lavender, and lime green.

Fluttering around the kitchen, Georgia hands me a pot-holder, directing me to check on the twelve sugar cookies shaped like the number sixteen, already in the oven.

They're a light golden brown and ready to come out.

They smell divine.

"You know, we've been baking birthday cookies for the twins for five years," she explains, sliding one cookie sheet out of the oven and another one in. "We stopped doing cake after their eleventh birthday—the year they got into a huge fight over which flavor; marble or red velvet."

Amelia laughs. "What a dumb thing to fight about." I know it's her because there's a monogram with her initials on the pocket of her baby blue tee shirt.

I make a mental note: Amelia—blue monogrammed tee shirt and jeans. Lucy: pajama bottoms and tank top.

Got it.

"Tossing sprinkles everywhere," Lucy adds.

"My husband was furious. Cake all over the kitchen," Georgia laughs at the memory with a smile, handing me a spatula. "Anyway, we decided that year to make cookies the birthday tradition. Easier and cleaner. Their friends love them during lunch, and I don't have to listen to the bickering."

"It's not bickering," Amelia disagrees. "It's—"

"—Debating."

"Well it's obnoxious," their mom says as we start to remove the cookies from the cookie sheets. Mrs. Ryan has a cooling rack on the counter. "Sweetie, would you hand me the wax paper?"

I mentally choose a cookie from the rack, anticipation making my stomach growl.

"She's talking to you," Lucy says, nudging me in the ribs with her pointy adolescent elbow. "Wax paper."

"Oh, sorry!" I apologize, springing into action.

"Shake a tail feather," Amelia teases. "No slacking on this job. We're known for our freakishly delicious birthday cookies."

"Freakishly large." Lucy smiles, going in to dip her finger in the pale pink frosting. Amelia slaps her hand away, pure disgust etched on her face.

"Stop. That's gross."

"Chill out, I washed my hands," Lucy rolls her eyes. "Hey, did you know Dex always complains because Mom never baked *him* special cookies—"

"—What did he want with cookies, anyway? He's a guy."

"Girls!" Georgia laughs. "I made him *cake*! Besides, when he was younger, we didn't have the money. All these ingredients you're throwing on each other for fun aren't cheap."

She's right; flour and sugar are everywhere, including on me. In my hair, on my clothes. I run a hand down the dainty, vintage apron wrapped around my waist, flattening out the wrinkles.

I love this stupid thing; I wonder if I could get away with wearing an apron on a regular basis as I lean against the counter, fingering several thin, charms on my necklace—one is a tiny, gold wishbone my sister bought me when I graduated from college two years ago, and I'm seldom without it.

When we were younger, my dad was big into duck hunting.

He would come home with the birds (gross, I know) and my mom would dress them for dinner, saving the wishbone for my sister, Morgan, and I to pull apart after our evening meal.

A friendly little competition, if I was lucky enough to snap off the wishbone, I usually said a prayer for stupid, trivial things; new clothes. A cool car. But the older I grew, my wishes became more altruistic; a steady job. Healthy family. Loyal friends.

I adore wishbones, just like I love throwing pennies into a wishing well, and making wishes when the clock strikes eleven-eleven.

Childish? Maybe.

But something so small has always filled me with tremendous hope; and I always hoped for love. No, not hoped—*wished*. Wished it from the depths of my soul.

Yeah, I get it; we're living in a world where feminism and female independence is a valuable asset. Two values that women have fought for centuries to obtain—but that doesn't make me want someone to share my life with any less.

Coming home to an empty apartment with no cat, no dog, or companionship *sucks*.

The twins' squabbling interrupts my daydreaming.

"We *know* the ingredients aren't cheap, Mom." The twins emphasize the same word, and reach for the jar of tiny purple candies at the same time, too.

"Then stop wasting sprinkles," Georgia chastises.

The twins exchange bemused glances. "But it's fun."

Inside the back pocket of my jeans, my phone vibrates, its chirpy little buzzing. I excuse myself to use the bathroom.

Tabitha: *Hey, what are you doing today*?

Me: *Playing baker—making delicious, gourmet cookies.*

Tabitha: *Shut up. LOL. For real though, what are you doing today?*

Me: *Why are you laughing?! That's what I'm doing!*

Tabitha: *This I gotta see; Collin's taking Greyson to pick out their parents' anniversary gift, then they're going* *to dinner. I'm bored. Let me jump in the shower quick and I'll be over in 20 minutes.*

Tabitha: *I wanna eat COOKIES!!!!*

Me: *NO! Don't! I'm not home...*

Tabitha: *Ugh, well that sucks! So where ARE you?*

Me: *I'm... at Dexter's, um... Mom's house?*

Tabitha: *WHAT??? Stop it, you are not.*

Me: *Shit, I shouldn't have told you.*

Tabitha: *Well that escalated quickly! I thought you weren't dating! Seriously though, what the HELL ARE YOU DOING AT HIS MOM'S HOUSE BAKING COOKIES?*

Me: *His sisters texted me and wanted me to bake with them today—they really like me, I guess, and they're young. What was I supposed to say???*

Tabitha: *Wait, is this the twins?*

Me: *Yeah.*

Tabitha: *How bout "Sorry twinsies! I might be lusting after your nerdy brother, but I'm NOT ACTUALLY DATING HIM!" There. That's what you could say.*

Me: **rolling my eyes* Oh, like it's that easy.*

Tabitha: *Yeah, it is actually. You just type it out and hit SEND. Please tell me Dexter is there with you.*

Me: *Um. No. He went in to work today, but I think one of the twins texted him. They were being really weird and sneaky, giggling over their phone a few minutes ago.*

Tabitha: *Sexer Dexer!*

Me: *That nickname is worse than Sexy Dexy.*

Tabitha: *I still can't believe you're at his mom's house. I'm literally dead over here. Dying. You have some lady balls. And also...super creepy.*

Me: *You told me to take him out of the friend zone!*

Tabitha: *Well yeah! But not like THIS!*

Tabitha: *Jeez Daff, the guy is going to piss his khakis when he finds you in his mom's kitchen baking it up with his family. That guy does NOT strike me as the type that likes surprises…*

Dexter

I don't like surprises.

Daphne Winthrop is the last person on Earth I expect to see when I walk into my Mom's house. Her kitchen. And yet—there she is. Standing among the chaos, wielding a spatula and wearing the cutest fucking shamefaced expression I've ever seen.

And the sexiest fucking apron.

Stunned from shock and faltering beneath the threshold, I take in the rest of her from head to toe; long hair in a pretty little ponytail. Silver hoop earrings. Gray short sleeve tee shirt over faded skinny jeans with ripped up knees, a yellow and white polka dot apron is tied around her slim waist.

Bare feet with bubble-gum pink nails.

Those cute feet.

I stare at those pink nails dumbly until she wiggles her toes, and slowly raise my head to meet her gaze.

"Hi." Her mouth tips into a bashful little smile.

What is she doing in my Mom's kitchen? I mean—obviously she's baking, but… what the hell is she doing in my mom's kitchen?

My mom rolls her eyes. "Dex you're being weird. Don't just stand there gawking at the poor girl. Come in here and give her a proper hello."

Still, I'm rooted to the spot. "What's… going on?"

What is she doing in my Mom's kitchen?

Mom ignores me. "Don't be rude. And can you grab us the broom from the hall closet since you're just standing there? Make yourself useful."

"It's okay Georgia," Daphne lays the utensil on the counter next to a black wire cookie rack I've seen on my mom's counter a thousand times, wipes her hands on the apron around her waist, and starts towards me. "He's just surprised to see me, that's all. I didn't tell him I was coming over."

It doesn't escape my notice that she's calling my mom Georgia with familiarity. My brows shoot into my hairline as Daphne reaches me, eyes sparkling with mischief. She goes up on the balls of her feet and leans in.

"Surprise?"

Her words are a light whisper right in the sensitive spot beneath my ear, the tip of her nose brushing gently against my lobe. Her warm breath rests a heartbeat too long on my skin to be accidental, and when she pulls away, I raise my hand.

"You have a little flour… right… there." I brush it off her cheek with a slow, gentle swipe.

She bites her lower lip demurely. "I haven't greeted you properly, have I?" Her soft lips connect to my jaw line the briefest of seconds; so quickly I might have imagined it.

"Hi."

Confused *as shit* but smiling like an idiot, I finally return her greeting. "Hi."

Daphne reaches up, removes my old University baseball hat, and runs her fingers over my scalp, giving my hair a tussle.

Christ her fingers feel good; *too* fucking good.

"The twins texted me an invite to help bake their birthday cookies; I could hardly say no," she says by way of explanation. "I didn't realize it would be quite this big a production."

I adjust my glasses and narrow my eyes.

My sisters—who aren't usually this quiet—hum happily over near the sink, sneaking covert glances over their shoulders and doing that weird telepathic Twin Speak crap they do when they don't want to talk out loud. Or are up to no good.

I stare the twins down hard.

"*Gee*, what a coincidence. Because they texted me, too. An S.O.S—something about needing help with their *economics* homework."

The girls make a display of loudly running the faucet, filling the sink with suds, clanking dishes around in the water, and avoiding my suspicious gaze.

"Hey, don't ignore me." I cross my arms, moving towards my younger sisters. "Correct me if I'm wrong, but I believe the phrase you used in the text was *DEFCON 5 Level Economics shit only you can help us with.* Do I have that right Lucy? Econ shit?" I use air quotes to illustrate my point, but they're determined to ignore me.

Silence.

"Do you even *take* economics?" I practically shout.

Lucy's shoulders shake with merriment as Amelia splashes her with bubbles. "*Moron*. I knew you'd get us into trouble."

"It was your idea!"

Now they're openly bickering, and once they get

started…

"Shut *up* Amelia. Seriously. This was *your* idea—"

"You don't have to *do* everything I *tell* you to do, *Lucy*, God! Be a think-for-yourselfer every once in a while —"

"—You're so annoying. Stop making that ugly face at me—"

"—This is *your* ugly face. *Duh.*"

My mom has this shrill, nervous laugh she employs when she panics—the situations usually involve my sisters, their weird twin crap, or the occasional fight between my aunts—to break up the tension.

She unleashes it now.

Anxiously walking up behind Daphne, she begins hastily loosening the apron strings behind her back while my sisters continue arguing back-and-forth. Daphne's arms go up as Mom quickly removes the apron, draping it over her arm and shooing at us. "There now! Dexter, sweetie, now's a good time for you to take Daphne somewhere nice. Run along. Daphne, you can leave your car here and come grab it later. Shoo! Go!"

Lucy flicks Amelia with sudsy water.

My mom's voice gets louder. "Run along now. We'll finish this up later. The twins can clean up this mess; the two of you can go grab an early dinner if you get moving."

Before I can object, Daphne is being ushered into her jacket, shoes are being laid at her bare feet, and we're being escorted towards the front door.

Practically pushed out into the cold.

Porch light goes on.

Just as the door is being closed behind us with a resounding thud and the deadbolt slides into place, from the corner of my eye I catch sight of the twins through the crack—high-fiving.

Those little, meddling—

"I think your mom and sisters are playing matchmaker," Daphne says quietly beside me once we're standing on the porch, stuffing her hands in her pockets to keep them warm. The air is so chilly we can see our breath.

"They already think we're dating." I point out.

Daphne gives a little nod, hands sinking deeper into her pockets. "Maybe."

My gaze lands on the SUV I drove tonight instead of my Audi; and for once I'm glad for it. With the weather turning, it's the safer of my two vehicles.

Still, not wanting to be presumptuous, I delay moving towards it.

Daphne does not. "Well, I guess we can't stand out here all night; we'll freeze. We could go… do something?"

Her voice is encouraging. Excited.

Naw. Can't be.

"But it's Saturday."

Tilting her chin up, she regards me under the glow from my parents' porch light. Her bright green eyes are sparkling up at me. "True. It *is* Saturday. But can you think of a better place to be right now? I can't."

It sounds like she's flirting.

"You know, there's a reason I didn't tell your sisters no."

Oh jeez—she's definitely flirting.

Daphne Winthrop is standing on my mother's porch on a Saturday night, flirting. With me. I roll this concept around in my head, mentally calculating what little I know about women and trying to determine her motives.

If I didn't know any better, I would think she wanted …

Shit.

Me.

In the cool night air, I give my head a shake; it makes no sense. None at all.

Not to be rude, but, "Daphne, why are you here?" I ask cautiously. Deliberately.

"I-I was invited."

"Okay." My eyes scan the empty yard and I exhale, the air from my warm breath forming another gray puff of smoke. "That's it? That's the reason?"

I'm not playing dumb; I genuinely can't figure out her motives.

"I'm sorry." She looks down at her feet, studying the wooden floor boards of the deck below us. Her voice is small. "I wasn't thinking; honestly, I didn't have plans other than *maybe* going to another movie by myself and stuffing my face with popcorn, and your family is so wonderful. Plus…"

Her voice trails off.

"Plus… *what*?" I'm desperate for her to finish that sentence; it holds so much possibility.

Daphne looks up and out into the dark side yard. "Plus. I—This is going to sound so lame."

God I want to reach out and touch her. "No it won't."

"I thought we could be friends."

Friends.

Friends?

Fuck.

Hey, I'm a smart guy—not *completely* delusional—

and know my chances of dating someone like Daphne Winthrop are slim to none; but a guy can dream. It's not like I'm lying in bed at night, closing my eyes and jerking-off while picturing her naked in my mind.

Okay, I *am*—but it was only once.

Fine. Three times.

With a resound sigh, I motion towards my car. "Hungry?"

She gives me a megawatt smile, her green eyes shining under the soft glow of the lamp light.

Gorgeous.

"*Starving*."

"Fine, let's go get something to eat. *Friend*."

Daphne

I thought we could be friends.

Just friends?

Why would I even say something like that?

I am such a liar.

Dexter

The twins are spying.

When we come back to my parents' place after our brief dinner, they're barely concealed behind the sheer curtains draped across their second story window; their nosey silhouettes are pressed against the glass conspicuously, glaringly obvious given the fact they never shut the lights off in their shared bedroom.

The sheers flutter, pulled back, whipping back and forth when one twin shoves the other aside, vying for more window space. I can't tell who is who, but when one gets jostled back, more prodding ensues.

They'll *never* make it in espionage.

I don't fight back the chuckle at their blatant lack of stealth; amused, I can't even muster up the energy to be irritated.

Or maybe I'm just happy.

Shit, that's got to be it.

Daphne and I walk unhurriedly through my parents' manicured lawn to the car parked in the shadows next to the house. Her body shivers.

"Cold?"

"Yeah, kind of. *Brrrr.* I have to remember mittens next time I leave the house with the seasons changing."

"I have some in my car—let me go grab them."

"Gosh, no! That's okay," she protests—but I'm already halfway across the lawn to my car, pulling open the door and digging through the glove box to retrieve the gloves.

Ah, here they are.

I hold up them up for inspection, blowing inside one, then the other, to warm them as I jog back to Daphne. Even in the dim shadows I can see her beaming when I hold out the first glove.

I hold it steady as she slides her hands in to each one.

She gives her hands a wiggle, smile widening. "Thank you."

The yard is quiet; we have no neighbors and my parents live on a wooded lot. Besides my snooping fifteen-year-old sisters spying from upstairs, we're completely alone.

"You're welcome."

She leans her shoulder against the door of her silver car, nothing but the sound of our breathing and the jingling of her cars keys in the still night air.

I clear my throat. "So."

"*So…*" Daphne shifts on her heels, dragging out the word like it's actually a question. It sounds diminutively more meaningful than a regular *so*, so… I'm actually really confused.

I'm tempted to repeat the word one more time, but fight the power. Removing my glasses, I lift the hem of my blue cable knit sweater to clean the lenses.

Instinctually, I feel Daphne move in closer; my personal space instantly becomes warmer.

"Can you see without those?"

I chuckle, the sound reverberating against the silence, and tease, "I can see *you*, if that's what you were wondering."

Even without my glasses, I can see her biting down on that pouty lower lip with her teeth to hide a shy smile. She cocks her head up at me. "Maybe it was."

I don't know how to respond to that.

"Aren't you curious, Dexter?" She whispers in the shadow, her warm breath forming a small puff of steam around her words in the cold, night air.

"Curious about what?"

God, even *I* can hear how fucking ridiculous that sounds. *Curious about what?* my inner thoughts mock. My friend Collin would be kicking my ass right now if he heard how much I sounded like a pussy. I have no game when it comes to women.

"Curious about… nothing." Daphne fakes a laugh, giving her head a little shake. "Nothing."

Except it doesn't feel like nothing. It sounds like she's asking for something in a language I don't speak. And I might not know shit about women, but I know that right now, she's flirting with me.

Or not.

Shit, I can't tell.

"Thanks for putting up with me tonight." She goes for the door handle of her car, pausing before pulling it open. "Your family is pretty… spectacular. I know you weren't expecting me today, so it was a relief when you didn't freak out."

"No problem. Don't worry about it."

"Right. Well…" Daphne lowers herself into the driver's seat, buckles her seat belt, and looks up at me with those eyes. Those dejected green eyes. "Good night, Dexter."

I push the glasses up the bridge of my nose. "Night."

Watching as she pulls out of the drive and her taillights slowly fade into the dark distance, I turn, glancing up towards the twins' bedroom window. Arms crossed, their double disappointment is palpable even from two stories up.

Fuck.

Ten

Dexter

"Sir?" Vanessa's voice crackles out of the intercom sitting on my desk. Sir? It still makes me cringe every time she or anyone from the office calls me that moniker. I'm twenty-six for Christ Sake; I might be one of the youngest junior traders for my company, but when Vanessa calls me Sir, I always expect my dad to come waltzing into the room.

"I have Brian Sullivan on hold from Nordic Acuities." Vanessa prods. "He hasn't heard a response on the email he sent through yesterday, and called to verify you'd responded. Can you check your outgoing messages and get back to me?"

I lean forward, tapping on the TALK button. "Yup. I'll do it now."

Tapping on my mouse, I open Outlook and go straight

to the outgoing mail.

Sent to: Collin Keller, Calvin Thompson. Subject: Joke of the day.

Sent to: Brian Sullivan. Subject: Merger

The wheels of my desk chair swivel as I roll back towards the intercom button. "Vanessa? It's still in the queue. Please call Brian and tell him I'm re-sending it right over."

"Thank you, Sir."

"Please stop calling me Sir—I'm only fifteen years younger than you."

"I'll stop calling you Sir when you head back to being an intern on the lower floors. Sir." I can hear her smirking.

Smart ass.

"Fine." I shift in my seat, hand hovering about the mouse pad. "I'm going to take forty-five minutes for lunch today, but I'm eating at my desk. Hold any correspondence until," I glance at my clock. "Until one thirty, please."

The intercom continues to crackle. And chuckle. "Got it."

My fingers move the cursor over my screen, moving to the corner of the monitor to close the window, eyes continuously scanning the screen. They land on the joke I'd sent Collin this morning, the brief memo mentioning a clients no-contact policy.

My message to Daphne.

As I—

Wait.

Rewind.

My eyes do a double take, my head actually swiveling

despite the screen being dead center in front of me.

Message to *Daphne*? What the shit is this?

Clicking the message open, my heart actually begins rapidly palpitating—so strong I can feel it beating in my neck.

Holy Christ.

To: dwinthrop_vp@publicrelations.info
From: DRyan@halyarcapitolinvsec.co
Subject:

Hello Daphne. I hope you had a lovely evening the other night after making cookies with my awesome sisters. They had a blast with you. I'm sorry I suck and let you drive away without asking you on a date. I was wondering if you'd be at their actual birthday party in two weeks. It's on a Sunday. I'm too shy and lame to tell you in person, but I think you're beautiful. I have horrible luck with girls because as you noticed I'm kind of a geek but not as boring as people think I am. For example, I love hiking in the mountains and ski trips. I would never say this to your face.

Yours Truly,
Dexter Ryan

I squint at the screen, reading and re-reading, praying to God that I'm not seeing what I'm actually seeing.

Too shy and lame?

What in the actual shit is this?

WHAT IN THE ACTUAL SHIT IS THIS?

Not only did I *not* send this, it sounds like a fucking fifteen-year old teenager wrote it—specifically *two* of them—and makes me look like a freaking moron. My face burns scarlet and my knuckles, which aren't touching any keys, are white.

White.

This positively *reeks* with the stench of Lucy and Amelia. Those nosey, meddling, conniving little brats have done some really stupid shit in their lives—like the time they switched places so Lucy could take an Algebra exam for Amelia but forgot to swap outfits.

They're constantly trying to Parent Trap unsuspecting people.

And I have no clue what that even means.

Those pranks were bad, but interfering in my personal business is going too far. I'm going to ring their scrawny, pubescent necks when I get my hands on those two.

I cannot even control my breathing, and although I don't have asthma, it feels like I'm having an asthma attack. Or a panic attack.

Daphne *read* this shit. Fucking read it.

How do I know? My *reads* are on. Read: 10:37am

She probably thinks I'm a blabbering idiot.

My stomach drops.

I take a few calming breaths—then a few more—before cracking my knuckles and suspend my hands above the keyboard, at the ready. How do I reply? What the hell do I say that's not going to sound *asinine*? Do I apologize? Explain that my darling sisters hacked my phone when I was home and sent the email for me? Yeah. Cause that's not going to sound idiotic and implausible.

My hands get buried in my hair and I tug.

How did they even manage it?

Those little…

Without further ado, my fingers nimbly fly over the keyboard, tapping out the following, professional and apologetic reply to Daphne.

To: dwinthrop_vp@publicrelations.info
From: DRyan@halyarcapitolinvsec.co
Subject: My sincerest apologies

Hello, Daphne. In regards to the recent message sent to your email account from mine; that note was sent by my sisters, in an obviously immature attempt to get your attention. It was obviously poor manners and an error in judgment on their part. I apologize for any level of embarrassment you might have felt receiving it, which may far exceed mine. Furthermore—

I'm distracted momentarily by the phone next to the computer buzzing, the email notification in the top left corner lighting up with a soft blue blinking light.

Shit. That could be Brian Sullivan already replying.

I lift the cell, swiping the screen down and tap to open the email browser.

For the second time in a short timeframe, my stomach drops as I stare at Daphne Winthrop's email address in my inbox, the Subject line reading: *I don't know what to say.*

I can't make myself tap her reply open it; I cannot.

Instead, I sit back in my desk chair palming the phone in my right hand and staring at that email address and short fucking sentence, trying to decipher what it could mean without opening the message.

I don't know what to say other than:

… that letter you sent had to have been a joke.

… I can't believe a grown-ass man wrote that.

… you should be embarrassed and *never* allowed near woman.

Shit, what does it actually say? I'm dying to open it at the same time I dread it. My thumb hovers, millimeters from an answer. I push the black glasses I wear to work up my nose, a thin layer of perspiration dampening my forehead.

Christ I'm pitiful.

Clicking my phone off, I set it on my desktop and frown scornfully, while the apology message I'd been composing to Daphne looms in front of me on the screen of my laptop. Mocking.

I hit 'Save' and watch the file float to the lower right hand corner drop box, the cursor on the screen blinking an entreaty. Blinking for me to click open the ominous new message from Daphne Winthrop.

To: DRyan@halyarcapitolinvsec.co
From: dwinthrop_vp@publicrelations.info
Subject: I don't know what to say

Dexter. To say I was surprised to get your message is an understatement… Excited and surprised. After seeing StarGate the other weekend, I was sure you were going to ask me on a date until your Aunt interrupted… and I was disappointed you asked me to Grace's engagement party as your Fake Date. I would have absolutely been proud to go as your official date. I think you're charming and disarming, and since we're being direct—very handsome. So yes. Yes! I would love to go on a date with you. I've been waiting for you to ask since the movie theater. Here is my cell phone number again just in case you lost it: 298-555.9392 Well, better get back to work! LOL.

Talk to you soon, I hope.

Daphne

To: dwinthrop_vp@publicrelations.info
From: DRyan@halyarcapitolinvsec.co
Subject: Confession time.

Dear Daphne,

I have a confession to make since we're being honest and it's easier for me to hide behind technology. Alright, here it is: my sisters wrote that first message behind my back and I found the email by accident, and I was furious. But now? I'm glad. As horrible and stupid as their message made me sound, and as embarrassed as I am that they did it, I'm glad.

DPR

To: DRyan@halyarcapitolinvsec.co
From: dwinthrop_vp@publicrelations.info
Subject: Me too.

Dexter, I should have guessed that you didn't write that first note. I guess I was so excited to receive it that… it didn't occur to me that you wouldn't use words like "Lame" and "Geek" in an email to describe yourself, because you are NEITHER of those things. LOL! Oh lord, you must have died when you saw their note. What a couple of beasts! You're right though. I'm glad they did it because… when would you have gotten around to telling me how you felt? I'd be old and gray by then!

Daphne

To: dwinthrop_vp@publicrelations.info
From: DRyan@halyarcapitolinvsec.co
Subject: You'd be waiting a long time

Dear Daphne,

Honestly? I'm not surprised by them messaging you; they've been doing stuff like this since they were old enough to understand what a prank was. But that doesn't mean I didn't want to *kill* them. When I found the message "I" sent you, I couldn't even read through the whole thing—I could only see red. I mean—what made them think I'd call myself lame? But enough about me; do you have any brothers/sisters that drive you insane?

DPR

To: DRyan@halyarcapitolinvsec.co
From: dwinthrop_vp@publicrelations.info
Subject: Not a Lonely Only

Dexter, Fortunately and Unfortunately, I have a sister although my mom says sometimes my Dad acts like a small child, so it's like having three kids. Haha. Growing up, I always wish I had a twin. I think your sisters are badass—I'm totally digging their Twin Voodoo and am kind of jealous, not gonna lie.

They're so pretty and cute for evil masterminds.

So… got anything planned for the weekend? Did you see the commercial on the Sci-Fi channel for the Star Trek Comic Con thing?

Daphne

To: dwinthrop_vp@publicrelations.info
From: DRyan@halyarcapitolinvsec.co
Subject: Me finally asking you

Dear Daphne,

I don't usually go to Comic Con events… I'm more of a laid back, lazy poster yielding nerd. I don't get all crazy and I don't have any collectible figurines still in the boxes, LOL; fine. A few. But yeah. I did see that commercial but that's the twins' family birthday with the whole Ryan side of the family. Grace, Elliot—the whole crazy clan. Are you brave enough? Would you have any interest in going? It's this Sunday around three.

Eleven

Daphne: *Okay, just to clarify… am I going with you this weekend to your sisters' party as a [fill in blank]?*

Dexter: *Date?*

Daphne: *Yes. I'm sorry to ask and I know it's awkward but it will drive me crazy not knowing. But we did go on that FAKE date… so this one is… [fill in blank]?*

Dexter: *Not fake. This is me—for once in my life—sucking it up and putting myself out there; Yeah. I'd like it to be a date. How does two o'clock sound?*

Daphne: *I would love that. Two o'clock.*

Dexter: *It's a date.*

Daphne: *Hey, it's me. Do you think your mom needs me to bring anything this weekend for the party? Like fruit or something…?*

Dexter: *No, don't worry about it. She'll have enough*

food there to feed a small herd of elephants. Or assholes.

Daphne: :) *Truth? I only asked you that as an excuse to text you. Is that weird?*

Dexter: *No weirder than you showing up to bake cookies at my mom's house…*

Daphne: *Oh god! Please don't remind me. Tabitha told me that was a horrible idea; I should have listened, but awkwardly... I was already in your mom's apron.*

Dexter: *Truth? I think I dreamt about that apron.*

Dexter: *Is that weird?*

Daphne: *Maybe someone else might think so, but I don't. LOL.*

Dexter: *I hope you don't think I'm being too forward, but I bought the twins a gift and signed your name to their card... I figured, since they already think we're dating, it would be okay.*

Daphne: *You are so sweet. Yes. That's absolutely okay.*

Daphne: *Shoot. I have a meeting in three minutes. Better get moving. Talk later?*

Daphne: *I'm back. Curious about what gift we're giving the twins?*

Dexter: *A spy kit.*

Twelve

Daphne

The twins love their spy kit.

Fully equipped with magnifying glass, finger printing kit, and baggies to store collected evidence, the cheap child's spy kit has the sisters bent at the waist, laughing hysterically. Before moving on to open their next gift, Lucy removes the kit's rubber gloves, snaps them at the wrist, and asks the family members crowded around the room who wants to be their first victim.

Half the room laughs uproariously; their Uncle Derek throws his arms up, demanding to be finger printed.

"Now maybe they'll leave me alone," Dexter gripes beside me as we stand in the threshold of the living room, watching the twins rip through the rest of their gifts like seven-year-old kids. "Even if the kit is just a toy, look at how happy they are."

"You know what I always wanted growing up?" I muse. "A metal detector; a real one—not one of those cheap, crappy ones."

Dexter laughs. "Me too! Imagine all the shit we'd find. Coins, jewelry."

"Pirate's booty, for sure," I tease. "Sunken treasure."

"Oh, now we're taking this metal detector in the ocean? Shit, I was thinking just parks and the beach. The ocean opens up a whole world of possibilities. What body of water would we explore first?"

I tap my chin, pretending to think. "I've actually given this some thought. It would definitely need to be somewhere near Spain."

"Okay Magellan." Dexter's burst of surprise is loud and raucous. "Why Spain?"

I roll my eyes, and give him a smirk of superiority. "All the shipwrecks from the explorers crossing over? Sheesh."

He's not convinced. "But aren't the best places to scuba dive in the Caribbean?"

My head gives a little shake. "No, no, no—I'm not talking about scuba diving; that's all surface stuff. We'd need to dive down deep—"

"—What the hell are you yammering on about over here? All I heard was *blah blah I'm a giant nerd who gave my sisters a spy kit*."

I inwardly groan, pivoting on my heel at the interruption.

Elliot. Of course.

He holds a beer towards Dexter as an offering.

My date takes it, hesitantly, his demeanor going from flirty and fun to guarded in a matter of nanoseconds.

My lips clamp shut, pursing with displeasure; not at the interruption, but at the rude way he went about it. Good lord, didn't his mother teach him any manners? You don't walk over and insult someone. I glance over at his mother, Aunt Tory, who sits perched daintily on the couch, sipping out of a champagne glass. Coiffed, strikingly made-up to the nines and discernibly high-maintenance, I acknowledge that she doesn't *look* like she's spent Elliot's childhood years teaching him modesty.

I also acknowledge that perhaps he doesn't know any better, and allow him some leeway. After all, the guy probably can't help himself.

He was raised this way.

"Hey Elliot," I start. "It's good to see you again."

Lie #1.

"Right? It's nice not to have the huge crowd we had at Gracie's party—now we can actually talk without all the music and annoying dancing," he schmoozes. The charming smile doesn't reach his calculating brown eyes.

"Oh, totally," I agree. *Lie #2*.

Elliot moves closer, his elbow giving Dexter an almost unperceivable nudge, jostling my date towards the wall. Away from me.

My green eyes become slits. This guy is certifiable.

"What are you doing after this?" He wonders aloud, blatantly ignoring his cousin. "It's a Sunday night but we should still do something."

"What a great suggestion; we should." *Just not with you, asshole*. "Dexter sweetie, let's do something after this."

The patronizing bastard scoffs. "Come on now, get real. You don't think I know what's going on here?"

My mouth falls open—actually falls open at his audacity—the anger inside me beginning its slow roll up my throat, past my lips. My claws come out. "Wow. Just… *wow*. You know something pal, you are seriously one shitty—"

"Cousin!" The twins announce, appearing out of nowhere, their lithe arms going around Elliot's shoulders. For once, their timing is impeccable.

Amelia gives her brother a quick peck on the cheek. "Dex, mom wants you to run upstairs and grab that picture of you and Dad from the Vacation from Hell of 2010. You know the one—where Lucy and I are both crying in the background—"

"—and you and Dad are smiling at the camera—"

"—and Mom looks like she's about to lose her mind—" Amelia giggles.

"—She says it's in your closet." Lucy finishes.

"Daphne, you should definitely go with him," they say together, grinning their identical grins. Their eyes are wide. Calculating.

They know exactly what's going on and suddenly… I adore them. I adore these perfect, weird, sassy human beings.

"So, this is your childhood bedroom, huh? The room you grew up in? I didn't get a tour when I was here baking cookies with your sisters."

"Yup, this was my room for eighteen years. Where all the magic *didn't* happen."

Yeah, it's not exactly a babe magnet: shocking blue stripped wallpaper with an orange basketball border. Vintage Sci-Fi poster of 3,000 Leagues Under the Sea. A poster of Doctor Zvago. Academic Decathlon trophies shining on an oak shelf. His High School diploma and medals hanging from blue and red ribbons.

It's sparse; clean. Slightly juvenile—but then again, it *is* the room from his childhood.

"Give me a minute to find the picture my Mom wanted, okay? Sit tight. I know it's in here somewhere..." Dexter disappears into the closet, and the sound of shoes, totes and clutter being shifted ensues. "*Shit, there used to be a box in here with…*" Clatter. Bang. "*Where the hell is it…*"

His muffled voice fades in and out of the walk-in closet, where I hear the distinct sound of a box being pulled open as he hunts for this elusive, lost photograph. I wander to the far side of the room, trailing a hand lightly over the Star Wars comforter laid out over the twin bed, my fingertips gliding along the course cotton fabric.

Darth Vader occupies the entire bed.

"I wonder why your mom hasn't redecorated in here. You've been moved out how long?" I ponder out loud, more to myself than anyone else.

His voice filters into the room from the deep pit of his closet, loud enough to be heard over the chatter and laughter of his rambunctious family floating up the stairs and through the vents in the floorboards.

"Uh, I moved out eight years ago?" Dexter sticks his head out, peering at me from behind the doorjamb, holding a tiny action figure towards me. "Hey, I know I said I didn't have many of these, but check this out! I totally forgot about this collection! I wonder where the rest of them are…"

I bounce on the bed, excited, extending my arms to take it. "Whoa! You have a Battlestar Galactica Cylon Centurion action figure! Where did you get that?"

He holds it towards me, faltering mid-step. "Wait. You actually *know* what this is?"

He looks suitably impressed.

I roll my eyes. "Dexter. I was at StarGate alone on a Saturday night—of course I know what a Cylon Centurion is." I grab at it, turning it this-way-and-that to examine it. "In perfect condition, too."

Dexter pauses in the doorway of the closet, pupils dilating, the figurine all but forgotten as he watches me, eyes blazing. "Shit Daphne, you're kind of turning me on right now with all this geek talk."

"Is that so?" I lean back on his pillows, channeling my inner Tabitha, the Cylon still in my hand. "In that case… Did you know the starship that became the Blockade Runner in *Star Wars: Episode four* was the original design for the Millennium Falcon?"

His nostrils flare and he takes a step closer.

I press on, willing him towards me. "Did you know," I start slowly. Very slowly, each word pronounced barely above a whisper. "That they still haven't named Yoda's species?"

Oh my god, where is all this random trivia coming from?

Dexter removes his glasses, setting them on a nearby dresser. Unwavering, the brown irises practically sizzle as he focuses every iota of his attention on me.

I stare *holes* into those glasses.

"Can you see without those?" I tease quietly as he

stalks forward.

He chuckles then, the sound low and deep against the silence of the bedroom. My teeth bite down on my lower lip to hide a shy smile. "*Can* you?"

His moves closer, closer still. "I see *you*, if that's what you mean."

Swallowing my nerves, I murmur, "Did you know…"

"Did I know what? Talk nerdy to me, Daphne." He falls to the carpet, on his knees between my legs, running his hands up the length of my thighs. "Don't stop."

Up and down, up and down my thighs his palms go.

"D-did you k-know," I gulp when he leans in, his delicious lips consuming the pulse in my neck. My heart beats wildly outside of my chest, and I struggle to catch my breath. "Throughout the course of the Battlestar Galactica series, Sheba never fires her laser pistol. Not even once."

"Actually, I *did* know that." Dexter's nose skims idly up the column of my neck, his lips trailing along behind.

"You're such a geek." I breathe.

"So are you." Up and down, up and down my thighs his palms leisurely go.

"Dexter, what are you waiting for?"

A pause. "I don't know."

A sigh. "Stop thinking and *just do it.*"

"Know what? Call me a glutton for punishment, but I kind of want…" The question purrs next to my ear. "I kind of want to hear you say it."

That I can do.

With a tiny nod and a tilted neck, I whisper into the room, "Kiss me."

Kiss me.

He does.

Large hands cupping my face, Dexter's thumbs tenderly stroke my cheekbones before he lowers his mouth. Our lips connect with the very barest of contact before touching, a veritable shockwave ricocheting to every nerve ending in my body; like a tiny voltage of electricity.

Every cell tingles, every nerve quivers—and all we're doing is kissing.

Softly at first, our kisses are small exploratory ones. Small yes, but bound to leave imprint after imprint on my heart.

I hesitate, pulling back; wanting to remember this moment forever, certain that *this* will be my last first kiss.

Dexter's brows furrow, concerned, drawing his hands away. "What's wrong?"

I grab them, holding them steady. Holding them on my flesh, not wanting to lose the connection.

"Nothing's wrong," I murmur. "Everything is *right*."

The mattress dips when I lean in towards him, settling my lips back on Dexter's mouth.

His lips part.

Our tongues tentatively meet in a painfully slow dance.

It's tender. It's sexy.

It's torture.

Our lips press harder, tongues searching. Urgently now.

"Oh my god," Dexter moans into me. "It feels so fucking good kissing you." His fingers tangle their way into my hair, running through the strands before cupping the back of my neck in his large palm. "I could kiss you forever."

"Yes please," I manage to whimper into his warm, open mouth. Tongues tangle, wet and delicious and positively intoxicating.

A labored groan. "Shit, we shouldn't have started this."

"Why?"

A deep, virile growl. "Because I won't want to stop."

"Then we won't."

"Daphne…" His lithe fingers *toy* with the tiny pearl button at the collar of my demure cotton shirt—the one I wore specifically to impress his grandmother—plucking at it but leaving it intact. Ugh, the *tease*. "My grandparents are downstairs in the…"

His voice falters when I reach between us, running my index and middle finger inside the waistband of his jeans; up the front of his rigged zipper, grasping somewhat desperately for the outline of his—

"You're right, you're right," I chant. "We need to stop."

"We need to stop," he repeats with determination, his breathing arduous; a pearl button slides free. Then another. Then, "Stop me, Daphne."

He tongue dampens my neck, sucking gently.

Now we're both moaning.

Mmmm.

"Oh god Dexter, *I can't*, I can't, your hands feel *too* good."

Breathing heavy, and with one last kiss to my temple, he releases me to stand. Pushing from his knees to a stand, he backs away, his fingers flex and immediately fly to run through his hair; sexual tension crackling through the air with rapid alacrity.

Without meaning to, my eyes shoot to the bulge between his thighs—to his glaringly obvious arousal.

My girly parts whimper in dismay.

I stand too, pressing my fingers against my swollen lips; they're raw and painfully tender and wonderful. I give them a few light swipes as if to quell the pain before holding out my trembling hands.

"Look at me; I'm shaking."

A second ticks by.

Then another.

Then another.

Then…

"Ah, *fuck it*."

We crash feverishly into each other then, my back hitting the blue wallpapered wall, shaking a nearby shelf. I don't know who's tugging the hem of my shirt free from the waistband of my jeans—his grasping hands or mine or both—but together, we frantically free all the buttons until my shirt's pulled open.

Finally, blessedly ripped open.

I moan in relief when Dexter connects with my bare skin. The tips of his fingers travel up my bare stomach, his palms a tense, restrained caress against my flesh.

Over my bra. Over the swell of my breasts.

My body strains up to meet his touch.

His head dips. He reaches down, grabs my ass in both his palms and hauls me to the dresser.

Lips. Teeth. Skin.

Tongue.

"I'm a horrible person," I gasp. "This is so wrong—your grandmother is downstairs."

He stifles my protests with his mouth, his sexy, *smart*,

skillful mouth… we can't get our tongues deep enough as he lifts me with a grunt, knocking a lamp to the carpeted floor with a loud thump and sitting me in the center of his dresser.

The light bulb hits the ground and shatters.

He rocks his hips into me, pounding the dresser into the drywall as we paw at each other, rattling the framed High School diploma hanging above the Debate team medals that jingle and sway on their hooks.

We don't notice.

We don't care.

He feels so good, he feels so good, he feels so—

Daphne

"Uh, Daphne *might* want to put her shirt back on. Just sayin—"

"—And fix her hair."

The twins stand in the open doorway of Dexter's old room, identical expressions fixated on us, unreadable. Completely pokerfaced—as if they hadn't just walked in on Dexter and I in the middle of us dry humping against the wall and tearing at each other's clothes. As if my shirt wasn't open and my breasts weren't threatening to spill out of my bra.

Like this kind of thing casually happens every Saturday.

I fumble blindly for the buttons on my shirt, fitting each tiny pearl through its hole, mindlessly shoving them through, desperate to match them up but not taking the time to actually do it properly.

I need to get my breasts covered.

The twins saunter a little farther into Dexter's room, past the dresser I'm perched on to study the spines of his collection of high school yearbooks.

"Mom sent us looking for you, F-Y-I, so don't get your boxers in a twist. You know the drill: we can't light the candles or sing Happy Birthday until everyone is—"

"—Present and accounted for," the twins parrot, prattling on as if nothing was amiss.

"And since they think you've been MIA for the past…"

Amelia checks the time on her phone.

"Twenty minutes."

"—Even though *everyone* heard the loud banging coming from up here." Lucy crosses her arms and purses her lips. "What the heck did you think you were doing?"

Amelia snorts. "You should know better than this Dex, going at it in *this* house? Remember how thin the walls are? You can't even—"

"—Whisper without someone hearing it through the vents."

They stare at us, Amelia raising her eyebrows and Lucy tapping her foot on the carpeted floor.

"Well?"

"Are you coming downstairs or what?"

Dexter and I stare after them as they airily saunter back out into the hallway, not a care in the world. And that thing I said before about *adoring* them?

Yeah.

Forget I mentioned it.

Dexter

Things go from bad to worse when we descend the stairs, my cousin Elliot waiting at the bottom, hand wrapped around the finial post of the wooden rail.

He starts in as soon as the twins usher Daphne into the kitchen, out of earshot.

"Jesus fucking Christ, Dexter." Elliot hisses, grabbing my arm the second I round the staircase in the foyer. He strong-arms me through the hall, cornering me near my dad's office. "Were you *seriously* fucking your hot girlfriend with a party going on?"

I register *hot* and *girlfriend*, cataloging them in my brain for future use. Aggravated, I give him a glower.

"Why would you even ask me that?"

Elliot claps a hand on my shoulder, emitting a low whistle. I shrug him off. "Several reasons. One: she looks thoroughly *fucked*. Or drunk, and Aunt Georgia isn't serving alcohol. So which is it?"

"Would you please stop using the word fuck when you're talking about Daphne?"

Elliot crosses his arms, pleased with himself. "Two: I notice you aren't denying fucking her."

I shake my head, pushing away from the wall, willing him to walk away.

He doesn't comply. "Three: *everyone* heard the

moaning. I'll admit, it was pretty hot and I was getting off on it until your Dad cranked the stereo and your mom did that weird laugh thing she does when she's about to lose her shit."

My back turned to him, I walk towards the kitchen leaving him trailing after me. "We weren't having sex in my room so shut the fuck up about it."

He's skeptical. "Well then you should have. Christ, man up, dude. Your girlfriend is a hot piece of ass. What she sees in you is—"

"—None of your business, you douchenozzle." An agitated feminine voice interrupts from behind, startling us both. I expect to find Daphne coming to my defense when I spin on my heel, but instead I find…

The twins.

Great. More drama; just what I need.

"You're being a real dickshitter," Lucy scowls. "Why are you always such an ass?"

Elliot's eyes bug out of his head at their foul language. I mean—all dressed up in their conservative birthday dresses, they hardly look like the truckers they're beginning to sound like.

"What the hell Dex—are you going to let her—them—talk to me like that?"

The twins cross their arms and Amelia *hmphs*. "Are you even listening to yourself?"

Lucy laughs. "All we need to do is go back in the kitchen and tell Aunt Tory you're—"

"—In here using profanity and talking shit about Daphne." Amelia's own use of profanity is not lost on me.

"Maligning her."

The girls nod. "If you scare her off after we worked

so hard to get her here…"

Lucy makes a slicing gesture across her neck with her hand: *dead.*

"Wait. How do you know the word malign?" Sorry, I can't help asking.

"Maligning?" The twins cross their arms and roll their narrowed eyes, speaking at the same time. "AP English."

"What's AP English?" Elliot probes.

More eye rolling. "Advanced Placement."

This gives me pause. Because, "If you're in AP English, why'd you write such a shitty letter to Daphne when you hijacked my email—you know what? Never mind. I don't want to know. Jesus you two, please just go back to your party."

Both my sisters stand tall, unflinching. "We'll wait here while you finish him off." Lucy gives her chin an encouraging nod in Elliot's direction.

Finish him off? "Okay tiny Godfathers, bring it down a notch. This isn't the mob."

Elliot glances at me with disbelief still etched across his brow. And pity. "Shit man, are they always like this?"

I chuckle, smacking my cousin on the back and moving him towards the party. "Unfortunately, yeah."

God, I really do love those two.

Crazy little weirdos.

Daphne

"So, this is me."

"Yup, this is you." Dexter taps on the steering wheel with his palm, glancing out the window up at my condo. My little front porch light glows in the dark, illuminating my dark gray front door and the adorable painted snowman leaning up against the brick wall. The light also bounces off the lenses of his glasses, making it hard to read his expression.

Pulling his car neatly into a parking spot in front of my awning, I unbuckle my seatbelt but make no move to exit the vehicle when he shifts into park.

The engine idles.

The radio is silent.

"Are you sure you don't want to go do something? It's still pretty early."

Nine o'clock on the dot on a Sunday night.

"Don't feel obligated to continue this farce of an evening." His chuckle is sardonic and patronizing. "Although I do appreciate the sentiment."

Farce? Obligated?

"Obligated? I thought this was a date."

Dexter laughs again, pushing his sexy tortoiseshell glasses up the bridge of his nose. The buttoned up collared shirt beneath his winter jacket peeks through, and my eyes travel of the column of his neck to his strong jaw line.

The place where I want to put my lips.

"Dexter, if Elliot said something to upset you, I—"

"—Let me stop you right there." He twists his body to face me from the driver's seat. "Nothing—and I mean nothing—Elliot says upsets me; it's the fact that he *says* anything at all and there's nothing I can do about it. He's not some guy off the street. He's family. So as much as I want to smash his face in, I can't. Because my freaking grandmother is usually in the other room."

He's pissed off and agitated and *passionate*.

"Elliot's always been like this, and thank god it's not just with me. He's a dick to our cousin John, too, and Little Erik who's what—ten years younger than him? What an ass. You don't do that shit to a kid." He lets out a puff of frustration. "Anyway. I'd love to deck him, but I never will, and that's the pisser of it."

Ass. Punch. Dick. Deck. *Pisser*.

Oh my god, why is this turning me on?

There's something wrong with me, I know it. Maybe it's been too long since I've had sex and I'm going through some kind of withdrawal, where mundane words trigger dirty, dirty thoughts.

I watch words and sentences come out of Dexter's beautifully sculpted lips, but I stop hearing them all, so lost in thought. So lost in the thought of him taking me inside and—

My head tips to the side and I study him.

I look up.

"What's… that *look?*"

Crap, he's studying me now, too, but his look isn't one of desire. It's one of confusion.

I know, I know, it's shameful! But he's so kind and patient and sweet and handsome and I like him and I want... everything. I want everything with him.

I need to know if he wants it too, but…

Guh!

"Why don't I walk you to the door."

Of its own volition, my head gives a nod.

Grabbing my purse from the backseat of his Audi while he jogs around to open the passenger side door, I step out, one leg after the next. Put one foot in front of the other as we walk unhurriedly to the front door.

Keys in hand, they jingle in the silent night, but I make no move to fit them into the lock, just like Dexter makes no move to kiss me. In fact, rather than move closer, his hands disappear into the pockets of his navy pea coat, stuffed inside protectively. Whether it's against me, or the cold, frigid air, is beyond me.

"Thanks for inviting me along today, despite all the crazy." A smile tips my lips. "Your sisters are really something. Do you even realize how much they love you?"

"Of course I know how much they love me. They have to; I'm their brother."

"No, I mean—they really love you. They set this whole thing up; getting me to your mom's house to bake cookies so I'd be thrust in your path. Emailing me from your phone. Breaking up the tension with Elliot and threatening to cut a bitch." This earns me a low chuckle. "You are their everything. It's…"

"I haven't thought of it that way. They're such pains in my ass most of the time it's easy to lose sight behind their intentions."

"I bet. But truly—they adore you." My hand finds the

sleeve of his thick, wool coat, and I squeeze, relishing the feel of him under my gloved hand. "*I* adore you, Dexter."

With a nervous blush that has nothing to do with the cold, I glance from under my long lashes into his brown eyes and wait for his reaction.

Pleasure curves his mouth. "You do?"

"I do."

He hums. "That's good because I adore *you*."

"You do?"

His head dips. "Yeah."

Beneath the awning of my tiny condo, under the winter stars, our lips touch for the second time tonight. And when he finally digs his hands out of his pockets, our fingers lace together.

I shiver.

"You need to get inside," he murmurs at the corner of my mouth. "It's freezing."

"Dexter," I breath, a tad wistful. "Come inside with me."

My key goes in the lock. Feet hit the tiled foyer; shoes get kicked off. Large hands find the base of my neck, pulling me in hungrily and pushing my back against the wall in the entryway.

"I really *do* want to talk and get to know you, I swear I do." He breaths into my hair. "But all I can think about right now is—"

"—Ripping all my clothes off and—"

"—hauling you to the bedroom."

Oh jeez, we're doing our own version of the Twin Speak thing, finishing each other's sentences, the words flowing out our mouths as our lips and bodies collide. My hands fist the collar of his coat, seeking out the row of toggles barring me from unbuttoning his dress shirt.

Dexter sheds his coat, thank god; it drops to the floor in a heap, followed by his knit hat, gloves and—only Dexter would remove his socks.

Grinning like a fool I shuck my own coat, hat and gloves, adding them to the pile on the floor.

Leading Dexter up the stairs and down the narrow hallway to my bedroom, I turn to face him once we're through the threshold of my door. Instead of a hurried frenzy to tear at each other's clothes, we face each other, drinking each other in from head to toe. Admiring each other.

Reveling in each other.

My chest swells with complete happiness when Dexter's hand gently cups my cheek, his fingers stroking my jaw line as he watches me, one part captivated—the other part aroused.

My eyes flutter shut when he leans in to land a kiss to the corner of my lips. The curve of my cheekbones. My eyelids.

Pleasure sends a ripple of tingles surging throughout my body, tipping my head back, giving him the access he needs to—

Gently suck on my neck.

His tongue slides leisurely along the column of my throat until his nose is buried in the hair behind my ear. A moan escapes my lips as our breathing becomes labored—I swear we're both panting; but is that his breath or mine?

Our tongues are sliding together when our bodies finally meet; my body sighs in relief. Exhales. Vibrates on high with anticipation.

"I love these glasses," I slur, finger tracing the frame at his temple, back-and-forth…then back again.

"What?" Dexter sounds as drunk as I feel.

"Your glasses, your glasses, God I love your glasses."

"You don't say?" More kisses against my neck. "That's got to be a first."

His ministrations on my body feel so good I can barely roll my eyes. "S-somehow, I doubt that. *Mmm…* you would be surprised at how… *your tongue feels so good...* many women find glasses and bowties and suspenders sexy."

"I only need *one* woman to find it sexy."

"I do, I do," I chant, finally groaning into his mouth when our mouths meet; finally, blessedly meet.

"Take them off me," he demands.

So I do.

I do; and he's gorgeous.

Fourteen

Dexter

Holy shit.

Daphne Winthrop is taking off my shirt.

Tugging the hem from the waistband of my dark jeans… hands splayed on my smooth chest, her soft palms running over my abs and pec muscles. Fingers trace my hardening nipples.

I bite down on my lower lip, nostrils flaring. At my sides, I clench and unclench my fists. The desire to wrap my hands around her waist is unbearable when she finally pushes the dress shirt down over my shoulders, down my arms, down to the floor.

Daphne Winthrop is taking off my pants.

Belt.

Then, before I can wrap my brain around it, the snap on my fly is popped open, the zipper slowly being tugged down. So slowly the simple sound of the metal track coming undone has my dick throbbing painfully hard.

Anticipation pulses through my veins, every fantasy I've ever had can't beat this reality as my pants get pushed down around my ankles.

I step out of them, and am slowly propelled towards the bed in nothing but my boxer briefs. My legs hit the mattress as she propels me back, back, back.

"Lay down against the headboard?" comes her quiet request. "I want you to watch me undress. Is that okay?"

Somehow, I manage to nod.

Swallow air.

Breathe Dexter, I remind myself. Breathe.

Holy shit. Daphne Winthrop is about to strip all the clothes off her gorgeous body and get naked.

For me.

She starts at the top button of her collared shirt, plucking one free from the hole, then another.

One.

Two.

My eyes are riveted to that gap of exposed skin; fucking riveted as a third button is plucked free, followed by a fourth. Her hands pause momentarily to part the seam of her shirt, the creamy expanse of cleavage sacredly, beatifically—*oh shit*—full. I've heard the phrase "spilling over" a few times, but I've never seen boobs overflowing a bra in person.

I force my face to remain impassive; willing my jaw to stay closed.

Instead of unbuttoning the rest of her pretty, preppy shirt, her hands glide to the waistband of her jeans. The snap on her fly opens; zipper forced down. I watch as her hands drift over her pale, perfect skin and push the denim down over her slim hips.

White lace boy shorts.

Flawless porcelain skin.

Daphne steps out of her skinny jeans, leaving them on the carpet in a heap, and strides slowly forward, fingers poised on the fifth button of her shirt as she comes to stand next to the bed.

With baited breath, I wait.

Daphne

He can't take his eyes off me, and quite honestly, he's holding so still I'm afraid he's stopped breathing. Dexter is completely… motionless. Crap. What if the sight of my near naked boobs gave the guy a stroke?

I pause, waiting to unbutton number five. "Dexter?"

His mumbled, incoherent, "Huh?" puts a coy smile on my lips, giving me leave to continue my strip tease.

Climbing up onto the bed, I crawl towards him in the center of the mattress and note with satisfaction his nostrils flaring when I straddle his hips. Dexter's hungry eyes roam my body as I pull off my pale pink shirt, dragging it slowly down my arms. Unceremoniously, I toss it on the ground next to the bed.

"*Oh shit*," he groans when I reach back and unclasp my bra; it joins my shirt and jeans in a pile on the floor.

Only underwear separates us now.

I lean forward, my breasts rubbing against his chest, the sound of his gravelly groan and my moan filling the air. My hands roam his smooth pecs; Dexter is toned perfection. Olive skin that's sinewy and trim and hard with perfect nipples. I run my trembling hands over them now, fingering one in a leisurely… burning… tease.

Beneath me, his hips give a jerk, and I rotate my pelvis onto his straining erection; it's just *begging* for attention.

Begging.

Begging and hard and rubbing so painfully good against my center that a stifling whimper gets caught in my throat as Dexter finally leans forward to capture my lips with his.

Suddenly, I'm on my back, his mouth and tongue are everywhere.

My neck.

My collarbone.

My breasts.

Oh god, my breasts. I arch my back into his mouth as he *sucks and licks and squeezes*, the pressure building between my legs so agonizing that when I pull his hair, we both gasp out in pleasure.

"You are going to drive me out of my damn fucking mind," he rasps, grinding and grinding his dick into the apex of my thighs, his head still bent at my breasts. His large hand cups one, squeezing gently. "Jesus Christ you feel so good."

I glance down between our bodies at our pelvises pressed together, feeling my eyes glaze over with arousal. Excitement. Wanting to *feel* him, I find the elastic waistband of his boxers, my fingers trailing along the edge before going under. Inside.

Grasping the hard, rigid length of him.

Stroking him up and down as he whimpers and moans into my mouth; it's a low, tortured guttural sound that has me desperately pushing his underwear down his hips, my palms smoothing over his firm backside.

Dexter flexes as I squeeze and knead, pulling him down into me by the ass cheeks, eventually, he kicks off the offensive boxers.

"Get on your back," I whisper when he's scrumptiously naked.

I start at his neck, languidly lavishing kisses along the pulse beating erratically in his throat—his heart. Kiss his stomach, lick his abs, his belly button and below…

I suck.

And swirl.

And suck.

"*Oh fuck, oh f-fuck,*" he chants, clutching the bedspread with a vice grip in his fantastically large palms. "*Fuck, oh fuck.*"

He's babbling and grimacing in agony and it's glorious. His dirty cursing only serves to make my lady parts tingle. Ache.

"Shit...stop, baby, I want to fuck you... stop, Daphne ... don't stop. Oh...f-fuck."

He comes, his head falling back against the pillow.

Dexter

"You're so beautiful," I murmur into her ear, my cock already hard again. "So beautiful."

I can't even believe this shit is real; that I'm in her bed and she's spread out next to me, my hand roaming her smooth, naked skin.

And that she's letting me.

Or that she's encouraging me.

My dick has literally *never* been in a girl's mouth.

And Daphne Winthrop *blew* me.

On purpose.

Speaking of which… her hand clasps mine, dragging it down under the covers and onto her right breast; I begin a slow caress with my thumb that has her throwing her head back on the pillow and breathlessly saying my name.

Not gonna lie: I push the bedspread down so I can watch my hand stroke her boobs. They're full and round in my palm, her nipples pink and perfect. Obviously watching myself fondle her tits makes my dick throb; I'm starring in my own goddamn sexual fantasies for Christ sake.

"*You're* beautiful." Her hand is on my inner thigh, then my pulsating cock, as she whispers in my ear. Licks it. "Everything about you turns me on."

"Daphne, I can't believe I'm about to say this, but…" Shit. Fuck. Damn. "I… don't have a condom."

Her hand grazes my cheek. “It’s okay, baby. I do, I do. I mean… it’s a *hundred* years old, but… I’m also on the pill so…”

Within moments the package is being ripped open, the condom is on and I’m sliding home, the only coherent thoughts after that?

If I died right now, I’d already be in heaven.

Daphne

"I love Star Wars," I slur as he rotates his hips—pressing me harder against the wall, his hands gripping my ass and squeezing. "I love it."

"Oh yeah?" Grunt. Pant. Groan.

"*Yes*, oh…oh! Yes." My toes curl.

"Fuck yeah you love Star Wars," Dexter moans as he grinds and grinds those lean, sexy hips, his hand gripping my backside. Gripping my ass. "Uh… god… fu-ck*kk*…"

"Dexter, *oh god*, mmm*nuh*…."

"Daphne, baby," his voice is strained. "I could live inside you."

"*Yes*," I beg. "Yes, please."

Yes.

Yes.

Yes.

Tabitha: *So. "Baking cookies" is your new code word for sex?*

Me: *Yeah, pretty much. Dexter is… I don't even have the words.*

Tabitha: *I believe the phrase you're searching for is*

"Orgasmic."

Me: *You're not allowed to say shit like that. Only I am.*

Tabitha: *Le'sigh. Fine. But I'm using your story in a book; sorry, I won't be able to help myself...*

Me: *I'd argue with you but I know it would be pointless. At least make my character gorgeous and smart and hilarious.*

Tabitha: *You just described yourself ;)*

Me: *Aww, that's why I love you so much.*

Tabitha: *So this thing with Dexter... can you see it getting serious?*

Me: *Oh gosh—YES! Yes, he's... awesome. LOL. Just the thought of him has me...*

Tabitha: *Wanting to "bake cookies?"*

Me: *Dozens and dozens of cookies...*

Epilogue

Daphne

Six or 8 months later…who really knows?

"I wonder what the occasion is," I mumble to a beautiful, blonde haired Greyson in the kitchen of her brother Collin's new condo. His second condo in a year, but… somehow this doesn't feel like a house warming party. "What's up with this little shin-dig they decided to throw last minute?"

He and Tabitha have been living together for the past six months—dating for eight—and tonight they're throwing an impromptu…whatever this party is.

"Well," she says conspiratorially, giving me a nudge and grabbing a handful of chips. "*My* theory is that they're going to announce an engagement. At least, I *hope* that's what this is. They can't keep having these house warming parties."

I glance around at the room full of people; Tabitha's parents. Collin and Greyson's parents. Greyson and her rugged, rugby playing boyfriend Calvin. More family. More friends. A crowded room gathered in Tab and Collin's spacious high-rise condo.

"Or maybe this is about one of her books?" I speculate. Tabitha is an author, and she's on book number three. "Maybe she's made a best seller list somewhere?"

Greyson doesn't look convinced. "Maybe. But I'm still putting my money on an engagement. Do you see the way my brother is following her around, waiting on her hand and foot?"

I had noticed that. Collin fetching her water. Rubbing her shoulders while she spoke to her parents. Bringing her little plates of food. Touching her.

Hmmm.

I'm not convinced this is them springing an engagement on us. That's not Tabitha's style. "Maybe, but they haven't even been together for a year."

Collin's sister looks at me, incredulously. "Those two? Are you kidding me? They were crazy about each other from day one. Almost inseparable."

I scrunch my face. "I think you're remembering it wrong. Collin harassed her, embarrassed her, and she spent *how* many weeks avoiding him. When you say 'crazy about each other,' you're thinking of you and Calvin."

Greyson and her boyfriend are in crazy, mad, love with each other, and have been since the day they met; the day she created a fake boyfriend named Cal Thompson to keep her nosy friends off her back.

Almost the same way Dexter had asked me to be his fake girlfriend for one night so his family wouldn't meddle in his love life.

Actually, come to think of it, all three of us—Greyson, Tabitha and I—lied at the beginning of our relationships; Greyson lied about inventing a fake boyfriend, Tabitha lied about being an author and hid her books from everyone, and I lied about being Dexter's girlfriend.

What pretty little liars we all turned out to be; thank god everything ended well for us.

"Having a good time?" I ask, sidling up to Dexter. He slides a hand around my waist, pulling me in. Pulling me close and planting a quick kiss on my neck, just under my ear; my favorite spot.

I shiver every time.

"I'm having a good time; I just wish Collin hadn't invited my sisters. Why would he do that? They're driving me crazy. I mean—just look at them over there." He nods to the opposite side of the room to where the twins are holding court, gesturing wildly and laughing uproariously.

I have a sneaking suspicion they're re-enacting the moment they came to Dexter's defense the night of their 16th birthday party, telling their cousin Elliot to kiss off. Called him a douchebag. Went Twin Gangsta on his cocky ass.

Even though that was more than six months ago, retelling that story is one of their favorite things to do in mixed company.

And they do it so well. So vividly.

So loudly.

The tips of Dexter's ears turn pink when Lucy throws her arms in the air, shouting, "We'll wait here while you finish him off!" The declaration is loud enough to be heard by everyone in the room.

My boyfriend groans. "Why do they insist on telling that story?" He runs a hand through his neatly combed hair, and my eyes follow his movements, trailing down the column of his neck to the exposed skin at his collar. "It's so embarrassing."

The top two buttons of his dress shirt, undone. For Dexter, this is as laid-back and casual as he gets. He does own tee shirts; I've seen them in his closet, and a few times on the weekends. But he likes to be dressed up. Pressed. Tidy.

It's my job to muss him up.

I press my mouth against his neck for a quick kiss, sniffing his deliciously male cologne. His woodsy shampoo. "Mmm, you smell good."

"Daphne, stop. You're going to make me—"

"—Hard?"

I love how open he is now; how uninhibited we are together. How honest and affectionate.

"Just hearing you say that word makes it worse." The low baritone of his voice gets lower, and he watches when I bite down on my lower lip, dragging my teeth back and forth.

I glance down the dark hallway off the living room, one eyebrow raised in thought. "Want to check out the spare bedroom?"

My meaning is clear.

Dexter swallows, his Adam's apple bobbing and eyes rapidly getting hazy behind the rim of his glasses. *Sexy*

Dexy indeed.

He gives a curt nod. *Yes.*

Grabs my hand. Hauls me down the dark corridor to the second door on the left, my body humming with need and anticipation with what's going to happen when we close the door to that dark spare room behind us.

Door locked, it's empty and pitch black.

Eyes straining, I can barely make out any furniture, let alone Dexter's fingers when he finds the tie of my emerald green wrap dress—the one I borrowed from Tabitha, fell into like with, and haven't given back. Wrapped around my waist, the soft cotton fits my body like a second skin, flattering my curves to perfection.

Large hands slide across the bare skin between the plunging wrap neckline, sliding into the cup of my bra, palm gently kneading my breast. Heaven. It feels like heaven.

Muffled sounds reverberate from the party outside, but we don't care.

"You're so sexy," he purrs in the dark, his lips finding purchase on my collarbone. "I've been wanting to touch you all night. Untie this dress and have my way with you."

"Yes," I breath into his mouth with a sigh; the mouth that I dream about each and every night; those lips that make all the aching in my body go away.

At some point I'm lifted onto the top of a dresser.

Fumbling hands find his belt buckle. Unzip his fly. Push the dark, dressy denim down his lean hips along with his navy boxer-briefs. Untie the sash around my waist. Push apart the cotton of my dress. Push aside my lacey, nude underwear.

My hands roam his torso, his taunt abs, his firm pecs.

I love his body.

I love his glasses.

I love his mind.

"I love you," I whisper when he pushes into me with a loud groan, condoms forgone when we became exclusive (not that there was any doubt we wouldn't be).

He thrusts once, then stills. "Did you just say that you love me?"

"Yes." I bob my head in the dark even though he can't see me. "Yes, yes, I love you." I wriggle my pelvis, hoping to urge him on.

He pulls out slowly. Pushes in slowly.

Again and again and again.

"God Daphne, oh god." He buries his nose in my hair, inhaling with a long drag. "I'm so in love with you."

Rocking. Pushing. Pulling.

The dresser hits the wall with every mad thrust, our loud moans and mutters drowned out only by the sound of party-goers in the next room. Vaguely I hear Tabitha's distinctive laugh, but my neck is rolling to the side and I'm drunk on the oxytocin surging through my body.

"I love you… oh! Oh god… mmmm…"

Bang.

Bang.

Bang. A picture on the wall behind my back falls, hits the hard wooden top of the dresser, and crashes to the ground with the telltale sound of broken glass.

We don't care.

We can't stop.

"Oh shit, oh fuck," Dexter grunts when we come at the same time. A wet kiss is planted at my temple, his chest heaving from his accelerated heart rate.

Then, after a lengthy silence, "How are we going to explain that broken whatever-that-is to Collin and Tabitha?"

He pulls away from my body, and I fumble to find the ties of my dress. "I'll probably just tell her the truth. I don't think she'll be mad."

I hear the sound of his zipper being pulled up, his belt being buckled. "Where's the damn light switch?"

Hands pat the wall, his voice fading as he nears the door.

The lights go on.

I blink rapidly to block out the blinding light, seeing nothing but…

Pink.

Pink, pink and more pink.

A white crib against the wall. A rocking chair with a little gray stuffed elephant in the corner. The letters "LKE" monogrammed in white, interlocking script in the center of the opposite, powder pink wall.

"Holy. Shit." Dexter breaths.

My mouth falls open, and I slap my hand over it to conceal my dread. "Oh my god. We just *sullied* a baby nursery with our fornicating!"

Which means…

"Oh my god. Tabitha is pregnant."

And not just pregnant—but *pregnant* pregnant. As in: she must be at least twenty weeks along if they already know the sex, have picked out a name, and decorated an entire nursery.

All the pieces of the puzzle slide into place: new bigger condo closer to the suburbs. Tabitha quitting her day job and writing from home. Collin taking that desk job at his firm so he wouldn't have to do any more traveling.

Her loose fitting shirt. Collin practically glued to her side all night, fawning all over her.

This party.

"Oh my god," I repeat with a horrified gasp. "Dexter. They're telling everyone tonight. That's what this is."

"*A baby*." We say the words together in wonderment.

"A girl," I breathe, the first twinge of envy planted inside my soul.

"Holy shit." He's rooted to the floor. "Collin is having a fucking baby."

He says it with such shock that I can't help but wonder…

"Do…" I gulp nervously, smoothing a hand down my dress to flatten the wrinkles out. "Do you want kids?"

I have to ask because, well. *I* do. Want kids, that is—so terribly. And I might only be twenty-five years old, but my biological clock has been ticking since the moment I met Dexter.

He is *it* for me.

"Of course I want kids."

I am *it* for him; I can see it in his eyes.

Hormones raging, our shy gazes meet.

Then our mouths clash.

"I love—" I murmur into the corner of his mouth.

"—You."

"We can't stay in here." One of us whispers.

"How are we going to—"

"—Look them in the eye?"

Eventually we come up for air, fixing our clothes, and my long hair. One last, long lingering kiss before together, we step through the door.

Dexter

Daphne loves me.

Yeah, we've been dating for the past few months, but I didn't actually think *she'd* be the one to blurt it out first; I assumed it would be me.

And now that I know, I can't stop watching her from across the room. My girlfriend. My best friend.

Loves me.

I watch as she flits from aunt to uncle, to college friends. I watch as she shimmies to the make-shift bar and pours herself a glass of wine. Grabs a beer from the ice bucket.

Watch as she makes her way towards me, this beautiful, gorgeous woman.

I push the glasses up my nose, shifting my focus to Collin as he leans in and whispers something in Tabitha's ear. She nods, biting her lower lip.

He clears his throat, preparing to speak, and I know exactly what's about to come next.

Daphne makes it to my side in time, handing me a beer bottle as Collin announces, "Everyone. Can I have your attention for a second?"

His arm goes protectively around Tabitha, and now that I know their secret, my eyes fly to her stomach. Straining to glean any signs of a baby bump, but not seeing one.

"First of all, thank you all for coming on such short notice. We have some exciting news that we didn't want to share online, and we're glad you could all make it." His voice breaks with a crack, emotion playing with every breath taken. "Tabitha and I… we…"

He looks at his parents.

Her parents.

Tabitha reaches between them and clasps his hand and I see him squeeze it.

Solidarity.

A team.

"Tabitha and I…" he begins again, clearing his throat and blowing out a puff of air. "We haven't been together long—not even a year, but when you know, you know, right?" The small gathered crowd chuckles. "For me, meeting Tabitha was love at first sight."

The room gives a collective '*Awwwww.*'

Collin looks over at me, and our eyes meet. I've known the guy almost my entire life and I can say with certainly that right now, he might sound confident—but he definitely looks like he's going to barf.

I give him a firm, *You got this, buddy* and an encouraging thumbs up.

Message received. "Anyway, we brought you here to tell you that… we're in love and, well. There's no easy way to say this, so… Mom. Dad. *Everyone*—we got married at the courthouse last week and… we're having a baby!"

For a second, no one moves.

The room is deafeningly silent.

"Surprise!" Tabitha radiates joy, hands flying to her

belly.

But then…

Both their mothers start to cry. All at once, everyone starts hugging. Excited chatter, a champagne bottle is uncorked and flies across the room. Wine is being poured.

It's a veritable love fest.

Greyson and Cal sidle up to Daphne and I get elbowed in the ribs by Collin's stunning kid sister.

She chuckles. "Well, since we're all sharing news, this might be a good time to go tell my parents Cal and I are moving in together this summer. There's no way they can get mad at us after *that* little announcement!"

With a laugh, they head off towards their parents, hand-in-hand.

"Wow, this whole night has been surreal," Daphne says beside me, leaning into me when I slide my arm around her waist. "First my friends all fall in love, then they're moving in together, then they're having babies…"

I plant a kiss on the top of her head. "We'll get there."

Her breath hitches. "Yeah?"

"Yeah."

She beams up at me, smiling wide. "I love you *so* much."

"I love you, too."

And you know what?

We do get there.

Exactly seventeen months and four days later.

For more information about Sara Ney and her books, visit:

Facebook
www.facebook.com/saraneyauthor

Twitter
twitter.com/saraney

Goodreads
www.goodreads.com/author/show/9884194.Sara_H_Ney

Website
http://kissingincars.weebly.com

Other Titles by Sara

The Kiss and Make Up Series
Kissing in Cars
He Kissed Me First
A Kiss Like This

#ThreeLittleLies Series
Things Liars Say
Things Liars Hide
Things Liars Fake

With M.E. Carter

FriendTrip
FriendTrip: WeddedBliss (a FriendTrip novella)

Made in the USA
Coppell, TX
07 December 2024

41968178R00277